OXFORD WORLD'S CLASSICS

THE POETIC EDDA

The collection of Norse–Icelandic mythological and heroic poetry known as the *Poetic Edda* contains the great narratives of the creation of the world and the coming of Ragnarok, the Doom of the Gods. The mythological poems explore the wisdom of the gods and giants and narrate the adventures of the god Thor against the hostile giants and the gods' rivalries amongst themselves. The heroic poems trace the exploits of the hero Helgi and his valkyrie bride, the tragic tale of Sigurd and Brynhild's doomed love, and the terrible drama of Gudrun, daughter of Giuki, Sigurd's widow, and her children. Most of the poems exist in a single manuscript written in Iceland around 1270, but many of them pre-date the conversion of Scandinavia to Christianity and allow us to glimpse the pagan beliefs of the North.

Carolyne Larrington studied medieval English and Old Icelandic as an Oxford undergraduate; her doctoral thesis on Old Icelandic and Old English wisdom poetry was published by Oxford University Press in 1993 as *A Store of Common Sense*. Her other books include *The Feminist Companion to Mythology* (1992) and *Women and Writing in Medieval Europe* (1995) and she has published several articles on Old Norse poetry. She taught Old Norse and medieval English literature in Oxford for some years, making frequent research trips to Iceland and the rest of Scandinavia. She is now a Senior Research Fellow at De Montfort University, Leicester.

OXFORD WORLD'S CLASSICS

For over 100 years Oxford World's Classics have brought readers closer to the world's great literature. Now with over 700 titles—from the 4,000-year-old myths of Mesopotamia to the twentieth century's greatest novels—the series makes available lesser-known as well as celebrated writing.

The pocket-sized hardbacks of the early years contained introductions by Virginia Woolf, T. S. Eliot, Graham Greene, and other literary figures which enriched the experience of reading. Today the series is recognized for its fine scholarship and reliability in texts that span world literature, drama and poetry, religion, philosophy and politics. Each edition includes perceptive commentary and essential background information to meet the changing needs of readers.

OXFORD WORLD'S CLASSICS

The Poetic Edda

Translated with an Introduction and Notes by
CAROLYNE LARRINGTON

OXFORD
UNIVERSITY PRESS

OXFORD
UNIVERSITY PRESS

Great Clarendon Street, Oxford OX2 6DP

Oxford University Press is a department of the University of Oxford.
It furthers the University's objective of excellence in research, scholarship,
and education by publishing worldwide in

Oxford New York

Athens Auckland Bangkok Bogotá Buenos Aires Calcutta
Cape Town Chennai Dar es Salaam Delhi Florence Hong Kong Istanbul
Karachi Kuala Lumpur Madrid Melbourne Mexico City Mumbai
Nairobi Paris São Paulo Shanghai Singapore Taipei Tokyo Toronto Warsaw

with associated companies in Berlin Ibadan

Oxford is a registered trade mark of Oxford University Press
in the UK and in certain other countries

Published in the United States
by Oxford University Press Inc., New York

© Carolyne Larrington 1996

The moral rights of the author have been asserted

Database right Oxford University Press (maker)

First published as a World's Classics paperback 1996
Reissued as an Oxford World's Classics paperback 1999

All rights reserved. No part of this publication may be reproduced,
stored in a retrieval system, or transmitted, in any form or by any means,
without the prior permission in writing of Oxford University Press,
or as expressly permitted by law, or under terms agreed with the appropriate
reprographics rights organizations. Enquiries concerning reproduction
outside the scope of the above should be sent to the Rights Department,
Oxford University Press, at the address above

You must not circulate this book in any other binding or cover
and you must impose this same condition on any acquirer

British Library Cataloguing in Publication Data

Data available

Library of Congress Cataloging in Publication Data

Edda Sæmundar. English.
The Poetic Edda / translated with an introduction and notes by
Carolyne Larrington.
(Oxford world's classics)
Includes bibliographical references and index.
1. Mythology, Norse—Poetry—Translations into English.
I. Larrington, Carolyne. II. Series
PT7234.E5L37 1996 839'.61—dc20 96-5465

ISBN 0-19-283946-2

7 9 10 8 6

Printed in Great Britain by
Clays Ltd, St Ives plc

FOR JOHN

CONTENTS

Contents

ACKNOWLEDGEMENTS

I SHOULD like to express my warmest and most respectful gratitude to Ursula Dronke, who first taught me Old Norse and introduced me to the poetry of the *Edda* and whose own edition of the *Poetic Edda* is brilliant and inspirational. Every scholar of the *Edda* owes a great debt to Anthony Faulkes, whose model translation of the *Snorra Edda* has been constantly at my elbow, and to Beatrice La Farge and John Tucker whose translation and updating of the Neckel-Kuhn glossary has been invaluable. Margaret Clunies Ross, Britt-Mari Näsström, Matthew Driscoll, Andrew Wawn, Paul Acker, Judy Quinn, and Beatrice La Farge have all contributed in one way or another to the interpretations in this volume. Judy Jesch has urged the project to completion, and Sarah Clarke has been a thoughtful and willing undergraduate reader of the translations and notes. Numerous Oxford Old Norse students who attended my 'Mythological Poems of the Edda' classes have also contributed. Naturally, none of the above are in the slightest responsible for the errors and solecisms which remain entirely my own responsibility.

INTRODUCTION

THE old, one-eyed god Odin hangs nine days and nights on the windswept ash-tree Yggdrasill, sacrificing himself to himself; the red-bearded Thor swings his powerful hammer against the giant enemy; the ravening wolf Fenrir leaps forward to seize the Father of the Gods in his slavering jaws, the terrible passion of Brynhild for the dragon-slayer hero Sigurd culminates in her implacable demand for his murder—all these famous scenes from Old Norse myth and legend are found in their oldest and most original form in the *Poetic Edda*. From the creation of the world out of the yawning void of Ginnungagap to the destruction of the gods in the mighty conflagration of Ragnarok, the poetry of the *Edda* gives some of the best evidence for the religious beliefs and the heroic ethics of the pagan North before its conversion to Christianity around the year 1000. Its stories are the interpretative key not only to modern depictions of northern myth and legend, in painting, sculpture, literature, and the operas of Richard Wagner—and much of the imagery employed in Third Reich political propaganda—but also to the complex and highly sophisticated court poetry of medieval Scandinavia, a poetic style which employs mythological and legendary material in its rhetoric of allusion.

The *Poetic Edda* is distinct from the famous Icelandic sagas, such as *Njals saga*, since these are written in prose and tell the stories of historical persons; however some of its heroic themes are played out in works such as *Laxdœla saga* and *Gisla saga*. In an earlier form, the *Poetic Edda* is a major source for Snorri Sturluson's great mythographic treatise, the *Prose* or *Younger Edda*. As a body of heroic and mythological poetry, the *Poetic Edda* is comparable in scope to such great masterpieces of world literatures as the Finnish *Kalevala*, Ovid's *Metamorphoses*, Hesiod's *Theogony*, or the *Mahabharata*; yet the *Edda*'s generic range, incorporating as it does, comedy, satire, didactic verse, tragedy, high drama, and profoundly moving lament, surpasses all these. Despite this, the poetry is not difficult to understand:

its language is neither obscure nor complex, but rather strikingly simple and direct. Since the rediscovery of the *Poetic Edda* in the late seventeenth century, its themes have captured the imaginations of many artists: Thomas Gray, William Morris, W. H. Auden in Britain, Richard Wagner, August Strindberg, and Carl Larsson in Europe, and have even inspired the great Argentinian author, Jorge Luis Borges.

The Codex Regius, the manuscript in which the *Poetic Edda* is preserved, is an unprepossessing-looking codex the size of a fat paperback, bound in brown with brownish vellum pages; it is now kept in the Arnamagnæan Institute in Reykjavik. Most of the mythological and heroic poems it contains are only in this single manuscript, abbreviated in what follows as manuscript R. In the 1270s, somewhere in Iceland, an unknown writer copied these poems down, preserving them as a major source of information about Old Norse myth and legend, and as a majestic body of poetry. Six of the mythological poems are found wholly or in part in two other manuscripts, one of which is AM 748 4 to (hereafter A). Certain other poems in the Eddic style are recorded elsewhere: the most important ones, *Baldr's Dreams*, the *List of Rig*, the *Song of Hyndla*, and the *Song of Grotti*, are included here. Although the poems were recorded in the late thirteenth century, it is thought that most of the mythological verse and a few of the heroic poems pre-date the conversion of Scandinavia to Christianity in the late tenth century. No satisfactory method has yet been found to date the poems relative to one another, nor has it proved possible to localize them to Norway or Iceland. It has been argued that the description of the end of the world (*Ragnarok*) in the *Seeress's Prophecy* is reminiscent of volcanic eruption and hence may be Icelandic in origin, while the absence of wolves or bears in Iceland may point to a Norwegian homeland for poems in which these are mentioned, such as the *Sayings of the High One*, but even if Icelanders did not encounter wolves every day, they knew quite well what they were. In general, the mythological poems are thought to predate most of the heroic poems, though some of the latter, the *Lay of Hamdir* and the *Lay of Atli* in particular, are believed to be among the earliest Eddic poems.

Why the name 'Edda'? Snorri Sturluson, an Icelandic author and historian who lived between 1179 and 1241, wrote a treatise on Norse poetry which he called an *edda*, a word whose etymology is uncertain but which clearly means 'poetics' where it occurs in fourteenth-century Icelandic. When Bishop Brynjolf Sveinsson presented a manuscript which had come into his possession to the Danish king in 1643—hence the name Codex Regius—he was well aware of its importance, for like most Icelanders, he had believed that the mythological poems which Snorri quoted from extensively in his *Edda* had been utterly lost. Thus Bishop Brynjolf connected his collection with the name 'Edda' found in Snorri, and assumed that the poems constituted part of that 'great body of human wisdom which Sæmund the Wise collected', as he wrote to a friend at the time. The famous Icelandic scholar Sæmund the Wise (1056–1133) had studied at Paris and was a byword for learning. Thus the contents of the Codex Regius came to be known, erroneously, as the *Sæmundar Edda*, or the *Elder Edda*, while Snorri's treatise (which is likely to have been written before the Codex Regius was compiled) is known as the *Snorra Edda*, the *Prose Edda*, or the *Younger Edda*. The Codex Regius remained in Copenhagen until the principal Icelandic manuscripts began to be returned to Iceland in the early 1960s to be preserved in the Arnamagnæan Institute. Too precious to be risked in an aircraft at that time, the manuscript travelled back on a ship with a military escort, to be welcomed by crowds and public acclaim at the Reykjavik docks.

Snorri's *Edda* and Other Related Works

In order to explain the many mythological and heroic allusions in Norse poetry Snorri set out, in a more or less systematic way, the main myths and heroic legends of the Scandinavians. His selection was no doubt affected by his primary purpose of clarifying poetic allusions, and it is probable, as Anthony Faulkes suggests, that the pagan religion was never systematically understood by those who practised it. Rather it was 'a disorganized body of conflicting traditions that was probably never reduced in heathen times to a consistent orthodoxy such as Snorri attempts to present'.[1] Nevertheless, Snorri's *Edda* is the only near-contemporary account of Norse myth and legend beyond the *Poetic Edda*, and, as such, frequent reference will be made to it in this volume to throw light upon the allusions and obscurities in our poems. Two other texts will be referred to frequently in the Notes. One is *Ynglinga saga*, one of the constituent sagas in Snorri's great history of the kings of Norway, *Heimskringla* (*Circle of the World*). *Ynglinga saga* is the first saga in *Heimskringla* and as such contains much legendary and semi-mythological material. The other text is *Volsunga saga*, written down in the early to mid-thirteenth century, thus at much the same time as Snorri was writing and the Codex Regius was being compiled. *Volsunga saga* tells the full story of Sigurd the Dragon-slayer, and that of his ancestors and descendants. In part it is based on Eddic poems, but here and there it has new information, and is invaluable for filling in the great gap in the *Poetic Edda* caused by some missing leaves between the *Lay of Sigrdrifa* and the *Fragment of a Poem about Sigurd*. Details of these, and other useful texts, are given in the Select Bibliography.

The Old Norse Cosmos

In explaining the mythological background of the Eddic poetry the modern scholar faces the same difficulties which Snorri Sturluson had to try to overcome in his *Edda*. A body of myths, often contradictory, incomplete, or obscure, has to be synthesized into a logical system. Just as Snorri could not help but be influenced by his Christian beliefs in his account—to the extent of providing an analogue to Noah's Flood in his version of the early history of the world—so we cannot now read the *Poetic Edda* without using Snorri to clarify and explain. In what follows, I offer a synthesis of Snorri, Eddic poetry, and certain skaldic verse which makes use of mythological motifs. The picture given is misleading in its coherence and clarity, yet essential for the understanding of the poems.

In the beginning there was only a chaos of unformed matter.

[1] Snorri Sturluson, *Edda: Prologue and Gylfaginning*, ed. A. Faulkes (London, 1988), p. xxvii.

In some poems the world is formed out of the body of Ymir, the primeval being, who is dismembered by the gods, in others the gods raise the earth out of the sea. The gods are descended from the giants: Odin and his mysterious brothers, Vili and Ve, are the sons of Bor, grandsons of Buri, who, according to Snorri, was licked out of the primeval ice by the cow Audhumla. The sun and moon are placed in the sky and time begins. The gods construct the home of the gods (Asgard) and a world for men (Midgard), and then they create the dwarfs who live in the earth and work in metal, followed by humankind. The first man and woman are created from driftwood found on the shore. Hereafter, unlike in Greek myth for example, humanity plays little part in the gods' adventures. Now history begins. The main tribe of gods, the Æsir, is visited by a female figure, Gullveig, probably a type of the goddess Freyia, who practises *seid*, a particularly disreputable kind of magic. The Æsir burn Gullveig three times but she is always reborn, and goes about among humans teaching them her magic. Possibly as a result of their mistreatment of Gullveig, the Æsir are challenged by another tribe, the Vanir, who demand a share of the sacrifices made to the gods and war breaks out. The Vanir seem to be undefeatable and so peace is negotiated and hostages are exchanged: the fertility deities, Freyr, Freyia, and their father, Niord, come to live among the Æsir permanently. To the Vanir are sent Hænir and Mimir. Hænir annoys the Vanir by refusing to participate in discussion and by constantly asking Mimir for his opinion, so the Vanir cut off Mimir's head, preserve it, and send it with Hænir back to the Æsir (*Ynglinga saga*, ch. 4).

In the centre of the universe is Yggdrasill, the World-Ash whose roots go far down below the earth. At their tips are the worlds of the dead, the hall of Hel, and the domain of the frost-giants. Beneath the tree are sacred wells which impart wisdom; these are presided over by the fates and can be reached by the rainbow bridge, Bifrost. Circling the world is the Ocean in which lurks the Midgard-serpent, a monstrous serpent which will attack the gods at the end of the world (Ragnarok). The gods possess many palaces (catalogued in *Grimnir's Sayings*); an important building in Asgard is Valhall (Valhalla) where Odin assembles dead heroes in preparation for the final battle at Ragnarok.

Gods and Goddesses

The Æsir are: Odin, the chief of the gods, deity of war, poetry, trickery, and wisdom. In the *Poetic Edda* Odin is to be found as a wanderer, disguised as a one-eyed old man obsessively seeking out wisdom, challenging it in others, or verifying the inescapable events of Ragnarok. Odin appears occasionally in the heroic poety as a patron of human heroes, watching their progress and sizing them up for a place in Valhalla. Odin's bearded son Thor is patron of farmers and sailors. Armed with his mighty hammer, Miollnir, he fights against the giants; though strong, he is sometimes foolish. Tyr is the god of justice; he is one-handed because he placed his hand in the jaws of the wolf Fenrir, as a pledge of good faith when the gods were trying to bind the monster with a deceptively weak-looking magic fetter. Scenting treachery, Fenrir only agreed on condition that one of the gods place his hand in his mouth, and when the magic bonds tightened on Fenrir, Tyr's hand was snapped off.[2] Loki is a strangely ambivalent figure, son of a giant and foster-brother of Odin. His loyalties are sometimes with the gods, sometimes with the giants. In certain myths he does his best to get the gods out of trouble, but in the story of the death of Baldr and the events which follow, his sympathies are clearly with the giants and at Ragnarok he will fight on their side. Loki is capable of shape-changing and is the father of the monsters Fenrir the wolf, the Midgard-serpent, and Hel, goddess of death. Hel is half corpse-blue, half human pink, according to Snorri.

Baldr, son of Odin and Frigg, is the most beautiful and most beloved of the gods. Through the machinations of Loki he is killed by his blind brother, Hod, with a mistletoe dart, and goes down to Hel. He will return after Ragnarok. Vali is born to avenge Baldr, while Vidar, another son of Odin, exists to avenge his father at Ragnarok. Other Æsir include Bragi, god of poetry, and Heimdall, watchman of the gods, who will blow his mighty Giallar-horn at the coming of Ragnarok, and whose hearing is lodged in the well of Mimir under Yggdrasill. Ull is patron of hunting, and shoots with a bow. More obscure figures, Vili and

[2] Snorri Sturluson, *Edda*, trans. A. Faulkes (London, 1987), p. 28.

Ve, brothers of Odin whom Frigg takes as husbands when Odin is away, and Lodur, a god who seems to play some part in the creation of humanity, as well as Hænir, whose adventures among the Vanir are mentioned above, scarcely figure in the extant stories.

The goddesses (Asynior) are less prominent in the Norse myths than in some other European mythologies. Frigg is the chief female of the Æsir, married to Odin, and mainly figured as the suffering mother of Baldr. Gefion is a patroness of human kings; she created the Danish island of Sjælland by ploughing out Swedish land, leaving the lake which is now Lake Mälar in central Sweden whose outline matches the shape of Sjælland. Snorri lists many other goddesses, some of whom are simply personifications of abstract qualities, such as Var, goddess of pledges, who is invoked in a marriage ceremony in *Thrym's Poem*. Nanna is the virtuous wife of Baldr. Golden-haired Sif is married to Thor. Idunn possesses the apples of immortality which keeps the gods young.

The Vanir are Niord, a sea-god, and his children, Freyr and Freyia. Both these last are associated with fertility. Certain giant women are connected with the gods: Skadi, daughter of the giant Thiazi, comes to Asgard seeking compensation for her father's death. She agrees to make peace if she can conclude a marriage with one of the Æsir. Skadi hopes to marry Baldr, but she is tricked into marrying Niord. The marriage is not a success, and the two separate. Gerd, daughter of the giant Gymir, is wooed by Freyr's servant Skirnir on Freyr's account in the poem *Skirnir's Journey*. Although it is not clear in that poem that a marriage is contracted, Snorri tells us in his history of the kings of Norway, *Heimskringla*, that the couple had a child, Fiolnir. Freyia is married to Od, an obscure figure who may be a doublet of Odin. She is said to have many other lovers, including her own brother, Freyr.

Giants and Other Beings

The giants are the oldest inhabitants of the universe and as such possess much wisdom which the gods covet. They live in the mountains to the east and are imagined both as hostile and bestial, particularly the frost-giants, and conversely as civil and cultivated, like the giant Ægir who feasts the gods in his hall. Giantesses especially may be hideous and haglike, little distinguished from troll-women, or radiantly lovely, like Gerd. The gods are intermittently threatened by the giants, who use cunning to try to obtain various treasures or women of the gods. The gods in return often raid Giantland to recover their women and possessions; sometimes they obtain giant women or such valuable cultural property as the mead of poetry.

Other beings who inhabit the mythic world are elves, who are very little mentioned; they have been interpreted as the spirits of dead male ancestors, the counterparts of the *disir*, who may be either female ancestors or fertility spirits, and who are often inimical to humans. Dwarfs are solely masculine and share some qualities with the giants. They work at smithing and produce ingenious treasures for the gods. Norns are figures of fate who may be present at a child's birth, prophesying his future, as in the *First Poem of Helgi Hundingsbani*. As determiners of fate, the norns are sometimes blamed when events go against human heroes or other mortal beings. Trolls and troll-women, monstrous, wicked, and often stupid creatures of folklore, live in the rocks. Valkyries have a double identity. On the one hand they are divine figures, women who serve mead to the dead warriors in Valhall, and who fulfil the will of Odin in overseeing battle and making sure that victory is awarded to the right man; on the other some valkyries are human in origin. When they fall in love with a hero they ensure victory for him, and eventually marry him, usually with disastrous results, though their love is strong. Shield-maidens are human girls who, scorning domesticity and female tasks, take up the warrior life; as such they can overlap with valkyries. Swan-maidens, who often share shield-maiden characteristics, have swan cloaks which enable them to transform themselves into birds, as in Tchaikovsky's ballet *Swan Lake*. Swan-maidens are common in Northern European folklore.

Mythic History

Our main Eddic source for the history of the gods is the poem the *Seeress's Prophecy* (*Voluspa*), a systematized and allusive account of the events which concern the gods. After the war between the Æsir and the Vanir the wall of Asgard is broken, and a wandering master-builder offers to repair it in a very short space of time, in exchange for the sun, the moon, and Freyia. If he takes any longer, he will forfeit his reward. The gods are confident that the task is impossible, but the smith has an unnaturally clever stallion to assist him and by the first day of winter it is clear that he will fulfil the contract. Loki is blamed for advising in favour of the bargain and so he changes himself into a mare and entices the stallion away. The smith loses his temper, revealing his giant nature; Thor strikes him down with his hammer, breaking the promises the gods had made to him. Within the text this breach of faith on thc part of the gods seems to be the first step in a moral decline. The binding of Fenrir, with the attendant broken promise which causes Tyr to forfeit his hand, the death of Baldr, and the binding of Loki with the guts of his own son forebode the destruction of the gods at Ragnarok (literally: the Doom of the Gods, though the word *rok* 'doom' is sometimes confused with *røkkr* 'twilight', most notably by Snorri, hence the alternative term 'Twilight of the Gods' or 'Götterdämmerung'). When the end comes, summer will disappear, winter will be vicious and constant. Then Yggdrasill will tremble, the fire- and frost-giants, with Loki at their head, will attack the gods. The first generation of gods will be destroyed and the earth collapse into the sea. However, the earth will rise again, and the younger generation of gods, and humans who have survived the catastrophe by hiding in Yggdrasill, will populate the world anew. Whether a new Golden Age returns, or whcther the new world is much like the old, with a balance of good and evil, depends on how one reads the final verses of the *Seeress's Prophecy*.

Heroes

The heroic poems of the *Edda* must originally have consisted of several different cycles about the individual heroes Helgi, Sigurd, Gunnar, and Hamdir. However, before the Codex Regius was compiled, much of the heroic poetry had alrcady bccn loosely joined together in the story of the Volsungs. Helgi still remains a separate figure, scarcely integrated into the Volsung clan. He is a hero whose fate is determined by his involvement with a valkyrie who helps him to victory over his enemies, then marries him. The marriage reveals her to be human, embroiled in family conflicts, and Helgi has to fight off her suitor to win her. Helgi dies as a result of his alliance with the valkyrie. Two different versions of the story of Helgi, slayer of Hunding, appear in the *Poetic Edda*: in the first, the poem concludes with Helgi's winning the hand of the valkyrie Sigrun; in the second, Helgi is killed after the marriage by Sigrun's brother in revenge for Helgi's slaying of their father. Helgi Hiorvardsson, whose story follows the pattern sketched above, dies at the hand of the valkyrie's thwarted suitor, bequeathing his lover to his brother. The name 'Helgi' means 'sacred' and at the end of the *Second Poem of Helgi Hundingsbani*, the compiler tells us that Helgi and his lover were reborn as another pair, Helgi and Kara, whose story has not survived. There is little evidence for belief in reincarnation in Norse religion, but it seems clear that the role of Helgi, lover of the valkyrie, can be filled by different heroes whose history offers a variation on the basic narrative pattern.

The poems which follow the three Helgi poems trace the history of Sigurd, son of Sigmund, slayer of the dragon Fafnir, and possessor of the treasure-hoard which was later to become known as the Rhinegold. After various adventures, including betrothing himself to a valkyrie, Sigrdrifa, Sigurd arrives at the court of the Giukungs, where he marries Gudrun. Sigurd assists Gudrun's brother Gunnar to win the hand of Brynhild, another valkyrie, who at some stage has become identified with Sigurd's earlier fiancée. Brynhild has sworn only to marry the man who knows no fear; this is Sigurd, but he is already married. Sigurd magically exchanges appearances with Gunnar and rides through a wall of flame to Brynhild's side. The two sleep together for three nights, with a drawn sword between them to safeguard Brynhild's honour. Brynhild marries Gunnar, believing him to be the man who crossed the flame-wall. At some point (presumably in the poems contained in the missing leaves of the manuscript) Brynhild discovers the truth and incites Gunnar and his brother Hogni to kill Sigurd, claiming that he had in fact been her lover, despite the oaths he had sworn to Gunnar. After his death she commits suicide. It is probable that Sigurd was originally a Helgi-type hero, destroyed by his involvement with a valkyrie. The addition of the battle with Fafnir and the involvement with Gudrun and her family are likely to have come later. Neither the compiler of the Codex Regius nor the author of *Volsunga saga* entirely succeed in rationalizing the Sigurd material. In the *Edda* Sigurd becomes involved with one valkyrie, Sigrdrifa, whom he encounters on the mountain Hindarfiall and who is never mentioned again, while in *Volsunga saga* the author replaces Sigrdrifa with Brynhild, only to have Sigurd encounter her again at her foster-father's house. Thus Sigurd betroths himself twice to Brynhild before he meets Gudrun. The complications can only be resolved through the introduction of a magic potion, which causes Sigurd to forget his prior betrothals to Brynhild entirely until he has won her for Gunnar.

Gudrun provides the link to the next instalment of the saga. Atli, originally the fourth-century leader Attila the Hun, is imagined to have been Brynhild's brother, and so the new cycle begins. After Sigurd's death Gudrun is unwillingly married to Atli; when he lures her brothers to his court and kills them for the treasure they had inherited from Sigurd, Gudrun kills him and her own sons by him in revenge. In the late poem *Oddrun's Lament*, yet another sibling is grafted onto the Brynhild–Atli family: Oddrun, who becomes the lover of Gunnar after Brynhild's death. The affair is discovered by Atli who has Gunnar killed. This motive for Gunnar's killing is found only in this poem and in *A Short Poem about Sigurd*, which is clearly dependent on *Oddrun's Lament*. Gudrun contracts a third marriage, bringing to it her daughter by Sigurd, Svanhild, and producing further sons, Hamdir and Sorli. Svanhild is sent in marriage to the tyrant Iormunrekk who has her trampled to death by horses when he believes her to be unfaithful to him with his son, Randver. In the last poem of the *Poetic Edda*, Gudrun dispatches her remaining sons on a doomed quest for revenge on Iormunrekk.

The figures in the Volsung poems belong partly in history, like Attila the Hun and Gunnar, king of the Burgundians, and partly in legend. There is influence from southern German texts, but the story of Sigurd, Gudrun, Brynhild, and Gunnar is quite distinct from the plot of the Middle High German epic, the *Nibelungenlied*, which uses the same characters. Here Gudrun metamorphoses into the monstrous Kriemhilt, bent on killing her brothers in revenge for Siegfried (Sigurd), and Etzel (Atli) is the well-meaning dupe of his terrifying wife. Richard Wagner made use of *Volsunga saga*, written down around 1300, as the main source for his Ring Cycle, though he employs the *Poetic Edda*, known to him from the works of Jakob and Wilhelm Grimm and from his own study of Old Norse, for the idea of *Götterdämmerung*.

Other Eddic Poems

The last four poems in this volume are recognizably Eddic though they are not found in the Codex Regius, but in manuscripts of Snorri's *Edda* or other late thirteenth-century codices. They are mythological in content: the *List of Rig*, though incomplete, tells how human society gains a class system and how the institution of kingship begins. *Baldr's Dreams* prophesies the death of Baldr, through the interaction of Odin and a dead seeress. Another seeress is questioned by Freyia in the *Song of Hyndla* about the genealogy of a human hero Ottar, who needs to know his lineage in order to lay claim to his inheritance. The *Song of Grotti* is sung by two giantesses who are forced to work for King Frodi, a semi-legendary Danish king, whose kingdom will be destroyed as a result of his mistreatment of them.

Reception

The Codex Regius was sent to Copenhagen in 1643; in 1665 Peder Hans Resen published an edition of the *Seeress's Prophecy* and *Sayings of the High One*, providing them with a Latin translation. With the addition of a text of Snorri's *Edda*, the Resen volume introduced Norse mythology to the world. A copy was given to the Bodleian Library in Oxford in the early 1670s; and the writer Robert Sheringham was able to draw on it for his study of the origins of the English published in 1670. A French diplomat, Paul Mallet, wrote a two-volume account of early Scandinavian beliefs and history in 1755 and 1766 entitled

Introduction à l'histoire de Dannemarc and *Monumens de la mythologie et de la poésie des Celtes*. Like many of his contemporaries, Mallet believed that the northern races were Celtic in origin, hence his title. In his work Mallet summarized parts of the *Seeress's Prophecy* and quoted from the *Sayings of the High One* in French translation, and also reproduced the first few verses of *Baldr's Dreams* which had been published by the Dane Bartholin in 1689. Mallet's book was translated by Thomas Percy under the title *Northern Antiquities* in 1770. Thus it was primarily from Percy that English Romantic writers learned about Norse myth and heroic legend, plundering *Northern Antiquities* for 'Gothick' detail, valkyries, vikings, shield-maids, and drinking out of enemy skulls (a fallacy based on a mistranslation). They also made 'versions' of the Norse heroic poems they found in Percy. Most notable was Thomas Gray's *The Descent of Odin*, expanding upon Mallet's excerpts from *Baldr's Dreams*, in his *Norse Odes* of 1768. In 1787 the Arnamagnæan Commission in Copenhagen began to publish a fully edited text of the Codex Regius and other Eddic poems, at last permitting proper scholarly study and translation of the contents. By 1797 Amos Cottle had produced a rhymed English translation of the first volume of the Copenhagen edition, based on the Latin translation. Cottle's level of understanding may be gauged by the fact that in *Thrym's Poem* he depicts Freyia as consenting to go to Giantland to marry Thrym, thus making a nonsense of everything which comes afterwards in the poem. For a direct and scholarly translation from Norse into English, the British public had to wait for Benjamin Thorpe's 1866 *Sæmundar Edda*. The final volume of the Copenhagen edition, containing the heroic poetry, did not appear until 1828. By this time the 'Gothick' enthusiasms of English poets were beginning to wane, just as such ghoulishly dramatic stories as the night spent by Sigrun with the dead Helgi and Gudrun's murder of her sons were becoming available to them.

More to Victorian taste were the Icelandic family sagas with their stories of grim courage, stark choices, and manly heroes. Victorian scholars and amateurs of Old Icelandic translated the sagas of Burnt-Njal and Grettir, and *Laxdæla saga* and *Eyrbyggja saga* among others. Though investigation of Norse myth revived, with the beginnings of the study of comparative mythology later in the century, Snorri's *Edda* proved a more manageable source of information than the *Poetic Edda*. William Morris and Eirikur Magnusson drew on some of the Sigurd poems, in addition to *Volsunga saga*, for their version of the Sigurd story, *The Story of Sigurd the Volsung and the Fall of the Niblungs* (1870), but it remains true that the first flush of interest in 'Eddick' verse in the late eighteenth century has never been surpassed. In the 1960s, following late on his pre-war journey to Iceland with Louis MacNeice, W. H. Auden (with P. B. Taylor) produced versions of the *Edda* poems. Although these scarcely give an accurate impression of the structure or sense of the poetry, they convey Auden's personal vision of the North with memorable phrases and striking simplicity. Nevertheless, in the twentieth century Snorri's *Edda* with its rationalized and systematic account of myth and the Norse heroes has been regarded as more straightforward than the difficult and allusive poetry of the *Poetic Edda* for English readers. Tales of the Norse gods and heroes have remained perennially popular as children's literature. In Europe the reinterpretation of Eddic themes and the Sigurd story by Wagner, and their consequent association with Nazi propaganda, has proved hard to shake off. However the last few decades have brought a renewed interest in myth—the runes which Odin won at such great cost are now a divinatory game for New Ageists, and neo-paganism has a limited following in Germany, England, and Scandinavia.

Critical Interpretation

The poems of the *Edda* were used in the nineteenth and early twentieth centuries primarily as source material for a number of larger projects—for reconstructing Indo-European mythic patterns, leading to an undue emphasis on seasonal and fertility motifs; for uncovering Germanic prehistory, giving life to forgotten heroes of the Migration Period (AD 400–600), and demonstrating Germanic ethics, customs, and heroic culture. More recently the poems have been acknowledged as worthy objects of study in their own right. Scholars ceased to rearrange or excise the stanzas of the longer mythological poems in order to recreate their vision of the 'original' poem, and began to concentrate on the unity and aesthetic value of the poems as they stand in the manuscripts. Since 1945 the poems have been interpreted according to structuralist, comparative, and, most recently, feminist theory and have proved amenable to investigation of their properties as texts intermediate between an oral and unrecoverable, and a fully literate, stage. Relating poems to 'real life', to particular historical moments, has been hampered by lack of knowledge about pagan religious ritual and the precise dates and origins of the poetry, but attempts at reading enduring Scandinavian social structures—ideas about kingship, the role of women, the function of feud—based on developments in anthropological theory yoked with a more flexible structuralist approach, have been relatively successful. The question of reception too has been raised: what might a late thirteenth-century readership for whom the Codex Regius was put together have understood from the poem?

The heroic poems are easier to characterize than the mythological ones since they form one long episodic cycle, yoking together Helgi, Sigurd, Gunnar, Gudrun, and her sons in the story of the hero and the valkyrie, in its different versions, and the subsequent history of the Niflung line. The plots centre on honour, revenge, love, and greed in an essentially aristocratic society. The hero is doomed to die young and faces his end with bravura and courage, glad not to die ignominiously in bed at the hands of a woman as Atli does. The heroine is left to grieve passionately for the greatness which has been lost and for her own plight. The women—Sigrun, Gudrun, Oddrun, Brynhild—voice the emotion and passion which the heroic mentality suppresses; powerful actors themselves in the unfolding drama, they should not be regarded as mere victims of male power politics.

The mythological poems seem to be organized by main protagonist, with poems featuring Odin followed by *Skirnir's Journey*, a poem about Freyr, poems about Thor, and then poems about marginally divine figures, Volund and Alviss. Twentieth-century critics have tended to stress the apocalyptic theme in the mythological poems, reading the Odinic poems, in which Odin seems desperate to learn the fate he cannot escape, as driving inexorably towards Ragnarok—a theme particularly congenial to a nuclear-age readership. Even the less solemn poems, *Harbard's Song* and *Loki's Quarrel*, have been adduced as evidence for the lack of unity and moral corruption among the gods, who thus deserve to be destroyed. Such an interpretation is both unhelpfully Christian and judgemental and also overlooks the space given to comic adventure in the triumphs of Thor over giants in *Thrym's Poem*, *Hymir's Poem*, and *All-wise's Sayings* and the apparently happy ending of *Skirnir's Journey*. Though the theme of Ragnarok is prominent in the *Seeress's Prophecy* and *Vafthrudnir's Sayings*, the mythological poems, despite Snorri's best efforts, cannot be synthesized into a single grand narrative. The poems, composed by different authors, at different times, in different genres, as monologues, dialogues, perhaps brief dramas, and as narrative, a millennium later speak individually to us in comic, tragic, grandiose, crude, witty, profound, and common-sense tones.

NOTE ON THE TRANSLATION

I HAVE used the usual conventions for spelling of Icelandic proper names, omitting accents and the consonantal nominative ending *-r*, except where it follows a vowel. The special Icelandic characters 'thorn' (þ) and 'eth' (ð) have been rendered as 'th' and 'd', spellings which occur in the *Poetic Edda* itself. Hooked 'o' and 'ø' have been printed as 'o', 'œ' and 'æ' both as 'æ', in accordance with modern Icelandic pronunciation; 'i' has been used for the semi-consonantal sound often written 'j'. Stress always falls on the first syllable in Norse names.

The Norse text used as the basis for translation is *Edda: Die Lieder des Codex Regius nebst verwandten Denkmälern*, i: *Text*, ed. G. Neckel, 5th edn., rev. H. Kuhn (Heidelberg, 1983). However, proper names are cited according to the normalized orthography of Jón Helgason as used in *Eddadigte*, ed. J. Helgason, 3 vols. (Copenhagen, 1955).

I have included a certain amount of cross-referencing to Snorri Sturluson's mythographical treatise, the *Prose Edda*, as it often clarifies or amplifies the material of the *Poetic Edda*, to *Ynglinga saga* (the first legendary saga in Snorri's history of the kings of Norway, *Heimskringla*), to *Volsunga saga*, which covers much of the ground of the heroic poetry, and to Saxo's *History of the Danish People*. The editions used are to be found in the Select Bibliography. Comment on particular points of difficulty can be found in the Explanatory Notes; the Annotated Index of Names gives basic information as to the identity of named characters.

Metre and Style

Eddic poetry is the kind of poetry found in the Codex Regius. It is simple, in comparison with the ornate and complex skaldic verse which was the court poetic style, and the subject of the later sections of Snorri's *Edda*. The kind of elaborate phrasing typical of skaldic diction, whereby the term (known as a kenning) 'battle-fish in the hawk's perch' means 'sword in the hand', is eschewed in Eddic verse. In the heroic poetry a warrior may be denoted as 'powerful apple-tree of strife', but such periphrases are relatively easy to decode. Eddic poetry depends for its effect rather upon stress and alliteration. The poems are composed in a restricted number of metres: *ljodahattr*, used for wisdom and dialogue poetry, has stanzas consisting in two halves, each composed of a long line with four stresses and two alliterative syllables, and a shorter line, with two stresses and two alliterative syllables, as in this example (vowels alliterate with one another):

x x x x
*H*iardir that vito, nær thær *h*eim scolo,
x x
oc *g*anga tha af *g*rasi;
x x x x
enn *o*svidr madr kann ævagi
x x
sins um *m*al *m*aga.

(*Sayings of the High One*, v. 21)

[Cattle know when they ought to go home, | and then they leave the pasture; | but the foolish man never knows | the measure of his own stomach.]

Fornyrdislag is the most frequent narrative metre, especially in the heroic poetry. It consists of four-line stanzas; a line consists of two half-lines, each with two stresses and one alliterating syllable:

x x x x
Her ma *H*odbroddr *H*elga kenna,
x x x x
*fl*otta traudan, i *fl*ota midiom;
x x x x
hann hefir *e*dli ættar thinnar
x x x x
*a*rf Fiorsunga, *u*nd sic thrungit.

(*Second Poem of Helgi Hundingsbani*, v. 20)

[Here Hodbrodd may recognize Helgi, | the fighter who does not flee in the midst of the fleet; | the homeland of your kin, | the inheritance of the Fiorsungs he has conquered.]

Galdralag (literally 'spell-measure') is different again, a repetitive metre found for example in *Sayings of the High One*, v. 144, while *malahattr* is an augmented *fornyrdislag*, found in the *Greenlandic Poem of Atli*. It has five stresses and two alliterating syllables in the first half-line and usually five stresses with one alliterating syllable in the second half-line.

Many poems change metre as they move from dialogue to narrative, or wisdom material to conversation. In the *Lay of Fafnir*, the dragon, Fafnir, and the hero, Sigurd, converse mostly in *ljodahattr* as they bandy gnomic sayings, but once the dragon is dead, the nuthatches who advise Sigurd to kill his foster-father, Regin the dwarf, and to set out to look for Sigrdrifa, mostly use *fornyrdislag*. Some poems have prose introductions giving a minimum of information necessary to understand the initial situation. In the cycle of poems about the hero Sigurd, someone, perhaps the compiler of the manuscript, has inserted some explanatory prose passages, covering parts of the story where perhaps no poem exists; elsewhere he draws attention to the conflicting traditions about where Sigurd's death took place.

The State and Presentation of the Text

Part of the Codex Regius is missing. Some leaves are lost in the Sigurd cycle, so that the end of the *Lay of Sigrdrifa* must be added from the prose account of Sigurd's life in *Volsunga saga*. When the manuscript begins again the story of Sigurd's marriage to Gudrun and Gunnar's wooing of Brynhild has been lost; the next poems deal with the aftermath of Brynhild's realization that she has been tricked into marrying the wrong man. Elsewhere in the manuscript lines have been lost and verses misplaced. The edition from which this translation has been made follows the manuscript fairly closely, but at times—for example, v. 48 of the *Seeress's Prophecy*—a verse has been moved to a different position in the text for the sake of clarity.

In the manuscript the poetry is written in continuous lines across the page, as if it were prose, in order to save space. We can only determine the boundaries of verses by applying metrical rules. In some cases verses contain lists which spill across several stanzas: in this translation, as in most editions, these verses are printed as if they were continuous, for example in the catalogue of dwarfs in the *Seeress's Prophecy*, vv. 11–16.

SELECT BIBLIOGRAPHY

The Poetic Edda

Dronke, Ursula (ed. and trans.), *The Poetic Edda*, i (Oxford, 1969). Model edition of the last four poems in the Codex Regius.

Helgason, Jón (ed.), *Eddadigte*, 3 vols. (Copenhagen, 1955). Contains the poems up to the *Lay of Sigrdrifa*.

La Farge, Beatrice, and Tucker, John (eds.), *Glossary to the Poetic Edda Based on Hans Kuhn's Kurzes Wörterbuch* (Heidelberg, 1992). Glossary to the Neckel–Kuhn edition, expanded and updated.

Neckel, Gustav (ed.), *Edda: Die Lieder des Codex Regius nebst verwandten Denkmälern*, i: *Text*, rev. Hans Kuhn, 5th edn. (Heidelberg, 1983). Still the most up-to-date edition of the complete *Poetic Edda*.

Other Texts

Egil's saga, trans. Christine Fell (London, 1975).

Grettir's saga, trans. Denton Fox and Hermann Palsson (Toronto, 1974).

Njals saga, trans. Magnus Magnusson and Hermann Palsson (Harmondsworth, 1960).

Saxo Grammaticus, *History of the Danish People*, trans. Peter Fisher, ed. Hilda Ellis Davidson, 2 vols. (Cambridge, 1979). A readable and lively translation with a compendious commentary.

Snorri Sturluson, *Edda*, trans. A. Faulkes (London, 1987). A translation of all of Snorri's poetic treatise.

Snorri Sturluson, *Edda: Prologue and Gylfaginning*, ed. A. Faulkes (London, 1988).

Tacitus, *The Agricola and the Germania*, trans. H. Mattingly, rev. S. A. Handford (Harmondsworth, 1970).

The saga of Gisli, trans. George Johnston (London, 1973).

Volsunga saga, trans. Jesse Byock (Enfield, Middx., 1993).

Ynglinga saga, in Snorri Sturluson, *Heimskringla*, trans. Lee Hollander (Austin, Texas, 1964). Reliable translation of Snorri's account of early Norwegian history.

On the Edda, Old Norse Myth, and Heroic Verse

Andersson, Theodore, *The Legend of Brynhild*, Islandica 43 (Ithaca, NY, 1980). A study of the Brynhild figure, incorporating material from the *Nibelungenlied* and other Scandinavian texts and tracing the probable development of the story.

Clover, Carol, and Lindow, John, *Old Norse–Icelandic Literature: A Critical Guide*, Islandica 45 (Ithaca, NY and London, 1985). Contains two very valuable essays, one by John Lindow on Norse myth and one by Joseph Harris on the *Poetic Edda*. Also full bibliography to 1984.

Clunies Ross, M., *Prolonged Echoes: Old Norse Myths in Medieval Northern Society*, i: *The Myths*, The Viking Collection 7 (Odense, 1994). A highly readable and learned discussion of the mythological materials in Snorri, the *Poetic Edda*, and other medieval sources.

Larrington, C. (ed.), *The Feminist Companion to Mythology* (London, 1992). Contains a chapter by the editor on the role of women in Scandinavian mythology and its later reception.

Page, R., *Norse Myths* (London, 1990). A sceptical, quirkily written account of the myths.

Simek, R. (ed.), *Dictionary of Northern Mythology*, trans. Angela Hall (Cambridge, 1993). Many entries on the protagonists of the myths, but excluding most human heroes.

Turville-Petre, E. O. G., *Myth and Religion of the North* (London, 1964). A standard introduction to Norse myth.

de Vries, Jan, *Heroic Song and Heroic Legend*, trans. B. J. Timmer (London, 1963). Ranges widely through Germanic material; a good popular overview.

MAIN GENEALOGIES OF GODS, GIANTS, AND HEROES

Note: in the tables below *m.* denotes 'married'; = denotes 'had sexual relationship with'.

GIANTS

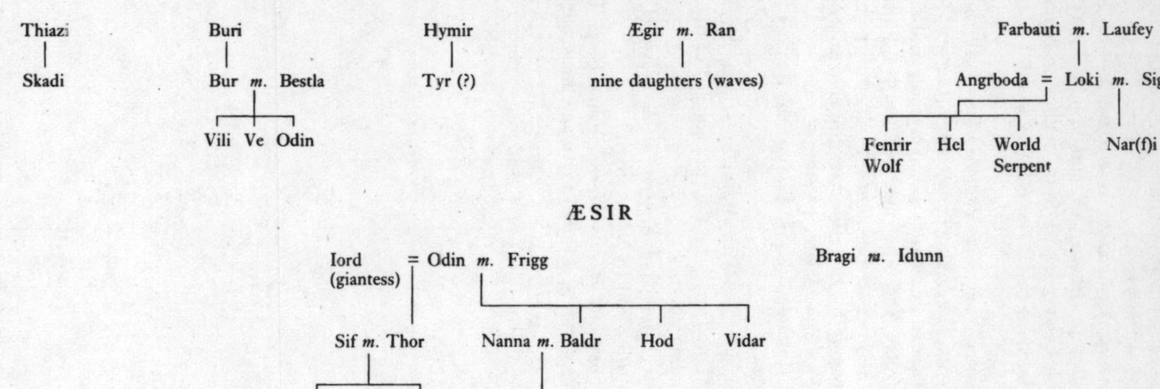

VANIR

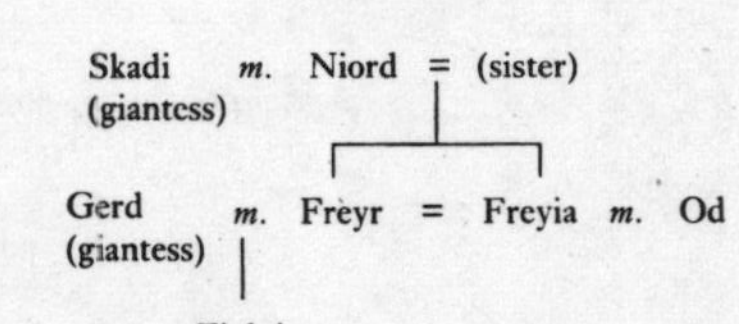

THE VOLSUNGS

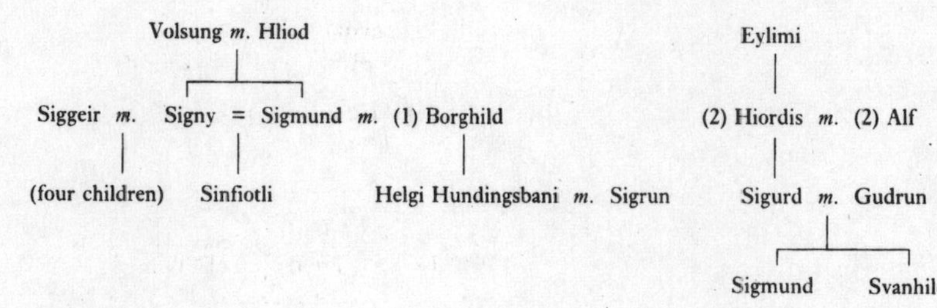

THE GIUKUNGS

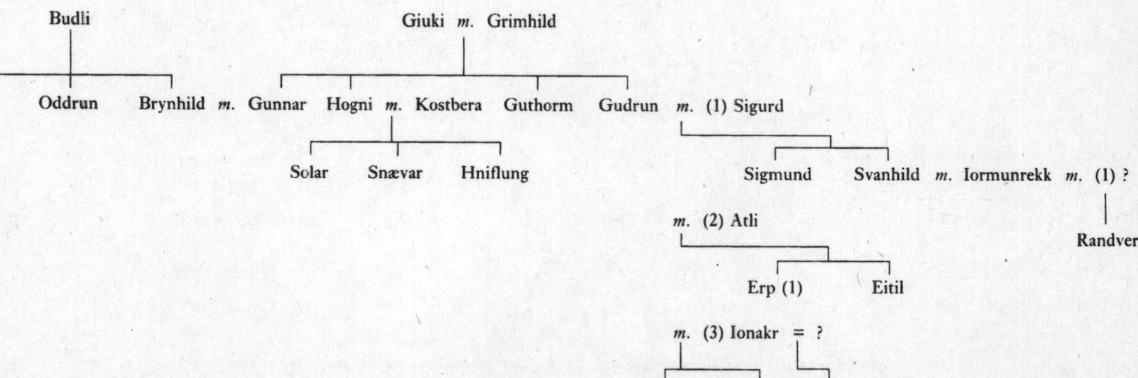

THE POETIC EDDA

The Seeress's Prophecy

The *Seeress's Prophecy* (*Voluspa*), composed mainly in the *fornyrdislag* metre, is recited by a seeress who can remember before the beginning of the world and who can see as far ahead as after Ragnarok—the Doom of the Gods. Odin ('Father of the Slain' in v. 1) is interrogating the seeress to find out what is to come; her reply moves swiftly and allusively through the history of gods and men. The account begins with the creation of the earth (vv. 3–5), then time is created (v. 6). The gods build temples and enjoy a golden age (vv. 7–8) until they are disrupted by three girls from Giantland. This somehow leads to the creation of the dwarfs (vv. 9–16). Humanity is created in vv. 18–19 and the fates arrive in v. 20. Now history begins: a mysterious female manifests herself amongst the Æsir, a woman well-versed in magic (vv. 21–2); as a consequence the Æsir find themselves at war with the Vanir (vv. 23–4). Peace is concluded and the gods have to repair damage to Asgard; a giant offers to rebuild the walls in a very short space of time in exchange for the sun, moon, and Freyia. The gods agree, thinking the task impossible, but the builder nearly succeeds and Thor has to destroy him, breaking the gods' promises of safe-conduct (vv. 25–6). At v. 28 we reach the present, with Odin questioning the seeress about what is to come. The Doom of the Gods is signalled by the death of Baldr and its consequences (vv. 31–5); the end of the world by images of punishment and social collapse (vv. 36–45). Ragnarok approaches: the World-Ash Yggdrasill trembles and the giants advance (vv. 46–52). Odin is killed by the wolf Fenrir, Freyr by Surt; Thor and the Midgard-serpent kill each other. Odin is avenged by his son Vidar and the world disappears in fire (vv. 53–8). In the verses which follow, the earth rises anew from the sea and some of the Æsir, including Baldr, return to live peacefully together (vv. 59–64). In v. 65 the coming of a mysterious figure is signalled; some commentators have taken this to be a Christian reference to the Last Judgement. In the final verse the sinister dragon Nidhogg is seen as the seeress sinks out of her trance. Does evil still exist in the new world, or have we returned to the present where the dragon is a portent of Ragnarok?

The *Seeress's Prophecy* is usually dated to the late tenth century when the pagan religion was beginning to be superseded by Christianity. One scholar has suggested that the poem is a kind of sacred text of the Scandinavian religion, composed just before the beliefs were to be eradicated by Christianity. The poem exists in two manuscripts, in rather different versions, and many of its verses are also to be found in Snorri's *Edda*. All verses ascribed to the poem are given here; the verse numbering follows the text in Neckel and Kuhn's edition.

1 Attention I ask from all the sacred people,
greater and lesser, the offspring of Heimdall;*
Father of the Slain, you wished that I should declare
the ancient histories of men and gods, those which I
remember from the first.

2 I, born of giants, remember very early
those who nurtured me then;
I remember nine worlds, I remember nine giant women,*
the mighty Measuring Tree down below the earth.

3 Young were the years when Ymir made his settlement,*
there was no sand nor sea nor cool waves;
earth was nowhere nor the sky above,
chaos yawned, grass was there nowhere.

4 First the sons of Bur brought up the earth,*
the glorious ones who shaped the world between;
the sun shone from the south on the hall of stones,
then the soil was grown over with green plants.

5 From the south, Sun, companion of the moon,
threw her right hand round the edge of the heaven;
Sun did not know where her hall might be,
the stars did not know where their place might be,
the moon did not know what power he had.

6 Then all the Powers went to the thrones of fate,
the sacrosanct gods, and considered this:
to night and her children they gave names,
morning they named and midday,
afternoon and evening, to reckon up the years.

7 The Æsir met on Idavoll Plain,
they built altars and high temples;
they set up their forges, smithed precious things,
shaped tongs and made tools.

8 They played chequers in the meadow, they were merry,
they did not lack for gold at all,
until three giant girls came,*
mighty and powerful, out of Giantland.

9 Then all the Powers went to the thrones of fate,
the sacrosanct gods, and considered this:
who should form the lord of the dwarfs
out of Brimir's blood and from Blain's limbs?*

10 Then Motsognir became the greatest of
all the dwarfs, and Durin another;
Many manlike figures they made,
dwarfs from the earth, as Durin recounted.

11 New-moon and Dark-of-moon, North and South,*
East and West, Master-thief, Delayer,
Bivor, Bavor, Bombur, and Nori,
An and Anar, Great-grandfather and Mead-wolf.

12 Liquor and Staff-elf, Wind-elf and Thrain,
Known and Thorin, Thror, Colour and Wise,
Corpse and New-advice: now I have rightly
—Regin and Counsel-sharp—reckoned up the dwarfs.
13 Fili and Kili, Foundling and Nali,
Haft and Vili, Hanar and Sviur,
Frar and Hornborer, Fræg and Sea-pool,
Loamfield, Iari, Oakenshield.
14 Time it is to tally up the dwarfs in Dvalin's lineage,
the people of Lofar,
those who sought out from the stony halls
the dwelling of Loamfield on Iorovellir.

15 There were Draupnir and Dolgthrasir,
Greyhair, Mound-river, Lee-plain, Glow,
Skirvir, Virvir, Skafid, and Great-grandfather.
16 Elf and Yngvi, Oakenshield,
Fialar and Frosty, Finn and Betrayer;
they'll be remembered while mankind endures,
the long tally of ancestors of Lofar.

. . . . . .

17 Until three gods, strong and loving,*
came from that company to the world;
they found on land Ash and Embla,*
capable of little, lacking in fate.

18 Breath they had not, spirit they had not,
character nor vital spark nor fresh complexions;
breath gave Odin, spirit gave Hænir,
vital spark gave Lodur, and fresh complexions.

19 I know that an ash-tree stands called Yggdrasill,
a high tree, soaked with shining loam;
from there come the dews which fall in the valley,
ever green, it stands over the well of fate.

20 From there come three girls, knowing a great deal,
from the lake which stands under the tree;
Fated one is called, Becoming another—
they carved on wooden slips—Must-be the third;
they set down laws, they chose lives,
for the sons of men the fates of men.

21 She remembers the first war in the world,*
when they buttressed Gullveig with spears
and in One-eye's hall they burned her;*
three times they burned her, three times she was reborn,
over and over, yet she lives still.

22 Bright One they called her, wherever she came to houses,*
the seer with pleasing prophecies, she charmed them
with spells;
she made magic wherever she could, with magic she
played with minds,
she was always the favourite of wicked women.

23 Then all the Powers went to the thrones of fate,
the sacrosanct gods, and considered this:
whether the Æsir should yield the tribute
or whether all the gods should partake in the sacrifices.

24 Odin shot a spear, hurled it over the host;
that was still the first war in the world;
the defensive wall was broken of the Æsir's stronghold;
the Vanir, indomitable, were trampling the plain.

25 Then all the Powers went to the thrones of fate,
the sacrosanct gods, and considered this:
who had mixed the air with wickedness,
or given Od's girl to the giant race.*

26 Thor alone struck a blow there, swollen with rage,
he seldom sits still when he hears such things said;
the oaths broke apart, the words and the promises,
all the solemn pledges which had passed between them.

27 She knows that Heimdall's hearing is hidden
under the radiant, sacred tree;
she sees, pouring down, the muddy torrent
from the wager of Father of the Slain; do you
understand yet, or what more?*

28 Alone she sat outside, when the old man came,
the Terrible One of the Æsir and he looked in her eyes:
'Why do you question me? Why do you test me?
I know everything, Odin, where you hid your eye
in the famous well of Mimir.'
Mimir drinks mead every morning
from Father of the Slain's wager—do you understand
yet, or what more?

29 Father of Hosts chose for her rings and necklaces,
he got wise speech and a rod of divination;
she saw widely, widely into all the worlds.

30 She saw valkyries coming from far and wide,
ready to ride to the Gothic nation;
Skuld held one shield, Skogul another,
Gunn, Hild, Gondul, and Spear-Skogul;
now the ladies of the General, the valkyries are counted up,
ready to ride the earth.

31 I saw for Baldr, for the bloody god,
Odin's child, his fate concealed;
there stood grown—higher than the plain,
slender and very fair—the mistletoe.

32 From that plant which seemed so lovely
came a dangerous, harmful dart, Hod began to shoot;
Baldr's brother was born very quickly;*
Odin's son began fighting at one night old.

33 Nor did he ever wash his hands nor comb his hair,
until he brought Baldr's adversary to the funeral pyre;
and in Fen-halls Frigg wept
for the woe of Valhall—do you understand yet, or what more?

34 Then oppressive bonds were twisted,
rather severe fetters, made of Vali's entrails.*

35 She saw a captive lying under the grove of hot springs,
that evil-loving form, Loki she recognized;
there sits Sigyn, not at all happy
about her husband—do you understand yet, or what more?

36 From the east falls, from poison valleys,
a river of knives and swords, Cutting it is called.

37 To the north there stood on Dark-of-moon Plains,
a hall of gold, of the lineage of Sindri;*
and another stood on Never-cooled Plain,
the beer-hall of the giant who is called Brimir.

38 A hall she saw standing far from the sun,
on Corpse-strand; its doors look north;
drops of poison fall in through the roof-vents,
the hall is woven of serpents' spines.

39 There she saw wading in turbid streams
men who swore false oaths and murderers,
and those who seduced the close confidantes of other men;
there Nidhogg sucks the bodies of the dead—
a wolf tears the corpses of men—do you understand yet, or what more?

40 In the east sat an old woman in Iron-wood
and nurtured there offspring of Fenrir;
a certain one of them in monstrous form
will be the snatcher of the moon.

41 The corpses of doomed men fall,
the gods' dwellings are reddened with crimson blood;
sunshine becomes black the next summer,*
all weather is vicious—do you understand yet, or what more?

42 He sat on the mound and plucked his harp,
the herdsman of the giantess, cheerful Eggther;
a rooster crowed in Gallows-wood,
that bright-red cockerel who is called Fialar.

43 Golden-comb crowed for the Æsir,
he wakens the warriors at the Father of Hosts';*
and another crows down below the earth,
a sooty-red cock in the halls of Hel.

44 Garm bays loudly before Gnipa-cave,*
the rope will break and the ravener run free,
much wisdom she knows, I see further ahead
to the terrible doom of the fighting gods.

45 Brother will fight brother and be his slayer,
brother and sister will violate the bond of kinship;
hard it is in the world, there is much adultery,
axe-age, sword-age, shields are cleft asunder,
wind-age, wolf-age, before the world plunges headlong;
no man will spare another.

46 The sons of Mim are at play and fate catches fire*
at the ancient Giallar-horn;
Heimdall blows loudly, his horn is in the air.
Odin speaks with Mim's head.

47 Yggdrasill shudders, the tree standing upright,
the ancient tree groans and the giant is loose;
all are terrified on the roads to hell,
before Surt's kin swallows it up.*

49 Garm bays loudly before Gnipa-cave,
the rope will break and the ravener run free,
much wisdom she knows, I see further ahead
to the terrible doom of the victorious gods.

50 Hrym drives from the east, he has his shield before
    him,*
the great serpent writhes in giant rage;
the serpent churns the waves, the eagle shrieks in
    anticipation,
pale-beaked he tears the corpse, Naglfar breaks loose.*

51 A ship journeys from the east, Muspell's people are
    coming*
over the waves, and Loki steers.
There are the monstrous brood with all the raveners,
The brother of Byleist is in company with them.*

48 What of the Æsir? What of the elves?
All Giantland groans. The Æsir are in council.
The dwarfs howl before their rocky doors,
the princes of the mountain wall—do you understand yet, or what more?

52 Surt comes from the south with the harm of branches,*
the sun of the slaughter-gods glances from his sword;
the rocky cliffs crack open and the troll-women are abroad,
men tread the road to hell and the sky splits apart.

53 Then the second grief of Frigg comes about*
when Odin advances to fight against the wolf,
and the bright slayer of Beli against Surt;*
then the beloved of Frigg must fall.

54 Then the great son of War-father,
Vidar, advances against the Beast of Slaughter;
with his hand he stabs his sword to the heart
of Loki's kinsman: then his father is avenged.*

55 In the air gapes the Earth-girdler,*
the terrible jaws of the serpent yawn above;
Odin's son must meet the serpent;
(the kin of Vidar is the death of the wolf).

56 Then the glorious son of Earth,
Odin's son, advances to fight against the serpent,*
in his wrath the defender of earth strikes,
all men must leave their homesteads;
nine steps Fiorgyn's child takes,
with difficulty, from the serpent of whom scorn is never spoken.

57 The sun turns black, earth sinks into the sea,
the bright stars vanish from the sky;
steam rises up in the conflagration,
a high flame plays against heaven itself.

58 Garm bays loudly before Gnipa-cave,
the rope will break and the ravener run free,
much wisdom she knows, I see further ahead
to the terrible doom of the victory-gods.

59 She sees, coming up a second time,
Earth from the ocean, eternally green;
the waterfall plunges, an eagle soars over it,
hunting fish on the mountain.

60 The Æsir meet on Idavoll
and they converse about the mighty Earth-girdler,
and they remember there the great events
and the ancient runes of the Mighty One.

61 There afterwards will be found in the grass
the wonderful golden chequers,
those which they possessed in the ancient times.

62 Without sowing the fields will grow,
all ills will be healed, Baldr will come back;
Hod and Baldr, the gods of slaughter, will live happily together
in the sage's palaces—do you understand yet, or what more?

63 Then Hænir will choose wooden slips for prophecy,
and the sons of two brothers will inhabit, widely,
the windy world—do you understand yet, or what more?

64 A hall she sees standing, fairer than the sun,
thatched with gold, at Gimle;
there the noble lords will live
and spend their days in pleasure.

65 Then the powerful, mighty one, he who rules over everything,
will come from above, to the judgement-place of the gods.

66 There comes the dark dragon flying,
the shining serpent, up from Dark-of-moon Hills;
Nidhogg flies over the plain, in his wings
he carries corpses; now she must sink down.

Sayings of the High One

Human social wisdom, teasing allusion to runic mysteries, spells, and charms combine in this poem to give a conspectus of different types of wisdom. Most of the poem is taken up with instruction on the subject of social behaviour, common sense and folly, moderation and friendship, composed in *ljodahattr*, the usual metre of wisdom verse. At times the poet steps forward to speak in his own voice, at times the first person merges with Odin, the god of wisdom, speaking from his own experience of questing after knowledge. The wisdom stanzas are organized by themes, connections made by juxtaposition or contrast. Towards the end of the poem Odin speaks more, of his sacrifice to learn the secrets of the runes and of his knowledge of spells, and narrates two adventures with women, and the metre is disrupted. *Sayings of the High One* (*Havamal*) is, no doubt, a redaction of several different poems unified by the theme of wisdom and by the central figure of Odin.

1 All the entrances, before you walk forward,
you should look at,
you should spy out;
for you can't know for certain where enemies are sitting
ahead in the hall.

2 Blessed be the givers! A guest has come in,
where is he going to sit?
He's in great haste, the one who by the hearth
is going to be tested out.

3 Fire is needful for someone who's come in
and who's chilled to the knee;
food and clothing are necessary for the man
who's journeyed over the mountains.

4 Water is needful for someone who comes to a meal,
a towel and a warm welcome,
a disposition, if he can get it, for good words
and silence in return.

5 Wits are needful for someone who travels widely,
anything will do at home;
he becomes a laughing-stock, the man who knows nothing
and sits among the wise.

6 About his intelligence no man should be boastful,
rather cautious of mind;
when a wise and silent man comes to a homestead
seldom does shame befall the wary;
for no more trustworthy a friend can any man get
than a store of common sense.

7 The careful guest, who comes to a meal,
keeps silent with hearing finely attuned;
he listens with his ears, and looks about with his eyes;
so every wise man informs himself.

8 This man is fortunate who can get for himself
praise and good will;
very difficult it is when a man lays claim
to what's in another's heart.

9 That man is fortunate who, in himself,
keeps his reputation and wits while he lives;
for men have often received bad advice
from another's heart.

10 No better burden can a man carry on the road
than a store of common sense;
better than riches it will seem in an unfamiliar place,
such is the resort of the wretched.

11 No better burden can a man carry on the road
than a store of common sense;
a worse journey-provisioning he couldn't carry over the land
than to be too drunk on ale.

12 It isn't as good as it's said to be,
ale, for the sons of men;
for the more he drinks, the less he knows
about the nature of men.

13 The heron of forgetfulness hovers over the ale-drinking;
he steals men's wits;
with the feathers of this bird I was fettered
in the court of Gunnlod.*

14 Drunk I was, I was more than drunk
at wise Fialar's;*
that's the best sort of ale-drinking when afterwards
every man gets his mind back again.

15 Silent and thoughtful a prince's son should be
and bold in fighting;
cheerful and merry every man should be
until he waits for death.

16 The foolish man thinks he will live for ever,
if he keeps away from fighting;
but old age won't grant him a truce
even if the spears do.

17 The fool gapes when he comes on a visit,
he mutters to himself or keeps silent;
but it's all up with him if he gets a swig of drink;
the man's mind is exposed.

18 Only that man who travels widely
and has journeyed a great deal knows
what sort of mind each man has in his control;
he who's sharp in his wits.

19 A man shouldn't hold onto the cup but drink mead in
moderation,
it's necessary to speak or be silent;
no man will blame you for impoliteness
if you go early to bed.

20 The greedy man, unless he guards against this tendency,
will eat himself into lifelong trouble;
often he's laughed at when he comes among the wise,
the man who's foolish about his stomach.

21 Cattle know when they ought to go home,
and then they leave the pasture;
but the foolish man never knows
the measure of his own stomach.

22 He's a wretched man, of an evil disposition,
the one who makes fun of everything;
he doesn't know the one thing he ought to know:
that he himself is not devoid of faults.

23 The foolish man lies awake all night
and worries about things;
he's tired out when the morning comes
and everything's just as bad as it was.

24 The foolish man thinks that everyone
is his friend who laughs with him;
he doesn't notice even if they say cruel things about him
when he sits among the wise.

25 The foolish man thinks that everyone
is his friend who laughs with him;
but then he finds when he comes to the Assembly*
that he has few to speak on his behalf.

26 The foolish man thinks he knows everything
if he takes refuge in a corner;
he doesn't know what he can say in return
if people ask him questions.

27 The foolish man in company
does best if he stays silent;
no one will know that he knows nothing,
unless he talks too much;
but the man who knows nothing does not know
when he is talking too much.

28 Wise that man seems who knows how to question
and how to answer as well;
the sons of men cannot keep secret
what's already going around.

29 Quite enough senseless words are spoken
by the man never silent;
a quick tongue, unless its owner keeps watch on it,
often talks itself into trouble.

30 Into a laughing-stock no man should make another,
though he comes on a visit;
many a man seems wise if he isn't asked questions
and he manages to lurk unscathed.

31 Wise that man seems who retreats
when one guest is insulting another;
the man who mocks others at a feast doesn't really
know
whether he's shooting off his mouth amid enemies.

32 Many men are devoted to one another
and yet they fight at feasts;
amongst men there will always be strife,
guest quarrelling with guest.

33 An early meal a man should usually eat,
unless he is going on a visit;
he sits and guzzles, acts as if he's starving,
and doesn't make any conversation.

34 It's a great detour to a bad friend's house,
even though he lives on the route;
but to a good friend's the ways lie straight,
even though he lives far off.

35 A man must go, he must not remain a guest
always in the same place;
the loved man is loathed if he sits too long
in someone else's hall.

36 A farm of your own is better, even if small,
everyone's someone at home;
though he has two goats and a coarsely roofed house,
that is better than begging.

37 A farm of your own is better, even if small,
everyone's someone at home;
a man's heart bleeds when he has to beg
for every single meal.

38 From his weapons on the open road
no man should step one pace away;
you don't know for certain when you're out on the
road
when you might have need of your spear.

39 I never found a generous man, nor one so hospitable
with food,
that he wouldn't accept a present;
or one so well-provided with money
that he wouldn't take a gift if offered.

40 On account of the property which he has amassed
a man shouldn't suffer need;
often what was meant for the lovable is saved for the
hateful,
much goes worse than is expected.

41 With weapons and gifts friends should gladden one another,
that is most obvious;
mutual givers and receivers are friends for longest,
if the friendship is going to work at all.

42 To his friend a man should be a friend
and repay gifts with gifts;
laughter a man should give for laughter
and repay treachery with lies.

43 To his friend a man should be a friend
and to his friend's friend too;
but a friend no man should be
to the friend of his enemy.

44 You know, if you've a friend whom you really trust
and from whom you want nothing but good,
you should mix your soul with his and exchange gifts,
go and see him often.

45 If you've another, whom you don't trust,
but from whom you want nothing but good,
speak fairly to him but think falsely
and repay treachery with lies.

46 Again, concerning the one whom you don't trust,
and whose mind you suspect:
you should laugh with him and disguise your thoughts,
a gift should be repaid with a like one.

47 I was young once, I travelled alone,
then I found myself going astray;
rich I thought myself when I met someone else,
for man is the joy of man.

48 Generous and brave men live the best,
seldom do they harbour anxiety;
but the cowardly man is afraid of everything,
the miser always sighs when he gets gifts.

49 My clothes I gave along the way
to two wooden men;*
champions they thought themselves when they had
clothing,
the naked man is ashamed.

50 The withered fir-tree which stands on the mound,
neither bark nor needles protect it;
so it is with the man whom no one loves,
why should he live for long?

51 Hotter than fire between bad friends
burns affection for five days;
but it dies down when the sixth day comes,
and all that friendship goes to the bad.

52 Not very much need a man give,
often you get praise for a little;
with half a loaf and a tilted cup
I've got myself a companion.

53 Of small sands, of small seas,
small are the minds of men;
for all men aren't equally wise,
men everywhere are half wise, half not.

54 Averagely wise a man ought to be,
never too wise;
for he lives the best sort of life,
the man who knows a fair amount.

55 Averagely wise a man ought to be,
never too wise;
for a wise man's heart is seldom cheerful,
if he who owns it's too wise.

56 Averagely wise a man ought to be,
never too wise;
no one may know his fate beforehand,
if he wants a carefree spirit.

57 One brand takes fire from another, until it is consumed,
a spark's kindled by a spark;
one man becomes clever by talking with another,
but foolish by taciturnity.

58 He should get up early, the man who means to take
another's life or property;
the slumbering wolf does not get the ham,
nor a sleeping man victory.

59 He should get up early, the man who has few workers,
and go about his work with thought;
much he neglects, the man who sleeps in in the
mornings,
wealth is half-won by the vigorous.

60 Of dry wood and thatching-bark
a man can know the measure;
and of the wood which can get one through
a quarter- or a half-year.

61 Washed and fed, a man should ride to the Assembly,
though he may not be very well dressed;
of his shoes and breeches no man should be ashamed,
nor of his horse, though he doesn't have a good one.

62 The eagle snaps and cranes his neck when he comes to
the sea,*
to the ancient ocean;
so does a man who comes among the multitude
and has few people to speak for him.

63 Asking questions and answering, this every wise man
should do,
he who wants to be reputed intelligent;
one may know, a second should not,
the whole world knows, if three know.

64 Every man wise in counsel
should use his power in moderation;
for when he mingles with warriors he finds out
that no one is boldest of all.

65 For those words which one man says to another,
often he gets paid back.*

66 Much too early I've come to many places,
but sometimes too late;
the ale was all drunk, or sometimes it wasn't yet brewed,
the unpopular man seldom chooses the right occasion.

67 Here and there I'd be invited to someone's home
when I had no need of food for the moment;
or two hams would be hanging in a trusty friend's house
when I'd already eaten one.

68 Fire is best for the sons of men,
and the sight of the sun
his health, if a man can manage to keep it,
living without disgrace.

69 No man is completely wretched, even if he has bad luck;
one man is blessed with sons,
another with kinsmen, another has enough money,
another has done great deeds.

70 It is better to live than not to be alive,
it's the living man who gets the cow;
I saw fire blaze up for the wealthy man,
and he was dead outside the door.

71 The lame man rides a horse, the handless man drives herds,
the deaf man fights and succeeds;
to be blind is better than to be burnt:
a corpse is of no use to anyone.

72 A son is best, even if he is born late,
when the father is dead;
seldom do memorial stones stand by the wayside,
unless one kinsman raises them for another.

73 Two are the conquerors of one, the tongue is the slayer
  of the head,
hidden under every fur coat I expect to find a hand.*

74 Night is eagerly awaited by the man who can rely on
  his provisions;
short are a ship's yards,
changeable are autumn nights,
many kinds of weather in five days,
and more in one month.

75 Even a man who knows nothing
knows that many are fooled by money;
one man is rich, another is not rich,
he should not blamed for that.

76 Cattle die, kinsmen die,*
the self must also die;
but glory never dies,
for the man who is able to achieve it.

77 Cattle die, kinsmen die,
the self must also die;
I know one thing which never dies:
the reputation of each dead man.

78 Fully stocked folds I saw for Fitiung's sons,*
now they carry beggars' staffs;
wealth is like the twinkling of an eye,
it is the most unreliable of friends.

79 The foolish man, if he manages to get
money or the love of a woman,
his arrogance increases, but not his common sense;
on he goes deeply sunk in delusion.

80 That is now proved, what you asked o
of the potent famous ones
which the great gods made
and the mighty sage stained,*
then it is best for him if he stays silent.

81 At evening should the day be praised, the woman when
she is cremated,
the blade when it is tested, the girl when she is
married,
the ice when it is crossed, the ale when it is drunk.

82 In a wind one should cut wood, in fine weather row on
the sea,
in darkness chat with a girl: many are the eyes of the
day;
use a ship to glide along, a shield for defence,
a sword for blows, and a girl for kisses.

83 By the fire one should drink ale, one should slide over
the ice,
buy a lean horse and a rusty blade,
fatten the horse at home and a dog on the farmstead.

84 The words of a girl no one should trust,
nor what a woman says;
for on a whirling wheel their hearts were made,*
deceit lodged in their breasts.

85 A stretching bow, a burning flame,
a gaping wolf, a cawing crow,
a grunting pig, a rootless tree,
a rising wave, a boiling kettle,
86 a flying dart, a falling wave,
ice of one night, a coiled serpent,
the bed-talk of a woman, or a broken sword,
the playing of a bear, or a king's child,

87 a sick calf, an independent-minded slave,
a seer who prophesies good, a newly killed corpse,
88 an early-sown field let no man trust,
nor too early in a son;
the weather determines the field and brains the son,
both of them are risky.

89 A brother's killer, if you meet him on the road,
a house half-burned, a too swift horse—
the mount is useless if he breaks a leg—
let no man be so trusting as to trust all these.

90 Such is the love of women, of those with false minds;
it's like driving a horse without spiked shoes over
slippery ice,
a frisky two year old, badly broken in,
or like steering, in a stiff wind, a rudderless boat,
or trying to catch when you're lame a reindeer on a
thawing hillside.

91 I can speak frankly since I have known both:
the hearts of men are fickle towards women;
when we speak most fairly, then we think most falsely,
that entraps the wise mind.

92 He has to speak fairly and offer money,
the man who wants a woman's love;
praise the body of the radiant woman:
he who flatters, gets.

93 No man should ever reproach
another for love;
often the wise man is seized, when the foolish man is
not,
by a delightfully fair appearance.

94 Not at all should one man reproach another
for what is common among men;
among the sons of men the wise are made foolish
by that mighty desire.

95 The mind alone knows what lies near the heart,
he alone knows his spirit:
no sickness is worse for the wise man
than to have no one to love him.

96 That I found when I sat among the reeds
and waited for my desire;
body and soul the wise girl was to me,
nevertheless I didn't win her.

97 Billing's girl I found on the bed,*
sleeping, sun-radiant;
the pleasures of a noble were nothing to me,
except to live with that body.

98 'At evening, Odin, you should come again,
if you want to woo yourself a girl;
all is lost if anyone knows
of such shame together.'

99 Back I turned, and thought I was going to love,
back from my certain pleasure;
this I thought that I would have,
all her heart and her love-play.

100 So I came afterwards, but standing ready
were all the warriors, awake,
with burning torches and carrying brands:
thus the path of desire was determined for me.

101 And near morning, when I came again,
then the hall-company were asleep;
a bitch I found then tied on the bed
of that good woman.

102 Many a good girl when you know her better
is fickle of heart towards men;
I found that out, when I tried to seduce
that sagacious woman into shame;
every sort of humiliation the clever woman devised for me,
and I didn't even possess the woman.

103 At home a man should be cheerful and merry with his guest,
he should be shrewd about himself,
with a good memory and eloquent, if he wants to be very wise,
often should he speak of good things;
a nincompoop that man is called, who can't say much for himself,
that is the hallmark of a fool.

104 I visited the old giant, now I've come back,*
I didn't get much there from being silent;
with many words I spoke to my advantage
in Suttung's hall.

105 Gunnlod gave me from her golden throne
a drink of the precious mead;
a poor reward I let her have in return,
for her open-heartedness,
for her heavy spirit.

106 With the mouth of the auger I made space for myself*
and gnawed through the stone;
over me and under me went the paths of the giants,
thus I risked my head.

107 The cheaply bought beauty I made good use of,
the wise lack for little;
for Odrerir has now come up*
to the rim of the sanctuaries of men.

108 I am in doubt as to whether I would have come
back from the courts of the giants,
if I had not made use of Gunnlod, that good woman,
and put my arms about her.

109 The next day the frost-giants went
to ask for the High One's advice, in the High One's hall;
they asked about Bolverk: whether he was amongst the gods,*
or whether Suttung had slaughtered him.

110 I thought Odin had sworn a sacred ring-oath,*
how can his word be trusted!
He left Suttung betrayed at the feast
and made Gunnlod weep.

111 It is time to declaim from the sage's high-seat,
at the spring of fate;
I saw and was silent, I saw and I considered,
I heard the speech of men;
I heard talk of runes nor were they silent about good counsel,
at the High One's hall, in the High One's hall;
thus I heard them speak:

112 I advise you, Loddfafnir, to take this advice,*
it will be useful if you learn it,
do you good, if you have it:
don't get up at night, except to look around
or if you need to visit the privy outside.

113 I advise you, Loddfafnir, to take this advice,
it will be useful if you learn it,
do you good, if you have it:
in the arms of a witch you should never sleep,
so that she charms all your limbs;

114 she'll bring it about that you won't care
about the Assembly or the king's business;
you won't want food nor the society of people,
sorrowful you'll go to sleep.

115 I advise you, Loddfafnir, to take this advice,
it will be useful if you learn it,
do you good, if you have it:
never entice another's wife to you
as a close confidante.

116 I advise you, Loddfafnir, to take this advice,
it will be useful if you learn it,
do you good, if you have it:
on mountain or fjord should you happen to be
travelling,
make sure you are well fed.

117 I advise you, Loddfafnir, to take this advice,
it will be useful if you learn it,
do you good, if you have it:
never let a wicked man know
of any misfortune you suffer;
for from a wicked man you will never get
a good thought in return.

118 I saw a man fatally wounded
through the words of a wicked woman;
a malicious tongue brought about his death
and yet there was no truth in the accusation.

119 I advise you, Loddfafnir, to take this advice,
it will be useful if you learn it,
do you good, if you have it:
you know, if you've a friend, one whom you trust,
go to see him often;
for brushwood grows, and tall grass,
on the road which no man treads.

120 I advise you, Loddfafnir, to take this advice,
it will be useful if you learn it,
do you good, if you have it:
draw to you in friendly intimacy a good man
and learn healing charms all your life.

121 I advise you, Loddfafnir, to take this advice,
it will be useful if you learn it,
do you good, if you have it:
with your friend never be
the first to tear friendship asunder;
sorrow eats the heart if you do not have
someone to tell all your thoughts.

122 I advise you, Loddfafnir, to take this advice,
it will be useful if you learn it,
do you good, if you have it:
you should never bandy words
with a stupid fool;

123 for from a wicked man you will never get
a good return;
but a good man will make you
assured of praise.

124 That is the true mingling of kinship when you can tell
someone all your thoughts;
anything is better than to be fickle;
he is no true friend who only says pleasant things.

125 I advise you, Loddfafnir, to take this advice,
it will be useful if you learn it,
do you good, if you have it:
even three words of quarrelling you shouldn't have with an inferior;
often the better retreats
when the worse man fights.

126 I advise you, Loddfafnir, to take this advice,
it will be useful if you learn it,
do you good, if you have it:
be neither a shoemaker nor a shaftmaker
for anyone but yourself;
if the shoe is badly fitting or the shaft is crooked,
then a curse will be called down on you.

127 I advise you, Loddfafnir, to take this advice,
it will be useful if you learn it,
do you good, if you have it:
where you recognize evil, speak out against it,
and give no truces to your enemies.

128 I advise you, Loddfafnir, to take this advice,
it will be useful if you learn it,
do you good, if you have it:
never be made glad by wickedness
but make yourself the butt of approval.

129 I advise you, Loddfafnir, to take this advice,
it will be useful if you learn it,
do you good, if you have it:
you should never look upwards in battle:*
the sons of men become panicked—
you may well be bewitched.

130 I advise you, Loddfafnir, to take this advice,
it will be useful if you learn it,
do you good, if you have it:
if you want a good woman for yourself to talk to as a
close confidante,
and to get pleasure from,
make fair promises and keep them well,
no man tires of good, if he can get it.

131 I advise you, Loddfafnir, to take this advice,
it will be useful if you learn it,
do you good, if you have it:
I tell you to be cautious but not over-cautious;
be most wary of ale, and of another's wife,
and, thirdly, watch out that thieves don't beguile you.

132 I advise you, Loddfafnir, to take this advice,
it will be useful if you learn it,
do you good, if you have it:
never hold up to scorn or mockery
a guest or a wanderer.

133 Often those who sit in the hall do not really know
whose kin those newcomers are;
no man is so good that he has no blemish,
nor so bad that he can't succeed in something.

134 I advise you, Loddfafnir, to take this advice,
it will be useful if you learn it,
do you good, if you have it:
at a grey-haired sage you should never laugh!
Often what the old say is good;
often from a wrinkled bag come judicious words,
from those who hang around with the hides
and skulk among the skins
and hover among the cheese-bags.

135 I advise you, Loddfafnir, to take this advice,
it will be useful if you learn it,
do you good, if you have it:
don't bark at your guests or drive them from your gate,
treat the indigent well!

136 It is a powerful latch which has to lift
to open up for everyone;
give a ring, or there'll be called down on you
a curse in every limb.

137 I advise you, Loddfafnir, to take this advice,
it will be useful if you learn it,
do you good, if you have it:
where you drink ale, choose the power of earth!*
For earth is good against drunkenness, and fire against sickness,
oak against constipation, an ear of corn against witchcraft,
the hall against household strife, for hatred the moon should be invoked—
earthworms for a bite or sting, and runes against evil;
soil you should use against flood.

138 I know that I hung on a windy tree*
nine long nights,
wounded with a spear, dedicated to Odin,
myself to myself,
on that tree of which no man knows
from where its roots run.

139 No bread did they give me nor a drink from a horn,
downwards I peered;
I took up the runes, screaming I took them,
then I fell back from there.

140 Nine mighty spells I learnt from the famous son
of Bolthor, Bestla's father,*
and I got a drink of the precious mead,
poured from Odrerir.

141 Then I began to quicken and be wise,
and to grow and to prosper;
one word found another word for me,
one deed found another deed for me.

142 The runes you must find and the meaningful letter,
a very great letter,
a very powerful letter,
which the mighty sage stained
and the powerful gods made
and the runemaster of the gods carved out.

143 Odin for the Æsir, and Dain for the elves,
Dvalin for the dwarfs,
Asvid for the giants,
I myself carved some.

144 Do you know how to carve, do you know how to interpret,
do you know how to stain, do you know how to test out,
do you know how to ask, do you know how to sacrifice,
do you know how to dispatch, do you know how to slaughter?

145 Better not to pray, than to sacrifice too much,
one gift always calls for another;
better not dispatched than to slaughter too much.
So Thund carved before the history of nations,*
where he rose up, when he came back.

146 I know those spells which a ruler's wife doesn't know,*
nor any man's son;
'help' one is called,
and that will help you
against accusations and sorrows
and every sort of anxiety.

147 I know a second one which the sons of men need,
those who want to live as physicians.

148 I know a third one which is very useful to me,
which fetters my enemy;
the edges of my foes I can blunt,
neither weapon nor club will bite for them.

149 I know a fourth one if men put
chains upon my limbs;
I can chant so that I can walk away,
fetters spring from my feet,
and bonds from my hands.

150 I know a fifth if I see, shot in malice,
a dart flying amid the army:
it cannot fly so fast that I cannot stop it
if I see it with my eyes.

151 I know a sixth one if a man wounds me
with the roots of the sap-filled wood:
and that man who conjured to harm me,
the evil consumes him, not me.

152 I know a seventh one if I see towering flames
in the hall about my companions:
it can't burn so widely that I can't counteract it,
I know the spells to chant.

153 I know an eighth one, which is most useful
for everyone to know;
where hatred flares up between the sons of warriors,
then I can quickly bring settlement.

154 I know a ninth one if I am in need,
if I must protect my ship at sea;
the wind I can lull upon the wave
and quieten all the sea to sleep.

155 I know a tenth one if I see witches
playing up in the air;
I can bring it about that they can't make their way back
to their own shapes,
to their own spirits.

156 I know an eleventh if I have to lead
loyal friends into battle;
under the shields I chant, and they journey inviolate,
safely to the battle,
safely from the battle,
safely they come everywhere.

157 I know a twelfth one if I see, up in a tree,
a dangling corpse in a noose:
I can so carve and colour the runes
that the man walks
and talks with me.

158 I know a thirteenth if I shall pour water
over a young warrior:
he will not fall though he goes into battle,
before swords he will not sink.

159 I know a fourteenth if I have to reckon up
the gods before men:
Æsir and elves, I know the difference between them,
few who are not wise know that.

160 I know a fifteenth, which the dwarf Thiodrerir
chanted before Delling's doors:
powerfully he sang for the Æsir and before the elves,
wisdom to Sage.

161 I know a sixteenth if I want to have all
a clever woman's heart and love-play:
I can turn the thoughts of the white-armed woman
and change her mind entirely.

162 I know a seventeenth, so that scarcely any
young girl will want to shun me.
Of these spells, Loddfafnir,
you will long be in want;
though they'd be good for you, if you got them,
useful if you learned them,
handy, if you had them.

163 I know an eighteenth, which I shall never teach
to any girl or any man's wife—
it's always better when just one person knows,
that follows at the end of the spells—
except that one woman whom my arms embrace,
or who may be my sister.

164 Now is the song of the High One recited, in the High
 One's hall,
very useful to the sons of men,
quite useless to the sons of giants,
luck to him who recites, luck to him who knows!
May he benefit, he who learnt it,
luck to those who listened!

Compare to behavior in LOTR + Beowulf.
who abides what? Role of King, wisdom + folly

How can one know; what do you do w/ knowledge
when you have it.

Vafthrudnir's Sayings

As the *Seeress's Prophecy*, *Sayings of the High One*, and *Grimnir's Sayings* show, Odin is characterized by his obsessive quest for wisdom, particularly for information about Ragnarok. In this poem he sets off, against his wife's advice, disguised as a poor wanderer, to test his wisdom against the giant Vafthrudnir, known only from this poem. Once Odin has proved his mettle, by answering questions which the giant puts to him, he is invited to risk his head in questioning the giant. *Vafthrudnir's Sayings* (*Vafthrudnismal*) belongs to the genre of the wisdom contest, known in many other cultures. Two protagonists ask each other questions or riddles, until one fails to answer. Thus the questioner must know the answer to his question; the answerer corroborates the interlocutor's information, rather than providing new facts. The trick question with which Odin wins the contest seems to be a favourite of his, since he also uses it to secure victory in a riddle contest against King Heidrek in *Heidreks saga*. Vafthrudnir's questions elicit simple mythological facts: the names of the horses who draw the day and the night, the name of the river which divides giants and gods and of the field on which the battle of Ragnarok will be fought. Odin's questions are more pointed: he draws out the history of the universe, its past (vv. 20–35), and present (36–43), culminating in questions about the future and Ragnarok (44–54). Some scholars have speculated that Odin's real aim is to discover his own fate (52–3); once he hears about the wolf, he brings the contest to a speedy end with his unanswerable question. Odin alone knows what he whispered into Baldr's ear, but it has been guessed that Baldr is assured of his return after Ragnarok, as the *Seeress's Prophecy*, v. 62, tells us, to rule over the gods who survive. As a contest between god and giant, *Vafthrudnir's Sayings* is mimetic of Ragnarok. Vafthrudnir's answers emphasize the ancientness and authority of the giants as the first of beings, but Odin's questions lead away from the giants and their claims, to the final triumph of gods and men. It is they, Odin's descendants and creations, if not Odin himself, who will survive the final conflagration. The giants may have had a past, but they have no future; Vafthrudnir's defeat in the contest symbolizes the final defeat in time of the giant race.

Odin said:

1 'Advise me now, Frigg, I intend to journey
to visit Vafthrudnir;
I've a great curiosity to contend in ancient matters
with that all-wise giant.'

Frigg said:

2 'I'd rather keep the Father of Hosts
at home in the courts of the gods,
for I have always thought no giant is as powerful
as Vafthrudnir is.'

Odin said:

3 'Much I have travelled, much have I tried out,
much have I tested the Powers;
this I want to know: what kind of company
is found in Vafthrudnir's hall.'

Frigg said:

4 'Journey safely! Come back safely!
Be safe on the way!
May your wisdom be sufficient when, Father of Men,
you speak with the giant.'

5 Then Odin went to try the wisdom
of the all-wise giant;
to the hall he came which Im's father owned;*
Odin went inside.

Odin said:

6 'Greetings, Vafthrudnir! Now I have come into the hall
to see you in person;
this I want to know first, whether you are wise
or very wise, giant.'

Vafthrudnir said:

7 'What man is this to whom I am addressing myself
in my hall?
May you not come out of our halls alive
unless you turn out to be the wiser one.'

Odin said:

8 'Gagnrad I am called; now I have come walking,
thirsty to your hall;
in need of hospitality and of your welcome,
I have journeyed long, giant.'

Vafthrudnir said:

9 'Why, Gagnrad, do you speak thus from the floor?
Go to a seat in the hall!
There we shall test which one knows more,
the guest or the old sage.'

Odin said:

10 'The poor man who comes to the wealthy one
should speak when needful or be silent;
to be too talkative I think will bring bad results
for the visitor to the cold-ribbed giant.'

Vafthrudnir said:

11 'Tell me, Gagnrad, since on the hall-floor
you want to try your luck,
what that horse is called who draws every
day to mankind.'

Odin said:

12 'Shining-mane, the shining one is called who draws
day to mankind;
the best of horses he is held to be among the
  Hreid-Goths,*
always that horse's mane gleams.'

Vafthrudnir said:

13 'Tell me, Gagnrad, since on the hall-floor
you want to try your luck,
what that horse is called who from the east
draws night
to the beneficent gods.'

Odin said:

14 'Frost-mane he is called, who draws every night
to the beneficent gods;
foam from his bit he lets fall every morning;
from there dew comes to the valleys.'

Vafthrudnir said:

15 'Tell me, Gagnrad, since on the hall-floor
you want to try your luck,
what that river is called which divides the earth
between the sons of giants and the gods.'

Odin said:

16 'Ifing the river is called, which divides the earth
between the sons of giants and the gods;
freely it will flow through all time,
ice never forms on the river.'

Vafthrudnir said:

17 'Tell me, Gagnrad, since on the hall-floor
you want to try your luck,
what that plain is called where in battle
Surt and the sweet gods will meet.'

Odin said:

18 'Vigrid the plain is called, where in battle
Surt and the sweet gods will meet;
a hundred leagues it is in each direction;
that is the ordained field.'

Vafthrudnir said:

19 'Wise you are, guest, come to the giant's bench,
and we will speak together in the seat;
we shall wager our heads in the hall,
guest, on our wisdom.'

Odin said:

20 'Tell me this one thing if your knowledge is sufficient
and you, Vafthrudnir, know,
from where the earth came or the sky above,
first, o wise giant.'

Vafthrudnir said:

21 'From Ymir's flesh the earth was shaped,*
and the mountains from his bones;
the sky from the skull of the frost-cold giant,
and the sea from his blood.'

Odin said:

22 'Tell me this second thing if your knowledge is sufficient
and you, Vafthrudnir, know,
from where the moon came, so that it journeys over
men,
and likewise the sun.'

Vafthrudnir said:

23 'Mundilfæri he is called, the father of Moon
and likewise of Sun;
they must pass through the sky, every day
to count the years for men.'

Odin said:

24 'Tell me this third thing, since you are said to be wise,
and you, Vafthrudnir, know,
where day comes from, he who passes over mankind,
or night with its new moons.'

Vafthrudnir said:

25 'Delling he is called, he is Day's father,
and Night was born of Norr;
new moon and dark of the moon the beneficent Powers
made
to count the years for men.'

Odin said:

26 'Tell me this fourth thing, since you are said to be wise,
and you, Vafthrudnir, know,
from where winter came or warm summer,
first among the wise Powers.'

Vafthrudnir said:

27 'Wind-cool he is called, Winter's father,
and Mild One, the father of Summer.'

Odin said:

28 'Tell me this fifth thing, since you are said to be wise,
and you, Vafthrudnir, know,
who was the eldest of the Æsir or of Ymir's descendants
in bygone days.'

Vafthrudnir said:

29 'Uncountable winters before the earth was made,
then Bergelmir was born,
Thrudgelmir was his father,
and Aurgelmir his grandfather.'

Odin said:

30 'Tell me this sixth thing, since you are said to be wise,
and you, Vafthrudnir, know,
from where Aurgelmir came among the sons of giants,*
first, o wise giant.'

Vafthrudnir said:

31 'Out of Elivagar sprang poison-drops,*
so they grew until a giant came of them;
[from there our clan all came,
thus they are all terrifying.']*

Odin said:

32 'Tell me this seventh thing, since you are said to be wise,
and you, Vafthrudnir, know,
how he got children, that fierce giant,
when he had no sport with giantesses.'

Vafthrudnir said:

33 'They said that under the frost-giant's arms
a girl and boy grew together;
one foot with the other, of the wise giant,
begot a six-headed son.'

Odin said:

34 'Tell me this eighth thing, since you are said to be wise,
and you, Vafthrudnir, know,
what you first remember or what you know to be earliest,
you are all-wise, giant.'

Vafthrudnir said:

35 'Uncountable winters before the world was made,
then Bergelmir was born;
that I remember first when the wise giant
was first laid in his coffin.'*

Odin said:

36 'Tell me this ninth thing, since you are said to be wise,
and you, Vafthrudnir, know,
where the wind comes from which goes over the waves,
which men never see itself.'

Vafthrudnir said:

37 'Corpse-swallower he is called, who sits at the end of the
world,
a giant in eagle's shape;
from his wings, they say, the wind blows
over all men.'

Odin said:

38 'Tell me this tenth thing, since all the fate of the gods
you, Vafthrudnir, know,
from where Niord came to the sons of the Æsir,
he rules over very many temples and sanctuaries
and he was not raised among the Æsir.'

Vafthrudnir said:

39 'In Vanaheim the wise Powers made him
and gave him as hostage to the gods;
at the doom of men he will come back
home among the wise Vanir.'*

Odin said:

40 'Tell me that eleventh thing, where men fight
in the courts every day.'

Vafthrudnir said:

41 'All the Einheriar fight in Odin's courts*
every day;
they choose the slain and ride from the battle;
then they sit the more at peace together.'

Odin said:

42 'Tell me this twelfth thing, why all the fate of the gods
you, Vafthrudnir, know;
of the secrets of the giants and of all the gods
tell most truly,
all-wise giant.'

Vafthrudnir said:

43 'Of the secrets of the giants and of all the gods,
I can tell truly,
for I have been into every world;
nine worlds I have travelled through to Mist-hell,
there men die down out of hell.'

Odin said:

44 'Much I have travelled, much have I tried out,
much have I tested the Powers;
which among men will live when the famous
Mighty Winter comes among men?'

Vafthrudnir said:

45 'Life and Lifthrasir, and they will hide
in Hoddmimir's wood;*
they will have the morning dew for food;
from them the generations will spring.'

Odin said:

46 'Much I have travelled, much have I tried out,
much have I tested the Powers;
from where will a sun come into the smooth heaven
when Fenrir has assailed this one?'

Vafthrudnir said:

47 'Elf-disc will bear a daughter,
before Fenrir assails her;
she shall ride, when the Powers die,
the girl on her mother's paths.'

Odin said:

48 'Much I have travelled, much have I tried out,
much have I tested the Powers;
who are those maidens who journey in troops,*
wise in spirit, over the sea?'

Vafthrudnir said:

49 'Three of the race of Mogthrasir's girls*
travel over the settlements,
they are bringers of luck in the world,
although they are raised among giants.'

Odin said:

50 'Much I have travelled, much have I tried out,
much have I tested the Powers;
which Æsir will rule over the possessions of the gods,
when Surt's fire is slaked?'

Vafthrudnir said:

51 'Vidar and Vali will live in the temples of the gods,
when Surt's fire is slaked;
Modi and Magni shall have Miollnir*
for battle-strength.'

Odin said:

52 'Much I have travelled, much have I tried out,
much have I tested the Powers;
what will Odin's life's end be,
when the Powers are torn apart?'

Vafthrudnir said:

53 'The wolf will swallow the Father of Men,
Vidar will avenge this;
the cold jaws of the beast he will sunder
in battle.'

Odin said:

54 'Much I have travelled, much have I tried out,
much have I tested the Powers;
what did Odin say into the ear of his son*
before he mounted the pyre?'

Vafthrudnir said:

55 'No man knows what you said in bygone days
into your son's ear;
with doomed mouth I've spoken my ancient lore
about the fate of the gods;
I've been contending with Odin in wisdom;
you'll always be the wisest of beings.'

Grimnir's Sayings

The prose introduction to *Grimnir's Sayings* (*Grimnismal*) gives an unexpected account of Odin and Frigg as rival patrons to two kingly candidates, the lost sons of King Hraudung. Odin uses cunning to give his protégé an unfair advantage, and then precipitates a matrimonial quarrel by pointing out the different fates which have overtaken their protégés. Frigg is swift to get her own back, accusing Odin's favourite of stinginess, a serious charge, given the near-sacred character which Germanic societies ascribed to hospitality. Frigg duplicitously ensures that Geirrod does mistreat his guest, relying on Odin's practice of disguising himself when visiting strange halls. Odin arrives at Geirrod's hall, calling himself Grimnir (the Masked One). Geirrod's methods of torture, starvation and heat, have been thought to recall shamanistic rituals allowing access to arcane knowledge kept hidden from the uninitiated; such practices could have been known to the Scandinavians from their northern neighbours, the Lapps. On the ninth night (nine is a magical number), Odin reveals himself. Geirrod realizes his mistake too late; as eventually happens to most Odinic protégés, the hero loses his patron's favour and is doomed to die. Geirrod's son, Agnar, who, significantly, bears his uncle's name and is now the same age as his uncle was when the brothers encountered their divine patrons, has recognized the responsibilities of the host in giving Odin a drink, and the god's favour now falls on him.

Like *Vafthrudnir's Sayings*, *Grimnir's Sayings* is obsessed with mythological facts: the topography of the world of the gods, rather than its history, is revealed in Odin's monologue. Stimulated by heat and hunger, Odin gradually reveals his divinity, first through demonstrating his mastery of arcane knowledge, wide-ranging and compendious, thematically arranged to allude to his physical torment and the judgement and revenge which will result from it. Finally, after the crucial v. 45, in which Odin asserts that right relations of sacrifice have been restored between gods and men by Agnar's action, he identifies himself in all his guises. Like *Sayings of the High One*, *Grimnir's Sayings* intends both to reveal mythological knowledge and to teach wisdom, a wisdom which comes too late for Geirrod, but which qualifies Agnar to become king in his father's place. The acquisition of all sorts of wisdom: runic, magical, gnomic, and mythological, as evidenced by the poems recounting the youth of Sigurd, is necessary for the hero to achieve the transition from fighter to ruler. In its context in the *Poetic Edda*, *Grimnir's Sayings* both completes the exposition of Odinic wisdom and looks forward to the exploration of kingship which develops in the heroic poems.

About the Sons of King Hraudung *King Hraudung had two sons; one was called Agnar, and the other Geirrod. Agnar was 10 years old, and Geirrod 8. They both rowed out in a boat with a trailing line after small fish. The wind drove them out into the ocean. In the dark that night, they were wrecked on land, and went ashore; they found a crofter. They stayed there for the winter. The old woman fostered Agnar, and the old man Geirrod. In the spring, the old man got them a ship. And when he and the old woman took them down to the shore, then the old man spoke privately to Geirrod. They got a breeze and came to their father's harbour. Geirrod was forward in the ship, he jumped ashore and pushed the ship out and said: 'Go where the trolls will take you!' The ship was driven out, and Geirrod went up to the house. He was greeted joyfully; his father had died. Then Geirrod was taken as king and became a splendid man.*

Odin and Frigg sat in Hlidskialf and looked into all the worlds. Odin said, 'Do you see Agnar, your foster-child, there raising children with a giantess in a cave? But Geirrod, my foster-child, is king and rules over the land.' Frigg says: 'He is so stingy with food that he tortures his guests if it seems to him that too many have come.' Odin says that is the greatest lie. They wagered on the matter.*

Frigg sent her handmaid, Fulla, to Geirrod. She told the king to beware lest a wizard, who had come into the country, should bewitch him, and said he could be known by this sign: that no dog was so fierce that it would attack him. And that was the greatest slander that Geirrod was not generous with food; however, he had the man whom no dog would attack arrested. He was wearing a blue cloak and called himself Grimnir, and would say nothing more about himself, though he was asked. The king had him tortured to make him speak and set him between two fires, and he sat there eight nights.

Geirrod the king had a son who was ten winters old, and he was called Agnar after Geirrod's brother. Agnar went to Grimnir and gave him a full horn to drink from, saying that the king was acting wrongly to have him, an innocent man, tortured. Grimnir drank it up. Then the fire had come so close that Grimnir's cloak burned. He said:

1 'Hot you are, fire, and rather too fierce;
go away, sparks!
My fur cloak singes, though I lift it in the air,
my mantle burns before me.

2 'Eight nights I have sat here between the fires,
and no one offered me food,
except Agnar alone, and he alone shall rule,
the son of Geirrod, over the land of the Goths.

3 'Blessed shall you be, Agnar,
since Odin bids you be blest;
for one drink you shall never
get a better reward.

4 'The land is sacred which I see lying
near the Æsir and elves;
but in Thrudheim Thor shall remain,
until the Powers are torn asunder.

5 'Yewdale it is called, the place where Ull*
has made a hall for himself;
Alfheim the gods gave to Freyr
in bygone days as tooth-payment.*

6 'There is a third home where the cheerful Powers
roofed the hall with silver;
Valaskialf it is called, which the God made for himself*
in bygone days.

7 'Sokkvabekk a fourth is called and cool waves
resound over it;
there Odin and Saga drink every day,*
joyful, from golden cups.

8 'Gladsheim a fifth is called, there gold-bright Valhall
rises peacefully, seen from afar;
there Odin chooses every day
those dead in combat.

9 'It's very easy to recognize for those who come to Odin
to see how his hall's arranged;
the hall has spear-shafts for rafters, with shields it is thatched,
mail-coats are strewn on the benches.

10 'It's very easy to recognize for those who come to Odin
to see how his hall's arranged;
a wolf hangs in front of the western doors
and an eagle hovers above.

11 'Thrymheim the sixth is called, where Thiazi lives,*
the terrible giant;
but now Skadi, the shining bride of the gods,*
lives in her father's ancient courts.

12 'Breidablik is the seventh, where Baldr has
a hall made for himself,
in that land where I know there are
the fewest evil plots.

13 'Himinbiorg is the eighth, and there, they say,
Heimdall rules over his sanctuaries;
there the glad watchman of the gods drinks good mead
in the comfortable hall.

14 'Folkvang is the ninth, and there Freyia arranges
the choice of seats in the hall;
half the slain she chooses every day,
and half Odin owns.

15 'Glitnir is the tenth, it has golden buttresses,
and likewise is roofed with silver;
and there Forseti lives most days*
and puts to sleep all quarrels.

16 'Noatun is the eleventh, where Niord has
a hall made for himself,
the prince of men, lacking in malice,
rules over the high-timbered temple.

17 'Brushwood grows and high grass
widely in Vidar's land;
and there the son proclaims on his horse's back
that he's keen to avenge his father.

18 'Andhrimnir has Sæhrimnir boiled
in Eldhrimnir,*
the best of pork; but few know
by what the Einheriar are nourished.

19 'Geri and Freki, tamed to war, he satiates,*
the glorious Father of Hosts;
but on wine alone the weapon-magnificent
Odin always lives.

20 'Hugin and Munin fly every day*
over the wide world;
I fear for Hugin that he will not come back,
yet I tremble more for Munin.

21 'Thund roars, the great wolf's fish*
swims in the stream;
the river's current seems very great for
those rejoicing in slaughter to wade.

22 'Valgrind it's called, standing on the plain,
sacred before the holy doors:
ancient is that gate, but few know
how it is closed up with a lock.

23 'Five hundred doors and forty
I think there are in Valhall;
eight hundreds of warriors will go together from one door*
when they go to fight the wolf.

24 'Five hundred daises and forty,
so I think Bilskirnir has in all;*
of all those halls which I know to be roofed,
my son's I think is the greatest.

25 'Heidrun is the goat's name, who stands on Father of Hosts' hall
and grazes Lærad's branches;*
she will fill a vat of shining mead,
that liquor cannot ever diminish.

26 'Eikthyrnir is the hart's name, who stands on Father of Hosts' hall
and grazes Lærad's branches;
and from his horns liquid drips into Hvergelmir,
from thence all waters have their flowing:

27 'Sid and Vid, Sækin and Eikin,*
Svol and Gunnthro,
Fiorm and Fimbulthul,
Rin and Rennandi,
Gipul and Gopul,
Gomul and Geirvimul,
they flow round the realm of the gods,
Thyn and Vin, Tholl and Holl,
Grad and Gunnthorin.

28 'Vina is one's name, another Vegsvinn,
a third Thiodnuma,
Nyt and Not, Nonn and Hronn,
Slid and Hrid, Sylg and Ylg,
Vid and Van, Vond and Strond,
Gioll and Leipt, they fall close to men,
and flow down from here to hell.

29 'Kormt and Ormt and the two Kerlaugar,
these Thor must wade
every day, when he goes to sit as judge
at the ash of Yggdrasill,
for the bridge of the Æsir burns all with flames,
the sacred waters boil.

30 'Glad and Golden, Glassy and Skeidbrimir,
Silvertuft and Sinir,
Brilliant and Hidden-hoof, Goldtuft and Lightfoot,
these horses the Æsir ride
every day, when they ride to sit as judges,
at the ash of Yggdrasill.

31 'Three roots there grow in three directions
under the ash of Yggdrasill;
Hel lives under one, under the second, the frost-giants,
the third, humankind.

32 'Ratatosk is the squirrel's name, who has to run
upon the ash of Yggdrasill;
the eagle's word he must bring from above
and tell to Nidhogg below.*

33 'There are four harts too, who gnaw with necks thrown
back
the highest boughs;
Dain and Dvalin,
Duneyr and Durathror.

34 'More serpents lie under the ash of Yggdrasill
than any fool can imagine:
Goin and Moin, they are Grafvitnir's sons,
Grabak and Grafvollud,
Ofnir and Svafnir I think for ever will
bite on the tree's branches.

35 'The ash of Yggdrasill suffers agony
more than men know:
a hart bites it from above, and it decays at the sides,
and Nidhogg rends it beneath.

36 'Hrist and Mist, I wish, would bear a horn to me,*
Skeggiold and Skogul,
Hild and Thrud, Hlokk and Herfiotur,
Goll and Geirolul,
Randgrid and Radgrid, and Reginleif;
they bear ale to the Einheriar.

37 'Arvak and Alsvid, they must pull wearily*
the sun from here;
and under their saddle-bows the cheerful gods,
the Æsir, have hidden iron bellows.

38 'Svalin is the name of a shield which stands before the sun,
before the shining god;
mountain and sea I know would burn up
if it fell away from in front.

39 'Skoll a wolf is called who pursues the shining god
to the protecting woods;
and another is Hati, he is Hrodvitnir's son,*
who chases the bright bride of heaven.

40 'From Ymir's flesh the earth was made,*
and from his blood, the sea,
mountains from his bones, trees from his hair,
and from his skull, the sky.

41 'And from his eyelashes the cheerful gods
made earth in the middle for men;
and from his brain were the hard-tempered clouds
all made.

42 'May he have Ull's protection, and that of all the gods,
whoever first quenches the flames;
for the worlds lie open for the sons of the gods
when they lift off the kettles.*

43 'Ivaldi's sons in bygone days*
made Skidbladnir,
the best of ships, for shining Freyr,
the beneficent son of Niord.

44 'The ash of Yggdrasill is the noblest of trees,
and Skidbladnir the best of ships,
Odin best of the Æsir, Sleipnir of horses,
Bilrost of bridges, Bragi of poets,
Habrok of hawks, and Garm of dogs.*

45 'My face have I now revealed before the sons of the
fighting gods,
now the wished-for sustenance will awaken;
all the Æsir it shall bring in
onto Ægir's benches,
at Ægir's feast.*

46 'I am called Mask, I am called Wanderer,*
Warrior and Helm-wearer,
Known and Third, Thund and Ud,
Hellblind and High;

47 'Sad and Svipal and Sanngetal,
War-merry and Hnikar,
Weak-eyed, Flame-eyed, Bolverk, Fiolnir,
Mask and Masked One, Maddener and Much-wise;

48 'Broadhat, Broadbeard, War-father, Hnikud,
Father of All, Father of the Slain, Atrid and
Burden-god;
by one name I have never been known
since I went among the people.

49 'Grimnir they called me at Geirrod's,
and Ialk at Asmund's,
and then Kialar, when I pulled the sledge;
Thror at the Assembly,
Vidur in battle,
Oski and Omi, Equal-high and Biflindi,
Gondlir and Harbard among the gods.

50 'Svidur and Svidrir I was called at Sokkmimir's,*
and I tricked the old giant then,
when I became the sole slayer of the famous
son of Midvidnir.

51 'Drunk are you, Geirrod! You've drunk too much;
you lose much when you lose
my favour, and that of all the Einheriar.

52 'Much I said to you but you remember little of it;
your friend has deceived you.
I see the sword of my friend lying
all covered in blood.

53 'Slaughter that wearies sword-edges the Terrible One
now wants to have;
I know your life is over;
the *disir* are against you, now you may see Odin,*
draw near to me if you can!

54 'Odin I am called now, Terrible One I was called
before,
I was Thund before that,
Vak and Skilfing, Vafud and Hroptatyr,
Gaut and Ialk among the gods,
Ofnir and Svafnir, all of which I think stem
from me alone.'

Geirrod the king sat with a sword on his lap, half drawn from the sheath. But when he heard that it was Odin who had come there, he stood up and intended to pull Odin away from the fire. The sword slipped from his hand, hilt downwards. The king lost his footing and plunged forwards, and the sword went into him, and he was killed. Odin disappeared. And Agnar was then king for a long time afterwards.

Skirnir's Journey

Freyr falls in love with a giant's daughter whom he sees from Odin's high-seat, Hlidskialf. According to Snorri (*Edda*, pp. 31–2) his love-sickness is a punishment for usurping Odin's place. Freyr's concerned parents, Niord and Skadi, ask their son's old friend and servant Skirnir ('Shining One') to help. Skirnir volunteers to go on a wooing mission and, after a remarkably smooth journey, effectively bullies the reluctant girl into agreeing to a rendezvous with Freyr. Snorri tells us in *Ynglinga saga*, ch. 10, that the pair married and had a son called Fiolnir who was the ancestor of the Yngling dynasty of Norwegian kings, and that in handing his sword over to Skirnir, Freyr leaves himself weaponless at Ragnarok. Although the poem has no especial connection with wisdom, it is composed mostly in *ljodahattr* dialogue. Several scholars have thought that, with its succession of lively scenes, *Skirnir's Journey* may well have been intended for dramatic presentation.

Freyr, the son of Niord, had seated himself in Hlidskialf and looked into all the worlds. He looked into Giantland and saw there a beautiful girl, as she was walking from her father's hall to the storehouse. From that he caught great sickness of heart. Skirnir was the name of Freyr's page. Niord asked him to go and talk to Freyr. Then Skadi said:

1 'Get up now, Skirnir, and go and ask to speak
with the young man
and ask this: with whom the wise, fertile one
is so terribly angry.'

Skirnir said:

2 'Harsh words I expect from your son
if I go to talk to the young man
and ask this: with whom the wise, fertile one
is so terribly angry.

3 'Tell me, Freyr, war-leader of the gods,
for I would like to know,
why do you sit alone in the long hall,
my lord, day after day?'

Freyr said:

4 'Why should I tell you, young man,
about my great sorrow of heart,
for the elf-ray shines day after day,
but not on my longings.'

Skirnir said:

5 'I don't think your longing can be very great,
if you, sir, will not tell me,
for we were young together in bygone days;
we two ought well to trust one another.'

Freyr said:

6 'In the courts of Gymir I saw walking
a girl pleasing to me.
Her arms shine and from there
all the sea and air catch light.

7 'More pleasing to me is the girl than any girl to any
man,
young in bygone days;
none of the gods and elves wishes that
we should be together.'

Skirnir said:

8 'Give me that horse which will carry me through the
dark,
sure, flickering flame,
and that sword which fights by itself
against the giant race.'

Freyr said:

9 'I'll give you that horse which will carry you through the
dark,
sure, flickering flame,
and that sword which will fight by itself
if he who wields it is wise.'

Skirnir said to the horse:

10 'It is dark outside, I declare it's time for us to go
over the dewy mountain,
to rush over nations;
we will both come back or the hideous giant
will take us both.'

Skirnir rode to Giantland to the courts of Gymir. There were savage dogs tied in front of the wooden fence which surrounded Gerd's hall. He rode to where a herdsman was sitting on a mound and greeted him:

11 'Tell me this, herdsman, as you sit on the mound*
and watch all the ways,
how I may come to talk with the young girl,
past the dogs of Gymir.'

The herdsman said:

12 'Are you doomed or are you dead already?
Conversation you shall never have
with Gymir's excellent daughter.'

Skirnir said:

13 'The choices are better than simply sobbing,
for a man who is eager to advance;
for on one day all my life was shaped,
all my span laid down.'

Gerd said:

14 'What is that noise of noises which I hear now
in our dwellings?
The earth trembles and all the courts of
Gymir shake before it.'

The serving-maid said:

15 'There is a man out here, dismounted from a horse,
he is letting his horse start grazing.'

Gerd said:

16 'Tell him to come in into our hall
and drink the famous mead;
though I am afraid that out here may be
my brother's slayer.*

17 'What are you of the elves or of the sons of the Æsir,
or of the wise Vanir?
Why do you come alone over the wild fire
to see our company?'

Skirnir said:

18 'I am not of the elves or of the sons of the Æsir,
or of the wise Vanir,
though I come alone over the wild fire
to see your company.

19 'Eleven apples here I have all of gold,*
those I will give you, Gerd,
to buy your favour, that you may say that Freyr is
the least hateful man alive to you.'

Gerd said:

20 'Eleven apples I will never accept
at any man's desire,
nor will Freyr and I settle down together
as long as our lives last.'

Skirnir said:

21 'I shall give you that ring, that which was burnt
with Odin's young son;
eight are the equally heavy ones, which drop from it
every ninth night.'*

Gerd said:

22 'I will not accept a ring, though it was burnt
with Odin's young son;
I lack no gold in the courts of Gymir,
sharing out my father's property.'

Skirnir said:

23 'Do you see this sword, girl, slender, inlaid,
which I have here in my hand?
Your head I shall cut from your neck
unless you say we are reconciled.'

Gerd said:

24 'Coercion I shall never endure
at any man's desire;
though I reckon this, if you and Gymir meet,
keen fighters, a battle is bound to occur.'

Skirnir said:

25 'Do you see this sword, girl, slender, inlaid,
which I have here in my hand?
Before these edges the old giant will fall,
your father will be doomed.

26 'I strike you with a taming wand, and I will tame you,
girl, to my desires;
there you shall go where the sons of men
shall never see you again.

27 'On an eagle's mound you shall sit from early morning,
looking out of the world, hankering towards hell;
food shall be more hateful to you than to every man is
the shining serpent among men.

28 'May you become a spectacle when you come out;
may Hrimnir glare at you, may everything stare at you,
may you become more widely known than the watchman
among the gods,*
may you gape through the bars.

29 'Madness and howling, tearing affliction and unbearable
desire,
may tears grow for you with grief!
Sit down, for I shall tell you
a heavy torment
and a double grief:

30 'Fiends will oppress you all the long weary day,
in the courts of giants;
to the halls of the frost-giants every day you shall
creep without choice,
without hope of choice;
weeping in exchange for joy you shall have,
and suffer grief with tears.

31 'With a three-headed giant you shall miserably linger out
your life,
or else be without a man!
May your mind be seized!
May pining waste you away!
Be like the thistle, that which is crushed
at the end of the harvest!

32 'I went to the forest, to the living wood,
to get a potent branch;
a potent branch I got.

33 'Odin is angry with you, Thor is angry with you,
Freyr will hate you;
most wicked girl, you have brought down upon you
the potent wrath of the gods.

34 'Hear o ogres, hear o frost-giants,
sons of Suttung, the troops of the Æsir themselves,
how I forbid, how I deny
pleasure in men to the girl,
benefit from men to the girl.

35 'Hrimgrimnir is the name of the giant who'll have you
down below the corpse-gates,
where bondsmen will give you at the roots of the wood
goat's piss to drink;*
finer drink you will never get,
girl, at your desire,
girl, at my desire!

36 '"Giant" I carve on you and three runes:*
lewdness and frenzy
and unbearable desire;
thus I can rub that off, as I carved that on,
if there is need of this.'

Gerd said:

37 'Be welcome now, lad, and receive the crystal cup,
full of ancient mead;
though I had never thought that I should ever love
one of the Vanir well.'

Skirnir said:

38 'All my errand will I know,
before I ride home from here,
when you'll grant a meeting
to the vigorous son of Niord.'

Gerd said:

39 'Barri is the name, as we both know,
of a peaceful grove;
and after nine nights, there to the son of Niord
Gerd will grant love.'

Then Skirnir rode home. Freyr stood outside and greeted him and asked for news:

40 'Tell me, Skirnir, before you throw the saddle from the
horse
and you step a foot further,
what you obtained in Giantland,
your desire or mine.'

Skirnir said:

41 'Barri is the name, as we both know,
of a peaceful grove;
and after nine nights, there to the son of Niord
Gerd will grant love.'

Freyr said:

42 'Long is one night, long are two,
how shall I bear three?
Often a month to me has seemed less
than half one of these pre-marital nights.'

Harbard's Song

Odin, in disguise, and Thor meet at a fjord crossing. Odin refuses to ferry Thor over the water and the two engage in a ritual exchange of insults. *Harbard's Song* (*Harbardzljod*) is both typical and atypical of this kind of exchange or 'flyting': a verbal battle common in Germanic literature; the best known example is perhaps the exchange between Hagen and the ferryman in the *Nibelungenlied*, ll. 1480 ff. Typically the winner is the contestant best able to prove his courage and manhood, while demonstrating the cowardice, laziness, and effeminacy of his opponent. In *Harbard's Song*, however, such is Odin's use of strategy and rhetoric, and so slow-witted is Thor, that Odin emerges a clear winner, despite the obvious advantages Thor has in strength and courage in battling against giants. The nub of *Harbard's Song* may be the statement in v. 24 that 'Odin has the nobles who fall in battle | and Thor has the breed of serfs', establishing the difference between the cults of the two deities, or, as Carol Clover has suggested, the poem may be intended as a parody of the usual 'flyting' poem. The poem is composed in a motley collection of metres, *ljodahattr*, *malahattr*, some unrecognizable metres, and some odd bits of prose. Many of the episodes alluded to by the two gods are unknown from any other sources; where additional information exists, it is outlined in the notes.

Thor was travelling from the east and he came to an inlet. On the other side of the inlet was the ferryman with his ship. Thor called:

1 'Who is that pipsqueak who stands on that side of the inlet?'*

He answered:

2 'Who is that peasant who calls over the gulf?'

Thor said:

3 'Ferry me over the water and I'll feed you in the morning;
I've a basket on my back, no food could be better;
I ate at leisure before I left home,
herrings and oatmeal—I've eaten my fill of these.'

The ferryman said:

4 'How proud you are of what you've done this morning!
You don't know clearly what's before you;
sad are your kin at home, I think your mother's dead.'*

Thor said:

5 'What you say now most people would think
great news, that my mother is dead.'

The ferryman said:

6 'It doesn't look as if you own three decent farms;
barelegged you stand, wearing your beggar's gear,
you don't even have any breeches.'

Thor said:

7 'Steer the oaken ship here—
I'll direct you to the landing stage—
anyway, who owns the ship which you're keeping next to the bank?'

The ferryman said:

8 'Hildolf he's called, the man who ordered me to keep it,
that warrior wise in counsel, who lives in Counsel-island Sound;
he told me not to ferry robbers or horse-thieves
but good men alone, and those whom I recognized clearly;
tell me your name if you want to cross the water.'

Thor said:

9 'I'd tell my name, even if I were an outlaw,
and my homeland to all: I am Odin's son,
brother of Meili, father of Magni,
powerful leader of gods; with Thor you're speaking here!
This I'll ask in return, what you are called.'

The ferryman said:

10 'I am called Harbard, I seldom conceal my name.'

Thor said:

11 'Why should you conceal your name, unless you have a quarrel with someone?'

Harbard said:

12 'But even if I had no quarrel, I'd defend my life
from such as you are, unless I were doomed.'

Thor said:

13 'It seems to me that it'd be an unpleasant labour
to wade over the water to you, and wet my balls.
I'll pay you back, you babe in arms,
for your jeering words, if I get over the water.'

Harbard said:

14 'Here I'll stand and wait for you;
you've encountered no sterner foe since the death of Hrungnir.'*

Thor said:

15 'This is what you're talking about: that Hrungnir and I fought—
the great-spirited giant whose head was made of stone;
and yet I killed him and made him fall before me.
What were you doing meanwhile, Harbard?'

Harbard said:

16 'I was with Fiolvar five winters long
on that island called All-green;
we fought there and wreaked slaughter,
we tried out many things,
had the choice of many a girl.'

Thor said:

17 'How did you turn the women to you?'

Harbard said:

18 We'd have had lively women, had they been loyal to us;
we'd have had wise women, had they been faithful to us;
they wound their ropes from the sand,
and from the deep valleys
they dug the ground;
I prevailed over them all with my plans;
I slept with the seven sisters,*
and I got their hearts, and pleasure from them all.
What were you doing meanwhile, Thor?'

Thor said:

19 'I killed Thiazi, the powerful-minded giant,*
I threw up the eyes of Allvaldi's son*
into the bright heaven;
they are the greatest sign of my deeds,
those which all men can see afterwards.
What were you doing meanwhile, Harbard?'

Harbard said:

20 'Mighty love-spells I used on the witches,
those whom I seduced from their men;
a bold giant I think Hlebard was,
he gave me a magic staff,
and I bewitched him out of his wits.'

Thor said:

21 'With an evil mind you repaid him for his good gifts.'

Harbard said:

22 'One oak-tree thrives when another is stripped,
each is for himself in such matters.
What were you doing meanwhile, Thor?'

Thor said:

23 'I was in the east, and I fought against giants,
malicious women, who roamed in the mountains;
great would be the giant race if they all lived,
mankind would be as nothing on the earth.
What were you doing meanwhile, Harbard?'

Harbard said:

24 'I was in Valland, and I waged war,
I incited the princes never to make peace;
Odin has the nobles who fall in battle
and Thor has the breed of serfs.'

Thor said:

25 'Unequally you'd share out forces among the Æsir,
if you had as much power as you'd like.'

Harbard said:

26 'Thor has quite enough strength, and no guts;
in fear and cowardice you were stuffed in a glove,*
and you didn't then seem like Thor;
you dared in your terror neither
to sneeze nor fart in case Fialar might hear.'

Thor said:

27 'Harbard, you pervert! I would knock you into hell
if I could stretch over the water.'

Harbard said:

28 'Why should you stretch over the water, since we have no quarrel?
What were you doing meanwhile, Thor?'

Thor said:

29 'I was in the east and I defended the river
where Svarang's sons attacked me;*
they pelted me with stones, yet they didn't get much advantage,
before me they had to sue for peace.
What were you doing meanwhile, Harbard?'

Harbard said:

30 'I was in the east and I was consorting with someone,
I sported with a linen-white lady and seduced her into a secret affair,
I made the gold-bright one happy, the girl gave me pleasure.'

Thor said:

31 'There were good things to be had from the girl there.'

Harbard said:

32 'I'd have needed your help, Thor,
to hold the linen-white girl.'

Thor said:

33 'I'd have helped you with that, if I could have managed it.'

Harbard said:

34 I'd have trusted you then, if you didn't betray my trust.'

Thor said:

35 'I'm not such a heel-biter as an old leather shoe in spring.'

Harbard said:

36 'What were you doing meanwhile, Thor?'

Thor said:

37 'Berserk women I fought in Hlesey;
they'd done the worst things, bewitched all men.'

Harbard said:

38 'That was a shameful deed, Thor, to fight against women.'

Thor said:

39 'They were she-wolves, and scarcely women,
they battered my ship which I had beached,
they threatened me with iron clubs, and chased Thialfi.
What were you doing meanwhile, Harbard?'

Harbard said:

40 'I was in the army, which set out here
to make battle-banners tower
and the spear red.'

Thor said:

41 'This is tantamount to saying that you want to wage war
upon us.'

Harbard said:

42 'I'll compensate you for that with a ring for the hand*
which arbitrators use, those who are willing to make a
settlement between us.'

Thor said:

43 'Where did you find such despicable words?
I've never heard words more despicable!'

Harbard said:

44 'I got them from those ancient men who live in the
woods at home.'*

Thor said:

45 'That's giving a good name to burial cairns, when you
call them
the woods at home.'

Harbard said:

46 'That's how I think of such things.'

Thor said:

47 'Your glibness with words will bring evil upon you,
if I manage to wade over the sound;
louder than the wolf I think you'll howl,
if you get a blow from my hammer.'

Harbard said:

48 'Sif has a lover at home, he's the one you want to meet,*
then you'd have that trial of strength which you deserve.'

Thor said:

49 'You speak carelessly of what seems worst to me,
coward, I know you're lying.'

Harbard said:

50 'Truth I think I'm saying, you're slow in your journey,
you'd now be well on your way, Thor, if you'd managed
to get in the boat.'

Thor said:

51 'Harbard, you pervert, you've held me up far too long!'

Harbard said:

52 'I never thought Asa-Thor would let
a ferryman make a fool of him.'

Thor said:

53 'I'll give you some advice now: row the boat here,
let's stop this mocking, come and meet the father of
Magni!'

Harbard said:

54 'Go around the inlet,
I'm not going to let you cross!'

Thor said:

55 'Show me the way since you won't ferry me over!'

Harbard said:

56 'It doesn't take long to show: it does take long to go;
a while to the stock, another to the stone,
keep to the left-hand road until you come to Verland;
there Fiorgyn will meet Thor, her son,
and she will show him the road of the kinsmen, to get to
Odin's land.'

Thor said:

57 'Can I get there today?'

Harbard said:

58 'With toil and difficulty, you'll be there by sunrise,
since I think it's thawing.'

Thor said:

59 'Short will our conversation be now, since you answer
me only with jeers.
I'll reward you for refusing to ferry me, if we meet
again.'

Harbard said:

60 'Go where the fiends'll get you!'

Hymir's Poem

Hymir's Poem (*Hymiskvida*) is badly preserved in the manuscript, but we can fill in the gaps from Snorri. The gods decided to have a feast and compel the giant Ægir to prepare it; this may reflect Scandinavian royal practices in which the king enforces his authority on his subordinates by visiting their homes and demanding to be feasted. Ægir, cunningly, demands an enormous cauldron in which to brew beer for the feast. This can only be obtained with great danger from the giant Hymir. Tyr, who was probably not the original protagonist of the poem, and Thor set off to try to obtain the cauldron. Like most encounters between Thor and the giants the adventure turns into a trial of strength. The gods are aided by giant women who give them advice at crucial moments. Embedded in the adventure of 'Fetching the Cauldron' is the tale of Thor and Hymir's fishing expedition, in which Thor almost catches the Midgard-serpent and demonstrates his strength.

1 Once, the victory gods ate their catch from hunting,
they were keen to drink before they got enough;
they shook the twigs and looked at the augury,*
they found that at Ægir's was an ample choice of
cauldrons.

2 The mountain-dweller sat ahead, cheerful as a child,
very like the son of the mash-blender;*
Odin's son looked into his eyes in defiance:
'You are going to have to prepare feasts for the Æsir.'

3 The contentious man annoyed the giant;
he began to think how to avenge himself on the gods;
he asked the husband of Sif to fetch him a cauldron,
'in which I can brew the ale for all of you'.

4 Nor could the glorious gods,
the mighty Powers, get one anywhere,
until Tyr the trustworthy
gave friendly advice to Hlorridi.*

5 'To the east of Elivagar
lives Hymir the very wise, at the end of heaven;
my father, the brave man, owns a cauldron,*
a capacious kettle, a league deep.'

6 'Do you know if we can get that cauldron?'
'If, friend, we use trickery to do it.'

7 They went out that day a long way
from Asgard, until they came to Egil.
He secured their goats with splendid horns,*
they went on to the hall which Hymir owned.

8 The lad found his grandmother, very ugly to him she seemed,*
nine hundred heads she had;
and another woman, all decked in gold, walked forward
with shining brows, bearing beer to her boy.

9 'Kinsman of giants, I'd like to hide you
two valiant men under the cauldron.
My dear husband, on many occasions,
is stingy to guests, bad-tempered towards them.'

10 Misshapen, stern-minded Hymir
came late back from hunting.
He went into the hall, the icicles tinkled
when he came in: the man's cheek-forest was frozen.*

11 'Greetings, Hymir, in such a good humour!
Now our son has come to your hall,
he whom we've missed on his long journeyings.
Hrod's adversary accompanies him,*
the friend of warriors, Veor is his name.

12 See where they sit under the gables of the hall,
they've hidden themselves so the pillar is in front of them.'

Asunder broke the pillar at the giant's gaze,
and the cross-beam broke in two.
13 Eight kettles smashed to pieces, but one of them,
a strong-forged cauldron, fell whole from the beam.

Forward they went, and the ancient giant
turned his gaze on his enemy.
14 His mind didn't speak encouragingly to him, when he
saw
the one who'd made the giantess weep walking across the
floor.*

Then three bulls they took.
The giant ordered them quickly to be boiled up.
15 Each one they made shorter by a head
and bore them afterwards to the cooking-pit.

Sif's husband ate before he went to bed,
alone he ate up two of Hymir's oxen.
16 It seemed to the grey-haired playmate of Hrungnir*
that Thor had consumed a considerable amount.

'Tomorrow evening we'll go hunting
for food that we three can live upon.'
17 Thor said he wanted to row out in the bay,
if the strong giant would give him bait.

'Go to the herds, if you've a mind to it,
breaker of giants, to look for bait!
18 I expect that it'll be easy
for you to get bait from the oxen.'

Thc lad went gliding swiftly to the woods,
there stood an ox, jet-black before him.
19 That slayer of ogres broke from the bull
the horns' high meadow, tore off its head.*

. . . .

(Hymir said)
'Your deed seems much worse,
steersman of ships, than if you had sat still quietly.'

20 The lord of goats told the monkey's offspring
to row the wave-horse out further;*
but the giant said, for his part,
he wasn't eager to row further out.

21 The brave and famous Hymir caught
two whales on his hook at once,
and back in the stern the kinsman of Odin,
Thor, cunningly laid out his line.

22 The protector of humans, the slayer of the serpent,*
baited his hook with the ox's head.
He whom the gods hate, the Circumscriber
beneath all lands, gaped at the bait.

23 Then very bravely Thor, the courageous one,
pulled the gleaming serpent up on board.
With his hammer he struck the head
violently, from above, of the wolf's hideous brother.*

24 The sea-wolf shrieked and the underwater rocks
re-echoed,
all the ancient earth was collapsing*
. . . . . .

then that fish sank into the sea.

25 The giant was unhappy as they rowed back,
at his oar Hymir didn't say a word;
changed tack completely:

26 'You'll be doing half the work with me
if you carry a whale home to the farm
or pen up our floating-goat.'*

27 Thor went forward and gripped the prow,
lifted up the sea-stallion with all the bilge-waters,
with the oars and with the bailer;
alone he brought the giant's sea-pig home to the farm,*
over the high, wooded ridge.

28 And still the giant, versed in contentiousness,
strove with Thor about his strength;
he said no man was strong, even if he knew how to row
powerfully, if he could not smash the crystal goblet.

29 And quickly Thor, when it was passed to him,
broke through the pillar with the glass;
sitting, he struck it against the column;
they carried it whole back to Hymir.

30 Until the lovely woman told him
some friendly advice which she knew:
'Smash it on Hymir's skull, the food-sated giant's,
that is harder than any cup!'

31 The strong man, lord of goats, rose with bent knees,
brought all his divine power to bear;
whole was the man's head above,
and the round goblet broke.

32 'A great treasure I know I've lost,
when I see the goblet smashed on my knee;'
the old man said, moreover: 'I cannot say
ever again, "now, ale, you are brewed!"

33 'Now it's up to you, if you can take
the ale-kettle out of our home.'
Tyr tried twice to move the cauldron,
both times the cauldron stayed immovable.

34 The father of Modi took it by the rim,
and rolled it along down onto the hall floor.
Sif's husband lifted the kettle up on his head,
the handle-rings jingled at his heels.

35 They'd not gone a long way
when the son of Odin looked once behind him;
he saw a many-headed army
coming from the cliffs, from the east with Hymir.

36 He lifted down the cauldron from his shoulders,
he swung Miollnir, eager for slaying,
and he killed all the mountain monsters.

37 They had not gone far, before Thor's goat
collapsed, half-dead, in front of them;
the draught-beast was lamed in its bones,
this the wicked Loki had caused.

38 But you have heard this already—anyone wiser about the gods
may tell it more clearly—
how he got recompense from the dweller on the lava,
how he paid for it with both his children.*

39 The mighty one came to the assembly of the gods,
bringing the kettle which Hymir had owned;
and the gods are going joyfully to drink
ale at Ægir's every winter.

??

Feast, cauldron & goblet,
God/giant rivalry.

Loki's Quarrel

Excluded from the feast at Ægir's hall, where all the other gods except Thor are celebrating, Loki forces his way in, compels Odin to assign him a seat, and insults each of the gods and goddesses in turn—hence the title *Loki's Quarrel* (*Lokasenna*). No one escapes his scorn and it is only when Thor returns from his journeying in Giantland and threatens Loki with his hammer, Miollnir, that Loki falls silent and consents to leave. The poem is cleverly structured so that Loki has two stanzas of insult, countered by one uttered by the victim in his or her defence, and one uttered by another of the company, serving to draw Loki's attention to the new speaker. In so far as we can verify the charges Loki lays against the gods and goddesses, they appear to have some foundation, though Loki speaks as if the gods were wayward human beings rather than divinities whose actions are attributes of their separateness and power. The poem may be early—and thus the composition of a poet who believes in the divinities he burlesques: a little comedy cannot hurt divinities whose cult is secure—or it may be late, and the mockery be directed by a Christian poet at heathen divinities whose immorality contrasts with the stern morality of the new religion. The prose introduction seems to misunderstand the poem; the latter suggests that Loki was never invited to the feast and gatecrashes it, insulting Ægir's servant as he does so.

About Ægir and the Gods *Ægir, who is also called Gymir, had brewed ale for the Æsir, when he got the great cauldron which has just been told about. To the feast there came Odin and Frigg, his wife. Thor did not come, because he was away in the east. Sif was there, Thor's wife, Bragi, and Idunn, his wife. Tyr was there; he was one-handed, for Fenrir the wolf tore his hand off when he was bound. There was Niord and his wife, Skadi, Freyr and Freyia, Vidar, son of Odin; Loki was there and the servants of Freyr, Byggvir and Beyla. Many of the Æsir and elves were there. Ægir had two servants, Fimafeng and Eldir. There was shining gold raised in the firelight; ale went the rounds; there was a great peace there. People praised the excellence of Ægir's servers. Loki could not bear to hear that, and he killed Fimafeng. Then the Æsir shook their shields and shrieked at Loki and chased him out to the woods, and they set to drinking.*

Loki came back and met Eldir outside; Loki greeted him:

1 'Tell me, Eldir, before you step
a single foot forward,
what the sons of the glorious gods here inside
are talking about over their ale.'

Eldir said:

2 'They discuss their weapons and their prowess in war,
the sons of the glorious gods;
among the Æsir and of the elves who are within,
no one has a friendly word for you.'

Loki said:

3 'I shall go in, into Ægir's halls
to see that feast;
before the end of the feast quarrelling I'll bring to the Æsir's sons
and thus mix their mead with malice.'

Eldir said:

4 'You know, if you go in, into Ægir's halls
to see that feast,
if shouting and fighting you pour out on the loyal gods,
they'll wipe it off on you.'

Loki said:

5 'You know, Eldir, that if you and I should
contend with wounding words,
I'd be rich in replies
if you're going to talk too much.'

Afterwards Loki went into the hall. And when those inside saw who had come in, they all fell silent.

Loki said:

6 'Thirsty I, Loki, come to these halls,
from a long way off,
to ask the Æsir that they should give me
a drink of the famous mead.

7 'Why are you so silent, you arrogant gods,
are you unable to speak?
Assign a seat and a place to me at the feast,
or tell me to go away!'

Bragi said:

8 'A seat and a place the Æsir will never assign
you at the feast,
for the Æsir know which men they should invite
to their splendid feast.'

Loki said:

9 'Do you remember, Odin, when in bygone days
we mixed our blood together?*
You said you would never drink ale
unless it were brought to both of us.'

Odin said:

10 'Get up then, Vidar, and let the wolf's father*
sit at the feast,
lest Loki speak words of blame to us
in Ægir's hall.'

Then Vidar stood up and poured a drink for Loki, and before he drank, he toasted the Æsir:

11 'Hail to the Æsir, hail to the Asynior
and all the most sacred gods!
—except for that one god who sits further in,*
Bragi, on the benches.'

Bragi said:

12 'A horse and a sword I'll give you from my possessions,
and Bragi will compensate you with a ring,
so you don't repay the Æsir with hatred;
don't make the gods exasperated with you!'

Loki said:

13 'Both horses and arm-rings you'll always
be short of, Bragi;
of the Æsir and the elves who are in here,
you're the most wary of war
and shyest of shooting.'

Bragi said:

14 'I know if I were outside, just as now I am inside
Ægir's hall,
your head I'd be holding in my hand;
I'd reward your lies with that.'

Loki said:

15 'You're brave in your seat, but you won't do as you say,
Bragi the bench-ornament!
You run away if you see before you
an angry man, brave in spirit.'

Idunn said:

16 'I ask you, Bragi, to do a service to your blood-kin
and all the adoptive relations,*
that you shouldn't say words of blame to Loki
in Ægir's hall.'

Loki said:

17 'Be silent, Idunn, I declare that of all women
you're the most man-crazed,
since you placed your arms, washed bright,
about your brother's slayer.'*

Idunn said:

18 'I'm not saying words of blame to Loki
in Ægir's hall;
I quietened Bragi, made talkative with beer;
I don't want you two angry men to fight.'

Gefion said:

19 'Why should you two Æsir in here
fight with wounding words?
Loki knows that he's joking
and all living things love him.'

Loki said:

20 'Be silent, Gefion, I'm going to mention this,
how your heart was seduced;
the white boy gave you a jewel
and you laid your thigh over him.'*

Odin said:

21 'Mad you are, Loki, and out of your wits,
when you get Gefion as your enemy,
for I think she knows all about the fates of men,
as clearly as I myself.'

Loki said:

22 'Be silent, Odin, you never know how to
apportion honour in war among men;
often you've given what you shouldn't have given,
victory, to the faint-hearted.'*

Odin said:

23 'You know, if I gave what I shouldn't have given,
victory, to the faint-hearted,
yet eight winters you were, beneath the earth,
a woman milking cows,
and there you bore children,
and that I thought the hallmark of a pervert.'*

Loki said:

24 'But you once practised *seid* on Samsey,*
and you beat on the drum as witches do,
in the likeness of a wizard you journeyed among
mankind,
and that I thought the hallmark of a pervert.'

Frigg said:

25 'Your actions ought never to be
spoken of in front of people,
what you two Æsir did in past times;
always keep ancient matters concealed.'

Loki said:

26 'Be silent, Frigg, you're Fiorgyn's daughter
and you've always been mad for men:
Ve and Vili, Vidrir's wife,*
both were taken into your embrace.'

Frigg said:

27 'You know that if I had in here in Ægir's hall
a boy like my son Baldr,
you wouldn't get away from the sons of the Æsir;
there'd be furious fighting against you.'

Loki said:

28 'Frigg, do you want me to say still more about
my wicked deeds;
for I brought it about that you will never again
see Baldr ride to the halls.'*

Freyia said:

29 'Mad are you, Loki, when you reckon up your
ugly, hateful deeds;
Frigg knows, I think, all fate,
though she herself does not speak out.'

Loki said:

30 'Be silent, Freyia, I know all about you;
you aren't lacking in blame:
of the Æsir and the elves, who are in here,
each one has been your lover.'

Freyia said:

31 'False is your tongue, I think you just want
to yelp about wicked things;
the Æsir are furious with you, and the Asynior,
you'll go home discomfited.'

Loki said:

32 'Be silent, Freyia, you're a witch
and much imbued with malice,
you were astride your brother, all the laughing gods
surprised you,
and then, Freyia, you farted.'*

Niord said:

33 'That's harmless, if, besides a husband, a woman has
a lover or someone else;
what is surprising is a pervert god coming in here
who has borne children.'

Loki said:

34 'Be silent, Niord, from here you were
sent east as hostage to the gods;
the daughters of Hymir used you as a pisspot
and pissed in your mouth.'*

Niord said:

35 'That was my reward, when I, from far away,
was sent as hostage to the gods,
that I fathered that son, whom no one hates
and is thought the prince of the Æsir.'

Loki said:

36 'Stop now, Niord, keep some moderation!
I won't keep it secret any longer:
with your sister you got that son,
though you'd expect him to be worse than he is.'

Tyr said:

37 'Freyr is the best of all the bold riders
in the courts of the Æsir;
he makes no girl cry nor any man's wife,
and looses each man from captivity.'

Loki said:

38 'Be silent, Tyr, you can never
deal straight with people;
your right hand, I must point out,
is the one which Fenrir tore from you.'*

Tyr said:

39 'I may have lost a hand, but you've lost the famous wolf;
evil has come to us both;
it's not pleasant for the wolf, who must in shackles
wait for the twilight of the gods.'

Loki said:

40 'Be silent, Tyr, it came about that your wife*
had a son by me;
not an ell nor a penny have you ever had for this
injury, you wretch.'

Freyr said:

41 'A wolf I see lying before a river mouth,
until the gods are torn asunder;
thus you shall be bound—unless you are now silent—
next, maker of harm!'

Loki said:

42 'With gold you bought yourself Gymir's daughter*
and so you gave away your sword;
but when the sons of Muspell ride over Myrkwood,*
do you know then, wretch, how you'll fight?'

Byggvir said:

43 'You know, if I had the lineage of Freyr,
and such an honourable seat,
smaller than marrow I would grind down that hateful crow
and lame him in every limb.'

Loki said:

44 'What's that little creature, that which I see wagging its tail
and snapping and gaping?
At Freyr's ears you're always found
and twittering under the grindstone.'

Byggvir said:

45 'Byggvir I'm called, and I'm said to be speedy
by all the gods and men;
thus I'm proud to be here where the kinsmen of Odin are
all drinking ale together.'

Loki said:

46 'Be silent, Byggvir, you never know how to
share out food among men;
and in the straw on the dais you make sure you can't be found
when men are going to fight.'

Heimdall said:

47 'Drunk you are, Loki, so that you're out of your wits,
why don't you stop speaking?
For too much drinking makes every man
not keep his talkativeness in check.'

Loki said:

48 'Be silent, Heimdall, for you in bygone days
a hateful life was decreed:
a muddy back you must always have*
and watch as guard of the gods.'

Skadi said:

49 'You're light-hearted, Loki; you won't for long
play with your tail wagging free,
for on a sharp rock, with your ice-cold son's guts,
the gods shall bind you.'*

Loki said:

50 'You know, if on a sharp rock, with my ice-cold son's
guts,
the gods shall bind me,
first and foremost I was at the killing
when we attacked Thiazi.'*

Skadi said:

51 'You know, if first and foremost you were at the killing
when you attacked Thiazi,
from my sanctuaries and plains shall always come
baneful advice to you.'

Loki said:

52 'Gentler in speech you were to the son of Laufey
when you invited me to your bed;*
we have to mention such things if we're going to reckon
up
our shameful deeds.'

Then Sif went forward and poured out mead for Loki into a crystal cup and said:

53 'Welcome, now, Loki, and take the crystal cup
full of ancient mead,
you should admit, among the children of the Æsir,
that I alone am blameless.'

He took the horn and drank it down:

54 'That indeed you would be, if you were so,
if you were shy and fierce towards men;
I alone know, as I think I do know,
your lover besides Thor,
and that was the wicked Loki.'*

Beyla said:

55 'All the mountains shake; I think Thor must be
on his way home;
he'll bring peace to those who quarrel here,
all the gods and men.'

Loki said:

56 'Be silent, Beyla, you're Byggvir's wife
and much imbued with malice;
a worse female was never among the Æsir's children,
you shitty serving-wench.'

Then Thor came and said:

57 'Be silent, you evil creature, my mighty hammer
Miollnir shall deprive you of speech;
the rock of your shoulders I shall strike from your neck,*
and then your life will be gone.'

Loki said:

58 'The son of Earth has now come in;
why are you raging so, Thor?
But you won't be so daring as to fight against the wolf,
when he swallows up Odin.'

Thor said:

59 'Be silent, you evil creature, my mighty hammer
Miollnir shall deprive you of speech;
I shall throw you up on the roads to the east,*
afterwards no one will see you.'

Loki said:

60 'Your journeys in the east you should never
brag of before men,
since in the thumb of a glove you crouched cowering, you hero!*
And that was hardly like Thor.'

Thor said:

61 'Be silent, you evil creature, my mighty hammer
Miollnir shall deprive you of speech;
with my right hand I'll strike you, with Hrungnir's killer,*
so that every one of your bones is broken.'

Loki said:

62 'I intend to live for a good time yet,
though you threaten me with a hammer;
strong leather straps you thought Skrymir had,
and you couldn't get at the food,
and you starved, unharmed but hungry.'*

Thor said:

63 'Be silent, you evil creature, my mighty hammer
Miollnir shall deprive you of speech;
the slayer of Hrungnir will send you to hell,
down below the corpse-gates.'

Loki said:

64 'I spoke before the Æsir, I spoke before the sons of the Æsir,
what my spirit urged me,
but before you alone I shall go out,
for I know that you do strike.

65 'Ale you brewed, Ægir, and you will never again
hold a feast;
all your possessions which are here inside—
may flame play over them,
and may your back be burnt!'

About Loki *And after that Loki hid in the waterfall of Franangr, disguised as a salmon. There the Æsir caught him. He was bound with the guts of his son Nari. But his son Narfi* changed into a wolf. Skadi took a poisonous snake and fastened it over Loki's face; poison dripped down from it. Sigyn, Loki's wife,* *sat there and held a basin under the poison. But when the basin was full, she carried the poison out; and meanwhile the poison fell on Loki. Then he writhed so violently at this that all the earth shook from it; these are now called earthquakes.*

Thrym's Poem

The comedy of *Thrym's Poem* (*Thrymskvida*) depends upon the characterization of Freyia and Thor, who are compelled to act against their reputations. Freyia is indignant when Loki and Thor suggest that she might marry a giant, though her reputation for promiscuity is such that taking a giant as a sexual partner might not be regarded as out of the question. Thor is the most masculine of the gods, and dressing up as a woman causes him acute embarrassment. The simple structure and repetition of the poem was suitable for adaptation into the ballad form and a number of versions of it are found among Danish and Swedish ballads.

1 Thor was angry when he awoke
and missed his hammer;
his beard bristled, his hair stood on end,
the son of Earth began to grope about.

2 And these were the first words that he spoke:
'Listen, Loki, to what I am saying,
what no one knows neither on earth
or in heaven: the hammer of the God is stolen.'

3 They went to the beautiful court of Freyia
and these were the first words that he spoke:
'Will you lend me, Freyia, your feather cloak,*
to see if I can find my hammer?'

Freyia said:

4 'I'd give it you even if it were made of gold,
I'd lend it to you even if it were made of silver.'

5 Then Loki flew off, the feather cloak whistled,
until he came beyond the courts of the Æsir
and he came within the land of the giants.

6 Thrym sat on a grave-mound, the lord of the ogres,
plaiting golden collars for his bitches;
he was trimming his horses' manes.

Thrym said:

7 'What's up with the Æsir, what's up with the elves?
Why have you come alone into the land of the giants?'
'Bad news among the Æsir, bad news among the elves;
have you hidden Thor's hammer?'

8 'I have hidden Thor's hammer
eight leagues under the earth;
no man will ever take it back again,
unless I am brought Freyia as my wife.'

9 Loki flew off, the feather cloak whistled,
until he came beyond the land of the giants
and he came within the courts of the Æsir.
He met Thor in the middle of the court,
and these were the first words that he spoke:

10 'Have you had any success for your efforts?
Tell me all the news while you're still in the air!
For tales often escape the sitting man,
and the man lying down barks out lies.'

11 'It was an effort and I've had some success:
Thrym has your hammer, the lord of the ogres;
no man will ever take it back from him again,
unless he's brought Freyia as his wife.'

12 Then they went to see the beautiful Freyia,
and these were the first words which he spoke:
'Dress yourself, Freyia, in a bride's head-dress!
We two shall drive to the land of the giants.'

13 Freyia then was angry and snorted in rage,
all the halls of the Æsir trembled at that,
the great necklace of the Brisings fell from her:*
'You'll know me to be the most sex-crazed of women,
if I drive with you to the land of the giants.'

14 Together all the Æsir came to the Assembly,
and all the goddesses came to the discussion,
and the mighty gods debated,
how Thor and Loki should get back the hammer.

15 Then Heimdall said, the whitest of the gods—
he can see far ahead as the Vanir also can:
'Let's dress Thor in a bridal head-dress,
let him wear the great necklace of the Brisings.

16 'Let keys jingle about him*
and let women's clothing fall down to his knees,
and on his breast let's display jewels,
and we'll arrange a head-dress suitably on his head!'

17 Then said Thor, the vigorous god:
'The Æsir will call me a pervert,
if I let you put a bride's veil on me.'

18 Then said Loki, son of Laufey:
'Be quiet, Thor, don't speak these words!
The giants will be settling in Asgard
unless you get your hammer back.'

19 Then they dressed Thor in a bride's head-dress
and in the great necklace of the Brisings,
they let keys jingle about him
and women's clothing fall down to his knees,
and on his breast they displayed jewels,
and arranged a head-dress suitably on his head.

20 Then said Loki, son of Laufey:
'I'll go with you to be your maid,
we two shall drive to the land of the giants.'

21 Quickly the goats were driven home,*
they hurried into the harness, they were going to gallop
well;
the mountains split asunder, the earth flamed with fire,
Odin's son was driving to the land of the giants.

22 Then said Thrym, lord of ogres:
'Be upstanding, giants, and spread straw on the benches!
Now they are bringing me Freyia as my wife,
the daughter of Niord from Noatun!

23 'Gold-horned cows walk here in the yard,
jet-black oxen to the giant's delight;
many treasures I possess, many necklaces I possess,
Freyia was all I seemed to be missing.'

24 They came together there early in the evening,
and ale was brought for the giants;
he ate one whole ox, eight salmon,
all the dainties meant for the women,
the husband of Sif drank three casks of mead.

25 Then said Thrym, lord of ogres:
'Where have you seen a lady eating more ravenously?
I have never seen any woman with a bigger bite,
nor any girl drink so much mead.'

26 The very shrewd maid sat before him,
she found an answer to the giant's speech:
'Freyia ate nothing for eight nights,
so madly eager was she to come to Giantland.'

27 He bent under the veil, he wanted to kiss her,
but he sprang back instead right down the hall:
'Why are Freyia's eyes so terrifying?
It seems to me that fire is burning from them.'

28 The very shrewd maid sat before him,
she found an answer to the giant's speech:
'Freyia did not sleep for eight nights,
so madly eager was she to come to Giantland.'

29 In came the wretched sister of the giants,
she dared to ask for the bride's wedding gift:
'Give me the red-gold rings from your hands,
if you want to merit my love,
my love and all my favour.'

30 Then said Thrym, lord of ogres:
'Bring in the hammer to sanctify the bride,
lay Miollnir on the girl's lap,
consecrate us together by the hand of Var!'*

31 Thor's heart laughed in his breast,
when he, stern in courage, recognized the hammer;
first he struck Thrym, lord of ogres,
and battered all the race of giants.

32 He killed the old sister of the giants,
she who had asked for the bridal gift;
striking she got instead of shillings,
and a blow of the hammer instead of many rings.

So Odin's son got the hammer back.

neat, self-contained episode. humorous, light hearted, witty. versified

The Lay of Volund

The Lay of Volund (*Volundarkvida*) appears to be a combination of two poems, the first the tale of the swan-maidens, the second the tale of Volund's imprisonment and his revenge. Volund is a strange character, neither human nor divine. At one point he is referred to as 'prince of elves'; since we know so little about elves in the Norse mythic scheme we cannot prove or disprove this attribution. Volund's story was known in England as well as Scandinavia. The Old English poem *Deor* refers allusively to the sufferings of 'Weland', and the misery of 'Beadohild' (Bodvild), while high-quality swords are sometimes called in Old English poetry 'Weland's work'. The smith is often regarded as an outsider and as possessing supernatural powers in a wide range of cultures. The antisocial noisiness of his work and the mysterious ability to transform unpromising lumps of metal into precious tools, weapons, and jewellery may account for this.

Nidud was the name of a king among the Swedish people. He had two sons and one daughter. She was called Bodvild. There were three brothers, sons of the Lappish king. One was called Slagfid, the second Egil, the third Volund. They stalked on snow-shoes and hunted wild animals. They came to Wolfdale and there built themselves a house. There is a lake which is called Wolf-lake. Early in the morning, they found three women on the shore, and they were spinning linen. Near them were their swan's garments; they were valkyries. There were two daughters of King Hlodver—Hladgud the swan-white, and Hervor, the strange creature—the third was Olrun, the daughter of Kiar of Valland. They took them home to the hall with them. Egil took Olrun, and Slagfid Swanwhite [i.e. Hladgud], and Volund Alvit [i.e. Hervor]. They lived together seven winters. Then the women flew off to go to a battle and did not come back. Then Egil went off on snow-shoes to look for Olrun, and Slagfid went looking for Swanwhite, and Volund sat in Wolfdale. He was the most skilful of men, that men know of, in the ancient stories. King Nidud had him seized, as is told of here:*

1 The maidens flew from the south across Mirkwood,
the strange, young creatures, to fulfil their fate;
there on the lake shore they sat to rest,
the southern ladies spun precious linen.

2 One of them took Egil to enclose in her arms,
the fair maid among men in bright embrace;
Another was Swanwhite, she wore swan feathers;
and the third, their sister,
wound her arms around the white neck of Volund.

3 They stayed thus for seven winters,
but all the eighth they suffered anguish,
and in the ninth necessity parted them;
the maidens hastened through Mirkwood,
the strange, young creatures, to fulfil their fate.

4 Then came from hunting the weather-eyed shooter;*
Slagfid and Egil found the hall empty;
they went in and out and looked about.
Egil went off east after Olrun,
and Slagfid went south after Swanwhite.

5 But Volund sat alone in Wolfdale.
He set red gold closely with gems,
he closed all the rings up well on a bast rope;
so he waited for his shining woman
if she were to make her way back to him.

6 That Nidud heard, lord of the Niarar,
that Volund sat alone in Wolfdale.
By night men journeyed, their corslets studded,
their shields glinted in the waning moon.

7 They dismounted from their saddles at the hall's gables,
they went in there all along the hall,
they saw on the bast rope rings threaded,
seven hundred in all, which the warrior owned.

8 And they took them off and they put them back,
except for one, which they left off.
Then there came from hunting the weather-eyed shooter,
Volund, travelling over the long road.

9 He went to roast the flesh of the brown she-bear;
high burned with kindling the very dry fir,
the wind-dried wood in front of Volund.

10 He sat on a bearskin, counted rings,
the prince of elves; he missed one.
He thought that the daughter of Hlodver
the strange, young creature, had come back again.

11 He sat so long that he fell asleep,
and he awoke deprived of joy,
he felt on his hands pressing, heavy bonds,
and on his feet fetters clasped.

12 'Who are the mighty men, those who have laid on me
these ropes of bast and bound me?'

13 Now Nidud called, lord of the Niarar:
'Where did you get, Volund, lord of elves,
this gold of ours in Wolfdale?'

14 'The gold was not there in Grani's road,*
far I think is our land from the hills of the Rhine.
I remember that we owned greater riches
when we were all safe at our home:

15 'Hladgud and Hervor, children of Hlodver,
Olrun, Kiar's daughter, was skilled in magic.'

16 She went in right along the hall,*
stood on the floor, said with low voice:
'He is not very gentle, this one who came out of the
forest.'

King Nidud gave Bodvild, his daughter, the gold ring which he took from Volund, from the bast rope, and he himself wore the sword which Volund owned. But the queen said:

17 'He bares his teeth in craving when the sword is shown
before him
and he recognizes Bodvild's ring;
similar are his eyes to a shining serpent.
Cut from him the might of his sinews*
and afterwards put him in Sævarstadir!'

Thus it was done: the sinews were cut at his knees and he was put on an island, near the land, called Sævarstadir. There he made for the king all kinds of treasures. No man dared go to him except the king alone.

Volund said:

18 'There shines at Nidud's belt a sword,
which I sharpened most skilfully as I knew how,
and I tempered as seemed to me most fitting;
that shining blade is forever carried far from me,
I shall not see that brought to Volund in the smithy;

19 'now Bodvild wears my bride's—
I shall not get compensation for this—red-gold rings.'

20 He sat, nor did he sleep, he struck with his hammer,
subtle things he created rather quickly for Nidud.
The two young men came to see precious things,
the sons of Nidud, to Sævarstadir.

21 They came to the chest, demanded the keys;
the evil intention was patent when they looked inside;
a multitude of necklaces, which seemed to the boys
to be of red gold, and treasures.

22 'Come alone, you two, come another day!
I shall have that gold given to you;
do not tell the maidens, nor the household,
any man, that you visit me!'

23 Early called one man to the other,
brother to brother: 'Let's go to see the rings!'
They came to the chest, demanded the keys;
the evil intention was patent when they looked inside.

24 He cut off the heads of those young cubs,
and under the mud of the smithy he laid their limbs;
and their skulls which were under the hair,
he chased outside with silver, gave to Nidud.
25 And from their eyes he shaped exotic stones,
he sent them to the cunning queen of Nidud;
and from the teeth of the two
he struck brooches; sent them to Bodvild.

26 Then Bodvild began
to praise the ring, which she had broken.
'I would not dare tell anyone except you alone.'

Volund said:

27 'I will so repair the break in the gold,
that your father will think it fairer,
and your mother much better,
and you yourself the same as before.'

28 He overcame her with beer, because he was more
experienced,*
so that on the couch she fell asleep.
'Now I have avenged my harm,
all except one of the wicked injuries!

29 'Lucky for me', said Volund, 'that I can use my webbed
feet,*
of which Nidud's warriors deprived me!'
Laughing, Volund rose into the air;
weeping, Bodvild went from the island,
she grieved for her lover's departure and her father's
fury.

30 Outside stood the cunning queen of Nidud,
and she went inside, all along the hall;
and he on the hall-wall sat and rested:*
'Are you awake, Nidud, lord of the Niarar?'

31 'I am always awake, deprived of joy,
I sleep very little since my sons died;
my head is icy, cold are your counsels to me,
I wish now that I could talk with Volund.

32 'Tell me, Volund, prince of elves,
what became of my healthy young cubs?'

33 'First you shall give me all these oaths,
by the side of a ship and the rim of a shield,
the back of a horse and the edge of a blade,
that you will not torment Volund's lady,
nor be the slayer of my bride,
though I have a wife who is known to you,
and we have a child inside your hall.

34 'Go to the smithy, the one which you built,
there you'll find bellows congealed with blood:
I cut off the heads of your young cubs,
and in the mud of the forge I laid their limbs.

35 'And their skulls which were under their hair,
I chased outside with silver, I sent them to Nidud:
and from the eyes I shaped precious stones,
I sent them to the cunning queen of Nidud;
36 and from the teeth of the two of them
I struck brooches; sent them to Bodvild.
Now Bodvild is with child,*
the only daughter of you both!'

37 'You could never have said anything which could grieve
me more,
nor could I, Volund, wish you any worse joy;
there is no man so tall that he could capture you from a
horse,
nor so powerful that he could shoot you down from
below,
there where you hover against the cloud!'

38 Laughing, Volund rose in the air,
and Nidud sadly sat there behind.

39 'Get up, Thakkrad, best of my thralls;
ask Bodvild, the white-lashed maiden,
to come in shining clothes to speak with her father.

40 'Is it true, Bodvild, what they said to me:
were you and Volund together on the island?'

41 'It is true, Nidud, what he said to you:
Volund and I were together on the island,
alone in that hour of terror; I should never have done it!
I did not know how to strive against him,
I was not able to strive against him!'

end of story rather abruptly. details + transactions missing: Revenge, loyalty & oaths

All-wise's Sayings

Thor intercepts a dwarf who apparently, and unbeknown to Thor, is intending to marry the latter's daughter. Thor proposes a wisdom contest in which he tests the dwarf's knowledge of the terminology used by the different races of being for natural phenomena. The dwarf knows a striking range of kennings and, perhaps, taboo words, but Thor's secret aim is to delay him until the sun comes up and turns him to stone. *All-wise's Sayings* (*Alvissmal*) is a catalogue poem, rather like *Vafthrudnir's Sayings* and *Grimnir's Sayings*, but it is not mythological information which is at issue; rather the interest is in the range of poetic synonyms which the dwarf has at his disposal.

1 'To spread the benches the bride is coming with me,
coming home now at this moment;
it may seem like rushing headlong into marriage to
    everyone;
but away from home one can get no rest.'

2 'What sort of man is that, why so pale about the nostrils,
did you spend the night with a corpse?
The image of an ogre you seem to be to me,
you are not meant for a bride.'

3 'All-wise is my name, I live below the earth,
my home is under a rock;
from the sea of wagons I've come on a visit,*
let no man break sworn pledges!'

4 'I shall break them, since I'm giving the bride
away as her father;
I wasn't at home when she was promised to you,
when that match was made among the gods.'

5 'Which warrior is this who reckons he'll manage the match
of the beautifully glowing lady?
—A vagabond, few people know you,
who has given you arm-rings?'

6 'Ving-Thor I'm called; I've journeyed afar—
I'm the son of Sidgrani;
not with my consent will you have that young woman
and have her hand in marriage.'

7 'Your consent I'd quickly like to get
and to have her hand in marriage;
I had rather have her than be without
the snow-white girl.'

8 'The love of the girl, wise wanderer,
you won't bc deprived of,
if you know how to tell me from all the worlds you've visited,
all that I want to know.

9 'Tell me this, All-wise—I foresee, dwarf,
that you have wisdom about all beings—
what the earth is called, which lies in front of men,
in each of the worlds.'

10 'Earth it's called among men, and ground by the Æsir,
the Vanir call it ways;
the giants evergreen, the elves the growing one,
the Powers above call it loam.'

11 'Tcll me this, All-wise—I foresee, dwarf,
that you have wisdom about all beings—
what the sky is called, known everywhere,
in each of the worlds.'

12 'Sky it's called among men, home of the planets by the gods,
wind-weaver the Vanir call it,
the giants call it the world above, the elves the lovely roof,
the dwarfs the dripping hall.'

13 'Tell me this, All-wise—I foresee, dwarf,
that you have wisdom about all beings—
what the moon is called, which men can see,
in each of the worlds.'

14 'Moon it's called by men, and fiery one by the gods,
in hell it's the whirling wheel,
the giants call it the hastener, the dwarfs the shiner,
elves call it counter of years.'

15 'Tell me this, All-wise—I foresee, dwarf,
that you know all the fates of men—
what the sun is called, which the sons of men see,
in each of the worlds.'

16 'Sun it's called by men, and sunshine by the gods,
for the dwarfs it's Dvalin's deluder,*
the giants call it everglow, the elves the lovely wheel,
the sons of the Æsir all-shining.'

17 'Tell me this, All-wise—I foresee, dwarf,
that you know all the fates of men—
what those clouds are called which mix with showers,
in each of the worlds.'

18 'Clouds they're called by men, and hope-of-showers by
the gods,
the Vanir call them wind-floaters,
hope-of-dew the giants call them, power-of-storms the
elves,
in hell the concealing helmet.'

19 'Tell me this, All-wise—I foresee, dwarf,
that you know all the fates of men—
what the wind is called, which blows so widely,
in each of the worlds.'

20 'Wind it's called by men, the waverer by the gods,
the mighty Powers say neigher,
whooper the giants, din-journeyer the elves,
in hell they call it stormer.'

21 'Tell me this, All-wise—I foresee, dwarf,
that you know all the fates of men—
what calm is called, which lies quiet,
in all the worlds.'

22 'Calm it's called by men, and lying quiet by the gods,
the Vanir call it wind-end,
the great lee the giants, day-soother the elves,
the dwarfs call it essence of day.'

23 'Tell me this, All-wise—I foresee, dwarf,
that you know all the fates of men—
what the ocean is called, which men row upon,
in each of the worlds.'

24 'Sea it's called by men, and endless-lier by the gods,
the Vanir call it rolling one,
home of the eel the giants, "lagastaf" the elves,*
the dwarfs the deep ocean.'

25 'Tell me this, All-wise—I foresee, dwarf,
that you know all the fates of men—
what fire is called, burning before the sons of men,
in each of the worlds.'

26 'Fire it's called among men, and spark by the Æsir,
burner by the Vanir,
ravener by the giants, burner-up by the dwarfs,
in hell they call it hurrier.'

27 'Tell me this, All-wise—I foresee, dwarf,
that you know all the fates of men—
what wood is called, growing before the sons of men,
in each of the worlds.'

28 'Wood it's called by men, and mane of the valleys by the gods,
slope-seaweed by humankind,
fuel by the giants, lovely boughs by the elves,
wand the Vanir call it.'

29 'Tell me this, All-wise—I foresee, dwarf,
that you know all the fates of men—
what night is called, whom Norr gave birth to,
in each of the worlds.'

30 'Night it's called among men, and darkness by the gods,
the masker by the mighty Powers,
unlight by the giants, joy-of-sleep by the elves,
the dwarfs call it dream-goddess.'

31 'Tell me this, All-wise—I foresee, dwarf,
that you know all the fates of men—
what that seed is called, which the sons of men sow,
in each of the worlds.'

32 Barley it's called by men, and grain by the gods,
the Vanir call it growth,
eatable the giants, 'lagastaf' the elves,
in hell they call it head-hanger.'

33 'Tell me this, All-wise—I foresee, dwarf,
that you know all the fates of men—
what ale is called, which the sons of men drink,
in each of the worlds.'

34 'Ale it's called among men, and beer by the gods,
the Vanir call it liquor,
clear-brew the giants, and mead in hell,
the sons of Suttung call it feasting.'

35 'In one breast I've never seen
more ancient knowledge;
with much talking I say I've beguiled you;
day dawns on you now, dwarf,
now sun shines into the hall.'

The First Poem of Helgi Hundingsbani

The two poems about Helgi Hundingsbani—the slayer of Hunding—and his namesake Helgi Hiorvardsson mark the beginning of the heroic poems in the Codex Regius manuscript. The relationship between the two Helgi Hundingsbani poems is unclear; it is quite likely that they represent much the same poem orally produced in different versions. All three Helgi poems centre on the meeting and battle adventures of the hero and his valkyrie lover. Valkyries were depicted as semi-divine figures, living in Valhall, serving mead to the warriors there, and hovering over battle choosing those who were going to die (hence the meaning of their name 'Choosers of the Slain'). But some valkyries were envisaged rather as human or superhuman. They were royal princesses who chose the valkyrie way of life in preference to that of a normal woman. The valkyrie would choose a hero, bring him good luck in battle while flying overhead with her companions, and eventually would become his bride. This would bring him into usually fateful collision with the valkyrie's kindred or with thwarted suitors. The name 'Helgi' means 'Sacred One'; the Helgi heroes are archetypal in their relation to the valkyrie bride and may even be reincarnated, as is suggested at the end of the poem of Helgi Hiorvardsson. Central to this poem—and to the other Helgi poems—is the 'flyting' here between Sinfiotli and Gudmund. The opponents accuse each other of unnatural behaviour, sexual deviancy, or taboo acts, as a prelude to battle. It is not always clear who is speaking, and I have punctuated the dialogue to reflect my understanding of who is speaking when. This poem ends with Helgi's successfully winning his bride; the other Helgi poems continue after this point. The events of the poem are summarized in *Volsunga saga*, chs. 8–9.

1 It was a long time ago that the eagles shrieked,
the sacred waters poured down from Himinfell;
then Helgi, the man of great spirit,
was born to Borghild in Bralund.

2 Night fell on the place, the norns came,*
those who were to shape fate for the prince;
they said the prince should be most famous
and that he'd be thought the best of warriors.

3 They twisted very strongly the strand of fate,
. . . in Bralund;*
they prepared the golden thread
and fastened it in the middle of the moon's hall.*

4 East and west they secured its ends,
the prince should have all the land between;
the kinswoman of Neri to the north*
threw one fastening; she said she'd hold it for ever.

5 [Not] one thing grieved the kinsman of the Ylfings*
and that girl who'd given birth to the dear one:
one raven said to another—he sat on a high tree,
they were hoping for food: 'I know something.

6 'The son of Sigmund stands in his byrnie,*
one day old; now dawn has come;
sharp his eyes like a fighter;
he's the friend of wolves, we should be cheerful.'*

7 To the men it seemed that he was a prince,
they said to one another that a good year had come;
the noble lord himself came from the tumult of battle
to bring a shining leek to the young nobleman.*

8 He gave Helgi a name, gave him Hringstadir,
Sunfell, Snowfell, and Sigarvoll,
Hringstod, Highmeadow, and Himinvangi,
provided with a blood-snake the brother of Sinfiotli.*

9 Then he began to grow in the bosom of his friends,
the shining-born elm-tree, radiant delight;*
he paid out and gave gold to the retinue,
the prince did not spare the blood-inlaid treasure.

10 For a short time the prince waited for war,
until the leader was fifteen years old;
then he brought about the killing of Hunding the hard,
who for a long time ruled over lands and men.

11 Afterwards they demanded, the sons of Hunding,
riches and rings from Sigmund's son,
yet they intended to repay the prince
for his great ravaging and the death of their father.

12 The prince did not let compensation be in question,
nor the descendants be given kin-payment at all;
he said they might hope for a great storm
of grey spears and the wrath of Odin.

13 The chieftains go to the sword-meeting
which they'd set up at Logafell;
the peace of Frodi was torn between the enemies;
eager for slaughter on the island ran Odin's hounds.*

14 The prince sat down, when he'd killed
Alf and Eyiolf, beneath Arastein,
Hiorvard and Havard, the sons of Hunding;
he'd brought down all of the spear-champion's clan.

15 Then a light shone from Logafell,
and from that radiance there came bolts of lightning;
wearing helmets at Himinvangi [came the valkyries].
Their byrnies were drenched in blood;
and rays shone from their spears.

16 Soon he asked when he left the wolf-lair,
the prince asked if the southern goddesses
would wish to go home with the warriors
when night fell; the elm bows were shrilling.

17 Hogni's daughter, from her horse,
—the shield-din was over—said to the prince:
'I think that we ought to have other business
than drinking beer with the breaker of rings.*

18 'My father has promised his girl
to Granmar's fierce son;
but, Helgi, I call Hodbrodd
a king as bold as the kitten of a cat.*

19 'The prince will come in a few nights
unless you challenge him to battle
or seize the girl from the warrior.'

20 'Don't be afraid of the slayer of Isung!
There'll be noise of battle unless I am dead.'

21 The all-powerful one sent messengers from there,
through air and sea, to assemble his army,
ample river-fire he offered*
the warriors and their sons.

22 'Tell them quickly to go to their ships
and to be ready to sail from Brand-island!'
The prince waited there until there came to him
huge numbers of men from Hedins-island.

23 And there straight away at Stafnsness
they pushed out the boats trimmed with gold;
Helgi asked Hiorleif this:
'Have you inspected the valiant young men?'

24 The young king spoke to the other—
said it would take a long time to count off
Crane-bank
the long-necked ships beneath the sailors,
journeying outwards from Orvasund:

25 'Twelve hundred trusty men;
though in Highmeadow there's twice as many,
the king's war-troop; we may expect battle din.'

26 So the leader ordered the tents in the prow dismantled,
awakened the crowd of warriors,
and the fighters see the dawn;
and the nobles hoisted up
the well-sewn sail in Varinsfjord.

27 There was the splash of oars and the clash of iron,
shield smashed against shield, the vikings rowed on;
hurtling beneath the nobles
went the leader's ship far from the land.

28 Then it could be heard: they'd met together,
the sister of Kolga and the longships,*
as mountains or surf might break asunder.

29 Helgi ordered the high sail to be set,
his crew did not fail at the meeting of the waves,
when Ægir's terrible daughter
wanted to capsize the stay-bridled wave-horse.

30 And Sigrun above, brave in battle,
protected them and their vessel;
the king's sea-beasts twisted powerfully
out of Ran's hand towards Gnipalund.*

31 So in Una-bay in the evening
the splendid ships are floating;
and the others in person from Svarinshaug*
with an anxious mind came to look at the army.

32 Gudmund asked, divinely-descended,
'Who is that ruler who leads the troop,
who's brought the dangerous men to the shore?'

33 Sinfiotli said—he'd slung on the yard-arm
his red shield, the rim was all of gold;
he was a lookout-man who knew how to answer
and how to debate with the princes:

34 'Say this evening, when you're giving
pigs and bitches their feed to chew,*
that these are the Ylfings come from the east,
eager for fighting to Gnipalund.

35 'Hodbrodd will find Helgi there,
the prince who never flees, aboard his ship,
a man who's often given food to the eagles,
while you were kissing slave-women at the grindstone.'

36 'Little must you recall, lord, the old stories,
when you taunt the princes with untruths;
you have eaten the leavings of wolves
and been the slayer of your brother,
often you've sucked wounds with a cold snout;
hated everywhere, you've crept into a stone-tip.'*

[*Sinfiotli said:*]

37 'You were a sorceress on Varins-island,
a deceitful woman, you made up slander;
you said that you did not want to have
any warrior in his armour except Sinfiotli.*

38 'You were, you harmful creature,
a witch, horrible, unnatural,
among Odin's valkyries,
all the Einheriar had to fight,
headstrong woman, on your account.

39 'Nine wolves on Saga's headland
we engendered; I alone was their father.'

[*Gudmund said:*]

40 'You were not the father of any ferocious wolf,
though you were older than them all, as far as I remember,
after the giant girls castrated you
on Thorsness by Gnipalund.

41 'You were Siggeir's stepson, you lay under the home haystacks,*
used to wolves' howling, out in the woods;
every kind of shameful thing has happened to you,
when the breast of your brother you tore.
You made yourself infamous for abominable deeds.

42 'You were a mare for Grani on Bravoll plain,*
a gold bit in your mouth, you were ready to leap;
I've ridden you to exhaustion over many a stretch of road,
under my saddle, a jaded hack, down the mountain
path.'

[*Sinfiotli said:*]

43 'You seemed to be a youth devoid of morals,
when you milked Gullnir's goats,
and another time as Imd's daughter*
in tattered clothes. Do you want to keep talking?'

[*Gudmund said:*]

44 'Rather I should like to make ravens sate themselves
on your corpse, at Frekastein,
than give your bitches dog-food to devour
or be feeding your pigs; may ill-luck befall you!'

[*Helgi said:*]*

45 'It would be much more fitting for you, Sinfiotli,
to go to battle and make the eagle happy,
than to be bandying useless words,
though these generous princes may be bitter enemies.

46 'I expect no good from Granmar's sons,
though the princes, truth to tell, have had some success;
they have proved at Moinsheim,
that they have the temperament for wielding swords.'

47 They allowed Svipud and Sveggiud*
to run powerfully to Solheim,
over the dew-sprinkled dales, the dark slopes,
the valkyrie's airy sea trembled where the kinsmen passed.

48 The prince met them on the meadow slope,
forcefully they said that the lord had come;
Hodbrodd stepped forward, wearing his helmet,
he pondered his kinsmen riding towards him:
'Why do the Niflungs look so troubled?'

49 'They've beached on the sand swift ships,
harts of mast-rings, long rowlocks,
many shields, smooth-planed oars,
the troop of the splendid king, the cheerful Ylfings.

50 'Fifteen companies came on shore;
yet out in Sogn there are seven thousand,
drawn up by the palisade before Gnipalund,
dark-coloured sea-beasts all decked with gold.
That mighty host is very huge indeed.
Helgi will not delay the meeting of swords.'

51 'Let the bridled horses gallop to the battle,
Spurwolf ride to Sparins-heath,
Melnir and Mylnir to Mirkwood,
let no man linger behind,
those who know how to brandish wound-flames.

52 'Summon to you Hogni and the sons of Hring,
Atli and Yngvi, Alf the old;
they are eager to advance to war,
let's offer the Volsungs some resistance!'

53 A storm there was then, as they came together,
of pale spear-points at Frekastein;
always was Helgi, slayer of Hunding,
foremost in the host, where men were fighting,
eager in the battle, extremely averse to flight;
that prince had a hard acorn of a heart.

54 Helmeted valkyries came down from the sky
—the noise of spears grew loud—they protected the
prince;
then said Sigrun—the wound-giving valkyries flew,
the troll-woman's mount was feasting on the fodder of
ravens:*

55 'Unscathed, prince, you'll rule over men,
upholder of Yngvi's line, and enjoy your life,
since you have brought low the king who scorns flight,
the one who dealt death to the sea-king.

56 'And it's fitting, lord, that you should have
both red-gold rings and the powerful girl;
unscathed, lord, you'll enjoy both
Hogni's daughter and Hringstadir,
lands and victory now the battle is over.'

The Poem of Helgi Hiorvardsson

Helgi Hiorvardsson is a kind of doublet of Helgi Hundingsbani whose two poems surround his in the manuscript. The *Poem of Helgi Hiorvardsson* (*Helgakvida Hiorvardssonar*) follows the basic plot of the other Helgi poems, except with an added prelude telling of the winning of Helgi's mother. This sets up Helgi's first adventure, killing his mother's disgruntled wooer; then comes a 'flyting' between the hero's lieutenant, Atli, and a troll-woman, Hrimgerd, the marriage with the valkyrie, and death at the hands of the son of his former enemy. Compared with the other two Helgi poems, the plot in this poem is incoherent. The flyting between Atli and Hrimgerd has no relevance to the plot and the vow of Hedin has no tragic consequences—he simply acquires his half-brother's bride after his death.

About Hiorvard and Sigrlinn *Hiorvard was the name of a king. He had four wives. One was called Alfhild, their son was Hedin; the second was called Særeid, their son was called Humlung; the third was called Sinriod, their son was Hymling. King Hiorvard had sworn an oath to marry the woman whom he had heard was most beautiful of all. He heard that King Svafnir had a daughter who was loveliest of all, who was called Sigrlinn.*

Idmund was the name of his earl. Atli was his son and he went to ask for Sigrlinn on the king's behalf. He spent the whole winter with King Svafnir. There was an earl called Franmar, Sigrlinn's foster-father; his daughter was called Alof. The earl advised that the girl not be betrothed and Atli went home.

Atli, the son of the earl, was standing one day in a certain grove; there was a bird sitting in the branches up above him and it had heard that his men were saying that the most beautiful women were those married to Hiorvard. The bird squawked; Atli listened to what it said. It said:

1 'Have you seen Sigrlinn, daughter of Svafnir,
the loveliest girl in the world of desire?
even if the wives of Hiorvard seem pleasing
to men in Glasilund.'

Atli said:

2 'Will you speak further, bird so wise-minded,
to Atli, Idmund's son?'

The bird said:

'I will if the chieftain will give me a sacrifice,
and I may choose what I wish from the king's court.'

Atli said:

3 'Don't choose Hiorvard, nor his sons,
nor the lovely brides of the king,
nor the brides who belong to the ruler;
let's make a good bargain, that's the hallmark of friends.'

The bird said:

4 'I'll choose temples, with many sanctuaries,
gold-horned cattle from the prince's farm,
if Sigrlinn sleeps in his arms
and willingly goes with the prince.'

This was before Atli set off, and when he got home and the king asked him for news, he said:

5 'We've had difficulties, not achieved our mission,
exhausted our horses on mighty mountains,
then we had to ford the Sæmorn;
Svafnir's daughter was refused us,
the girl endowed with rings whom we wished to have.'

The king commanded them to go a second time and he himself went. And when they came up on top of the mountain they saw in Svavaland the country all on fire and dust-clouds from horses' hoofs. The king rode on down the mountain and encamped for the night by a river. Atli kept watch and went over the river. He found a house. A great bird was sitting on the house, keeping watch, but it had fallen asleep. Atli hurled a spear at the bird and killed it, and in the house he found Sigrlinn, the king's daughter, and Alof, the earl's daughter, and took them away with him. Earl Franmar had changed himself into an eagle and had been keeping them safe from the army by magic. Hrodmar was the name of a king who was Sigrlinn's suitor. He had killed the king of Svavaland and was raiding and burning the land. King Hiorvard married Sigrlinn, and Atli married Alof.

Hiorvard and Sigrlinn had a tall and handsome son. He did not speak and he had no name. He sat on a burial-mound* and saw nine valkyries ride past. One was the most striking of all. She said:*

6 'It'll be a long time, Helgi, before you can distribute rings,
apple-tree of strife, or rule over Rodulsvoll*
—early shrieked the eagle—if you are always silent,
even if, prince, you have a stern temperament.'

7 'What will you give me with the name Helgi,*
bright-faced lady, since you have bestowed it?
Consider well before you answer!
I won't accept it unless I can have you also.'

8 'I know of swords lying on Sigarsholm,
four less than fifty;
one of them is better than all the rest,
the evil one among battle-needles, its hilt inlaid with gold.

9 'There's a ring on the hilt, there's courage in the middle,
and terror in its point, for him who manages to own it;
a blood-dyed snake lies along the edge
and on the boss a serpent chases its tail.'

Eylimi was the name of a king. His daughter was Svava. She was a valkyrie and rode through air and sea. She gave Helgi that name and often protected him in battles. Helgi said:

10 'You are not, Hiorvard, well advised,
war-leader of the people, though you are famous;
you let fire consume the settlements of the princes,
even if they do no harm to you.

11 'But Hrodmar will distribute rings,
those which our kinsmen used to own;
that king is little anxious about his life,
he expects to have the inheritance when there's no heir alive.'

Hiorvard answered that he would give Helgi a troop of men if he wanted to avenge his grandfather. Then Helgi went to look for the sword which Svava had directed him to. Then he and Atli set off and killed Hrodmar and did many remarkable and brave deeds. He killed the giant Hati, who was sitting on a certain cliff. Helgi and Atli moored their ships in Hatafjord. Atli kept watch for the first part of the night. Hrimgerd, Hati's daughter, said:

12 'Who are those men in Hatafjord?
Shields are hanging outside your ships;
you're acting rather boldly, I don't think you're afraid of much;
tell me the name of the king!'

Atli said:

13 'Helgi is his name, and you can never*
bring harm to the prince;
there are iron plates on the prince's ships,
no troll-women can attack us.'

14 'What is your name (said Hrimgerd), mighty warrior,
what do men call you?
The prince trusts you, since he lets you watch
in the pleasant prow of the ship.'

15 'Atli I'm called, atrocious I shall be to you,*
I am most hostile to ogresses;
I've often stayed at the dew-washed prow
and tormented night-riding witches.

16 'What is your name, corpse-greedy hag?
Troll-woman, name your father!
You ought to be nine leagues underground
with fir-trees growing from your breast!'

17 'Hrimgerd I'm called, Hati is my father,
the most terrible giant I know of;
many brides he's taken from their dwellings,
until Helgi hacked him down.'

18 'Ogress, you stood before the prince's ships
and blocked the fjord mouth;
the king's men you were going to give to Ran,*
if a spear hadn't lodged in your flesh.'

19 'Deluded you are now, Atli, I reckon you must be dreaming,
you're scowling with drooping brow;
it was my mother who lay in front of the prince's ships,
I drowned Hlodvard's sons in the ocean.

20 'You'd neigh, Atli, if you hadn't been gelded,*
Hrimgerd's raising up her tail;
I think your heart, Atli, is in your hindquarters,
though you have a stallion's voice.'

21 'I'd seem like a stallion to you if you wanted to try it,
if I came on land from this ship;
I'd lame every part of you if I were in earnest,
you'd drop your tail, Hrimgerd!'

22 'Atli, come on land, if you trust in your strength,
and let's meet at Varins-bay!
Warrior, you'd get your ribs straightened out,
if you got into my clutches.'

23 'I can't come before the warriors awake
and they keep watch for the king;
nor should I be surprised if, you witch, you came close,
and bobbed up from under the ship.'

[*Hrimgerd said:*]

24 'Wake up, Helgi, and give Hrimgerd compensation,
since you struck down Hati;
if for one night she can sleep with the prince,
then she'll have redress for her wrongs.'

25 'Shaggy is the name of the one who'll have you, you're
hideous to humankind;
that monster lives on Tholley;
a very wise giant, but the worst of lava-dwelling ogres,
he's a fitting mate for you.'

26 'You'd rather have her, Helgi, the one who was spying
out the harbours
the other night with the men;
the sea-golden girl surpassed me in strength;
here she landed from the ship
and moored your vessel so.
She alone is preventing me from destroying
the prince's men.'

27 'Listen now, Hrimgerd, if I give redress for your grief,
answer the prince directly:
was it just one creature who protected the lord's fleet,
or many journeying together?'

28 'Three times nine girls, but one girl rode ahead,
white-skinned under her helmet;
the horses were trembling, from their manes
dew fell into the deep valleys,
hail in the high woods;
good fortune comes to men from there;
all that I saw was hateful to me.'

29 'Look east now, Hrimgerd! Since Helgi has struck you
with fatal runes,
both on land and sea the prince's ships are safe
and so are the prince's men.

30 'It's day now, Hrimgerd, Atli has kept you talking
until you laid down your life;
as a harbour-mark you look ridiculous,
there transformed into stone.'

King Helgi was a great fighter. He came to King Eylimi and asked for his daughter, Svava. Helgi and Svava exchanged vows and loved one another very much. Svava stayed at home with her father, and Helgi went raiding. Svava was a valkyrie just as before.

Hedin was at home with his father, King Hiorvard, in Norway. Hedin was going home alone from the woods one Yule evening and he met a troll-woman; she was riding a wolf and had serpents as reins. She offered Hedin her company. 'No', he said. She said: 'You'll pay for this when it comes to drinking to pledges.' In the evening pledges were made. The sacrificial boar was led out, men put their hands on it and then they made their vows with the pledging-cup. Hedin vowed to have Svava, daughter of Eylimi, the beloved of his brother Helgi, and he repented so much of this that he went wandering away to the south and encountered his brother Helgi. Helgi said:

31 'Welcome, Hedin! What news
do you bring from Norway?
Why, prince, have you left your country
and come alone to meet us?'

32 'A terrible crime has come upon me:
I have chosen that royally born
bride of yours with the pledging-cup.'

33 'Do not reproach yourself! For both of us, Hedin,
what's said over ale must come true;
the prince has challenged me to an island duel,*
in three nights' time, I shall go there;
I have my doubts as to whether I'll return;
it may turn out well if I don't.'

34 'You're saying, Helgi, that Hedin deserves from you
good will and the greatest of gifts;
it would be more fitting to bloody your sword on me
than to grant peace to your enemies.'

Then Helgi said that he suspected that he was doomed and it was his fetch who had visited Hedin when he met the woman riding on the wolf.*

Alf, son of Hrodmar, was the king who had staked out the duelling-ground for Helgi three nights later. Then Helgi said:

35 'She rode on a wolf, as it grew dark,
that lady who offered him company;
she knew that Sigrlinn's son
would be killed at Sigarvoll.'

There was a great fight and Helgi received a death-wound.

36 Helgi sent Sigar to ride
for the only daughter of Eylimi;
told her to get ready quickly
if she wanted to see the prince alive.

37 'Helgi has sent me here to you, Svava,
to speak to you in person;
the lord says he wants to see you
before the splendidly born man draws his last breath.'

38 'What has happened to Helgi, Hiorvard's son?
A terrible fate has been sought out for me;
if the sea has washed over him, or the sword has bitten
into him,
I shall wreak vengeance on men.'

39 'He fell here in the morning at Frekastein,
the prince who was best under the sun;
Alf has achieved total victory,
though there was no need for it to have happened.'

40 'Greetings, Svava! You must steady your feelings,
this will be our last meeting in the world;
the prince has been made to bleed below,
a sword has pierced close to my heart.

41 'I beg you, Svava—bride, do not weep!—
that you will listen to what I say,
that you will share a bed with Hedin
and live in love with the young prince.'

42 'I said in my dear homeland,
when Helgi chose me, gave me rings,
that I would not willingly, if my lord were gone,
hold a prince of no reputation in my arms.'

[*Hedin said:*]

43 'Kiss me, Svava! Never will I come
to see Rogheim or Rodulsfiall,
until I've avenged the son of Hiorvard,
he was best of princes under the sun.'

Helgi and Svava are said to have been reincarnated.

A Second Poem of Helgi Hundingsbani

The second poem about Helgi Hundingsbani has several elements in common with the first: the hero's gaining of his nickname, his love for the valkyrie, and a very reduced form of the flyting found in the *First Poem of Helgi Hundingsbani*. It is quite likely that the scribe of the manuscript intended readers and reciters to leaf back to the first poem and read the flyting there, rather than recopying it. This poem is notable for the sense of conflict Sigrun feels between her love for Helgi and her loyalty to her family, and for the extravagantly Gothic ending in which Sigrun and Helgi spend a final night together in the burial-mound.

King Sigmund, son of Volsung, married Borghild of Bralund. They called their son Helgi after Helgi Hiorvardsson. Hagal was Helgi's foster-father.

Hunding was a powerful king. Hundland is named after him. He was a great warrior and had many sons who went raiding. There was hostility and enmity between King Hunding and King Sigmund; each killed the kinsmen of the other. Sigmund and his clan were known as Volsungs and Ylfings.

Helgi went in disguise to reconnoitre King Hunding's court. Hæming, son of King Hunding, was at home. And when Helgi went away, he met a shepherd boy and said:

1 'Tell Hæming that Helgi remembers
whom the warriors struck down in his coat-of-mail.
You've had a grey wolf within your court,
he whom King Hunding thought was Hamal.'

Hamal was Hagal's son. King Hunding sent men to Hagal to search for Helgi. And since Helgi couldn't escape any other way he put on a serving-woman's clothes and went to grind at the mill. They searched and couldn't find him. Then Blind the malevolent said:

2 'Piercing are the eyes of Hagal's maidservant,*
that's not a low-born person standing at the grindstone;
the stones are breaking, the wooden stand is splitting.

3 'Now the prince has got a harsh sentence,
the noble has to grind foreign barley.
It would be more fitting to have in those hands
a sword hilt than a grinding-handle.'

Hagal answered and said:

4 'It's not so surprising that the stand is juddering,
as the king's daughter turns the handle;
she sped above the clouds
and dared to fight like a viking,
before Helgi captured her;
she's the sister of Sigar and Hogni,
that's why the Ylfing girl has terrifying eyes.'

Helgi got away onto a warship. He killed King Hunding and after that was called Helgi Hundings-killer. With his fleet he lay in Bruna-bay and there they butchered cattle on the beach and ate them up raw. Hogni was the name of a king. His daughter was Sigrun, she was a valkyrie and rode through air and sea; she was Svava reincarnated. Sigrun rode to Helgi's ship and said:

5 'Who has brought these ships to anchor by the steep shore,
where, warriors, do you come from?
What are you waiting for in Bruna-bay,
which way do you set your course?'

6 'Hamal has brought these ships to anchor by the steep shore,
we come from Hlesey;
we're waiting for a breeze in Bruna-bay,
to the east we wish to set our course.'

7 'Where have you, prince, stirred up war
or fed the goslings of Gunn's sisters?*
Why is your corslet spattered with blood,
why are you eating raw meat, still wearing your helmets?'

8 'The descendant of the Ylfings fought most recently
west of the sea, if you wish to know,
where I was hunting bears in Bragalund*
and gave food with sword-points to the eagle's race.

9 'Now I've told you, girl, why the battle came about;
and so on the ship we were eating meat scarcely roasted.'

10 'War you're describing; King Hunding
fell on the field, before Helgi;
it came to battle, in revenge for kinsmen,
blood streamed along the edges of the swords.'

11 'How did you know, wise lady,
that we are those avengers?
There are many keen prince's sons,
who look like us kinsmen.'

12 'I was not far away, leader of the battle,
yesterday morning, when the prince lost his life;
though I see that the clever son of Sigmund
is giving news of the battle in secret slaughter-runes.

13 'I glimpsed you once before on the longships,
where you fought in the bloody bow of the ship
and cold and wet the waves were playing.
Now the prince wants to conceal himself from me
but Hogni's girl recognizes Helgi.'

Granmar was the name of a powerful king who lived at Svarinshaug. He had many sons: Hodbrodd, secondly Gudmund, the third Starkad. Hodbrodd was at a meeting of kings; he betrothed himself to Sigrun, Hogni's daughter. But when she heard that, she rode with her valkyries through air and sea to find Helgi.

*Helgi was at Logafell and had fought with the sons of Hunding. There he brought down Alf and Eyiolf, Hiorvard and Hervard; he was exhausted from battle and he was resting below Arastein. There Sigrun found him and flung her arms around his neck and kissed him and told him what her errand was, as it says in the 'Old Poem of the Volsungs':**

14 Sigrun went to see the cheerful prince,
she caught Helgi by the hand;
she kissed and greeted the king in his helmet,
then the king began to love the woman.

15 She said she'd already loved with all her heart
the son of Sigmund before she'd seen him.

16 'I have been betrothed to Hodbrodd among the fighters,
but another prince I wish to have;
though, lord, I fear the anger of kinsmen,
I have broken my father's lovingly given word.'

17 Hogni's girl did not dissemble,
she said she wanted Helgi's love.

18 'Don't worry about Hogni's anger,
nor the wrath of your kinsmen.
Young girl, you will live with me;
I've no fear, good lady, of your family.'

Helgi assembled a great fleet and went to Frekastein, and on the ocean they ran into a terribly dangerous storm. Lightning flashed above them and the ships were struck. They saw nine valkyries riding up in the air, and recognized Sigrun among them. Then the storm abated and they got safely to land. The sons of Granmar were sitting up on a cliff, when the ships sailed into land. Gudmund leapt on his horse and rode down to a cliff near the harbour to reconnoitre. The Volsungs lowered their sails. Then Gudmund Granmarsson said, as is written above in the 'Poem of Helgi':

Who is that ruler who leads the troop,
who's brought the dangerous men to the shore?

19 'Who is the prince who steers the ships,
and has the golden war banners at his prow?
Peace, it seems to me, is not at the forefront of your vessels;
a red battle-glow hangs over the vikings.'

Sinfiotli said:

20 'Here Hodbrodd may recognize Helgi,
the fighter who does not flee, in the midst of the fleet;
the homeland of your kin,
the inheritance of the Fiorsungs, he has conquered.'

[*Gudmund said:*]

21 'Thus we should at Frekastein
meet together, settle the matter;
Hodbrodd, it's a case for taking revenge,
where we have long had to take the lower part.'

[*Sinfiotli said:*]

22 'Rather, Gudmund, you'll be herding goats
and clambering down the rocky clefts,
in your hand you'll have a hazel switch;
you prefer that to the judgement of swords.'

[*Helgi said:*]

23 'For you, Sinfiotli, it would be more fitting
to draw up for battle and make the eagles glad,
than to be bandying useless words,
even if these chieftains are bitter enemies.

24 'I don't expect good from Granmar's sons,
though the princes, truth to tell, have had some success;
they have proved at Moinsheim
that they have the temperament for wielding swords;
the chieftains are far too bold.'

Sinfiotli, Sigmund's son, answered, as is also written. Gudmund rode home with the news of invasion. Then Granmar's sons assembled an army. Many kings came to join them. There was Hogni, Sigrun's father, and his sons, Bragi and Dag. There was a great battle and all of Granmar's sons were killed and all of the chieftains except for Dag, Hogni's son, who obtained a truce and swore oaths to the Volsungs. Sigrun went among the slaughtered and found Hodbrodd on the point of death. She said:

25 'Sigrun from Sefafell
will not sink into your arms, King Hodbrodd;
ebbing is the life—often the grey stud-horse of the troll-woman*
gets the corpses—of Granmar's sons.'

Then she met Helgi and was extremely joyful. He said:

26 'It was not all good fortune for you, foreign woman,
though I think the norns had some part in it;*
this morning at Frekastein
Bragi and Hogni were killed, I was their slayer.

27 'And at Styr-cleft King Starkad,
and at Hlebiorg the sons of Hrollaug;
I saw that fiercest-minded of kings
defending his trunk—his head was gone.

28 'All the rest of your kinsmen
were lying on the ground, corpses they'd become;
you could not stop the battle, it was fated for you
that you'd be cause of strife among powerful men.'

Then Sigrun wept. He said:

29 'Be comforted Sigrun! You've been our battle-goddess;
the princes could not struggle against fate.'
'I'd choose now that those who are gone might live again
and that I could still hold you in my arms.'

Helgi married Sigrun and they had sons. Helgi did not live to old age. Dag, Hogni's son, sacrificed to Odin for revenge for his father. Odin lent Dag his spear. Dag encountered Helgi, his brother-in-law, at a place called Fetter-grove. He pierced Helgi with the spear and Helgi fell there. And Dag rode to the mountains and told this news to Sigrun:

30 'Sister, I am reluctant to tell you of grief,
for I have been forced to make my sister weep:
there fell this morning below Fetter-grove
the lord who was the best in the world
and who stood on the necks of chieftains.'

31 'May all the oaths which you swore
to Helgi rebound upon you,
by the bright water of Leift
and the cool and watery stone of Unn.

32 'May the ship you sail on not go forward,*
though the wind you need has sprung up behind;
may the horse you ride on not go forward,
though your enemies are about to catch you.

33 'May the sword that you wield never bite for you,
unless it's whistling above your own head.
The death of Helgi would be avenged on you,
if you were a wolf out in the forest
with nothing of your own and deprived of happiness,
if you had no food except when you glutted yourself on corpses.'

Dag said:

34 'Sister, you are mad, you are out of your wits,
that you should wish this evil on your brother;
Odin alone caused all the misfortune,
for he cast hostile runes between the kinsmen.

35 'Your brother offers you red-gold rings,
all Vandilsve and Vigdal;
take half of our homeland to pay for your loss,
ring-adorned woman and your sons.'

36 'I shall not sit so happily at Sefafell,
neither early nor at night-time will I desire to live,
unless light should shine on the company of the prince,
unless Vigblær were to gallop here under the prince,
tamed to his gold bridle, and I could welcome the warrior.

37 'Helgi so terrified
all his enemies and their kin,
just as panicking goats run before the wolf
down from the mountain filled with fear.

38 'So was Helgi beside the chieftains
like the bright-growing ash beside the thorn-bush
and the young stag, drenched in dew,
who surpasses all other animals
and whose horns glow against the sky itself.'

A burial-mound was made for Helgi. And when he came to Valhall Odin asked him to rule over everything with him. Helgi said:

39 'Hunding, you shall fetch the foot-bath*
for every man and kindle the fire,
tie up the dogs, watch the horses,
feed the pigs before you go to sleep.'

One evening Sigrun's maid went past Helgi's mound and saw Helgi riding into the mound with a large number of men. The maid said:

40 'Is this some kind of delusion, that I think I can see
dead men riding, or is it Ragnarok?
Are you spurring your horses onward,
or have the fighters been allowed to come home?'

Helgi said:

41 'It is not a delusion that you think you see,
nor the end of mankind, though you gaze upon us,
though we spur our horses onwards,
nor are the fighters allowed to come home.'

The maid went home and told Sigrun:

42 'Go outside, Sigrun, out from Sefafell,
if you want to meet the leader of the army;
the mound has opened up, Helgi has come;
his wounds are bleeding, the prince asks you
to staunch his injuries.'

Sigrun went into the mound to Helgi and said:

43 'Now I am so glad, at our meeting,
as are the greedy hawks of Odin*
when they know of slaughter, steaming food,
or, dew-drenched, they see the dawn.

44 'First I want to kiss the lifeless king,
before you throw off your bloody mail-coat;
your hair, Helgi, is thick with hoar-frost,
the prince is all soaked in slaughter-dew,*
Hogni's son-in-law has clammy hands.
How, lord, can I find a remedy for this?'

45 'You alone, Sigrun, from Sefafell,
cause Helgi to be soaked in sorrow-dew;
you weep, gold-adorned lady, bitter tears,
sun-bright southern girl, before you go to sleep;
each falls bloody on the breast of the prince,
cold as dew, burning hot, thick with grief.

46 'We ought to drink this precious liquid,*
though we have lost our love and our lands;
no man should sing a lament for me,
though on my breast wounds can be seen;
now the lady is enclosed in the mound,
a human woman with us, the departed.'

Sigrun made up a bed in the mound.

47 'Here I've made you, Helgi, a bed all ready;
descendant of the Ylfings, now free from care
in your arms, lord, I'll sleep,
as I would with the prince, when he was living.'

48 'I say that nothing could be less expected,
neither early nor late at Sefafell,
that you should sleep in the arms of a dead man,
white lady, in the tomb, Hogni's daughter,
and you alive, and royally born.

49 'It is time for me to ride along the blood-red roads,
to set the pale horse to tread the path in the sky;
I must cross the bridge in the sky-vault,
before Salgofnir awakens the victorious people.'*

Helgi and his men rode away, and the women went back to the house. The next evening Sigrun had the maid keep watch by the mound. And at dusk, when Sigrun came to the mound, she said:

50 'He would have come by now, if he meant to come,
the son of Sigmund, from Odin's halls;
hopes of seeing the prince come here are fading,
now the eagles roost on the ash-branches
and all the household head for the dream-assembly.'*

51 'Do not be so mad as to go alone,
high-born lady, into the home of ghosts;
they are all much more powerful at night, lady,
the dead creatures, than when day dawns.'

Sigrun did not live long from sorrow and grief. There was a belief in the pagan religion, which we now reckon an old wives' tale, that people could be reincarnated. Helgi and Sigrun were thought to have been reborn. He was Helgi Haddingia-damager, and she was Kara, Halfdan's daughter, as is told in the 'Song of Kara', and she was a valkyrie.*

The Death of Sinfiotli

Sigmund, son of Volsung, was king in France. Sinfiotli was his eldest son, the second was Helgi, the third Hamund. Borghild, Sigmund's wife, had a brother called [?]. And Sinfiotli, her stepson, and [?] were both wooing the same woman, and for that reason Sinfiotli killed him. And when he came home, then Borghild told him to go away, but Sigmund offered her compensation, and she had to accept that. But at the funeral feast Borghild was carrying the ale around. She took poison, put it in a great, full horn, and gave it to Sinfiotli. But when he looked in the horn, he realized that there was poison in it and he said to Sigmund, 'This drink is cloudy, father.' Sigmund took the horn and drank it all. It is said that Sigmund had such a mighty constitution that no poison could harm him, neither outside nor inside; and all his sons could withstand poison on their skin. Borghild gave another horn to Sinfiotli, and it all happened as before. And the third time she brought him a horn and taunted him with not drinking it. He spoke to Sigmund as before. He said, 'Let your moustache strain it, son!' Sinfiotli drank it and died immediately. Sigmund carried him in his arms for a long time, and came to a long, narrow fjord, and there was a little ship and a man in it. He offered to take Sigmund over the fjord. But when Sigmund put the corpse in the ship, it was fully loaded. The man said that Sigmund would have to walk round the fjord and he pushed out the boat and disappeared.**

Sigmund lived in Denmark, Borghild's kingdom, for a long time after he married her. Then he went south to France, to the lands he had there. He married Hiordis, daughter of King Eylimi. Sigurd was their son. Sigmund was killed in battle by the sons of Hunding and then Hiordis married Alf, son of King Hialprek. Sigurd lived with them in his childhood.

Sigmund and all his sons surpassed all men in strength and size and courage and all accomplishments. Sigurd, however, was the most remarkable of all, and in the old tradition everyone says he was the greatest of all men and the most redoubtable war-leader.

Gripir's Prophecy

Gripir's Prophecy (*Gripisspa*) is clearly a late poem, dependent upon the other poems which follow it in the Sigurd cycle, and possibly upon an early version of *Volsunga saga*. Its function is to summarize the story of Sigurd, foretelling everything which will happen to him. It introduces the characters which follow, but adds little, artistically or thematically, to the later poems of the cycle. *Volsunga saga*, ch. 16, mentions the meeting between uncle and nephew but, wisely, does not recount the contents of the prophecy.

Gripir was the son of Eylimi, the brother of Hiordis; he ruled over nations and was the wisest of all men, and was prophetic. Sigurd was riding by himself and came to the hall of Gripir. Sigurd was easy to recognize. He met a man outside the hall and spoke to him. He was called Geitir. Then Sigurd greeted him and asked:

1 'Who lives here in these dwellings?
What do warriors call that mighty king?'
'Gripir he is called, that leader of men,
he who resolutely rules the land and the warriors.'

2 'Is that wise king at home in this land?
Will the prince come to speak with me?
An unknown man needs to speak to him,
I should like quickly to meet Gripir.'

3 'The gracious king will ask Geitir
who that man might be who would speak with Gripir.'
'Sigurd I am called, son of Sigmund,
and Hiordis is the prince's mother.'

4 Then Geitir went to say to Gripir:
'Here is a man outside, come from I know not where;
he is striking to look at;
he would like, lord, to meet you.'

5 The lord of men went out of the hall
and greeted him warmly, the prince who had come:
'Welcome here, Sigurd, you should have come before now!
And you, Geitir, look after Grani!'*

6 They began to speak and they discussed many things,
there where they met, the sagacious men.
'Tell me if you know, uncle,
how Sigurd's life will turn out.'

7 'You will be the most glorious man under the sun
and the highest born of all princes,
well endowed with gold, and slow to retreat,
striking to look at and wise in your words.'

8 'Say, honest king, wise man, plainly
as I ask, tell Sigurd if you think you can foretell:
what will first happen as part of my fate
when I have gone out of your courtyard?'

9 'First, prince, you will avenge your father,
and repay for all the sorrow of Eylimi;*
bravely you will bring down the bold sons of Hunding;
you'll have the victory.'

10 'Tell me, shining king, kinsman so wise,
as we speak our thoughts: do you see mighty deeds
ahead of Sigurd, those which under
the vault of heaven would be highest?'

11 'You alone will kill the shining serpent,
the greedy one who lies on Gnita-heath;
you will be the killer of both Regin and Fafnir;
Gripir says what is right.'

12 'There'll be wealth enough if I manage that
killing among men, as you surely say;
ponder my course and speak at more length;
what more will my life be?'

13 'You will find Fafnir's lair
and gather up the beautiful treasure,
load the gold on Grani's back;
ride to Giuki's, the prince prominent in war.'*

14 'Still you must, prophetic prince,
tell your thoughts to the warrior, say more;
I am Giuki's guest, and I go away from there;
what more will my life be?'

15 'The prince's daughter, bright in her mail-shirt,
sleeps on the mountain after the killing of Helgi;*
you must strike with your sharp sword,
cut the mail-shirt with the slayer of Fafnir.'

16 'The mail-shirt is cut open, the lady begins to speak,
the woman awakened from sleep;
what will the lady wish to say to Sigurd,
which will bring good luck to the prince?'

17 'She will teach you powerful runes,
all those which men wish to know,
and how to speak every single human tongue,
medicine with healing knowledge; may you live blessed,
king!'

18 'Now that is over, the wisdom is learned,
and I am ready to ride from there;
ponder my course and speak at more length;
what more will be in my life?'

19 'You will come to the dwellings of Heimir
and be a cheerful guest of the king;
that has passed, Sigurd, that which I knew already;
you should not question Gripir any further!'

20 'Now grief seizes me with the words which you say,
for you see further ahead, prince;
you know of great misery for Sigurd;
and you, Gripir, won't tell me of it.'

21 'Your youth lay before me
most clearly to look at;
it is not true that I am reckoned to be wise
or at all prophetic, I've told you what I know!'

22 'I know of no man on earth
who could be more prophetic than you, Gripir;
you must not hide it, though it be unpleasant,
or if harm is afoot in my circumstances.'

23 'There is no shame laid down for your life;
accept that from me, shining prince,
for as long as men survive, warrior who offers battle,
your name will be uppermost.'

24 'This is the worst I can imagine, Sigurd parting
from the prince with things as they are;
show me all the road which is laid down from me,
if you will, my illustrious uncle.'

25 'Now shall I speak clearly to Sigurd,
the prince has forced me to this point;
it's quite certain that there is no lie,
on one day death is intended for you.'

26 'I do not want the wrath of the powerful king,
his good advice, Gripir, I'd rather accept;
now I will know clearly, though it be undesirable,
what there is to be seen ahead for Sigurd.'

27 'A lady there is at Heimir's, pleasing to look at,
Brynhild she is called by the warriors,*
the daughter of Budli, and the fierce king,
the stern-minded Heimir has brought her up.'

28 'What is it to me, if the girl should be
pleasing to look at, brought up at Heimir's?
That you must, Gripir, say quite clearly,
since you foresee all this fate ahead.'

29 'She'll rob you of most of your happiness,
pleasing to look at, the foster-child of Heimir;
no sleep will you have, nor will you care for lawsuits,
you'll take no notice of anyone unless you can see the girl.'

30 'What comfort in this is laid down for Sigurd?
Tell me that, Gripir, if you think you see it;
shall I get the girl, obtain her with a dowry,
that beautiful daughter of the prince?'

31 'You two will swear all your oaths
very strongly; few will you keep;
when you've been for one night the guest of Giuki
you won't recall the wise fosterling of Heimir.'

32 'What is this, Gripir, that you are putting to me!
Do you see faithlessness in this prince's temperament,
if I shall tear asunder the oaths to that girl
whom I thought I loved with all my heart?'

33 'Prince, victim of another's treachery you'll be,
Grimhild's counsels will prevail;
she'll offer you the bright-haired girl,
her daughter, she'll play a trick on the prince.'

34 'Shall I then become kin to Gunnar
and enter wedlock with Gudrun?
Well married this prince'd be then,
if hateful grief didn't seize me.'

35 'Grimhild will thoroughly deceive you,
she'll urge you to woo Brynhild for Gunnar,
the king of the Goths; speedily you'll promise
to journey for the ruler's mother.'

36 'Harm lies ahead, I can see that,
Sigurd's plans will clearly go astray,
if I shall woo the splendid woman
for another, the woman I love well.'

37 'All of you will swear oaths,
Gunnar and Hogni, and you, prince, the third;
for you'll exchange appearances on the road,
Gunnar and you; Gripir does not lie!'

38 'What's the point of that? Why should we exchange
appearance and behaviour when we're on the road?
Some further deception goes with this,
something completely terrible; but tell me, Gripir!'

39 'Gunnar's complexion you'll have and his bearing,
your own eloquence and powerful intellect;
you'll betroth to yourself the high-minded woman,
fosterling of Heimir; nothing will prevent this.'

40 'This is the worst that I can imagine, I, Sigurd, will be reviled
by men for this; I should not wish
to entrap with cunning the noble bride
whom I know to be the best.'

41 'You'll sleep, lord of the spear-point,
splendid man, with the girl, as if she were your mother;
and so, prince of the people, as long as men survive,
your name will be uppermost.

43 'Together will both weddings be celebrated,*
Sigurd's and Gunnar's in the halls of Giuki;
for you'll change back your shapes when you come home,
each of you will have his own spirit back.'

42 'Gunnar will wed the good woman,
famous among men, so you tell me, Gripir,
though for three nights the warrior's resolute bride
has slept with me? That would be unexampled!

44 'How afterwards can our kinship prosper
between men? Tell me Gripir;
is it Gunnar who later will have pleasure in this
or will it be me myself?'

45 'Though you recall your oaths you'll keep silent,
you love Gudrun and want good for her;
and Brynhild the bride will think herself disparaged,
the lady will find means to get her revenge.'

46 'What compensation will that bride accept,
when we've woven for her such deceit?
From me the lady had oaths I'd sworn,
none fulfilled, and little pleasure.'

47 'To Gunnar she'll say very clearly
that you did not truly keep your oaths,
those in which the shining king, heir of Giuki,
trusted you, prince, with all his heart.'

48 'What is this, Gripir? What are you telling me!
Will these stories be proved true of me?
or will that woman, worthy of praise,
lie about herself and me? Gripir, tell me that!'

49 'In her anger and her great grief
the powerful lady will not act so well towards you;
never will you harm the good lady,
though the king's wife plots treachery against you.'

50 'Will Gunnar the wise follow her urging
—and Guthorm and Hogni—after this?
Shall the sons of Giuki, despite our kinship,
redden their blades in my blood? Gripir, tell me more!'

51 'Gudrun will become grim in her heart
when her brothers bring about your death,
and no joy will afterwards come
to the wise lady; Grimhild's the cause of this.

52 'Console yourself with this, lord of the spear-point,
this luck is laid down in the prince's life:
no mightier man will walk on the earth,
under the dwelling of the sun, than you, Sigurd, are
thought to be.'

53 'Let's part and say farewell, one can't overcome fate;
now, Gripir, you have done as I asked you to do;
gladly you'd have told me of a life
more pleasant, if you'd been able!'

The Lay of Regin

The *Lay of Regin* (*Reginsmal*) consists of a number of different sequences of verses, most of which have little to do with Regin himself. The poet introduces the theme of the cursed gold, the ransom for Otter which forms Fafnir's hoard, and sketches the future strife it will cause; he sets up the prickly relationship between Regin and Sigurd, and introduces Odin as patron of the Volsung clan. Like other poems pertaining to the youth of Sigurd, part of the poem consists of wisdom, signalled by a change in metre from *fornyrdislag* to *ljodahattr*. Loki asks Andvari for mythological information and Sigurd questions Hnikar (Odin) about battle-omens. By the end of the poem the narrative groundwork has been done and Sigurd is ready to face the dragon—his greatest adventure.

Sigurd went to Hialprek's stud and chose himself a horse who was afterwards called Grani. Then Regin came to Hialprek's; he was the son of Hreidmar; he was a very skilful man in making things and a dwarf in height; he was wise, ferocious, and knowledgeable about magic. Regin offered to foster Sigurd and to teach him, and he loved him a great deal. He told Sigurd about his parents and these events: Odin, Hænir, and Loki had come to Andvara-falls; in those falls there were a great many fish. There was a dwarf called Andvari; he had spent a long time in the falls in the form of a pike and got himself food in that way. 'Otter is the name of our brother,' said Regin, and he used often to go in the falls in the form of an otter. He had caught a salmon and was sitting on the river bank, eating it with his eyes shut. Loki struck him with a stone and killed him. The Æsir thought this was great good fortune and flayed off the otter's skin for a bag. The same evening they stayed the night with Hreidmar and showed what they had caught. Then we seized them and made them ransom their lives by filling the otterskin bag with gold and also by covering the outside with red gold. Then they sent Loki to collect the gold. He went to Ran, and borrowed her net and then went to Andvara-falls and spread the net ahead of the pike; and he jumped into it. Then Loki said:*

1 '"What is that fish which courses through the water,
which doesn't know how to avoid danger?
Your head you can save from hell;
find the serpent's flame for me!"*

2 '"Andvari is my name, Oin is my father's name,
I have spent much time in the falls;
a norn of misfortune shaped my fate in the early days,*
so that I have to spend my time in the water."

3 '"Tell me, Andvari," said Loki, "if you want to retain
your life in the halls of men:
what requital do they get, the sons of men,
if they wound each other with words?"*

4 '"A terrible requital the sons of men get,
they have to wade in Vadgelmir;*
for untrue words, when one man lies about another,
for a long time he'll suffer the consequences."

'Loki saw all the gold which Andvari possessed, and when he had handed over the gold, he had one ring left, and Loki took that from him. The dwarf went into a rock and said:*

5 '"That gold, which Gust owned,
will be the death of two brothers,
and cause of strife between eight princes;*
my treasure will be no use to anyone."

'The Æsir gave Hreidmar the money and spread out the otterskin and stretched its legs. Then the Æsir had to heap up the gold to cover it. And when that was done, Hreidmar went forwards and saw a single hair, and said it must be covered. Then Odin produced the ring, Andvari's Jewel, and covered the hair.

6 '"The gold now is given to you" (said Loki), "and you
have
a great payment for my head;
for your son no good fortune is ordained;
it will be the death of both of you!"

'Hreidmar said:

7 "Gifts you gave, you did not give them as love-gifts,
you did not give them wholeheartedly;
your lives I would have taken from you
if I had known of this deceit before."

8 '"It is worse still—or so I think—
the strife of doomed kinsmen,
the princes are not yet born for whom I believe*
this hatefulness is intended."

9 '"Red gold", said Hreidmar, "I think I'll have at my disposal
as long as I may live;
I don't fear your threat in the slightest, now go home,
go away from here!"

'Fafnir and Regin demanded a share of the compensation from Hreidmar for their brother Otter. He refused. And Fafnir stabbed his father with a sword while he was asleep. Hreidmar called to his daughters:

10 '"Lyngheid and Lofnheid!
know that my life is snatched from me,
need makes men do many things!"
Lyngheid answered:
"Few sisters will, even if missing a father,
avenge their wrongs on a brother!"

11 '"Yet you should nurture a daughter" (said Hreidmar), "you wolf-hearted girl,
if you don't get a son with a king;
give the girl to a man, when in great need,
then their son will avenge your wrongs!"*

'Then Hreidmar died, and Fafnir took all the gold. Then Regin asked for his inheritance from his father, and Fafnir refused. Then Regin asked Lyngheid, his sister, for advice, how he should recover his inheritance. She said:

12 '"You should ask your brother cheerfully
for your inheritance, with a friendly demeanour;
it is not fitting that you should demand the treasure
from Fafnir with a sword!"'

Regin told Sigurd these things. One day when he came to Regin's house, he was warmly greeted. Regin said:

13 'The offspring of Sigmund has come here,
the man full of mighty plans, to our halls;
he has more courage than an older man,
I have expectation of winnings from a ravening wolf.

14 'I must nurture the battle-brave prince;
now the offspring of Yngvi has come to us;
he will be the most powerful prince under the sun,
the web of his fate spreads through every land.'

Sigurd stayed with Regin after that, and he told Sigurd that Fafnir was lying on Gnita-heath in the shape of a dragon; he had a helmet of dread, which all living creatures were terrified of.*

Regin made Sigurd a sword which was called Gram. It was so sharp that he put it in the river Rhine and let a hank of wool drift on the current, and the hank was sliced apart as if it were water. With this sword, Sigurd sliced through Regin's anvil.

After that Regin egged Sigurd on to kill Fafnir. He replied:

15 'Loudly would the sons of Hunding laugh,
they who snatched the life of Eylimi,
if the prince had a greater lust
to gain red gold than to avenge his father.'

King Hialprek gave Sigurd ships and a crew to avenge his father. They ran into a great storm and were weathering a certain rocky headland. There was a man standing on the cliff who said:

16 'Who are they, riding the sea-king's horses
on the high waves, on the resounding sea?
The sail-steeds are spattered with spray,
the ocean-chargers cannot stand up to the wind.'

Regin answered:

17 'It is Sigurd and myself in the wooden ship;
we've been given a wind which is going to be our death;
the steep breaker is falling higher than stern and prow,
the roller-steeds are plunging; who is asking about it?'

18 'Hnikar they called me, when young Volsung*
gladdened the raven when there was fighting;
now you may call the old man on the cliff
Feng or Fiolnir; I would like passage!'

They turned towards the land, and the old man went aboard the ship, and the tempest abated.

19 'Tell me, Hnikar, all you know about two matters:
omens of gods and men,
which omens are best, if one has to fight
when swords are swinging?'

Hnikar said:

20 'There are many good omens if men knew them,
while swords are swinging;
a trusty omen for the warrior, I believe,
is the company of the dark raven.

21 'That is a second omen, if you have gone outside
and are ready to set off;
if you see standing on the pathway
two men eager for glory.

22 'That is a third omen, if you hear a wolf
howling under ash-branches,
good luck will be ordained for you against the warriors
if you catch sight of them first.

23 'No man should fight facing into the late-
shining sister of the moon;*
those who know how to look properly
get the victory, those who urge sword-play
and know how to draw up an army or a wedge-shaped
column.*

24 'That is great misfortune, if you stumble
when you risk yourself in battle;
guileful *disir* stand on both sides of you*
and want to see you injured.

25 'Combed and washed every thoughtful man should be
and fed in the morning;
for one cannot foresee where one will be by evening;
it is bad to rush headlong before one's fate.'

Sigurd fought a great battle against Lyngvi, son of Hunding, and his brothers. Then Lyngvi and his three brothers were killed. After the battle Regin said:

26 'Now the bloody eagle is carved on the back*
of the slayer of Sigmund with a sharp sword!
None is more successful than the heir of the king,
who reddened the earth and gave joy to the raven!'

Sigurd went home to Hialprek. Then Regin egged Sigurd to kill Fafnir.

The Lay of Fafnir

Perhaps unexpectedly, the *Lay of Fafnir* (*Fafnismal*) does not give the details of an exciting dragon-fight like the one at the end of the Old English poem *Beowulf*. Rather, Sigurd stabs Fafnir from below while hiding in a pit and the rest of the poem is taken up with conversation between Sigurd and the dragon he has fatally wounded, a tetchy interchange between Sigurd and Regin, and the advice of the nuthatches, whose conversation Sigurd comes to understand through the accidental tasting of Fafnir's blood. Sigurd and Fafnir's dialogue alternates between hostility and mutual respect; when Regin returns, the seeds of mistrust which Fafnir has sown in Sigurd's mind, and the arrogant way in which the foster-father orders Sigurd about as if he were an apprentice rather than a fully-fledged hero, combine to create resentment in the young man. The motif of wisdom accidentally acquired from licking the thumb when cooking appears also in Irish, in the tales of the hero Finn mac Cool, who gains knowledge when cooking the Salmon of Wisdom for his master. Birds often give prophetic and insightful advice in the *Edda*. In the *Poem of Helgi Hiorvardsson* Atli makes a compact with a bird, and in the *List of Rig* young Kon is directed towards conquest by a wise bird. The nuthatches point Sigurd both towards a match with Gudrun, daughter of Giuki, and to the rescue of the valkyrie Sigrdrifa.

Sigurd and Regin went up onto Gnita-heath and there they found Fafnir's tracks, where he crawled down to the water. Then Sigurd dug a great pit in the path, and he got into it. And when Fafnir crawled away from the gold, he snorted out poison and it fell down onto Sigurd's head. And when Fafnir crawled over the pit, Sigurd stabbed him to the heart with his sword. Fafnir shook himself and flailed with his head and tail. Sigurd jumped out of the pit and both looked at one another. Fafnir said:

1 'A boy! just a boy! Of whom were you born, boy?
Whose son are you
that you should redden your shining sword on Fafnir?
The blade stands in my heart.'

Sigurd concealed his name, because it was an old superstition to believe that the words of a dying man had great power if he cursed his enemy by name. He said:

2 '"Pre-eminent beast" I'm called, and I go about*
as a motherless boy;
I have no father, as the sons of men do,
I always go alone.'

Fafnir said:

3 'Do you know, if you had no father, as the sons of men do,
of what wonder you were born?'

Sigurd said:

4 'My lineage, I think, will be unknown to you,
as am I myself;
Sigurd I am called—Sigmund was my father—
I who've killed you with my weapons.'

Fafnir said:

5 'Who egged you on, why were you urged
to attack my life?
Shining-eyed boy, you had a fierce father,
[innate qualities show quickly].'*

Sigurd said:

6 'My courage whetted me, my hands assisted me
and my sharp sword;
few are brave when they become old,
if they are cowardly in childhood.'

Fafnir said:

7 'I know, if you did succeed in growing up in the bosom of your friends,
you would be seen to fight furiously;
but now you are a captive, a prisoner of war;
they say the bound man is always trembling!'

Sigurd said:

8 'You taunt me now, Fafnir, because I'm far away
from my father's inheritance;
but I'm no captive, though I was taken prisoner;
you've found that I'm a free agent!'

Fafnir said:

9 'Spiteful words you think you hear in everything,
but I'll tell you one thing true:
the resounding gold and the glowing red treasure,
those rings will be your death!'

Sigurd said:

10 'Power over his property every man shall have
always until his last day comes,
for on one day only shall every man
depart from here to hell.'

Fafnir said:

11 'The judgement of the norns you'll get in sight of
land,*
and the fate of a fool;
you'll drown in the water even if you row in a breeze;
all fate is dangerous for the doomed man.'

Sigurd said:

12 'Tell me, Fafnir, you are said to be wise*
and to know a great deal;
which are those norns who go to those in need
and choose mothers over children in childbirth?'*

Fafnir said:

13 'From very different tribes I think the norns come,
they are not of the same kin;
some are of the Æsir, some are of the elves,
some are daughters of Dvalin.'*

Sigurd said:

14 'Tell me, Fafnir, you are said to be wise
and to know a great deal,
what that island is called where Surt and the Æsir together
will mingle sword-liquid together.'*

Fafnir said:

15 'Mismade it's called, and there all the gods
shall sport with their spears;
Bilrost will break as they journey away,
and their horses will flounder in the great river.

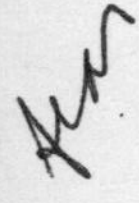

16 'The helm of terror I wore among the sons of men,*
while I lay upon the necklaces;
more powerful than all I thought myself to be,
I didn't encounter many foes.'

Sigurd said:

17 'The helm of terror protects no one,
where angry men have to fight;
a man finds that out when he comes among the multitude;
that no one is bravest of all.'

Fafnir said:

18 'Poison I snorted, when I lay upon
the mighty inheritance of my father.'

Sigurd said:

19 'Mighty dragon, you snorted great blasts
and you hardened your heart;
men are the more ferocious
when they have that helmet.'

Fafnir said:

20 'Now I advise you, Sigurd, and you take that advice
and ride home from here!
The resounding gold and the glowing red treasure—
those rings will be your death!'

Sigurd said:

21 'You've given your advice, but I shall ride
to where the gold lies in the heather,
and you, Fafnir, lie in mortal fragments,
there where Hel can take you!'

Fafnir said:

22 'Regin betrayed me, he'll betray you,
he'll be the death of us both;
I think Fafnir must give up his life;
you had the greater strength.'

Regin had disappeared while Sigurd was killing Fafnir and came back as Sigurd was wiping the blood off his sword. Regin said:

23 'Hail to you, Sigurd, now you've won the victory
and have brought down Fafnir;
of those men who tread upon the earth
I say you've been raised the least cowardly.'

Sigurd said:

24 'There's no knowing for certain when all are come together,
all the sons of the glorious gods,
who has been brought up the least cowardly;
many a man is bold when he does not redden his sword
in another's breast.'

Regin said:

25 'You're cheerful now, Sigurd, and pleased with your winnings,
as you dry Gram on the grass;
my brother you've wounded,
yet in part I myself brought it about.'

Sigurd said:

26 'You arranged that I had to ride here
over the sacred mountains;
his treasure and his life the shining dragon would still possess,
if you hadn't challenged my courage.'

Then Regin went to Fafnir and cut out his heart with a sword called Ridil, and then he drank the blood from his wound. Regin said:

27 'Sit down now, Sigurd, and I'll go to sleep,
roast Fafnir's heart in the flame;
that heart I'll have to eat after the drink of blood.'

Sigurd said:

28 'You went far off while in Fafnir I was reddening
my sharp sword;
my strength I needed against the dragon's might,
while you lurked in the heather.'

Regin said:

29 'Long you'd have left the old giant*
lurking in the heather
if you'd not used the sword which I myself made
and that sharp blade of yours.'

Sigurd said:

30 'Courage is better than the power of a sword,
where angry men have to fight;
for I've seen a brave man fighting strongly
conquer with a blunt sword.

31 'Bravery is better than cowardice
to have in battle-sport;
cheerfulness is better than snivelling,
whatever may be at hand.'

Sigurd took Fafnir's heart and roasted it on a spit. And when he thought that it was done, and the juice was dripping out of the heart, he prodded it with his finger to see if it was done. He burnt himself and stuck his finger in his mouth. And when the heart-blood of Fafnir came on his tongue, he understood the speech of birds. He heard that there were nuthatches twittering in the branches. The nuthatch said:

32 'There sits Sigurd, splattered with blood,
roasting Fafnir's heart on a spit;
the destroyer of rings would seem wise to me*
if he were to eat the shining life-muscle.'

A second nuthatch said:

33 'There lies Regin plotting to himself,
he wants to betray the boy, the one who trusts him,
in anger sharp words he's uttered,
that smith of evil wants to avenge his brother.'

A third one said:

34 'Shorter by a head he should send the old sage
off to hell from here!
Then all the gold he alone would possess,
that heap which lay under Fafnir.'

A fourth one said:

35 'Wise he'd seem to me if he knew how to get
the friendly advice of you sisters;
if he thought about himself and made the raven happy;
I expect a wolf to be around when I see his ears.'*

A fifth one said:

36 'The warrior isn't so wise
as I thought a war-leader ought to be,
if he lets one brother get away,
when he's snatched the life of the other.'

A sixth one said:

37 'He'll be extremely foolish if he still spares
the murderous enemy,
there Regin is lying and plotting against him;
he doesn't know how to guard against such a thing.'

A seventh said:

38 'Shorter by a head he should leave the frost-cold giant*
and make him lose the rings;
then the treasure which Fafnir owned
would be in one man's control.'

Sigurd said:

39 'Fate doesn't make Regin so powerful that he's going
to bear a fatal point against me,
since those two brothers are going, very quickly,
to set off for hell from here.'

Sigurd cut off Regin's head and then he ate Fafnir's heart and drank the blood of both Regin and Fafnir. Then Sigurd heard the nuthatches saying:

40 'Gather up, Sigurd, the red rings;
it would not be kingly to be afraid of anything!
I know a girl, the fairest by far,
endowed with gold, yet you could win her.

41 'Green ways lie straight towards Giuki,
fate points forward for a wide-travelling man.
There the lavish king has raised up a daughter.
There, Sigurd, you may obtain a wedding settlement.

42 'There is a hall on high Hindarfell,
outside it is all surrounded with flame;
wise men have made it
out of radiant river-light.

43 'I know on the mountain the valkyrie sleeps,
and the terror of the linden plays about her;*
Odin stabbed her with a thorn;*
the goddess of flax had brought down*
a different fighter from the one he wanted.

44 'Young man, you shall see the girl under the helmet,
who rode away from battle on Vingskornir.
Sigrdrifa's sleep may not be broken
by a princely youth, except by the norns' decree.'

Sigurd rode along Fafnir's track to his lair and found it open and with doors and door-frames of iron. All the beams of the house were of iron, and they were driven down into the earth. There Sigurd found a huge amount of gold and filled two chests with it.

Then he took the helmet of terror and a gold mail-shirt and the sword Hrotti and many other treasures, and loaded Grani with it, but the horse would not proceed until Sigurd climbed onto his back.

The Lay of Sigrdrifa

As directed by the birds at the end of the previous poem, in the *Lay of Sigrdrifa* (*Sigrdrifumal*) Sigurd sets out towards the sleeping valkyrie. Releasing her from her spell, he asks her for advice and Sigrdrifa obliges with runic and gnomic wisdom. Pages are missing from the Codex Regius manuscript towards the end of the poem, so it remains incomplete. The events which occur in the missing pages are summarized at that point.

Sigurd rode up onto Hindarfell and headed south towards the land of the Franks. On the mountain he saw a great light, as if fire were burning, and gleaming up against the sky. And when he came there, there stood a shield-wall with a banner flying over it. Sigurd went into the shield-wall and saw someone lying there asleep and fully armed. First he took off the helmet, then he saw that it was a woman. Her corslet was tight, as if it had grown into her flesh. So with his sword Gram he cut from the neck of the corslet downwards, and so along both the arms. Then he took the corslet off her, and she woke up, sat up, looked at Sigurd, and said:

1 'What bit into my corslet? Why was my sleep disturbed?
Who has taken from me my pallid coercion?'
He answered:
'Sigmund's son—the sword of Sigurd,
which a short time ago was cutting the raven's
corpse-plain.'*

2 'Long I slept, long was I sleeping,
long are the woes of men;
Odin brought it about that I could not break
the spell of drowsiness.'

Sigurd sat down and asked her name. She took a horn full of mead and gave him a memory-drink.

3 'Hail to the day! Hail to the sons of day!
Hail to night and her kin!
With gracious eyes may you look upon us,
and give victory to those sitting here!

4 'Hail to the Æsir! Hail to the goddesses!
Hail to the mighty, fecund earth!
Eloquence and native wit may you give to us two famous ones
and healing hands while we live!'

She was called Sigrdrifa and was a valkyrie. She said that there were two kings who were fighting one another; one was called Helmet-Gunnar, he was old and a great warrior and Odin had promised him victory; and:

'the other was Agnar, the brother of Auda,
whom no creature wanted to protect.'

Sigrdrifa brought down Helmet-Gunnar in battle. And Odin pricked her with a sleep-thorn in revenge for this and said that she would never again fight victoriously in battle and said that she should be married. 'And I said to him that I had sworn a great oath in this matter, never to marry a man who was acquainted with fear.' He asked her to teach him wisdom, if she had information about all the worlds. Sigrdrifa said:*

5 'Beer I give you, apple-tree of battle,*
mixed with magical power and mighty glory;
it is full of spells and favourable letters,
good charms and joyful runes.

6 'Victory-runes you must cut if you want to have victory,
and cut them on your sword-hilt;
some on the blade-guards, some on the plates,
and invoke Tyr twice.

7 'Ale-runes must you know if you do not want another's wife
to beguile your trust, if you believe her;
on a horn they should be cut and on the back of the hand,
and mark your nail with "Naud".*

8 'The cup should be signed over and guarded against mischief,
and garlic thrown in the liquid;
though I know that for you there will never be
mead blended with malice.

9 'Helping-runes you must know if you want to assist
and release children from women;
they shall be cut on the palms and clasped on the joints,
and then the *disir* asked for help.*

10 'Sea-runes you must cut if you want to have guaranteed
the sail-horses on the sea;
on the prow they must be cut and on the rudder,
and burnt into the oar with fire;
however steep the breakers or dark the waves,
yet you'll come safe from the sea.

11 'Limb-runes you must know if you want to be a healer
and know how to see to wounds;
on bark they must be cut and of the tree of the wood,
on those whose branches bend east.

12 'Speech-runes you must know if you want no one to repay
sorrow with enmity;
wind them about, weave them about,
set them all together
at that meeting where people must go
to fully constituted courts.

13 'Mind-runes you must know if you want to be
wiser in spirit than every other man;
Hropt interpreted them,
cut them, thought them out,
from that liquid which had leaked
from the skull of Heiddraupnir
and from Hoddrofnir's horn.*

14 'On the cliff he stood with Brimir's sword,*
a helmet he had on his head;
then Mim's head spoke*
wisely the first word
and told the true letters.

15 'On a shield they should be cut,
the one which stands before the shining god,
on the ears of Arvak and the hoof of Alsvinn,*
on that wheel which turns under [H]rungnir's chariot,
on Sleipnir's teeth and on the sledges' strap-bands;
16 on the bear's paw and on Bragi's tongue,
on the wolf's claw, and the eagle's beak,
on bloody wings and on the arch of the bridge,
on hands which deliver and on the trail of a helpful man,
17 on glass and on gold, and on the amulets of men,
in wine and on wort and on the seat of honour,
on the point of Gungnir and the breast of Grani,
on the nail of the norn, and the beak of the owl.

18 'All were shaved off, those which were carved on,
and scattered with the sacred mead
and sent on wandering ways;
they are among the Æsir, they are among the elves,
some are with the wise Vanir,
some with humankind.

19 'Those are book-runes, those are helping-runes,*
and all the ale-runes,
and valuable runes of power,
for those who can, without confusing them, without destroying them,
possess them for good;
use them, if you get them,
until the gods are torn asunder!

20 'Now you must choose, since choice is offered to you,
maple of sharp weapons,*
speech or silence—you can make up your own mind,
all harms are measured out.'

21 'I may not avoid it, even if I knew myself doomed,
I am not born a coward;
your loving advice I want in its entirety,
as long as I live.'

22 'That I advise you firstly, that towards your kin
you should be blameless;
be slow to avenge although they do harm,
though that is said to benefit the dead.

23 'That I advise you secondly, that you do not swear an
oath
unless it is truly kept;
terrible fate-bonds attach to the oath-tearer;
wretched is the pledge-criminal.

24 'That I advise you thirdly, that at the Assembly
you do not contend with a fool;
for the stupid man often permits himself to say
worse words than he knows.

25 'Everything is lost if you are silent in response;
then you seem to be born a coward
or else it is spoken truly;
dangerous is one's reputation
unless it is for good;
on another day let his spirit pass on
and thus repay his lies in public.

26 'That I advise you fourthly, if a witch, full of malice,
lives on your route,
it is better to go on than to be her guest,
though night overtake you.

27 'Eyes that can spy out ahead are what the sons of men
need,
where angry men shall fight;
often malevolent women sit close to the roads,
those who deaden swords and spirits.

28 'That I advise you fifthly, though you see
fair ladies on the benches,
silver-decked women, don't let them disturb your sleep
nor entice them to you to kiss.

29 'That I advise you sixthly, though among men
talk over ale becomes offensive,
when drunk you should not quarrel with a warrior;
wine steals many a man's wits.

30 'Songs and ale have been cause of sorrow*
to many a man;
slayers of some, misfortune for some;
manifold is the grief of men.

31 'That I advise you seventhly, if you are feuding
with a man of courage,
it is better to fight than to be burnt inside*
by powerful opponents.

32 'That I advise you eighthly, that you should guard
against evil
and distance yourself from shame;
do not entice girls nor any man's wife,
nor encourage sexual excess.

33 'That I advise you ninthly, that you bury corpses
where you find them on the ground,
whether they are dead of sickness or else drowned,
or men killed by weapons.

34 'A warm bath shall be made for those who are departed;
hands and head be washed,
combed, and dried before they go in the coffin,*
and bid them sleep blessedly.

35 'That I advise you tenthly, that you never trust
the oaths of a wrongdoer's brat,
whether you are his brother's slayer
or you felled the father;
the wolf is in the young son,
though he seems to be gladdened by gold.

36 'Quarrels and enmity are not, I think, asleep,
any more than grief;
common sense and weapons are necessary for the prince
to acquire,
for him who shall be foremost among men.

37 'That I advise you eleventhly, that you beware
in every direction your friends;
a long life I think the prince will [not] have;
powerful quarrels have sprung up.'

The poem ends here; it is possible to reconstruct what must have happened in the missing leaves of the manuscript from *Volsunga saga*. The valkyrie (here, Sigrdrifa, in *Volsunga saga*, Brynhild) and Sigurd betroth themselves to each other—a fact which has no relevance to the story as it develops—and Sigurd sets off for the court of Giuki. On the way he stops at the house of Heimir where he falls in love with Brynhild. It seems likely that two stories are conflated in the Sigurd cycle: in one the hero is betrothed to the valkyrie won by crossing a flame-wall, in another he becomes entangled with the Giukung family and is destroyed by his sister-in-law's passion for him. But the plots are imperfectly merged: in the *Edda* the two separate women remain, whereas in *Volsunga saga* the author simplifies by making Brynhild the only woman with whom Sigurd becomes involved. Thus in the saga Sigurd meets Brynhild three times—on the mountain, at Heimir's, and when he woos her for Gunnar; his failure to recognize her at the third meeting is explained by a drink of forgetfulness. Sigurd is made to appear more heartless than he really is, and the simplified plot involves the author of *Volsunga saga* in an implausible second meeting at Heimir's. At the court of Giuki Sigurd is given a magic drink which makes him forget Brynhild and he agrees to marry Gudrun, sister of Gunnar. The Codex Regius takes up the story once again after Sigurd has agreed to help woo Brynhild for Gunnar. The marriages of Sigurd to Gudrun and Brynhild to Gunnar have taken place; Sigurd has remembered his previous promise but resolves silently to make the best of things. When Gudrun quarrels with Brynhild and reveals to her the shape-changing deception involved in her wooing, Brynhild decides to destroy Sigurd. Even though, according to *Volsunga saga*, ch. 31, he offers to leave Gudrun and marry her, Brynhild remains implacable.

Fragment of a Poem about Sigurd

The Codex Regius picks up the story of Sigurd some verses into a poem narrating the aftermath of Brynhild's demand that Sigurd be killed. In this poem Sigurd is murdered outside in the forest by Guthorm, younger brother of Gudrun, aided by Gunnar and Hogni, and the focus is on Brynhild's reaction to the death. The speaker of the first stanza seems to be Hogni, responding to Gunnar's request for help in disposing of his brother-in-law. Gunnar elaborates the problem in v. 2.

1 'What harm can Sigurd have done
that you want to deprive the brave one of life?'

2 'To me Sigurd gave oaths,
oaths he gave, and all were false;*
thus he deceived me when he should have been
completely trustworthy in every oath.'

3 'Brynhild is stirring up disaster for you,
she's urging hatred, that wrong be done;
she begrudges Gudrun her good marriage match,
and also that she has to take her pleasure with you.'

4 Some roasted wolf, some sliced-up serpent,
wolf-meat they gave Guthorm to eat,*
before they could, desiring his ruin,
lay their hands on the wise man.

5 Dead was Sigurd on the south side of the Rhine,
a raven called out loudly from a tree:
'Atli will redden his blades in your blood,
your oaths will destroy you, you warlike men.'

6 Outside stood Gudrun, daughter of Giuki,
and this was the first thing that she said:
'Where is Sigurd, lord of warriors,
now my kinsmen are riding ahead?'

7 Hogni alone gave her an answer:
'Sigurd we've hacked into pieces with a sword,
the grey horse droops his head over the dead prince.'

8 Then said Brynhild, Budli's daughter:
'Now you'll enjoy the use of weapons and lands;
Sigurd alone would have held it all,
if a little longer he'd kept his life.

9 'It wouldn't have been fitting that he should have ruled
over the inheritance of Giuki and all the hosts of
Goths,*
when he had fathered five sons,
eager in battle, to rule the people.'

10 Then Brynhild laughed—all the hall resounded—
just once she laughed with all her heart:
'Long may you enjoy your lands and your followers,
now you've brought the wise prince to his death.'

11 Then said Gudrun, Giuki's daughter:
'Many abominable words you've said;
may fiends take Gunnar, murderer of Sigurd!
Thoughts bent on wickedness shall be revenged.'

12 It was late in the evening, much was drunk,
there all sorts of pleasant words were spoken;
all went to sleep when they went to their bed,
Gunnar stayed awake for a very long time.

13 His foot began to twitch, he muttered many things,
the destroyer of armies began to ponder
what the two of them had said in their curses,
the raven and the eagle, as they'd ridden home.

14 Brynhild awakened, Budli's daughter,
lady of the Skioldings, a little before dawn:
'Urge me on or hinder me—the harm is done now—
sorrow to be told of or else let be!'

15 Everyone was silent at these words,
little could they understand the behaviour of women,
now that, weeping, she began to speak of
that which, laughing, she'd asked the men for.

16 'I thought, Gunnar, that I was having a bad dream,
it was chilly in the hall, and my bed was cold;
and you, lord, were riding, bereft of happiness,
with chains you were fettered among a troop of foes.
So from all of you of the Niflung line
your strength will pass away: you are oath-breakers.

17 'You clearly did not remember, Gunnar,
that you both let your blood run into a trench;*
now you have repaid him badly for that,
when he wanted to make himself the most pre-eminent
of men.

18 'Then that was proved when the brave man
came riding to ask for my hand,
how the destroyer of armies had previously*
kept his oaths to the young prince.

19 'A wound-wand, braided round with gold,*
the splendid king laid between us,
the outer edges were forged in fire,
and the inner ones patterned with acid-marks.'

About the Death of Sigurd *In this poem the death of Sigurd is related and here it is said that they killed him outside. But some say this, that they killed him inside, sleeping in his bed. And Germans say that they killed him out in the forest. And the 'Old Poem of Gudrun'* says that Sigurd and the sons of Giuki were riding to the Assembly when he was killed. But they all say that they treacherously betrayed him and attacked him when he was lying down and unarmed.*

The First Lay of Gudrun

There are three lays of Gudrun in the *Poetic Edda*; in this, the first (*Gudrunarkvida I*), Gudrun is struck dumb by her grief at Sigurd's death. Other women attempt to rouse her to tears by telling their own sad tales, but it is Gullrond, Gudrun's sister, who has the psychological acumen to display the covered body of Sigurd, bringing Gudrun to give vent to her sorrow. Gudrun's lament, reminiscent of Sigrun's in the *Second Poem of Helgi Hundingsbani*, vv. 37–8, is vividly poignant—she now feels 'as little as a leaf' and calls down curses on Gunnar and Hogni.

Gudrun sat over Sigurd's dead body. She did not weep like other women and she was on the point of collapsing with grief. Both men and women came to comfort her; it was not easy. People said that Gudrun had eaten some of Fafnir's heart and so she understood the talk of birds. This is also said of Gudrun:

1 It was long ago that Gudrun intended to die,
when she sat sorrowful over Sigurd;
she did not weep or strike her hands together,
or lament like other women.

2 The very wise warriors stepped forward,
they tried to ease her terrible grief;
even so Gudrun could not weep,
she was so impassioned, she might have burst asunder.

3 The gleaming wives of warriors,
adorned with gold, sat by Gudrun;
each of them told of their great grief,
the bitterest which had been visited on them.

4 Then said Giaflaug, Giuki's sister:
'I know that in the world, I'm most deprived of joy,
the heavy loss of five husbands has come upon me;
of three daughters, three sisters,
of eight brothers, I alone am living.'

5 Even so Gudrun could not weep;
she was so impassioned by the death of the young man
and so fierce in mind at the fall of the prince.

6 Then said Herborg, queen of the land of the Huns:
'I have a heavier grief to speak of:
my seven sons, in the lands in the south,
my husband, as the eighth, all fell in slaughter;
7 father and mother, four brothers,
the wind played too much with them on the waves,
the waves beat against thc gunwale.

8 'I myself had to honour, I myself had to bury,
I myself had to arrange their journey to Hel;
that I endured in one half-year,
so that no man could ever give me any joy.

9 'Then I was taken captive, war-prisoner,
that same half-year it befell me;
I had to adorn her, and tie on the shoes
of the war-leader's wife every morning.

10 'She raged at me in her jealousy
and struck me with savage blows;
nowhere have I found a better husband,
nowhere have I found a worse wife.'

11 Even so Gudrun could not weep;
she was so impassioned by the death of the young man
and so fierce in mind at the fall of the prince.

12 Then said Gullrond, daughter of Giuki:*
'You don't really know, foster-mother, though you are wise,
how to reply to a young wife.'
She advised against concealing the corpse of the prince.

13 She swept the covering from Sigurd
and pushed the blood-soaked pillows by the woman's knees:
'Look at your beloved, put your mouth to his moustache,
as you used to embrace the prince when he was alive.'

14 Gudrun looked at him one time only;
she saw the prince's hair running with blood,
the bright eyes of the lord grown dim,
the prince's breast scored by the sword.

15 Then Gudrun knelt, leaning on the pillow;
loosened her hair, scratched her cheeks,
and drops like rain ran down to her knees.

16 Then Gudrun wept, the daughter of Giuki,
so that her tears fell into her hair,
and the geese in the meadow cackled in reply,
the splendid birds which belonged to the girl.

17 Then said Gullrond, daughter of Giuki:
'Yours I know was the greatest love
of all people across the earth;
inside or outside, you were never happy
to be with anyone, my sister, but Sigurd.'

18 'So was my Sigurd, beside the sons of Giuki,
as if a leek were grown up out of the grass,
or a bright stone were threaded onto a string,
a precious gem, among the nobles.

19 'I thought myself also, among the prince's warriors,
to be higher than all of Odin's ladies;
now I am as little as a leaf
among the bay-willows at the death of the prince.

20 'I miss in his seat and in my bed
my friend to talk to, the kin of Giuki caused it;
the kin of Giuki caused my grief
and agonizing weeping for their sister.

21 'So may the people and land be laid waste on your account,
as you have caused it, with the oaths you swore;
you, Gunnar, shall never make use of the gold,
the rings will be the death of you,
since you swore oaths to Sigurd.

22 'In the meadow there was more merriment,
before my Sigurd saddled Grani,
and they went off to woo Brynhild,
that wicked creature, in an ill-fated hour.'

23 Then said Brynhild, Budli's daughter:
'Lacking may that woman be in husband and children,
who got you, Gudrun, to weep
and in the morning gave the runes of speaking!'*

24 Then said Gullrond, Giuki's daughter:
'Be silent, you monstrous woman, stop these words!
The nemesis of princes you have always been;
every wave of ill fate drives you along,
you wounding sorrow of seven kings,
woman who's been the greatest ruination to women's friendship.'

25 Then said Brynhild, Budli's daughter:
'Atli alone caused all the evil,
born of Budli, brother of mine,
26 when in the hall of the Hunnish people
he saw the fire of the serpent's bed shine on the prince;*
I have paid for this journey since then,
those sights are always before my eyes.'

27 She stood by the pillar, she called on all her strength;
from Brynhild, daughter of Budli,
fire burned from the eyes, poison she snorted,
when she looked at the wound upon Sigurd.

Gudrun went away from there to the woods in the wasteland, and went as far as Denmark, and stayed seven half-years with Thora, daughter of Hakon there.

Brynhild did not want to go on living after Sigurd. She had eight of her slaves killed and five serving-maids. Then she stabbed herself with a sword, as is told in the 'Short Poem about Sigurd'.

A Short Poem about Sigurd

Like *Gripir's Prophecy*, the *Short Poem about Sigurd* (*Sigurdarkvida in skamma*) is in part a prospective summary of events following the death of Sigurd, integrating the continuing story of Gudrun and her future husbands, and the fate of Gunnar and his doomed affair with Oddrun. The poem also gives in brief the story of how Sigurd came to be killed, although the details of how he came to forget his prior betrothal to Brynhild, and how the change of appearance with Gunnar was effected are not spelt out. The centre of poetic interest is the characterization of Brynhild, who moves from implacable, monstrous avenger to sorrowing, yet unregretful, bride in death. The contrast with Gudrun's impotence in this poem is striking. At seventy-one stanzas the poem is not especially short; a lost longer poem, explaining events between Sigurd's parting from Sigrdrifa and the decision to kill Sigurd, has been hypothesized from *Volsunga saga*.

1 Long ago it was that Sigurd visited Giuki,
the young Volsung had already killed;
he accepted promises from the two brothers,
oaths were given by the men so valiant in great deeds.

2 They offered him the girl and a great deal of treasure,
young Gudrun, Giuki's daughter;
they drank and debated many days together,
young Sigurd and the sons of Giuki,

3 until they went to woo Brynhild,
and Sigurd rode in company with them;
the young Volsung knew the way,
he would have married her if fate had allowed it.

4 The man from the south laid a naked sword,*
a slender inlaid blade, between them both;
nor did he seek to kiss the woman,
the southern king did not take her in his arms;
the girl so young he gave to Giuki's son.

5 She had not known of any shame in her life,
nor of the injury that had befallen her,
no disgrace that was or could be imagined.
The terrible fates intervened in this.

6 Outside she sat alone, in the evening,
then quite openly she began to speak:
'I shall have Sigurd—or I shall die—
that young man I'll have in my arms.

7 'The words I'm speaking now I'll be sorry for later,
Gudrun is his wife, and I am Gunnar's;
the hateful norns decreed this long torment for us.'*

8 Often she went outside, filled with anger,
on the ice of the glaciers, every evening,*
and he and Gudrun went to bed
and Sigurd wrapped her in the bedclothes,
the southern king caressing his wife.

9 'I am deprived of both happiness and husband,
I'll pleasure myself with my savage thoughts.'

10 Then in her malice she began to goad to slaughter:
'Gunnar, you will altogether lose
my lands and lose me myself;
I shall never be satisfied with you, prince.

11 'I shall go back to where I was before,
among my close relatives, my near-born kin;
there I shall sit and sleep away my life,
unless you manage to kill Sigurd
and become superior to other lords.

12 'Let the son go the same way as the father!*
Don't nurture for long the young wolf;
for to which man would revenge come easier—
afterwards in recompense—than if the son were still
alive?'

13 Gunnar was angry and cast down,
he wrapped himself in thought and sat all day;
he did not know at all clearly
what would be most honourable for him to do
or what would be best for him to do,
he knew he would have to rid himself of the Volsung
and he knew Sigurd would be a great loss.

14 Different plans he weighed up for hours at a time,
it was not customary in those days
for women to abandon the royal state;
he got Hogni to promise to keep counsel,
for him he knew he could completely trust.

15 'Brynhild I like better than all other women,
Budli's girl is a prize among ladies;
rather would I lose my life,
than lose the treasure of that girl.

16 'Will you, for our sake, betray the prince for money?
It's good to have hold of the metal of the Rhine*
and pleasantly to enjoy wealth
and, sitting comfortably, to revel in the hall.'

17 Hogni replied, he had only one answer:
'It is not fitting for us to do this,
cutting asunder with a sword
the oaths we've sworn, the pledges made.

18 'We don't know of happier men anywhere on earth
while we four rule the people*
and the southern leader is alive,
nor of a mightier clan in the world
if we should in time bring up five sons
of good family to augment our kin.

19 'I know quite well how things stand:
Brynhild's passions are far too great.'

20 'We should prepare Guthorm for the killing,
our younger brother, not so experienced;
he was away when the oaths were sworn,
when the oaths were sworn and the pledges made.'

21 Easy it was to egg on the undaunted man,
the sword stood in Sigurd's heart.

22 The man eager for battle pondered revenge in the bedchamber*
and then he hurled at the undaunted one;
at Guthorm there flew the weapon of Gram
the powerful, wonderfully bright iron from the king's hand.

23 The enemy fell from the blow into two pieces;
arms and head flew in different directions
and his legs fell over backwards.*

24 Sleeping was Gudrun in bed,
quite carefree next to Sigurd;
but she awoke far away from joy
when she found herself swimming in her lover's blood.

25 She clapped together her hands so loudly*
that the man of mighty spirit heaved himself up in the bed:
'Do not weep, Gudrun, so fiercely,
young bride, you have brothers still alive.

26 'I have an heir, too young,
he doesn't know how to get away from this hostile place;
they have thought up, fatefully and sinisterly,
a new plan which they've carried out.

27 'No sister's son, though seven should be nurtured,
like him would ride afterwards to the Assembly;*
I know well why this is happening:
Brynhild alone has caused all this misery.

28 'The girl loves me before all other men,
but to Gunnar I did no harm;
I did not violate the kinship or the oaths,
so I ought not to be called his wife's lover.'

29 The woman gave a sigh, the king gave up his life,
she clapped together her hands so loudly
that the goblets in the corner echoed her
and the geese in the meadow cackled in reply.

30 Then Brynhild, Budli's daughter,
laughed once with all her heart,
when in her bed she was able to hear
the echoing weeping of Giuki's daughter.

31 Then said Gunnar, the fierce fighter:
'You're not laughing, you evil woman,
merrily in the bedchamber, because you have any good in mind.
Why have you lost your pallor,
nourisher of evil? I think you must be doomed.

32 'You deserve more than all women
that we should strike down Atli before your eyes,
so you should see on your brother bloody wounds,
flowing gashes, that you might bind up.'

33 'No man'll taunt you, Gunnar, you struck home all right,
Atli won't care about your enmity;
of the two of you he'll breathe the longer,
he'll always have the greater strength.

34 'I must tell you, Gunnar, though you know it already,
how you so quickly fell into guilt;
I was not too young, nor was I constrained at all,*
I had great supplies of gold in my brother's hall.

35 'Nor did I wish that I should have a husband,
before you Giukungs rode into the courtyard,
three sovereign kings on horseback—
a journey that should never have happened.

39 'To him I'd betrothed myself
when he sat on Grani's back with his gold;
his eyes were not like those of you brothers,
nor was he like you in any respect;
though you thought yourselves sovereign kings.

36 'And then Atli said to me in private*
that he would never share out the property,
neither gold nor land, unless I let myself be betrothed,
nor any portion of my goods and wealth,
which had been given to me so very young,
the wealth counted out for me, so very young.

37 'Then my mind was in doubt about this,
whether I should fight or kill in battle,
a brave woman in a corslet, against my brother.
That might become well known among the nations,
and make strife the lot of many a man.

38 'We reconciled our disagreement;
I had a greater desire to accept treasure,
red-gold rings from the son of Sigmund,
nor did I wish for any other man's wealth.

40 'I loved only one, I did not love any others,
the valkyrie of necklaces was never fickle;*
all that will Atli discover,
when he asks about the journey of death I'll achieve
41 —that no light-minded woman should ever
keep company with another woman's man;
then there'll be vengeance for all my sorrows.'

42 Up rose Gunnar, prince of the retinue,
and he put his arms round the neck of his wife;
they all attempted in different ways
with all their hearts to dissuade her.

43 Quickly from her neck each she pushed from her,
she let no man dissuade her from the long journey.

44 Then he asked Hogni for secret counsel:
'I want all the men to go into the hall,
yours and mine together—for now there's great need—,
to see if we can stop the woman's death-journey,
else more harm will come of it;
so let us then do what's necessary, devise some plan.'

45 Hogni then gave just this answer:
'Let no man hinder her from the long journey,
let her never be born again!
From her mother's womb she was born awkward,
she was ever born to misery
and to cause grief of heart to many a man.'

46 Downcast he turned from the conversation,
to where the necklace-lady was sharing out her treasure.

47 She looked at all her property,
dead were her maids and the ladies of her hall;*
she put on a golden mail-coat—her intention was not good—
before she pierced herself with the edge of the sword.

48 She fell backwards against the pillow;
wounded with the sword, she considered what to say:

49 'Now they should come, those who want gold,
or who want something to remember me by;
I'll give to each a fine-worked jewel,
embroidered coverlets, bright clothing.'

50 All were silent, they considered what to say,
and very slowly they all gave their answer,
'Enough women have died, we want to live on,
let the hall-servants achieve such honour.'

51 Then, thinking hard, the linen-wearing woman,
still so young, said these words:
'I do not want someone who's reluctant
or hard to persuade to lose her life for our sake.

52 'Though the less treasure
will burn with your bones when you come down,
—no treasures of Menia—to visit me.*

53 'Sit down, Gunnar! Now I shall tell you,
your radiant bride has no hope of life;
your vessel is not safe in harbour
even if I've breathed my last.

54 'You and Gudrun will be reconciled sooner than you
think;
the wise woman will have, beside the king,*
sad memories of her dead husband.

55 'A girl will be born, her mother will raise her;
she'll be more radiant than the bright day,
Svanhild, brighter than a ray of the sun.

56 'You must give Gudrun, destroyer of many men,
to some good man, to a marksman;
she will not be happily married, married against her
wishes;
Atli will wish to wed her,
born of Budli, my brother.

57 'Much I remember: how they acted against me,
those who betrayed me, caused me pain;
deprived of joy was I while I lived.

58 'You'll want to marry Oddrun,*
but Atli won't permit it;
you'll have secret embraces,
she'll love you as I ought to have done,
if a good fate had been granted to us.

59 'Atli will persecute you, he'll prepare wickedness,
you'll be lodged in a narrow snake-pit.*

60 'Not much later this will happen,
that Atli will breathe his last,
lose his happiness and the lives of his sons.
For Gudrun will smear their bed with blood,
with sharp edges, from her wounded heart.

61 'It would be more fitting for our sister Gudrun
to follow her first husband in death,
if she were given good advice
or if she had a spirit like mine.

62 'Slowly I speak now, but she will never
give up her life on my advice;
her the high waves will carry
over to Ionakr's ancestral land.

63 'Carefully she'll rear up Ionakr's sons;
she'll send Svanhild from that land,
her daughter and Sigurd's.

64 'Bikki's counsel will bitterly grieve her,*
for Iormunrekk lives to wreak havoc;
then all the line of Sigurd will have passed away,
Gudrun will have more to weep for.

65 'I must ask you for one thing only,
this will be my last request in this world:
let a pyre be built on the meadow
with enough space for all of us,
those who died with Sigurd.

66 'Cover the pyre with shields and hangings,
skilfully patterned foreign weaving, and many foreign slaves;
burn the southern man beside me.

67 'On the southern man's other side
burn my maids adorned with jewellery,
two by his head and two hawks,
then everything will be orderly.

68 'Lay between us the ring-hilted sword,
the sharp-edged iron, as it lay before,
when we two together lay in one bed,
when we had the name of being man and wife.

69 'The door of the hall, decorated with a ring,
must not jangle at his heels,*
if my travelling from here is to accompany him;
our journey must not be wretched.

70 'So five serving-girls accompany him,
eight servants of good family,
the slave who grew up with me, my patrimony,
which Budli gave to his child.

71 'Much I have said, I would say more,
if more time for speech were granted to me;
but my voice fails, my wounds are throbbing,
I said what was true and now I must depart.'

Brynhild's Ride to Hell

After her cremation, burnt in a wagon perhaps like that found in the Oseberg ship-burial in Norway, Brynhild sets off to the kingdom of the dead to be reunited with Sigurd. As she approaches the borders of Hel's land, she encounters a dead giantess who challenges her—the settlement where the giantess lives is her grave-mound. Brynhild, still proud and undaunted, tells the story of her life, making clear the conflation with the valkyrie history of Sigrdrifa, and goes on her way.

After Brynhild's death two pyres were made, the other one was for Sigurd, and that was kindled first, and Brynhild was burnt on the second one, and she was in a wagon draped with costly woven tapestries. It is said that Brynhild drove the wagon along the road to hell and went past a settlement, where a certain giantess lived. The giantess said:

1 'You shall not journey through
my homestead set with stone;
it would befit you better to be at your weaving
than to be going to visit another woman's man.

2 'What are you coming to see, from the southern land,
with your giddy mind, in my houses?
Goddess of gold, if you wish to know,
you, gentle lady, have washed your hands in a man's blood.'

Then Brynhild said:

3 'Don't reproach me, lady who lives in the rock,
even though I've often been on viking expeditions;
I shall be accepted as of better ancestry than you
wherever people compare our lineage.'

The giantess said:

4 'Brynhild, you were Budli's daughter,
born to the worst luck in the world;
you have deceived the children of Giuki
and destroyed their good dwelling-places.'

Brynhild said:

5 'I must tell you, I, the wise lady in the wagon,
you very stupid woman, if you wish to know,
how the heirs of Giuki treated me,
deprived me of love, and violated their oaths.

6 'The wise king had our magic garments—
eight sisters we were together—put under an oak;*
I was twelve years old, if you want to know,
when I gave my promise to the young prince.

7 'They all called me in Hlymdale,
anyone who knew me, War-lady in the helmet.

8 'Then I let the old man of the Gothic nation,
Helmet-Gunnar, quickly go off to hell;
I gave the young man victory, the brother of Auda;
Odin was very angry with me for that.*

9 'With shields he enclosed me in Skata-grove,
with red ones and white ones, shields overlapping;
that man he ordered to break my sleep
who in every land knew no fear.

10 'Around my hall to the south,
the destroyer of all wood he set blazing up high;*
there he told one warrior to ride over it,
he who brought me the gold which lay under Fafnir.

11 'The good man rode on Grani, saddled with gold,
where my foster-father commanded his halls;
he alone seemed better than all men,
the Danish viking among the retinue.*

12 'We slept and we were enclosed in one bed together,
as if he were my brother born;
nor did we lay one arm over another
for the eight nights of our lying together.

13 'And yet Gudrun accused me, Giuki's daughter,
that I had slept in Sigurd's arms;
then I discovered what I wish I'd never known,
that they'd betrayed me in my taking a husband.

14 'Men and women, those who are living,
must spend all too long in terrible sorrow
but we shall never ever part,
Sigurd and I will be together—now, ogress, sink!'

The Death of the Niflungs

This short prose passage, probably written by the compiler of the Codex Regius in order to pull together the poems which follow, explains how the story of Atli and Gudrun, and the death of the brothers, follows from the killing of Sigurd, and allows the inclusion of the two poems about Gudrun which follow. Certain details in the passage are not borne out by the poetry: Gudrun does not ask her sons by Atli to plead for the life of Gunnar and Hogni in either of the poems about their deaths, but the compiler seems to be seeking a better motivation for the murder of the two boys than simple revenge upon their father.

Gunnar and Hogni took all the gold, Fafnir's inheritance. There was a feud between the sons of Giuki and Atli. He blamed the Giukungs greatly for the death of Brynhild. In compensation, they were to marry Gudrun to him, and they had to give her a drink of forgetfulness before she agreed to marry Atli. Her sons with Atli were Erp and Eitil, and Svanhild was Gudrun's daughter by Sigurd.

King Atli invited Gunnar and Hogni to visit him and sent Vingi or Knefrod as messenger. Gudrun knew his treacherous plans and sent a message in runes saying that they should not come, and as a token she sent Hogni the ring, Andvari's Jewel, and twisted round it a wolf's hair.

Gunnar had asked for the hand of Oddrun, Atli's sister, and had not been given it; then he married Glaumvor, and Hogni married Kostbera. Their sons were Solar and Snævar and Giuki And when the Giukungs came to Atli, then Gudrun asked her sons to plead for the two brothers' lives. But they would not. The heart was cut out of Hogni, and Gunnar was put in a snake-pit. He played his harp and put the serpents to sleep, but an adder bit him in the liver.

The Second Lay of Gudrun

Another poem in which Gudrun recounts her sorrows up until the death of her brothers. Her narrative fills in the events between the end of the *First Lay of Gudrun* and the *Lay of Atli*, summarizing the events surrounding the death of Sigurd and explaining how she comes to marry Atli, against her will. The poem is probably one of the later ones in the collection; *Volsunga saga*, ch. 34, fills out the events in the interval between the death of Sigurd and the marriage to Atli.

King Thiodrek was with Atli and had lost almost all his men there. Thiodrek and Gudrun exchanged the story of their woes. She spoke to him and said:

1 'Radiant I was, the loveliest of girls,
my mother brought me up in the women's quarters,
I loved my brothers greatly; until Giuki endowed me with gold,
endowed me with gold and gave me to Sigurd.

2 'So was Sigurd beside the sons of Giuki
like a green leek grown up out of the grass,*
or a high-antlered stag among the sharp-eyed beasts,
or red-glowing gold next to dull silver.

3 'Until my brothers begrudged it me
that I should have a husband most prominent among all;
they could not sleep, they could not judge cases,
until they had put Sigurd to death.

4 'Grani ran from the Assembly, the uproar could be heard,*
and then Sigurd himself did not come;
all the saddle-horses were dripping with sweat,
exhausted by their labours beneath the killers.

5 'Weeping I went to talk to Grani;
cheeks wet with tears, I asked the horse for news;
Grani drooped his head then, hid it in the grass,
the horse knew that his master was not living.

6 'Long I turned it over, long my thoughts ran on,
until I questioned the king about the prince.

7 'Gunnar looked down, Hogni told me
about Sigurd's bitter death:
"Struck down, he lies beside the river,
the slayer of Guthorm, given to the wolves.

8 '"Look for Sigurd there on the roads southwards!
There you'll hear the ravens shriek,
the eagles shriek; rejoicing in the carrion,
the wolves are howling over your husband."

9 '"How, Hogni, can you bring yourself to tell
of such terrible harm to me, bereft of joy?
May the ravens tear out your heart
across the wide land, you wicked man."

10 'Hogni answered once only,
not inclined to be cheerful, out of great grief:
"More tears you'd have, Gudrun, from this,
if ravens were to tear out my heart."

11 'Away I went from the conversation,
to the wood, to gather the leavings of the wolves;
I could not weep nor strike my hands together,
nor lament as other women do,
there I sat close to death over Sigurd.

12 'The night seemed to me as dark as the dark of the moon,
as I sat grieving over Sigurd;
it seemed to me the best of all things
if the wolves took my life
or if they burned me up like birchwood.

13 'I walked from the mountain, five days together,
until I recognized the high hall of Half.

14 'I sat with Thora seven half-years,
Hakon's daughter in Denmark;
she embroidered in gold for my pleasure
southern halls and Danish swans.

15 'We also made pictures of men's war-play together,
and the warriors of the prince on our handiwork;
red shields, Hunnish fighters,
sword-warriors, helmet-warriors, the retinue of the prince.

16 'The ships of Sigmund glided from the land,
fierce wild boar inlaid on the prows;
we showed in our weaving how they fought
Sigar and Siggeir, south in Fion.

17 'Then Grimhild learned, queen of the Goths,
what my state of mind was;
she stopped embroidering and called to her sons,
insistently she asked this:
which man would compensate the sister for her son,
who would pay for the slain husband?

18 'Eagerly Gunnar offered gold
to settle the matter, and so did Hogni;
she asked this: that everyone who was willing to go
should saddle a horse, prepare a wagon,
ride a horse, fly a hawk,
shoot arrows from a yew bow.*

19 'Valdar with the Danes, with Iarizleif,
Eymod the third, with Iarizskar—
in they went, all most princely,
the troops of the Langobards; they had red cloaks,
ornamented byrnies, towering helmets,
girded with short-swords, they had dark hair.

20 'Each wanted to pick out treasure for me,
pick out treasure and speak comforting words,
to see if they could bring me from my great sorrow,
win my trust: I could not come to trust them.

21 'Grimhild brought me a cup to drink from,
cool and bitter, I could not remember the past;*
that drink was augmented with fateful power,
with the cool sea, with sacrificial blood.

22 'On the drinking-horn were all kinds of runes,
cut and red-coloured—I could not interpret them—
a heather-fish, an uncut corn-ear*
of the land of the Haddings, the entrails of beasts.*

23 'Many evil things were mixed into that drink,
the herbs of all the woodland, and burnt acorns,
the dew of the hearth, the innards from sacrifice,
boiled pig's liver, since it blunted the past.

24 'And then was forgotten, the things which had been known,
all the prince's death in the hall;
three kings came to kneel at my feet
before she herself spoke to me.

25 '"Gold I will give you, Gudrun,
a great deal of treasure from your dead father,
red-gold rings, all the precious bed-hangings
of Hlodver's hall, for the fallen prince;

26 '"Hunnish girls to do your delicate weaving,
to work in gold for your pleasure;
you alone shall control the wealth of Budli,
be endowed with gold, and given to Atli."

27 '"I do not want to go to another man
nor to marry Brynhild's brother;
it is not fitting for me to have children
nor to live happily with the son of Budli."

28 '"Don't try to repay the men's wickedness,
though what we brought about before was evil;
you'll feel as if they were still alive,
Sigurd and Sigmund, if you have sons."*

29 '"I may not, Grimhild, fling myself into happiness,
nor comply with the hopes of that man brave in battle,
since the corpse-greedy wolf and raven bitterly drank
the heart-blood of Sigurd."

30 '"I have found the most highly-born
princc of all, thc most prominent of all;
him you'll be married to, or else till your life's end,
you'll be without a man if you won't take this one."

31 '"Stop offering me this unholy
kinship so insistently!
He will prepare a trap for Gunnar,
tear out the heart from Hogni.
Then I won't delay until I take
the life of the vigorous man,
of the sword-warrior."

32 'Weeping, Grimhild heard these words
which portended doom for her sons
and great harm to her boys:

33 '"Lands I'll give you, troops of men,
Vinbiorg, Valbiorg, if you'll take them;
possess them all your days, and be content, daughter!"

34 '"I'll choose him from among the kings
coerced into this by my kin;
he won't be a husband whom I can love
nor will the fate of my brothers protect my sons."

35 'Quickly each man was seen to his horse,
and the southern women lifted into the wagon;
seven days we rode over the chilly land,
and another seven we passed over the waves.
In the third week we came to dry land.

36 'There the door-guards opened the gates
of the high citadel, as we rode into the court.

37 'Atli awoke me, for I seemed to be
full of evil foreboding of the death of kinsmen.

38 'So recently the norns have wakened me,
he wanted me to interpret prophecies of trouble—
"I thought that you, Gudrun, daughter of Giuki,
ran me through with a poisoned sword."

39 '"Dreaming of iron represents fire,
of the anger of a woman, deception and delusion;
I shall have to cauterize your injuries,
for comfort and for healing, though it pains me to do it."

40 '"I thought that in the meadow the saplings had fallen,
those which I'd wanted to let grow tall,
were torn up by the roots, reddened with blood,
carried to the bench and offered to me to eat.

41 '"I thought that my hawks flew from my hand,
without their prey to a hall of evil;
their hearts I ate mixed with honey,
sorry in my heart, gorged on blood.

42 '"I thought that I loosed my pups from my grasp,
deprived of joy, both of them howled;
I thought their flesh became carrion,
disgusting corpses which I was meant to enjoy."

43 '"That means men will discuss sacrifice
and cut the heads off white sacrificial beasts;*
doomed, they will, in a few days,
be consumed by the retinue."

44 'I lay down then, I did not want to sleep,
obstinate in the bed of pain; that I remember well.'

The Third Lay of Gudrun

This poem is set between the death of Gudrun's brothers and her revenge, but is grouped with the *Second Lay* because of the similarity of title. The story is unknown from anywhere else and probably very late. The combination of possibly contemporary trial by ordeal and archaic Germanic punishment, drowning in a bog, is striking. Thiodrek is a character well known in both Norse and German heroic legend.

Herkia was the name of one of Atli's serving-maids; she had been his mistress. She told Atli that she had seen Gudrun and Thiodrek together. Atli was very upset. Then Gudrun said:

1 'What's the matter, Atli? Always, son of Budli,
you're downcast; why do you never laugh?
It would seem better to the warriors
that you should speak to people and look at me.'

2 'It grieves me, Gudrun, daughter of Giuki,
what Herkia told me in the hall,
that you and Thiodrek slept under one coverlet
and made yourselves comfortable in the bedlinen.'

3 'I'll swear you oaths about all this,
by the sacred white stone,
that with Thiodmar's son I never did anything
which a lady and man ought not to do together.

4 'Just once only did I embrace
the war-leader, the valiant prince;
but quite other was our conversation,
when we two, griefstricken,
spoke privately together.

5 'Thiodrek came here with thirty men,
not one of them lives now, out of thirty men;
you deprived me of brothers, of corslet-wearing men,
you deprived me of all my closest kin.

6 'Summon Saxi, the prince of the southerners!
He knows about the sacred, boiling cauldron.'

7 Seven hundred men entered the hall,
before the king's lady dipped her hands in the cauldron.

8 'Gunnar will not come now, I do not call for Hogni,
I shall not ever again see my sweet brothers;
with a sword Hogni would avenge such an insult,
now I have to purge this accusation myself.'

9 She stretched her bright hands down to the bottom
and there she seized the precious stones:
'Look now, warriors—acquitted am I,
by the sacred test—how this cauldron bubbles.'

10 Then Atli's heart laughed within him
when he saw Gudrun's hands all whole:
'Now Herkia shall go to the cauldron,
she who spoke slander of Gudrun.'

11 Everyone who watched watched wretchedly,
how Herkia's hands were scalded;
they took the girl away into a foul bog,*
Gudrun thus avenged her wrong.

Oddrun's Lament

An odd addition to the story of Gunnar and Atli, providing more motivation than is needed for Atli's killing of his brothers-in-law, but continuing the theme of the sorrows and suffering of women, which began with the laments of Svava and Sigrun in the Helgi poems and which has continued through the Gudrun laments.

About Borgny and Oddrun *There was a king called Heidrek; his daughter was called Borgny. Vilmund was the name of the man who was her lover. She could not give birth to her children until Oddrun, sister of Atli, came; she had been the lover of Gunnar, son of Giuki. About this tale, this is told.*

1 I heard said in ancient tales,
how a girl came to Mornaland;
no one on the face of the earth
was able to help the daughter of Heidrek.

2 Oddrun heard, sister of Atli,
that the girl was having terrible pains;
she brought from its stall the bridled horse
and saddled up the black steed.

3 She let the horse travel over the smooth paths
until she came where a high hall was standing;
and in she went along the hall
—she took the saddle off the hungry horse—
and, first of all, she spoke these words:

4 'What is best known in this land,
or what is most noteworthy in the land of the Huns?'
'Here lies Borgny, overcome with labour pains,
your friend, Oddrun—help her if you can!'

5 'Which prince has brought about this shame?
Why does Borgny have these sudden pains?'

6 'Vilmund he's called, a fighting man,
he kept the girl in warm coverlets
for five whole winters, so that she concealed it from her
father.'

7 There, I think, they did not speak much more:
the gentle lady went to sit by the girl's knees;
strongly Oddrun sang, powerfully Oddrun sang,
bitter spells for Borgny.*

8 A girl and a boy were able to kick on the earth,
cheerful children for the slayer of Hogni.*
Then the mortally sick girl began to speak,
for she had not spoken a word before.

9 'May all the kindly beings help you,
Frigg and Freyia and more of the gods,
as you warded away that dangerous illness from me.'

10 'I didn't kneel to help you because
you in any way deserved it;
I promised, and I fulfilled that promise, when I said I'd
come here,
that I should help any creature
who shared the inheritance of princes.'

11 'You're mad, Oddrun! you're out of your wits,
that you say so many spiteful words to me!
And I used to accompany you on mother Earth
as if we had been born of two brothers!'

12 'I remember what you said one evening,
when I was preparing the drink for Gunnar:*
you said that such behaviour would be a bad example
to women ever after; only I was capable of it!'

13 Then the woman with troubled heart sat down,
to recount her misery, her great griefs:

14 'I was brought up in the hall of princes
—most people rejoiced—according to men's counsel.

'I enjoyed my father's prosperity
for just five winters while my father lived.
15 Then he spoke of the highest matters,
the weary king, before he died:

'he said I should be endowed with red gold,
and given to the son of Grimhild in the south;

16 'and he commanded the helmet to be given to Brynhild,
he said she would be Odin's beloved girl.*
He said she should be reared as the most noble
girl in the world, unless fate intervened—

17 'Brynhild in the chamber worked at embroidery,
she had men and lands under her—
the earth resounded and the heaven,
when the slayer of Fafnir recognized the stronghold.

18 'Then war was fought with French swords
and the stronghold seized which Brynhild owned—
it was not long thereafter, rather it was pitifully soon,
that she knew all of their stratagems.

19 'Then she made harsh vengeance come about,
of that we have all had our fill:
that will be known to men in every land,
that she killed herself next to Sigurd!

20 'And I came to love Gunnar,
the giver of rings, as Brynhild ought to have.

21 'Soon they offered red-gold rings,
and no small compensation to my brother;
he offered for me fifteen farms,
the burden of Grani, if he wanted it.*

22 'But Atli said that he would never
want a dowry from the kin of Giuki.
Nor could we two struggle against our love,
so I leaned my head against the ring-breaker.*

23 'Many of my kin said
that we had been together;
but Atli said that I would not
act disgracefully or bring myself to shame.

24 'One cannot deny such things to another,
where love's involved!

25 'Atli sent his messengers
through the dark wood to test me out;
and they came where they should not have come,
where we spread for ourselves a single coverlet.

26 'Red-gold rings we offered to the warriors
that they should not tell Atli—
but they excitedly told Atli,
eagerly they hurried home.

27 'And they completely concealed it from Gudrun,
something she really ought to have known.

28 'Then the noise was heard of golden-hoofed horses,
when the heirs of Giuki rode into the courtyard;
out of Hogni they cut the heart,
and placed the other in the snake-pit.

29 'I'd just gone on that one occasion
to Geirmund, to brew beer for a feast;
the wise king began to play the harp,*
for he thought, the king of mighty lineage,
that I would come to help him.

30 'I heard it there in Hlesey,
how the strings were singing of strife;
I told my serving-maids to get ready,
I wanted to save the prince's life!

31 'We made the boat travel over the sea
until I saw all the courts of Atli.

32 'Then came the wicked one hurrying out,
the mother of Atli—may she shrivel away!—*
and she struck to Gunnar's heart
so that I could not protect the famous prince.

33 'Often I wonder how I can still—
goddess of the pillow—hold onto my life,*
when I thought that I loved the terribly brave man,
the sword-fighter as I loved myself!

34 'You sat and listened while I told you
many evil things about my fate and theirs.
Everyone lives by their desires—
now the weeping of Oddrun is over.'

· The Lay of Atli

In this tense, allusively told poem, the heroic deaths of Gunnar and Hogni are related. Atli, anxious to gain the treasure which had belonged to Sigurd, invites Gunnar and Hogni to visit him so he can capture them and force them to give him the treasure. After their deaths Gudrun takes a terrible revenge: like the Greek Procne she slaughters her children and feeds them to Atli and his warriors before killing Atli and burning down the hall. In German tradition Gudrun is the one determined to kill the brothers in revenge for the death of Sigurd; in Norse she is more loyal to her brothers than her husband. The *Lay of Atli* (*Atlakvida*) is likely to be one of the oldest in the *Edda*, the language sometimes elaborate, sometimes studiedly simple.

Gudrun, daughter of Giuki, avenged her brothers, as is very well known: first she killed Atli's sons, then she killed Atli and burned down the hall and all the courtiers. This poem was composed about it:

1 Atli sent a messenger to Gunnar,
a well-travelled man came riding, Knefrod was his name;
he came to the courts of Giuki and to Gunnar's hall,
the benches grouped around the hearth, and the
sweet-tasting beer.

2 The household all drank there—still they concealed their
thoughts in silence—
wine in the splendid hall, they anticipated the Huns'
hostility;
then Knefrod called out in a cold voice,
the man from the south—he sat on a high bench:

3 'Atli has sent me here, riding with a message,
on a horse gnashing at its bit, through Mirkwood the
unknown,
to invite you, Gunnar, you two, to come to our benches,*
with helmets grouped about the hearth, to visit Atli at
home.

4 'There you may both choose shields and smooth-planed ash spears,
golden helmets and a host of the Huns,
silver-gilt saddle-cloths, scarlet tunics,
lances with pennants, coursers gnashing at their bits.

5 'He said too that he would give you the plain of wide Gnita-heath,
whistling spears and gilded prows,
great treasures, farms on the Dneiper,
that famous forest which men call Mirkwood.'

6 Gunnar turned his head and said to Hogni:
'What do you advise, young man, when we hear of such things?
I didn't know of any gold on Gnita-heath*
that we did not own just as much.

7 'We have seven store-buildings full of swords,
each of them has a golden hilt;
I know my horse is the best, my blade the sharpest,
my bow graces the benches, and my corslets are of gold,
the brightest shield and helmet come from the emperor's hall;
one of mine is better than all of the Huns' might be.'

8 'What do you think the lady meant when she sent us a ring,
wrapped in the coat of the heath-wanderer? I think she was giving us a warning.*
I found a hair of the heath-wanderer twisted round the red-gold ring:
our way is wolf-beset if we go on this errand.'

9 No kinsman urged Gunnar, nor any close relative,
neither advisers nor counsellors, nor any powerful men;
Gunnar then said, as a king ought to,
splendid in his mead-hall, with great courage:

10 'Rise up now, Fiornir, send the golden goblets of the warriors
passing around the hall from hand to hand!

11 'The wolf will have control over the Niflungs' inheritance,
the old grey guardians, if Gunnar is going to be lost,
dull-coated bears will bite with vicious fangs,
make the bitch-pack rejoice if Gunnar does not return.'

12 The valiant troop, the men, weeping,
led forth the prince eager for war, from the young men's court;*
then said the young heir of Hogni:
'Go well now and wisely, where your spirit draws you.'

13 At full gallop the brave men spurred the bit-gnashing horses,
over the mountains, through unknown Mirkwood;
All the Hun borderlands shook as the resolute ones passed,
they drove the whip-shy horses over the green plains.

14 They saw the domain of Atli and thickly guarded watch-towers,
the warriors of Bikki standing on the high citadel,*
the hall towering over the southern folk encompassed with wooden benches,
with well-bound shields, shining targes,
lances with pennants, there Atli was drinking
wine in the splendid hall; the watchmen remained outside,
guarding against Gunnar, if they should come visiting
with whistling spears, making war against the prince.

15 Their sister very quickly perceived them come into the hall,
both her brothers, little beer had she drunk:
'Betrayed you are now, Gunnar; what, mighty lord, will help you
against the evil tricks of the Huns? Quickly, leave the hall!

16 'It would have been better, brother, if you'd come in a corslet,
with those helmets still grouped round the hearth, to see the home of Atli;
if you'd sat in the saddle all through sun-bright days,
made the norns weep at the pale, doomed corpses,*
taught Hun shield-maidens how to pull a plough,
and Atli himself you could have put in the snake-pit;
now that snake-pit is ready for you.'

17 'Too late now, sister, to collect the Niflungs,
a long time to wait for the arrival of a troop
of uncowardly men from the russet mountains of the Rhine.'*

18 They seized Gunnar and put him in fetters,
the friend of the Burgundians, and bound him fast.

19 Seven Hogni hacked down with a keen sword,
and the eighth he thrust into the hot fire;
so a brave man should defend himself against enemies,
as Hogni defended himself and Gunnar.

20 They asked the brave man, prince of the Goths,*
if he wanted to buy his life with gold.

21 'Hogni's heart must lie in my hand,
bleeding, cut out of the horseman's breast
with the sharp-biting knife from the prince's son.'

22 They cut the heart out of Hialli's breast,*
bleeding, laid it on a plate, and carried it to Gunnar.

23 Then said Gunnar, lord of men:
'Here I have the heart of Hialli the cowardly,
quite unlike the heart of Hogni the brave;
it quivers greatly as it lies on the plate;
it quivered twice as much when it was in the breast.'

24 Then Hogni laughed as they cut to his heart,
that living maker of mutilations, he never thought to cry out;
bleeding they laid it on a plate, and brought it to Gunnar.

25 Then Gunnar, the glorious lord of the Spear-Niflungs, said:
'Here I have the heart of Hogni the brave,
quite unlike the heart of Hialli the cowardly;
it scarcely quivers as it lies on the plate;
it did not quiver even that much when it was in the breast.

26 'Atli, now you'll be as far from my eyes*
as my jewels are going to be.
Now in me alone it is all concealed,
the hoard of the Niflungs, now Hogni is not alive.

27 'I was always in doubt while we were both alive,
now I am not, now I alone am living;
The Rhine shall rule over the strife-bringing metal,
the Æsir-given inheritance of the Niflungs,*
the splendid rings will gleam in the running water,
rather than the foreign rings shine on the hands of the Huns.'

28 'Drive out the chariot! now the captive is in chains.'*

29 Atli the powerful rode the horse with ringing mane,
surrounded by sword-armed men, their brother-in-law;
Gudrun of the line of heroes
struggled with her tears, left in the noisy hall.

30 'May it so befall you, Atli, as you gave in oath to Gunnar,
oaths you often swore and pledged early
by the sun curving to the south and the mountain of War-god,
by the marital bed and by Ull's ring.'

28 And on from there the ship of the bit*
drew the necklace-guardian warrior to death.

31 The living prince they placed in the pit
—a crowd of men did it—which was crawling
inside with snakes; and Gunnar, alone,
furiously struck his harp with his hand.*
The strings resounded; so should a brave ring-giver
guard his gold from enemies.

32 Atli turned his gravel-treading horse
towards his land, back from the murder;
there was a noise in the courtyard, crowded with horses,
men's weapon-song, they had come from the heath.

33 Out went Gudrun to meet Atli
with a golden goblet to render the prince his due:
'Lord, you may receive in your own hall,
gladly from Gudrun, little creatures gone into darkness.'*

34 Atli's ale-cups were ringing heavy with wine,
as all together in the hall the Huns assembled,
men with long moustaches, each one came in.

35 The bright-faced woman hastened to bring drink,
the terrible woman, to the nobles; she arranged morsels
with the ale
for the pale-faced men, then, sickened, she told his
shame to Atli.

36 'Your own sons'—sharer-out of swords—*
hearts, corpse-bloody, you are chewing up with honey;
you are savouring, proud lord, human flesh,
eating it as ale-appetizers and sending it to the high seat.

37 'You'll never again call to your knee
Erp or Eitil, two boys made merry with ale;
you'll not see them again amidst the seats,
generous with their gold, putting shafts on their spears,
trimming the manes or driving their horses.'

38 There was moaning on the benches, a terrible song of men,
howling under the battle-cloaks, the children of the Huns wept,
all but Gudrun, she who never wept
for her brothers fierce as bears and her dear sons,
young, innocent, whom she had with Atli.

39 Gold she scattered, the gosling-bright woman,
red-gold rings she gave to the house-servants;
she let fate culminate, and the shining metal flow,
she did not care at all, that lady, about the temple stores!

40 Unaware, Atli had drunk himself to exhaustion,
he had no weapon, he did not defend himself from Gudrun;
often their sport was better when they lovingly
would embrace each other frequently in front of the nobles.

41 With a sword-point she gave the bed blood to drink,
with a hand bent on death she loosed the dogs;
hurled before the hall doors a flaming brand; wakening the house-servants,
that bride made them pay for her brothers.

42 She gave to the fire all who were in there,
who after the death of Gunnar and Hogni had come from Mirkheim;
the ancient timbers fell, the temples went up in smoke,
the home of Budli's descendants, the shield-maids inside
burnt up, their lives stopped, they sank into the hot fire.

43 Now this story is all told; never since has a bride
in a byrnie acted so to avenge her brothers;
she brought death to three great kings,
that bright woman, before she died.

The 'Greenlandic Poem of Atli' tells this story more clearly.

The Greenlandic Poem of Atli

In comparison with the subtle and allusive style of the *Lay of Atli*, the *Greenlandic Poem of Atli* (*Atlamal*) is colloquial and idiomatic, closer to the prose sagas in tone. The protagonists live in farmsteads rather than great halls, and the action is localized in Denmark. Much of the poem is taken up with bickering between Gudrun and Atli, both reflecting on their marital disappointments. Atli is motivated by sheer enmity towards his brothers-in-law; lust for treasure plays no part. Otherwise, the story unfolds much as in the *Lay of Atli*, with some elaboration of the incident with Hialli into rather effective comedy. What the exact connection with Greenland was is unknown; clearly the compiler of the Codex Regius thought this poem had come from there and it seems quite likely that the harsh frontier conditions in the colony, so distant from the courtly world of Continental European literature, might have prompted the poem's recasting. The poem is composed in *malahattr*, a longer line which gives a sense of the story's leisurely unfolding.

1 People have heard of the enmity which happened long ago
when men met in counsel together, that was of benefit to very few;
they talked privately together, terror came of it afterward,
for them and for the sons of Giuki, who were utterly betrayed.

2 They brought the princes' fate to culmination—they should not have been doomed—
Atli was ill-advised, even though he had cunning;
he brought down a great support, injured himself terribly,
a hasty message he sent that his in-laws should come quickly.

3 The lady of the house was clever; she used her common sense,*
she heard what they were saying, though they spoke in secret;
the wise lady was at her wits' end, she wanted to help them,
they were going to sail over the sea, and she could not reach them.

4 She carved some runes, Vingi defaced them
—hastened on disaster—before he handed them over;
then they departed, the messengers of Atli,
over the Limfjord to where the courageous ones lived.

5 They were most welcoming, stoked up the fires,
they perceived no treachery in those who had come;
they accepted the gifts which the lovely lady had sent them,
hung them on the hall-pillar, did not think that significant.

6 Then came Kostbera, she was Hogni's wife,
a most circumspect woman, and greeted them both;*
and Glaumvor was also glad, who was married to Gunnar,
the wise lady was not discourteous, busied herself with the guests' needs.

7 Hogni they invited home, to see if the other one wished to come;
the duplicitous intention was clear if they'd been on their guard;
Gunnar said he'd come, if Hogni wished to,
Hogni didn't refuse if the other thought it best to go.

8 Pre-eminent women brought mead, much hospitality was shown,
many a horn went round until they had drunk enough.

9 The couple retired then, when they thought it time to do so.*
Kostbera had been taught, she knew how to interpret runes,
spelled out the letters in the light of the fire;
she held her tongue, bit back her words,
the runes were so confused they could scarcely be made out.

10 They went to bed then, Hogni and his wife;
the courtly lady had a dream, not at all did she conceal it,
the wise one told it to the prince as soon as she awoke:

11 'You intend to leave home, Hogni, listen to advice!
Few are very learned in runes—go some other time!
I interpreted the runes which your sister cut:
the radiant lady hasn't summoned you this time.

12 'I'm greatly surprised by one thing—I still can't make it out—
why the clever woman should carve so awry;
for they seemed to indicate an underlying meaning:
it would be the death of both of you if you hastened there now;
the lady's missed out a letter or else others have caused this.'

13 'All women think the worst,' said Hogni, 'I am not so inclined,
I shan't go looking for trouble unless there's something we have to pay them back for;
the prince will shower us with glowing red-gold arm-rings,
I am never afraid, though we hear dire things portended.'

14 'You'll meet your downfall if you set off there,
there's no loving welcome waiting for you this time.
I had a dream, Hogni, it's not concealed from me:
an evil fate will come upon you—or else I am simply too afraid.

15 'I dreamt your bedclothes were burning up in fire,
high flames were raging all through my buildings.'
'Here are linen garments lying, which have no value,
they'll soon be burnt up, as you saw the bedclothes burn.'*

17 'I thought I saw a bear come in here, smash up the panelling,
swing with his paws so that we were afraid;
many of us he held in his mouth so that we were helpless;
his lumbering made no small amount of noise.'

18 'That must mean a storm coming, it'll soon be dawn;
thinking of a white bear, that's a blizzard from the east.'*

19 'I thought I saw an eagle fly in here, all along the house,
something terrible will happen to us, he sprinkled us all with blood;
I thought from its threatening noise that it was the spirit of Atli.'

20 'We'll soon be slaughtering, then we'll see blood;
often it means oxen—dreaming of eagles;
Atli is well intentioned, whatever you dream.'
They left it at that, every conversation has an end.

21 The high-born ones awoke, they too had this example,
Glaumvor was anxious that there was disaster in her sleep;
Gunnar undertook that there were two ways of interpreting it.*

22 'I thought I saw gallows ready for you, you were to be hanged,
serpents gnawed at you, I lost you while you were still alive,
the doom of the gods came about; tell me what that meant!'

[Here a verse giving Gunnar's interpretation must have been omitted.]

24 'I thought a bloody sword was pulled out of your shirt,
it's painful to have to tell such a dream to a man so close to one;
I thought I saw a spear pierce right through you,
wolves were howling at both its ends.'

25 'That will be dogs running, barking a great deal,
the noise of dogs often stands for spears flying about.'

26 'I saw a river flowing through here, all along the house,
it roared in its course and crashed over the benches;
it broke the legs of both you brothers here,
nothing could stop the water—that must mean something.'

[Gunnar's reply is missing; the paraphrase in *Volsunga saga*, ch. 36, relates to cornfields.]

28 'I thought that dead women came here tonight,
they were not badly decked out, they wanted to choose you,
invite you very soon to their benches;
I declare that your *disir* are powerless to help you.'*

29 'It's too late to speak thus, all is now arranged;
I cannot escape this fate, since we intend to go;
everything seems to show that we haven't long to live.'

30 They saw it was getting light, said they were eager to get up,
though others wanted to detain them;
five journeyed together—another ten house-retainers
could have gone too—this was ill-advised.
Snævar and Solar, Hogni's sons,
Orkning the other was called who accompanied them,
Hogni's wife's brother, a cheerful shield-warrior.

31 The splendidly dressed ladies came too until the fjord separated them
the beautiful women kept dissuading them; they would not be prevented.

32 Glaumvor said, the wife of Gunnar,
she said to Vingi, since she felt it was warranted:
'I don't know if our feasting will be rewarded as we would wish;
the coming of a guest is a wickedness if something happens because of it.'

33 Then Vingi swore—he did not spare himself in this—
'May the giants seize this man if he lies to you,
may the gallows be ready for him if he should plot against your safety.'

34 Then Bera said, she felt cheerful:*
'Sail safely and achieve your errand victoriously!
Let it happen as I wish it, let no one contradict it.'

35 Hogni answered—he felt concern for his family—
'Be in good spirits, wise ladies, whatever happens!
Many say this—though often it turns out differently—
for many it makes no matter how they are accompanied from home.'

36 A long time they gazed before they turned away from each other;
I think their fates were laid down there when their ways parted.

37 Mightily they began to row, almost split the keel,
put their backs into the rowing, they became infuriated;
the oar-thongs snapped, the rowlocks shattered,
they didn't tie up the vessel before they left it behind.*

38 A little later—now I shall tell to the story's end—
they saw the buildings which Budli had owned;
loudly creaked the gate when Hogni hammered on it.

39 Then said Vingi, what he might have left unsaid,
'Go away from the house! It is dangerous to go near it,
soon I'll have destroyed you, shortly they'll hack you down;
I invited you here warmly but treachery lurked underneath,
or else you can wait here while I build you your gallows!'—

40 Then said Hogni—he didn't weigh his words much—
not one whit did he hesitate, as he afterwards proved:
'Don't try to frighten us, don't bother to keep talking!
If you drag out your words it will lengthen your miseries.'

41 They pushed Vingi aside and they knocked him into hell,
set about him with axes while he struggled for breath.

42 Atli and his men gathered, they put on their coats of mail,
when they were ready they went to the palisade;
they hurled insults at one another, all straightway stirred to fury:
'For a long time we've intended to take away your lives.'

43 'It doesn't really look as if you had decided any such thing;
you aren't even ready while we have struck down one,*
smashed him into hell, one of your number.'

44 Then they were furious when they heard these words,
moved their hands, caught hold of their javelin-loops,
they shot accurately, defending themselves with shields.

45 Inside they heard news of what was happening outside,
there was din before the hall: they heard a slave telling them.

46 Then Gudrun was wildly angry when she heard this terrible thing,
the necklaces weighing on her throat she hurled away from her entirely,
flung down the silver chain so all the links broke apart.

47 Then she went outside, flinging open the doors,
she advanced fearlessly to welcome the arrivals;
she embraced the Niflungs, it was the last time she greeted them,
heartfelt was her embrace, she added these words besides:

48 'I tried to give you protection by keeping you at home,
no one can defeat fate, and so you still came here.'
She spoke common sense to try to make peace between them,
they would not agree at all, both sides refused.

49 Then the high-born lady saw them play a wounding game,
she resolved on a hard course and flung off her cloak;
she took a naked sword and fought for her kinsmen's lives,
she was handy at fighting, wherever she aimed her blows.

50 Giuki's daughter brought down two fighters,
she struck at Atli's brother—he had to be carried thereafter:
she shaped her fighting so that she cut the leg from him.
51 Another she managed to strike so that he could not get up again,
she had him away into hell; nor did her hands tremble.

52 A battle came about there which was famous far and
wide;
that surpassed all others, what the children of Giuki
achieved;
people said of the Niflungs while they were still alive,
they'd lead their attack with swords, slash open
mail-coats,
hack at helmets, as their courage prevailed.

53 They fought most of the morning until midday came
and went,
all the dawn and the early day.
Before they'd fought to the end, the ground was awash
with blood;
eighteen, before they fell, they had overcome,
Kostbera's two boys and her brother.

54 Then the brave man began to speak, even though he
was enraged:*
'Terrible it is to look around us, you are to blame for this,
there were thirty formidable fighters,
now eleven remain alive, our men are decimated.

55 'There were four of us brothers when we lost Budli,
now Hel has half of us, two lie cut down there.

56 'Alliance with splendid men I made—I can't deny it—
I got a monstrous wife, I've had no benefit from it.
We've scarcely had any peace since you came among us,
you've deprived me of kinsmen, swindled me of property,
you sent my sister off to hell, that is what matters most
to me.'*

57 'Can you speak of such things, Atli, given what you've
already done:
you seized my mother and killed her, to have her treasure,
my wise cousin you starved to death in a cave;*
it seems to me cause for laughter when you recount
your injuries,
I thank the gods for it when things go badly for you.'

58 'I urge you, warriors, to greatly increase the grief
of this redoubtable woman; that I want to see;
do all you can to make Gudrun sob!
so that I might see her without a vestige of joy.

59 'Take Hogni and butcher him with a knife,
cut out his heart, be ready to do this;
Gunnar the fierce-spirited, string up on the gallows,*
hurry up with this—invite the snakes to come to him!'

Hogni said:

60 'Do as you wish, I'll cheerfully withstand it,
my courage you can test, I've borne sharper trials before;
you met some resistance when we were unwounded,
now we are injured you may do as you please.'

61 Beiti spoke—he was Atli's steward—
'Let's take Hialli and spare Hogni,
let's carry out a deed half done; he's fated for death,*
however long he lives, he'll always be called useless.'

62 The kettle-minder was terrified, he didn't stay in his place,
he knew how to be pusillanimous, he scrambled into every cranny;
said he was the wretched victim of their violence, to be thus rewarded for his hard work,
said it was a dark day for him to have to die and leave his pigs,
and all the fine provisions that he'd enjoyed before.

63 They took Budli's scullion and took out their knives,
the wicked slave howled before he felt the point;
said he would be at their disposal to dung the fields for them,
do the filthiest work, if that would improve his position;
Hialli said he'd be very glad if he could keep his life.

64 Hogni saw to this—few would act this way—
ensured that the slave would escape:
'I declare that for me it is a small matter to play this
game with you,
why would anyone here want to listen to his
screeching?'

65 Then they seized that great man, there was no chance
for the stout-hearted warriors to delay their action
longer;
Hogni laughed then so that the day-labourers heard it,*
he knew how to show his mettle and endured the
torture well.

66 Gunnar took his harp, moved it with his foot-twigs;*
plucked as well as he knew how to, so that the ladies
wept;
the men sobbed, those who heard it most clearly;
he related his fate to the powerful woman, so that the
rafters split.

67 Then the beloved men died, it was still early in the
day,
by their end they kept alive their fame for their
prowess.

68 Atli thought himself a great man, he had got the better
of both of them,
he told the wise woman of her loss and even taunted
her with it:
'Now it's morning, Gudrun, and you've lost those
faithful men,
you in part are to blame that this should be the result.'

69 'You're exultant now, Atli, you proclaim your murders,
regret will overcome you when you've lived to the end
of it all;
there will be a legacy—I can tell you truly of it:
evil will always befall you unless I die too.'

70 'I can't deny what you say: but I see another alternative,
twice as fitting—often we scorn what benefits us:
I'll comfort you with splendid treasure, with slave-girls,
snow-gleaming silver, just as you yourself desire.'

71 'There is no hope of this—I shall refuse these things,
I have broken agreements before for lesser reasons;
a demon I seemed before, I shall now improve on that,
I could endure everything while Hogni was still alive.

72 'We were brought up together in the same house,
we used to play games and we grew up in the grove;
Grimhild enriched us with gold and with neck-rings;
you can never compensate me for killing my brothers
nor ever bring me to be content with this.

73 'Women's lot is crushed by the dominion of men—
the trunk collapses when shorn of its branches,
a tree begins to topple if the root is cut from under it;
now you alone, Atli, wield all the power here.'

74 The prince's credulity was enough for him to believe this,
her treachery was clear if he had looked out for it.

Gudrun was impenetrable, she kept her own counsel,
pretended to be cheerful, played a double game.
75 She got ready a great ale-feast in memory of her brothers,
Atli agreed it should be held for his own men also.

76 They left matters so. The drink was brewed;
that was a banquet resulting in great turmoil;
fierce was her strong temperament, she maimed the line of Budli,
upon her husband she intended all-encompassing revenge.

77 She enticed the little ones to her and held them against the bedpost;
the fierce children were aghast but they did not cry,
they came into their mother's arms and asked what was intended.

78 'Don't ask any more! I'm going to destroy you both,
I've long wanted to cure you of old age.'
'Sacrifice, if you wish, your children, no one will prevent you,
your anger will not be slaked for long if you carry this out.'*

79 She ended then the brothers' childhood, that formidable woman,
acted fatefully, cut both their throats.
Then Atli asked where his boys had gone
playing their games, since he could not see them anywhere.

80 'I intend to go over to tell Atli.*
Grimhild's daughter will not conceal it from you;
it won't gladden you in the slightest, Atli, when you find out all.
A great disaster you stirred up when you killed my brothers.

81 'I've hardly slept since they died,
I promised you a grim reward, now I'm reminding you of it;
you said it was morning to me—I remember it so clearly—
and now it's evening, you must hear similar news.

82 'Your boys you have lost, as you ought never to have done.
You know, their skulls you had for ale-goblets.*
I augmented your drink by mixing it with their blood.

83 'I took their hearts and roasted them on a spit,
gave them to you—told you they were calf-meat;
you made all this happen, you wouldn't leave any scraps,
chewed it up greedily, relying on your back teeth.

84 'Now you know about your children—few could ask to hear worse—
I have chosen my course, this is no empty boasting.'

85 'You were savage, Gudrun, to be able to do such a thing,
to mix the blood of your children for me to drink;
you have wiped out your kindred, the last thing you should have done,
you give me little rest between the horrors.'

86 'Had I still one more wish, it would be to kill you,
few things are wicked enough to do to such a prince;
you've already committed, in a way that's unexampled,
foolishness and cruelty in this world;
now you've added to what we'd heard before,
seized this great crime, prepared your own funeral feast.'

87 'You should be burned on a pyre, and before that be stoned to death,
then you'll have got what you've been begging for.'
'Recount such sorrows to yourself early tomorrow morning!
I'll be journeying to a better place with a more splendid death.'

88 They sat in the same building, directing rancorous thoughts at each other,
threw out hateful words, neither was happy.

Hatred grew in Hniflung's heart, he was thinking of a great stratagem,*
he let Gudrun know that he felt loathing for Atli.

89 Then came into her mind the dealings with Hogni,
she said it would be his good fortune if he could bring about revenge;
then Atli was killed, little time did they wait,
Hogni's son struck him and Gudrun herself.

90 The brave man began to speak, dragged himself out of sleep,
realized at once he was wounded, he said he had no need of bandages:
'Tell me most truthfully: who has struck down Budli's son?
No little trick you've played on me, I reckon I've no hope of life.'

91 'Grimhild's daughter will not conceal from you:
I declare I brought it about that your life is over,
Hogni's son had some part in it—that your wounds weary you so.'

92 'You have waded deep into killing, though it was not right;
it is wrong to betray a friend who trusted you well.

'I left home, persuaded to woo you, Gudrun;
93 you were a highly esteemed widow, they said you were capable of great deeds,
there was no hope of a lie in that—as we discovered.
You came home here, an army of men came with us,
all our customs here were glorious.

94 'All the honour was here that distinguished men should have,
we had plenty of cattle, made great use of them;
we had great wealth, which we gave out to many.

95 'I paid a dowry for a famous bride to get a great deal of treasure,
thirty slaves and seven good slave-women
—it was honourable to do such—there was even more silver.

96 'You said that all this seemed as nothing to you,
while those lands lay unclaimed, my inheritance from Budli;
you undermined us so, you managed to get your share;
your mother-in-law you often made sit and weep,
no good-heartedness did I ever find in our household again.'

97 'You are lying now, Atli, though I don't really care;
I was hardly ever docile but you lorded it greatly.
You young brothers fought each other, sent strife round amongst yourselves,
half your line were sent off to Hel.
Everything which we should have enjoyed collapsed and disappeared.

98 'We were three brothers and a sister, we seemed to be unconquerable,
we left our country and went with Sigurd;
we hastened our ships onwards, each of us captained one,*
we roamed where our fate led us, until we came to the east.

99 'First we killed a king there, chose land in that place;
earls submitted to us—this demonstrated their fear;
by fighting we brought from outlawry those we wished to rescue,
we gave any man a fortune who had no wealth of his own.

100 'The southern prince died, my luck was speedily destroyed;
bitter torment it was for a young girl to be given the name of widow;
it seemed anguish for a survivor to come to Atli's house;
I had been married to a hero before—that was a cruel loss.

101 'You never came back from the Assembly—or so we heard—
having prosecuted a case or crushed an adversary's;
you always wanted to yield, you'd never stand firm in any matter,
you'd quietly let things be.'

102 'Now you're lying, Gudrun: that won't much improve
the fate of either of us—we have all suffered injury.
Now, Gudrun, out of kindness,
act in keeping with our honour when they carry me out.'

103 'I will buy a ship and a painted coffin,*
I shall wax the shroud well to enclose your corpse,
I'll consider all that's needful as if we were united.'

104 Atli became a corpse, made his kin's anguish grow.
The splendidly born lady did all as promised;
Gudrun the wise tried to kill herself—
but the days were long drawn out; she died on another day.

105 Fortunate is any man who afterwards can father
such heroic children as Giuki fathered.
After them in every land
their defiance lives on wherever people hear of it.

The Whetting of Gudrun

There are clearly close affinities between the *Whetting of Gudrun* (*Gudrunarhvot*) and the *Lay of Hamdir*, which follows it. They open with the same scene: Gudrun urging her sons by Ionakr to set out to the court of Iormunrekk to avenge the death of their sister. While the *Lay of Hamdir* follows the brothers' adventure, the *Whetting of Gudrun* stays with the heroine while she laments her past woes. At the close of the poem, once again, she seems intent on death.

When Gudrun had killed Atli she went to the sea, she waded out into the water and wanted to drown herself but she could not sink. She drifted across the fjord to the land of King Ionakr who married her.

Their sons were Sorli and Erp and Hamdir. Svanhild, Sigurd's daughter, was brought up there. She was married to Iormunrekk the powerful. Bikki was at his court. He advised that Randver, the king's son, ought to marry her, and then he told the king this.* The king had Randver hanged and Svanhild trampled under the feet of horses. And when Gudrun heard this, she spoke to her sons.*

1 Then I heard quarrelling of the most violent sort,*
speech uttered strongly out of great grief,
when the fierce-spirited Gudrun whetted for the fight,
with grim words, her sons.

2 'Why do you sit, why do you sleep away your life?
Why aren't you unhappy when you speak of cheerful things?
—since Iormunrekk your sister,
still so young, trampled with horses,
white and black, on the paved road,
with the grey horses of the Goths, trained to pace slowly.

3 'You haven't become like Gunnar and his brother,
nor any the more been brave as Hogni was—
you would have tried to avenge her,
if you had the temperaments of my brothers
or the fierce spirits of the kings of the Huns.'

4 Then said Hamdir, the strong-minded one:
'Little did you praise the achievement of Hogni,
when they awakened Sigurd from his sleep.
Your embroidered coverlets, the blue and white ones,
were red with your husband's blood, drenched in the blood of the murder.

5 'Vengeance for your brothers was wounding and painful
to you when you murdered your sons.
We could all have avenged on Iormunrekk*
our sister, all of the same mind.

6 'Bring out the treasures of the kings of the Huns.
You have stirred us up to a meeting of swords.'

7 Laughing, Gudrun went to the store-room,
she chose from the coffers the insignia of kings,
broad mail-coats, and took them to her sons.
Stirred to bravery they leapt on horseback.

8 Then said Hamdir, the strong-minded one:
'So will the spear-warrior come home to visit his mother,
brought low in the land of the Goths,
so that you may drink the funeral ale for us all,
for Svanhild and for your sons.'

9 Weeping, Gudrun, the daughter of Giuki,
went sorrowfully to sit on the threshold
and to recount, with tears on her face,
grievous stories, many times:

10 'Three fires have I known, three hearths have I known,
to three husbands' houses I was brought.
Sigurd alone for me was better than all others,
whom my brothers did to death.

11 'A heavier, more painful wound I have not seen nor felt—
yet they intended to hurt me more
when the princes gave me to Atli.

12 'My sharp young boys I called to secret counsel.
I could not get remedy for my wrongs
before I lopped off the heads of the Hniflungs.

13 'I went to the sea-strand, I was enraged with the norns;
I wanted to rush from their violent storms.
Great waves lifted me, did not drown me—
so I came to the land, I had to go on living.

14 'I entered the bed—I'd hoped for something better for myself—
for thc third time of a nation's king.
I had children, legal heirs,
legal heirs in Ionakr's sons.

15 'Then still with Svanhild sat her maids,
the one of my children whom I loved best with all my heart,
Svanhild in my hall
was like an illustrious ray of the sun.

16 'I dressed her in gold and splendid garments
before I gave her to the people of the Goths.
That was the cruellest of all my injuries,
when the white-blonde hair of Svanhild
in the mud they trod under the horses' hooves.

17 'And the most agonizing when they killed my Sigurd,
robbed him of victory, in our bed;
and the most terrible when the gleaming snakes
crept towards Gunnar's life;
and the sharpest when they cut to the heart
of the king, unafraid, they sliced into the living man.

18 'I remember many wrongs...

19 'Bridle, Sigurd, the dark-coloured, shining horse,
the swift-footed charger—let it gallop here.
Here there does not sit a daughter-in-law or daughter
who might give treasure to Gudrun.

20 'Do you recall, Sigurd, what we promised,
when we two lay in bed together,
that, brave warrior, you would visit me from hell,
and I would come to you from the world.

21 'Nobles, build high the oak-wood pyre!*
Let it be the highest under the heaven.
May fire burn up the breast so full of wrongs,
may sorrows melt, heavy about the heart.

22 'To all warriors—may your lot be made better;
to all ladies—may your sorrows grow less,
now this chain of griefs has been recounted.'

The Lay of Hamdir

This poem completes the story of the descendants of Gudrun with the two brothers, Hamdir and Sorli, dispatched by their mother to avenge the death of their sister. Thought to be amongst the oldest poems in the *Edda*, the *Lay of Hamdir* (*Hamdismal*) is defective in places and has some verses out of order, and strange, archaic diction. The story is allusively told; the brothers meet their half-brother on the way to Iormunrekk's court. He offers them help in riddling terms which they misunderstand, and they kill him. Thanks to their magical invulnerability, the brothers have surprising success in their revenge, maiming Iormunrekk and burning his severed limbs. It is only when Iormunrekk screams out the answer to their invulnerability—stoning them—that they realize why they needed their brother. He would have known to cut off the head and have silenced the king. The theme of hands and feet, the metaphor used in Erp's proverbial riddle, is taken up again in the torture scene.

1 There sprang up on the threshold grievous actions,
to make elves weep, their joy dammed up;*
early in the morning the wicked deeds of men,
every misery, kindle sorrow.

2 It was not today nor yesterday,
a long time has passed since then,
—few things are so long ago that this is not twice so long—
when Gudrun born of Giuki urged
her young sons to avenge Svanhild:

3 'Your sister—Svanhild was her name—
she whom Iormunrekk trampled with horses,
white and black, on the paved road,
with the grey horses, trained to pace slowly, of the Goths.

4 'You are thrust back, you great kings,
the last living strand of my lineage.

5 'I have come to stand alone like an aspen in the forest,
my kinsmen cut away as a fir's branches,
bereft of happiness, as a wood of its leaves,
when a girl cutting branches comes on a warm day.'

6 Then said Hamdir the strong-minded one:*
'Little did you praise the achievement of Hogni,
when they awakened Sigurd from sleep,
you sat in the bed and the killers laughed.

7 'Your embroidered coverlets, the blue and white ones,
woven by craftsmen, were red with your husband's blood.
There Sigurd died, you sat over the dead man,
gave no thought to happiness. That's what Gunnar thought up for you.

8 'Atli you intended to hurt by Erp's death
and by the loss of Eitil, but it was even worse for you;
every man should bring about death for others,
with a sword that bites into wounds, so that he does not hurt himself.'

9 Sorli said—he had good sense—
'I do not want to bandy words with mother;
each of you two thinks there's more to be said:
what are you asking for now, Gudrun, the lack of which makes you weep?

10 'Weep for your brothers and your dear sons,
close-born kinsmen, brought to strife;
for us both, Gudrun, you shall weep too,
we who sit here, doomed men on our horses; far from here we'll die.'

11 They went out of the courtyard, roaring in rage;
the young men then travelled over the wet mountains,
on the Hun-bred horses, to avenge the murder.

12 They met on the road a man full of clever stratagems:
'How can this swarthy dwarf give us any help?'

13 The son of a different mother answered, said he would give help*
to his kinsmen, as one foot does another.
'How can a foot help a foot,
or a hand made of flesh help a hand?'

14 Then Erp said—he spoke once only—
splendidly he pranced on the horse's back:
'It's no good showing the way to a cowardly man.'
They said the bastard was very confident.

15 They pulled from their sheaths the sheathed iron,
the edges of the sword, to the joy of the troll-woman;*
they diminished their might by a third,
they made the young lad sink to the ground.

16 They shook their fur cloaks, fastened on their swords,
the descendants of the gods put on splendid garments.

17 The roads lay ahead, they found the dreary path
and their sister's son wounded on the gallows,*
the wind-cold wolf-tree west of the settlement;
the incitement to cranes was bobbing about; it was not pleasant to remain there.

18 There was merriment in the hall, men made glad with ale,
and they did not hear the horses at all,
until an attentive man blew his horn.

19 They went to tell Iormunrekk
that men in helmets had been sighted:
'Think of some plan, princes have come,
the girl you trampled has powerful kindred.'

20 Iormunrekk laughed then, he smoothed his beard,
he looked forward to the violence, made battle-bold by wine;
he shook his dark hair, glanced at his shining shield,
he dangled in his hand the golden cup.

21 'Happy I'd think myself, if I were to see
Hamdir and Sorli in my hall;
I should tie up the boys with bow-sinews,
string the good sons of Giuki up on the gallows.'

22 Then spoke Hrodglod, who stood on the chamber threshold,*
the slender-fingered one said to that young man:
'Now they promise that which they cannot achieve—
can two men alone against ten hundred Goths
bind them or fight against them in the high fortress?'

23 There was tumult in the hall, ale-cups shattered,
men lay in blood shed from the breasts of Goths.

24 Then said Hamdir the strong-minded:
'You were looking forward, Iormunrekk, to our arrival,
brothers born of the same mother, coming into your citadel.
You see your own feet, you see your own hands,
Iormunrekk, hurled into the hot fire.'

25 Then the man roared, the one versed in powerful magic,
the lord in his mail-coat, roared as a bear roars:
'Stone the men, since spears will not bite on them,*
neither edges nor iron, on Ionakr's sons.'

[*Then said Hamdir the strong-minded*]:*

26 'Evil you brought about, brother, when you opened up that bag,*
for often from a bag comes bad advice.

27 'You'd have had a mind, Hamdir, if you'd known how to think;
much is lacking in a man when he lacks any common sense.'

28 'Off his head would be now, if Erp were alive,*
our brother bold in battle, whom we killed on the road,
the man so fierce in war—the *disir* urged me to do it—*
the man inviolate in fighting—they drove me to it.'

29 'I don't think it is for us to follow the wolves' example
and fight among ourselves, like the dogs of the norns,
reared up in the wilderness, those greedy beasts.

30 'We have fought well, we stand on Goth corpses,
weary from the sword-edge like eagles on a branch;
we have won great glory if we die now or yesterday,
after the norns have given their verdict, no man outlasts the evening.'

31 Then Sorli fell at the end of the hall,
and Hamdir sank behind the house.

That is called the ancient 'Lay of Hamdir'.

Baldr's Dreams

Alarmed by Baldr's bad dreams the Æsir send Odin down to Hel to seek an explanation. At the edge of Hel's kingdom Odin awakens a dead prophetess who tells him what he needs to know, that Baldr will soon be killed by his brother Hod. Odin ends the conversation by asking for a piece of mythological information which reveals his true identity to the prophetess. *Baldr's Dreams* (*Baldrs draumar*), like the poems which follow, is not found in the Codex Regius, but in another manuscript containing a number of fragmentary poems in the Eddic style.

1 All together the Æsir came in council*
and all the Asynior to speak together,
and what they talked of, those powerful gods,
was why Baldr was having sinister dreams.

2 Up rose Odin, the sacrifice for men,*
and on Sleipnir he laid a saddle;
down he rode to Mist-hell,
there he met a dog coming from hell.*

3 Bloody it was on the front of its chest
and long it barked at the father of magic;
on rode Odin, the road resounded,
he approached the high hall of Hel.

4 Then Odin rode by the eastern doors,
where he knew the seeress's grave to be;
he began to speak a corpse-reviving spell for the wise woman,*
until reluctantly she rose, spoke these corpse-words:

5 'Which man is that, unknown to me,
who is making me travel this difficult road?
I was snowed upon, I was rained upon,
dew fell on me, dead I've been for a long time.'

6 'Way-tame is my name, I'm the son of Slaughter-tame;
tell me the news from hell—I know what's happening in the world:
for whom are the benches decked with arm-rings,
the dais so fairly strewn with gold?'

7 'Here the mead stands, brewed for Baldr,
the shining liquid, a shield hangs above,
and despair over the Æsir.
Reluctantly I told you, now I'll be silent.'

8 'Don't be silent, prophetess! I want to question you,
until I know everything, I still want to know more:
who will be Baldr's killer
and who'll steal the life from Odin's son?'

9 'Hod will dispatch the famous warrior to this place;*
he will be Baldr's killer
and steal the life from Odin's son.
Reluctantly I told you, now I'll be silent.'

10 'Don't be silent, prophetess! I want to question you,
until I know everything, I still want to know more:
who will bring about vengeance on Hod for this wickedness,
who will bring Baldr's killer to the funeral pyre?'

11 'Rind will give birth to Vali in western halls,*
Odin's son will fight when one night old;
he won't wash his hands nor comb his hair,
until he's brought to the pyre Baldr's enemy.
Reluctantly I told you, now I'll be silent.'

12 'Don't be silent, prophetess! I want to question you,
until I know everything, I still want to know more:
who are those girls who weep for love*
and who throw up to the sky the corners of their head-dresses?'

13 'You are not Way-tame, as I thought,
rather you are Odin, the ancient sacrifice.'
'You are not a prophetess nor a wise woman,
rather you're the mother of three ogres.'

14 'Ride home, Odin, and be proud of yourself!
No more men will come to visit me,
until Loki is loose, escaped from his bonds,
and the Doom of the Gods, tearing all asunder,
approaches.'*

The List of Rig

The *List of Rig* (*Rigsthula*) tells how the god Heimdall sets out to create the structures of human society. He calls at three houses, observes the way of life there—dull and peasant-like, skilled and practical, noble and courtly respectively—and receives the hospitality of the couple in each house. Heimdall (Rig) sleeps between them in their bed that night. Later a child is born to the parents: to the first couple, Thrall, the lowest labourer; to the second couple, Farmer; to the third, Lord. These are the progenitors of each class, each marrying a suitable wife and producing a bevy of children with symbolic names to continue the line. The poem is incomplete, but the line of Lord seems to culminate in the birth of 'King', the youngest son. Where the poem breaks off, the boy destined for kingship is about to embark on conquering other territories, at the urging of a wise bird.

People say in the old stories that one of the Æsir, who was called Heimdall, went on a journey, and as he went along the sea-shore somewhere he came to a household and he called himself Rig. This poem is about that story.*

1 Long ago they say that along the green roads
a powerful, mature, and knowledgeable god went walking,
mighty and vigorous, Rig stepping along.

2 Further on he went walking in the middle of the roads,
he came to a house, the door was ajar;
in he stepped, there was a fire on the floor;
a couple sat there, grey-haired, by the hearth,
Great-grandfather and Great-grandmother
in an old-fashioned head-dress.

3 Rig was able to give them some advice;
moreover he sat in the middle of the bench,
and the couple of the household on either side.

4 Then Great-grandmother brought a coarse loaf,*
thick and heavy, stuffed with grain;
and she set too in the middle of the table
boiled meat in the bowls, put on the platter;
it was boiled calf-meat, the best of delicacies;
he got up from there, got ready to sleep.

5 Rig was able to give them some advice;
on top of that he lay in the middle of the bed,
with the couple of the household on either side.

6 There he was for three nights together;
then away from there he went in the middle of the roads,
nine months passed after that.

7 Great-grandmother had a baby, poured water over it,*
dark as flax, they called it Thrall.

8 He began to grow and to thrive well;
on his hands there was wrinkled skin,
crooked knuckles,
thick fingers, he had an ugly face,
a crooked back, long heels.

9 But also he began to grow in strength,
to weave bast rope to make baskets.
Brushwood he carried home the whole day long.

10 Then there came to the farm a bandy-legged girl;
she had mud on her soles, her arms were sunburned,
her nose was bent, her name was Slavegirl.

11 And then she sat in the middle of the bench;
the son of the house sat next to her;
they talked and they whispered, they went to bed together,
Thrall and Slavegirl, through hard-working days.

12 Children they had, they lived and they were happy;
I think they were called Weatherbeaten and Stableboy,
Stout and Sticky, Rough, Badbreath,
Stumpy, Fatty, Sluggard and Greyish,
Lout and Longlegs; they established farms,
put dung on the fields, worked with swine,
looked after goats, dug the turf.

13 Their daughters were Stumpina and Podgy,
Bulgy-calves and Bellows-nose,
Noisy and Bondwoman, Great-gabbler,
Raggedy-hips and Crane-legs.
From them are descended all the race of slaves.

14 Rig went on along the straight roads;
he came to a hall, the door was on the latch.
In he stepped, a fire was on the floor,
a couple sat there; they kept on working.

15 The man was whittling wood for a cross-beam.
His beard was trimmed, his hair above his brows,
his shirt close-fitting, there was a chest on the floor.

16 On it sat a woman, spinning with a distaff,
stretching out the thread, preparing for weaving;
a head-dress was on her head, a smock on her body,
a kerchief round her neck, brooches at her shoulders.
Grandfather and Grandmother keeping house.

17 Rig was able to give them advice;*
. . . .

(19) He rose from the table, got ready for bed;
on top of that he lay in the middle of the bed,
with the couple of the household on either side.

20 There he was for three nights together;
then away from there he went in the middle of the roads,
nine months passed after that.

21 Grandmother had a baby, poured water over it,
the woman swaddled it, red and rosy,
with lively eyes; they called it Farmer.

22 He began to grow and to thrive well;
he tamed oxen, worked the harrow,
he built houses and threw up barns,
made carts and drove the plough.

23 Then they drove home the woman with keys at her belt,
in a goatskin kirtle, married her to Farmer,
Daughter-in-law she was called, she wore a bridal veil;
the couple settled down together, exchanged rings,*
spread the bed-coverlets, made a household together.

24 Children they had, they lived and they were happy,
called Man and Soldier, Lad, Thane and Smith,
Broad, Yeoman, Boundbeard,
Dweller, Boddi, Smoothbeard and Fellow.

25 And these were called by other names:
Lady, Bride, Sensible, Wise, Speaker,
Dame, Fanny, Wife, Shy, Sparky,
from them descend all the race of farmers.

26 Rig went on along the straight roads;
he came to a hall, the doors looked south,
the door was half-open, there was a ring on the latch.

27 In he stepped, the floor was strewn with straw;
there sat the couple looking into one another's eyes,*
Father and Mother, busy with their fingers.

28 There sat the householder and twisted bow-strings,
bent elm, shaped arrows,
and the lady of the house was admiring her arms,
stroking the material, straightening the sleeves.

29 Her head-dress was set straight, there was a pendant on
her breast,
a short, full cape and a blue-stitched blouse;
her brow was brighter, her breasts more shining,
her neck was whiter than freshly fallen snow.

30 Rig was able to give them some advice;
moreover he sat in the middle of the bench,
and the couple of the household on either side.

31 Then Mother took an embroidered tablecloth,
of white linen, covered the table,
then she brought a fine loaf,
of white flour, and put it on the cloth.

32 She set out full dishes,
chased with silver, put them on the table,
dark and light pork-meat and roast birds;
there was wine in the cups, ornamented goblets;
they drank and they chatted, the day drew to a close.

33 Rig was able to give them some advice;
up he rose, got ready for bed;
there he was for three nights together;
then away from there he went in the middle of the
roads,
nine months passed after that.

34 Mother gave birth to a boy, wrapped him in silk,
poured water over him, had him named Lord;
blond was his hair, bright his cheeks,
piercing were his eyes like a young snake's.

35 Lord grew up there in the hall;
he began to brandish shields, fit bow-strings,
bend the elm bow, shape arrows,
hurl javelins, throw French spears,
ride horses, hunt with hounds,
wield a sword, practise swimming.

36 Then came Rig walking,
walking out of the thicket, taught him runes;
gave him a name, said he was his son;
then he told him to get ancestral property,
to get ancestral property, a long-established settlement.

37 Moreover he rode through the dark wood,
over the frost-covered mountains, until he came to a hall,
he hurled the shafted spear, brandished his linden shield,
made his horse gallop, wielded his sword;
he started a war, he reddened the plain with blood,
dead men fell, he fought for the land.

38 He alone then ruled eighteen settlements.
He began to use his wealth, offered to everyone
treasures and gifts, lean-ribbed horses,
squandered his rings, hacked up arm-rings.

39 Messengers came over the dewy roads,
came to the hall where Chieftain lived,
he had there the slender-fingered girl,
radiant and wise, they called her Erna.

40 They asked for her hand and home they drove her,
married her to Lord, she wore the bridal veil,
they lived together, loved one another,
raised a clan and enjoyed their lives.

41 Son was the eldest and Child the second,
Baby and Noble, Heir and Offspring,
Descendant and Kinsman—they played together—
Sonny and Lad—at swimming and chequers—
Lineage one was called, Kin was the youngest.

42 Lord's children grew up there,
tamed horses, brandished shields,
practised shooting, used ash spears.

43 But young Kin knew runes,*
life-runes and fate-runes;
and he knew how to help in childbirth,
deaden sword-blades, quiet the ocean.

44 He understood birds' speech, quenched fires,
pacified and quietened men, made sorrows disappear,
had the strength and vigour of eight men.

45 He contended in rune-wisdom with Lord Rig,
he knew more tricks, he knew more;
then he gained and got the right
to be called Rig and to know the runes.*

46 Young Kin rode through woods and thickets,
shooting bird-arrows, charming down the birds.

47 Then a crow said—it was sitting on a branch—
'Why, young Kin, are you charming down birds?
Rather you ought to be riding horses,
conquering armies.

48 'Dan and Danp own precious halls,
worthier territories than your clan own;
they know very well how to steer ships,
to assess a sword blade, to make red wounds.'

The Song of Hyndla

The *Song of Hyndla* (*Hyndluliod*) is two poems in one. The main story concerns the goddess Freyia who is anxious to assist her protégé Ottar in gaining his inheritance against the competing claims of someone called Angantyr. In order to do this Ottar needs to know all about his ancestry. Freyia disguises him as the pig with golden bristles, Battleswine, on which she rides and brings him to the giantess Hyndla to elicit the information he seeks. Freyia tries to flatter the giantess, calling her 'sister'; after some initial sparring the giantess settles down to recount the ancestors of Ottar. At verse 29 an interpolation, often known as the *Short Prophecy of the Seeress* (*Voluspa in skamma*), begins, listing the Æsir and referring very unclearly to 'one who is greater than all' who will come after Odin, conceivably an allusion to Christ. The poem concludes with further bickering between the goddess and the giantess. Little is known about most of the figures mentioned in the *Song of Hyndla*; where more information exists it is given in the notes.

This is the beginning of the 'Song of Hyndla', told about Ottar the foolish.

1 'Wake up, girl of girls, wake up, my friend,
Hyndla, sister, who lives in the rock cave!
Now it's the darkest of darkness, we two shall ride
to Valhall, to the sacred sanctuary.

2 'Let us ask Odin, lord of hosts, to be kindly to us,
he gives and pays out gold to the retinue;
he gave Hermod a helmet and corslet,
and to Sigmund a sword to keep.

3 'He gives victory to some, to some riches,
eloquence to many, and common sense to men;
he gives following winds to sailors, turns of phrase to poets,
he gives manliness to many a warrior.

4 'I must sacrifice to Thor, I must ask for this,*
that he should always be kindly towards you;
though he doesn't much care for giant women.

5 'Now take one of your wolves out of the stable,*
let him race beside my boar!'
'Your boar is slow at treading the paths of the gods;
I don't want to exhaust my excellent steed.

6 'Deceitful you are, Freyia, when you question me,
when you look at me that way,
when you're taking your lover on the way to Valhall,
young Ottar, son of Innstein.'

7 'You're confused, Hyndla, you must be dreaming,
when you say my lover is on the road to Valhall;
there my boar is glowing with his golden bristles,
Battleswine, whom those skilful dwarfs,
Dain and Nabbi, made for me.*

8 'Let's dismount to argue about this! We should sit down,
and talk about the lineage of princes,
about those men who are descended from the gods.

9 'They have wagered foreign gold,
young Ottar and Angantyr;
it's necessary to help, so that the young warrior
should get his inheritance from his kinsmen.

10 'He's made an altar for me, faced with stone,
now that stone has turned to glass;*
he's reddened the new altar with ox blood,
Ottar has always trusted in the Asynior.

11 'Now let's count up the ancestors
and the lineage of men born from them:
which are of the Skioldungs, which are of the Skilfings,
which are of the Odlings, which are of the Ylfings,*
which are born of farming stock, which are born of
fighting stock,
the greatest choice of men on the face of the earth?'

12 'You, Ottar, were son of Innstein,
and Innstein of Alf the old,
Alf of Ulf, Ulf of Sæfari,
and Sæfari from Svan the red.

13 'Your father had a mother adorned with necklaces,
I think her name was Hledis the priestess,
Frodi was their father, and Friaut the mother,
all that line is thought to be most superior.

14 'Ali was previously the most powerful of men,
highest among the Skioldungs, before Halfdan;
famous were the battles which they brought about,
his deeds were well known under heaven's vault.

15 'He made a mighty alliance with Eymund, best of men,
and he killed Sigtrygg with icy sword-edges;
he went to marry Almveig, best of women,
they had, they nurtured, eighteen sons.

16 'From them come the Skioldungs, from them the Skilfings,
from them the Odlings, from them the Ynglings,
from them the farming stock, from them the fighting stock,
the greatest choice of men on the face of the earth;
all these are your kin, Ottar the foolish.

17 'Hildigunn was her mother,*
child of Svava and Sækonung;
all these are your kin, Ottar the foolish;
it's important that you know it, do you want to know more?

18 'Dag married Thora, mother of champions;
mighty fighters sprang from that lineage:
Fradmar and Gyrd and both the Frekis,
Am and Iosurmar, Alf the old;
it's important that you know it,
do you want to know more?

19 'Ketil was their friend, heir of Klypp,
he was the maternal grandfather of your mother;
there Frodi came before Kari,
the elder son begotten by Alf.

20 'Nanna came next, Nokkvi's daughter,
her son was your father's brother-in-law;
forgotten is that kinship; I can recite further back.
I knew both Brodd and Horvir;
all these are your kin, Ottar the foolish.

21 'Isolf and Asolf, sons of Olmod
and of Skurhild, Skekkil's daughter;
you must count up a large number of men;
all these are your kin, Ottar the foolish.

22 'Gunnar the bulwark, Grim the inheritor,
Thorir Ironshield, Ulf the gaper.

23 'Bui and Brami, Barri and Reifnir,
Tind and Tyrfing and the two Haddings;*
all these are your kin, Ottar the foolish.

24 'Ani, Omi were both born
sons of Arngrim and Eyfura;
the din of the berserkers and all sorts of wickedness,
on land and on sea sped like flame;
all these are your kin, Ottar the foolish.

25 'I knew both Brodd and Horvir,
they were retainers of Hrolf the old,
all the children of Iormunrekk,
the kinsman by marriage of Sigurd—listen to my account—
of the grim fighter who slew Fafnir.

26 'He was a prince descended from Volsungs
and Hiordis from Hraudung,*
and Eylimi of the Odlings;
all these are your kin, Ottar the foolish.

27 'Gunnar and Hogni, heirs of Giuki,
and likewise Gudrun, their sister;
Guthorm was not of the line of Giuki,*
though he was brother of both of them;
all these are your kin, Ottar the foolish.

28 'Harald Battletooth, born of Hrœrek,
generous hurler of rings, he was son of Aud,
Aud the deep-minded, daughter of Ivar,
and Radbard was the father of Randver;
they were men blessed by the gods;
all these are your kin, Ottar the foolish.'

29 ['Eleven were the Æsir when all counted up,*
Baldr has slumped against a death-hummock;
Vali was born to avenge this,
the death of his brother, he slew the killer;
all these are your kin, Ottar the foolish.

30 'Baldr's father was heir to Bur,*
Freyr married Gerd, she was Gymir's daughter,
of the giant race, and Aurboda's;*
though Thiazi was their kinsman,
the giant who loved to shoot; Skadi was his daughter.

31 'Much we have told you, we will tell you more,
it's important that you know it, do you want to know more?

32 'Haki was the best by far of the sons of Hvædna,
and Hvædna's father was Hiorvard,
Heid and Horse-thief were Hrimnir's children.

33 'All the seeresses are descended from Vidolf,
all the wizards from Vilmeid,
and the *seid*-practisers from Svarthofdi,*
all the giants come from Ymir.

34 'Much we have told you, we will tell you more,
it's important that you know it, do you want to know more?

35 'One was born in bygone days,
with enormous power of the sons of men;
then nine women gave birth to him, to the spear-magnificent man,*
daughters of giants, at the edge of the earth.

36 'Much we have told you, we will tell you more,
it's important that you know it, do you want to know more?

37 'Gialp bore him, Greip bore him,
Eistla bore him and Eyrgiafa;
Ulfrun and Angeyia,
Imd and Atla and Iarnsaxa.*

38 'He was empowered with the strength of earth,
the cool waves of the sea, and sacrificial blood.

39 'Much we have told you, we will tell you more,
it's important that you know it, do you want to know more?

40 'Loki got the wolf on Angrboda,
and he got Sleipnir by Svadilfari;*
one monster was thought the most baleful,
who was descended from Byleist's brother.*

41 'Loki ate some of the heart, the thought-stone of a woman,
roasted on a linden-wood fire, he found it half-cooked;
Lopt was impregnated by a wicked woman,*
from whom every ogress on earth is descended.

42 'The ocean stirs up storms against heaven itself,
washes over the land, and the air yields;
from there come snow and biting winds;
then it is decreed that the gods come to their end.

43 'One was born greater than all,
he was empowered with the strength of earth;
he is said to be the wealthiest of princes,
closely related to all the families.

44 'Then will come another, even mightier,
though I do not dare to name his name;*
few can now see further than when
Odin has to meet the wolf.']

45 'Give some memory-ale to my boar,*
so that he can hold fast to all these words
from this conversation on the third morning,
when he and Angantyr reckon up their lineage.'

46 'Go away from here! I wish to sleep,
little did you get from me, few pleasant alternatives;
gallop away, noble lady, out into the night,
as Heidrun runs in heat among the he-goats.*

47 'You ran to Œdi, always full of desire,*
many have thrust themselves up the front of your skirt;
gallop away, noble lady, out into the night,
as Heidrun runs in heat among the he-goats.'

48 'I'll surround this place with troll-woman's fire,
so that you can never get away from here.'

49 'Fire I see burning and the earth aflame,
most when suffering will try to ransom their lives;
put this beer into Ottar's hand,
mixed with a great deal of poison and ill fortune.'

50 'Your curse will have no effect,
bride of the giant, you intend to call down evil;
he shall drink the precious liquid,
I pray that Ottar may thrive in all good things.'

The Song of Grotti

The Danish king Frodi acquires on a visit to Sweden two female slaves whom he takes home to grind with the magic millstone Grotti, which would grind out whatever the grinder asked for. At first the stone ground out riches and treasure, peace and happiness, but so relentless was Frodi as an employer, refusing to allow the women any rest, that by the end of the poem they are grinding out an army to fight against him. According to Snorri, *Edda*, p. 107, a sea-king called Mysing came and overthrew Frodi. Fenia, Menia, and Grotti were taken away on his ship and made to grind out salt. They ground so much that the ship sank under the weight and that is why the sea is salt to this day—a common European fairy-tale motif. The *Song of Grotti* (*Grottasongr*) is the work-song of the two girls as they grind under Frodi's orders.

1 Now there have come to the king's dwellings
two prescient women, Fenia and Menia,
the mighty girls were with Frodi,
Fridleif's son, to have at his pleasure.

2 They were led to the grindstone
and they ordered the grey stones to grind into motion;
he promised neither of them rest nor pleasure
until he had heard the slavegirls' song.

3 They kept up the noise of the never-silent mill:
'Let's set down the grinder, let's stop the millstones!'
He ordered the girls to keep grinding.

4 They sang and they turned the fast-revolving stone,
so that Frodi's household mostly fell asleep;
then said Menia, who'd come to the milling:

5 'Wealth let's grind for Frodi, grind out happiness,
grind many possessions on the wonderful stone!
Let him sit on his wealth, let him sleep on a quilt,
let him wake to happiness! That is well ground out.

6 'Here no one shall bring harm to another,
nor plot evil, nor conspire against someone's life,
nor shall he strike with a sharp sword,
though he should find, trussed up, his brother's slayer.'

7 He did not speak at all, except this one phrase:*
'You shan't sleep any longer than the cuckoo over the hall
or longer than I take to recite a single song.'

8 'Frodi, you were not being entirely wise,
eloquent lord of men, when you bought the slavegirls;
you chose them for their strength and for their appearance,
but you didn't ask about their lineage.

9 'Hrungnir was stern, as was his father,
though Thiazi was mightier than they;
Idi and Aurnir, our close kinsmen,
mountain-giants' brothers, we are descended from them.

10 'Grotti would not have come from the grey rock,
nor the hard stone block out of the earth,
nor would the mountain-giant girl keep grinding so,
if we had known nothing about it.

11 'Nine winters we were playmates,
mighty girls, nourished under the earth;
the girls were doers of mighty deeds,
we ourselves moved the flat-topped mountain from its place.

12 'We rolled the boulder from the giant's court,
so that the earth began shaking;
so we turned the fast-revolving stone,
the heavy boulder, so that men seized it.*

13 'And afterwards in Sweden,
we two prescient ones, we advanced against the army;
we fought against bearlike warriors, we broke shields,
we marched against the grey-corsleted army.

14 'We overthrew one prince, we supported another one,
we gave help to Gothorm's good troop;
there was no peace then before Knui fell.

15 'We continued for some seasons,
so that we became well known for our fighting deeds;
there we sliced with sharp spears
blood from wounds and made swords red.

16 'Now we have come to the dwellings of the king
without mercy, and live as slaves,
mud eats away at our feet, the rest of us is chilled
through,
we drag the calmer of strife; it's dull at Frodi's house.*

17 'Hands must rest, the stone will stand still,
I have ground my full share.'
'We may not give any rest to our hands
until it seems to Frodi we have ground out everything.'

18 'Hands shall grip the hard shafts,
the bloodstained weapons; wake up, Frodi!
Wake up, Frodi, if you want to hear
our songs and our ancient tales.

19 'I see fire burning east of the city,
warfare awakened, that must be a beacon;
an army is coming here very shortly,
it will burn the settlement despite the prince.

20 'You shan't hold onto the throne of Lejre,
the red-gold rings, nor this magic grindstone.
Let's seize the handle, girl, turn more swiftly!
We are not yet warmed by the blood of slaughtered men.

21 'My father's daughter ground fiercely,
for she saw the fate of a multitude of men;
the great shafts snapped away from the mill-frame,
shut up in iron, let's grind more!

22 'Let's grind more! The son of Yrsa,
will avenge Frodi on the Half-Danes;
he'll be famed as both her son
and brother; as we two know.'*

23 The girls ground, they used their strength,
the young girls were in a giant rage;
the shaped wood shook, the frame collapsed,
the heavy grindstone broke in two.

24 And the mountain-giant woman spoke these words:
'Frodi, we have ground to the point where we must stop,
now the ladies have had a full stint of milling!'

EXPLANATORY NOTES

Readers are also referred to the Annotated Index of Names, pp. 298–323.

The Seeress's Prophecy

Page

4 *offspring of Heimdall*: the offspring of Heimdall are the different classes of humankind (see the *List of Rig* below). The 'sacred people' in l. 1 are the gods.

nine giant women: who these may be is not certain, though nine giantesses are listed as mothers of a 'spear-magnificent man' in *Song of Hyndla*, vv. 35–7, probably Heimdall who is said to have had nine mothers in Snorri, *Edda*, pp. 25–6.

Ymir: the primeval being, according to this poem. In *Grimnir's Sayings*, vv. 40–1, Odin describes how the universe was created out of Ymir's dismembered body.

the sons of Bur: Odin and his brothers, Vili and Ve. Bur was the son of Buri, a being licked out of the primeval ice by Audhumla, the first cow, according to Snorri, *Edda*, p. 11.

5 *three giant girls*: who these giant girls might be is not at all clear. They seem to be inimical to the gods and their appearance marks the end of the Golden Age. Some critics have identified them as the fates who appear in v. 20.

Brimir: probably identical with Ymir. *Brim* normally means 'ocean', *blain* the 'dark or black one'.

New-moon and Dark-of-moon: this list of dwarf-names cannot be original to the poem; as the dwarfs have no further role in the *Seeress's Prophecy*, the catalogue is disproportionately long.

6 *until three gods*: one or more verses must be missing from before v. 17. The three gods are Odin, Hænir, and Lodur. Little is known of Hænir, though he returns after Ragnarok, and still less about Lodur who is mentioned only here and in a couple of kennings. Odin and Hænir are found together accompanied by Loki, at the beginning of the gods' contest with Thiazi, Skadi's father, in Snorri, *Edda*, p. 59. Earlier in Snorri's account of the creation of humanity, it is the sons of Bur (Odin, Vili, and Ve) who give life to mankind (Snorri, *Edda*, p. 13).

Ash and Embla: Ash and Embla (elm? vine?) are two pieces of driftwood washed up on the shore.

she: throughout the poem the pronoun used to denote the speaker varies between 'I' and 'she'. It seems most likely that they refer to a single seeress.

One-eye: Odin.

7 *Bright One*: (Heid) is usually thought to be a hypostasis of Freyia, like Gullveig in the previous verse, since Freyia is known to be skilled in *seid* (this particular form of magic). Thus the Vanir manifest themselves both in the divine and the human worlds, demanding a share of sacrifice (v. 23). The Æsir at first go to war over this but eventually concede the tribute.

Od's girl: Freyia who is married to Od.

wager of Father of the Slain: both Heimdall, watchman of the gods, and Odin have left some body part in the well. Odin exchanged one of his eyes for wisdom from Mimir, guardian of the well, while Heimdall seems to have forfeited his ear.

8 *Baldr's brother*: Vali, son of Odin by Rind, begotten solely to avenge Baldr's death. The story is told more fully in Saxo, *History of the Danish People*, Book 3, pp. 69–79.

made of Vali's entrails: this Vali is a son of Loki, probably identical with Nari, whose guts, according to the prose at the end of *Loki's Quarrel*, were used by the gods to bind Loki.

9 *Sindri*: the hall, then, must belong to the dwarfs.

the next summer: the poet may be thinking here of the effects of a volcanic eruption and consequent ash cloud, perhaps pointing to an Icelandic origin for the poem.

at the Father of Hosts': Valhall.

10 *Garm*: Garm seems to be a hound of hell, destined, according to Snorri, *Edda*, p. 54, to fight with Tyr at Ragnarok. Originally he may have been identical with Fenrir the wolf.

Mim: the sons of Mim are unknown. Mim in l. 4 seems to be identical with Mimir who, according to *Ynglinga saga*, ch. 4, was sent as a hostage to the Vanir, where he displayed remarkable wisdom. The Vanir beheaded him, preserved his head and sent it back to the Æsir along with Hænir.

Surt's kin: Surt is a fire-demon, so his kin is fire itself. What is swallowed is unclear—perhaps the road to hell.

Hrym: a frost-giant.

10 *Naglfar*: a ship made of the uncut nails of the dead (Snorri, *Edda*, p. 53).

Muspell's people: although in Old High German and Old Saxon *Muspilli* simply means 'the end of the world', the Norse poet understands it as a giant's name.

brother of Byleist: nothing is known about Byleist himself; his name only appears in kennings like this one, referring to Loki, whose brother he seems to be.

11 *harm of branches*: a kenning for fire.

second grief of Frigg: the death of Odin. Her first was the death of Baldr.

slayer of Beli: Freyr killed the giant Beli with a deer horn as he had given away his sword to Skirnir. See *Skirnir's Journey*.

Loki's kinsman: the wolf, son of Loki by the giantess Angrboda.

Earth-girdler: the mighty serpent, Iormungand, or the Midgard-serpent who lies in the outer ocean. Fathered by Loki, it is brother to Fenrir the wolf and to Hel. Thor has encountered it previously in a comic context in *Thrym's Poem*.

Odin's son: Thor is Odin's son by Earth. Instead of 'serpent' the R text has the word 'wolf' here, an error imported from v. 53.

Sayings of the High One

16 *Gunnlod*: this alludes to the story of the winning of the mead of poetry, told in full in Snorri, *Edda*, pp. 61–4. The mead originally belonged to two dwarfs, Fialar and Gialar, and was stolen by the giants. Odin had worked for a year as a thrall for the brother of Suttung, the giant who had the mead. When the year was up he went to Suttung (here confusingly called Fialar) to claim his reward of mead. By seducing Gunnlod, Suttung's daughter, he gained her help and escaped with the mead back to Asgard. The story is told in fuller detail in vv. 104–10 below.

Fialar: here a mistake for Suttung, owner of the mead.

17 *Assembly*: in both mainland Scandinavia and Iceland people would regularly meet at regional assemblies (Things) to resolve law cases.

21 *two wooden men*: these may be scarecrows, or they may be wooden idols, mentioned in some sagas. In the *saga of Ragnar Lodbrok*, ch. 20, some vikings come to a Baltic island where they find a huge, wooden idol. The idol speaks a verse complaining that once he used to be given food and clothing but now he is neglected.

22 *the eagle*: opinion is divided as to whether this is a sea-eagle on the look out for fish as prey, or a land eagle who has flown away from his accustomed habitat and so is disoriented.

23 *paid back*: this verse is missing some lines.

24 *a hand*: the metre has changed suddenly and the meaning is obscure. Possibly a rich outer garment may well conceal a hand ready to strike.

cattle die, kinsmen die: a parallel has been detected in the Old English poem *The Wanderer*: 'here cattle are transient / here property is transient, here a friend is transient' (l. 108). If there is a direct connection it most likely stems from the formulaic use of the words 'cattle' and 'kinsmen', an alliterating pair both in Old Norse, *fe* and *frændr*, and in Old English, *feoh* and *freond.*

Fitiung's sons: although they sound proverbial, Fitiung's sons are otherwise unknown.

25 *mighty sage stained*: the sage is probably Odin. Carved runic letters appear originally to have been filled in with some kind of paint.

whirling wheel: the image is of a potter's wheel or of a turning lathe; in its turning the wheel incorporates changeability into women's hearts. Some have seen the medieval image of the Wheel of Fortune here, but that deals with a human's external fate, not his internal character.

27 *Billing's girl*: this story is unknown from other sources, though the sequence of events is not difficult to follow. Odin importunes the wife or daughter of Billing (probably a giant). She puts him off until the evening; when he first comes to her hall everyone is still awake, the second time she has gone, leaving a bitch in her place. Billing's girl doubtless fears to reject Odin openly lest he bewitch her as he does Rind, who was fated to be the mother of Vali, avenger of Baldr. Her story is told in Saxo's *History of the Danish People*, Book 3, pp. 69–79.

28 *the old giant*: a further elaboration of the story of the mead of poetry begun in vv. 13–14.

auger: according to Snorri, *Edda*, p. 63, Odin makes use of an auger called Rati to bore his way into the mountain where Gunnlod is to be found, and, turning himself into a snake, wriggles in through the hole.

Odrerir: according to Snorri this is the name of one of the vats in which the mead of poetry was kept, though the name 'Stirrer of Inspiration' seems more likely to refer to the mead itself.

29 *Bolverk*: the name Odin had used when disguised as a thrall, and in his dealings with Gunnlod.

ring-oath: in Iceland oaths were sworn on large silver rings kept at the local temple and reddened with sacrificial blood.

Loddfafnir: the name is unknown from other sources. *Lodd-* seems to mean 'rags', while Fafnir is the name of the dragon Sigurd killed. The combination 'Ragged-dragon' may be a mocking term for someone who is not yet fully initiated into arcane knowledge.

32 *look upwards in battle*: the phenomenon warned against here is a kind of mass panic, frequently found in Irish sources, and for which an Irish loanword is used in the Norse.

34 *power of earth*: the substances mentioned may be invoked or be incorporated into some kind of ritual.

I hung on a windy tree: Odin performs a sacrifice by hanging for nine nights on the tree Yggdrasill, pierced with a spear in order to gain knowledge of the runes. The parallels with the Crucifixion are marked, though interpretation is controversial. The motif of the Hanged God is widespread in Indo-European and ancient Near Eastern religion, however, so direct Christian influence need not be present here.

Bolthor: Odin's maternal grandfather; Bolthor's son is therefore Odin's mother's brother, a particularly close relationship in Germanic society.

35 *Thund*: an Odinic name.

spells: the spells which Odin alludes to here broadly match those magical skills listed for him in *Ynglinga saga*, chs. 2 and 6.

Vafthrudnir's Sayings

40 *Im's father*: i.e. Vafthrudnir. Im is otherwise unknown.

41 *Hreid-Goths*: though the Goths lived in southern Sweden, this phrase probably means simply 'among men'.

43 *Ymir*: Ymir was the primeval giant, the earliest creature. This account of the creation of the world differs markedly from that in the *Seeress's Prophecy*. Snorri's *Edda*, pp. 11–12, elaborates the creation myth.

44 *Aurgelmir*: according to Snorri, *Edda*, p. 10, Aurgelmir was the name given to Ymir by the frost-giants.

45 *Elivagar*: the name seems to mean 'mighty waves', some sort of icy primeval matter. In his *Edda* (p. 10) Snorri says that they are a number of rivers.

from there . . . terrifying: lines 3–4 of this stanza are missing in R and are supplied from Snorri's *Edda*.

coffin: the word here means 'box, chest' and some scholars have suggested that it might equally be interpreted as 'cradle'. Snorri, *Edda*, p. 11, identifies it as 'ark', and introduces a Flood-narrative, borrowed from Christian tradition.

46 *home among the wise Vanir*: no other source tells of Niord's return to the Vanir, nor anything about his fate at Ragnarok.

Einheriar: the warrior dead who live in Valhall, and who will fight on the side of the gods at Ragnarok.

47 *Hoddmimir*: from the connection between Mimir and Yggdrasill noted in the *Seeress's Prophecy*, it is possible that Hoddmimir is another name for Mimir, and that the two survivors hide in Yggdrasill. We are not expressly told whether Yggdrasill survives Ragnarok or not.

maidens: these are probably the norns, spirits who rule over fate. See also the *Lay of Fafnir*, v. 13.

48 *Mogthrasir*: the name is unknown from elsewhere, though it seems to mean perhaps 'Striver for Sons'. His relevance to the norns, if the identification is correct, is unclear.

Vidar and Vali . . . Modi and Magni: sons of Odin and Thor respectively. Miollnir is Thor's weapon, his mighty hammer.

ear of his son: this refers to Baldr. No one but Odin knows what was whispered in Baldr's ear; it is assumed that it was a promise of resurrection.

Grimnir's Sayings

51 *Hlidskialf*: Odin's high-seat, from which he can see into all the worlds.

52 *Ull*: god of the bow. Since bows were normally made of yew, it is appropriate that the god should have his palace in Yewdale.

tooth-payment: a gift given to a child when it loses its first tooth. Freyr is the only god who seems to have had a childhood.

the God: according to Snorri, *Edda*, p. 20, this is Odin himself.

Saga: Snorri, *Edda*, p. 29, lists Saga as a separate goddess, based on this passage. Saga is likely to be another name for Frigg, however.

53 *Thiazi*: a giant who kidnapped Idunn, keeper of the apples of immortality, and was subsequently killed. See Snorri, *Edda*, p. 60.

53 *Skadi*: Thiazi's giantess daughter who gained Niord as a husband in compensation for her father's death. They were divorced, hence her separate habitation. See Snorri, *Edda*, pp. 23–4, 61.

54 *Forseti*: Baldr's otherwise obscure son. The name means 'Ruler', and is the title used by the president of Iceland.

Andhrimnir . . . Eldhrimnir: Andhrimnir is the cook in Valhall, Eldhrimnir the cooking-pot, and Sæhrimnir the boar whom the Einheriar eat every day, and who is rejuvenated every night.

Geri and Freki: Odin's wolves, whom he keeps as dogs.

Hugin and Munin: Odin's ravens. Their names mean 'Thought' and 'Memory' and they are also mentioned in *Ynglinga saga*, ch. 7.

Thund: this verse is very obscure. Thund is probably a river in which the 'wolf's fish', possibly the World-serpent, swims. Those 'rejoicing in slaughter' must be the Einheriar, on their way to Valhall.

55 *hundreds*: this is the so-called 'long hundred' = 120.

Bilskirnir: a hall belonging to Thor.

Heidrun . . . Lærad: Heidrun provides mead enough for all the Einheriar from her udder. Cf. Snorri, *Edda*, p. 33. The tree, Lærad, may be another name for Yggdrasill, but Snorri does not make the connection.

Sid and Vid: this list of river-names contains some real rivers such as the Rhine and Dvina, but the rest are mythical.

56 *Nidhogg*: a dragon, cf. the *Seeress's Prophecy*. Snorri, *Edda*, pp. 17–20, elaborates the description of Yggdrasill and Valhall.

57 *Hrist and Mist*: these, and the other names in the verse, are valkyries, Odin's warrior-maidens whose duties include choosing those doomed to die in battle, and serving the horns of mead in Valhall. Cf. Snorri, *Edda*, p. 31.

Arvak and Alsvid: horses who pull the sun. Snorri, *Edda*, p. 14, thinks that the bellows cool the horses, though they may function to keep the sun ablaze.

Skoll . . . Hrodvitnir: the wolf Skoll and his companion Hati are chasing the sun and moon. They will swallow them at Ragnarok (Snorri, *Edda*, pp. 14–15). Hrodvitnir may be another name for Fenrir.

Ymir's flesh: this allusion to the making of the world conflicts with the version we have in the *Seeress's Prophecy*, but agrees with *Vafthrudnir's Sayings*. See also Snorri, *Edda*, pp. 11–12.

58 *kettles*: the import of this verse is obscure. It is possible that the reference is to some kind of shamanistic rite involving heat and steam, perhaps with hallucinogenic herbs, to allow the initiate to see into another world.

Ivaldi's sons: these were dwarfs who not only made Skidbladnir, a ship which Freyr can fold up and put in his pocket, but also various other treasures, including Gungnir, Odin's spear, and Miollnir, Thor's hammer. For the full story, see Snorri, *Edda*, pp. 96–7.

Sleipnir . . . Bilrost . . . Garm: Odin's eight-legged horse is the offspring of Loki and the Giant-builder's stallion: Snorri, *Edda*, pp. 35–6. Bilrost is the rainbow bridge, Garm the dog whose baying portends Ragnarok.

Ægir's feast: a personification of the sea, possibly a giant. He hosts the feast in *Loki's Quarrel*. Agnar's horn, given to Odin, functions as a sacrifice, connecting the human hall with the divine assembly.

Mask: Odin reckons up a long list of names by which he is known. Some have meanings, others are obscure. Snorri draws on this list, among others, both for the names of his triple protagonists in the *Gylfaginning* section of his *Edda* and for his list of Odinic names in *Edda*, pp. 8–9 and 21–2.

59 *Sokkmimir's*: this story is otherwise unknown.

disir: fateful female deities who often contrive the death of heroes, notably in the Norwegian genealogical poem *Ynglingatal* (cited in Snorri's *Ynglinga saga*) and in the *Lay of Hamdir*.

Skirnir's Journey

63 *herdsman*: the watchman sitting on the mound, warning of danger is a familiar motif. Originally this figure—who may be identical with the brother Gerd mentions in v. 16—may have had to be overcome by Skirnir in battle.

64 *my brother's slayer*: what Gerd means by this remark is obscure. The only mythological figure who embraces her brother's slayer is Idunn, according to Loki in *Loki's Quarrel*, v. 17. It may be that in some version of the story the herdsman on the mound was Gerd's brother whom the hero had to kill to gain access to the bride.

eleven apples: apples are normally the attribute of Idunn, who kept the Æsir ageless with her apples of immortality. Eleven is not normally a significant number in Norse, and it may be there has been confusion between *ellifo*, 'eleven', as the manuscript reads, and *ellilyf*, 'eternal life', which would confirm the connection with Idunn.

64 *every ninth night*: this must be the famous ring Draupnir which belonged to Odin and which has the self-replicating property mentioned. Odin placed it on Baldr's funeral pyre and Baldr sent it back to him from Hel with the messenger, Hermod: Snorri, *Edda*, p. 50. How Skirnir has it within his gift is not clear.

65 *watchman of the gods*: Heimdall. Gerd, perched at the edge of hell on the eagle's mound, would become a kind of demonic Heimdall since he watches for Ragnarok at the edge of heaven.

66 *goat's piss*: the goat Heidrun supplies mead from her udders for the warriors in Valhall. Gerd would be enduring the very opposite of the splendid life lived among the gods.

67 *three runes*: runes were the pre-Christian writing system in Scandinavia. Each rune represented both a sound (e.g. 'h') and a concept (e.g. 'hail' for the 'h' rune); they could be used for magical purposes, both for good and evil. See the *Lay of Sigrdrifa*, vv. 6–13.

Harbard's Song

69 *pipsqueak*: Odin is usually imagined as an old man, and in this poem his assumed name 'Harbard' means 'Greybeard'. Thus Thor's ironic address sparks off the quarrel.

70 *your mother's dead*: this is not true, but part of Odin's psychological strategy; Thor's mother is Earth.

71 *Hrungnir*: a giant with a head of stone. Knowing that Thor was coming to attack him, but persuaded that he was approaching from underground, he stood on his shield and thus was an easy target. Hrungnir was armed with a whetstone, a fragment of which is still stuck in Thor's head. See Snorri, *Edda*, pp. 77–81.

72 *seven sisters*: who these women are is not clear, but Odin's riddling style and the references to sand and digging out valleys suggest that they may perhaps be the unpredictable waves, daughters of Ran, the sea-goddess.

Thiazi: the account of the death of Thiazi, recounted in Snorri, *Edda*, pp. 60, 86–8, citing Thiodolf of Hvinir's poem *Haustlong*, gives Thor no particular role in killing Thiazi. Loki claims the credit for it in *Loki's Quarrel*, v. 50.

Allvaldi's son: Thiazi. Snorri, *Edda*, p. 61, says that it was Odin who transformed Thiazi's eyes into stars as part of the Æsir's compensation to his daughter, Skadi. It is not known whether they were identified with any particular constellation.

73 *stuffed in a glove*: this is the well-known story of Thor's trip to Utgarda-Loki, recounted in Snorri, *Edda*, pp. 37–46. *En route* Thor and his companions stay overnight in, as they think, an oddly designed hall. They spend an anxious night, kept awake by a terrifying rumbling. The next morning they meet the giant Skrymir (here called Fialar, a common giant-name) whose snoring was the source of the rumbling. He points out that they have been using his glove as accommodation. Thor is worsted by the giants' magic in this tale, and his enemies delight in reminding him of it—cf. Loki in *Loki's Quarrel*, vv. 60, 62.

Svarang's sons: this story is unknown from other sources.

75 *ring for the hand*: this phrase must have some other meaning than its literal one, since Thor is so upset by it. One scholar has plausibly suggested that the ring may refer to the anus, and the offer thus be an invitation to homosexual activity.

the woods at home: this phrase could also mean 'the woods of the world'. Either way the connection with burial cairns is obscure, but the phrase appears in both manuscripts of the poem. The 'ancient men' are presumably the dead, a frequent source of wisdom in Norse.

Sif: Thor's wife. There is no record of Sif being unfaithful to Thor, though Loki claims in *Loki's Quarrel*, v. 54, that he has been her lover.

Hymir's Poem

78 *shook the twigs*: twigs or wooden slips seem to be involved in Norse prognostications, though how they are used is not clear. In the *Seeress's Prophecy*, v. 63, Hænir chooses slips of wood for divination. Probably a number of sticks carved with runic symbols were thrown.

mash-blender: this line is obscure, but the mountain-dweller (giant) seems to be Ægir, since he makes the stipulation about the cauldron and he is presumably a skilled brewer. Odin's son is Thor.

Hlorridi: a name for Thor.

79 *my father*: it would be surprising if the giant Hymir really were Tyr's father, but we know little about Tyr. Possibly Loki, whose father certainly was a giant, was the original companion on this adventure, as in *Thrym's Poem*. Thialfi, Thor's companion in other adventures, son of the giant Egil, may also have been the other protagonist.

79 *Egil . . . goats*: Egil is the father of Thialfi and Roskva. Thor's goats, which draw his chariot, could be cooked and eaten each night and reconstituted from the bones every morning. Egil's son, Thialfi, contrary to instructions, splits open a bone to get at the marrow and next day the goat is lame. Thor in anger demands the children as his servants in recompense. The story is told fully in Snorri, *Edda*, pp. 37–8, and alluded to in vv. 37–8 of this poem.

the lad: presumably Tyr.

cheek-forest: beard.

Hrod: an otherwise unknown giant.

80 *the one who'd made the giantess weep*: Thor, killer of giants.

playmate of Hrungnir: Hrungnir was a well-known giant; 'playmate of Hrungnir' is a kenning for 'giant'.

head: the ox's head is used for bait for the Midgard-serpent, and can be quite clearly seen in the illustration of this scene on the Gosforth Fishing Stone, a large standing stone from the late tenth or early eleventh century in Cumbria, England. Following is a lacuna. The missing text can be summarized from Snorri, *Edda*, pp. 46–7: Thor went on board the boat, and began to row very quickly. Then Hymir said that they had come to the waters where he usually sat and caught flatfish, but Thor said he wanted to row out much further; Hymir said that now they had gone so far out that it was dangerous because of the Midgard-serpent. Thor continued, but Hymir was very unhappy.

81 *lord of goats . . . wave-horse*: a series of zoological kennings. The lord of goats is Thor, since they pull his chariot; the monkey's offspring is an unusual designation for a giant, while the wave-horse is the boat.

slayer of the serpent: prolepsis. Thor and the Midgard-serpent will kill one another at Ragnarok. The Circumscriber (l. 3) is the Midgard-serpent, who encircles the world.

the wolf's hideous brother: the Midgard-serpent is the brother of Fenrir the wolf.

collapsing: another lacuna follows. Snorri, *Edda*, p. 47, says that Hymir was terrified when he saw the serpent, and the sea washing in and out of the boat. As Thor raised his hammer, the giant grabbed the bait-knife and cut Thor's line; the serpent sank into the sea. In Snorri's account, Thor throws Hymir overboard in disgust; here he survives in order to conclude the 'Fetching the Cauldron' story.

floating-goat: boat.

sea-pig: this is the whale rather than the boat.

83 *both his children*: this refers back to the story of the lamed goat (see note to v. 7, p. 274 above). It is likely these verses belong earlier in the poem, and thus that Thor's companion in the cauldron adventure might originally have been Thialfi, rather than Tyr.

Loki's Quarrel

86 *mixed our blood*: Odin and Loki had thus sworn blood-brotherhood in the past.

wolf's father: Loki is father of the wolf Fenrir.

further in: that is, in a more honourable seat.

87 *adoptive relations*: an obscure term perhaps meaning 'the Vanir' as opposed to the Æsir.

brother's slayer: the story is not known from elsewhere. However, the motif of the wooer who has to kill his bride's male relations to gain her is a common one—see the *Second Poem of Helgi Hundingsbani*.

88 *thigh*: the story is unknown: however, we do know from Snorri that Gefion bartered sex for territory in her dealings with Gylfi, the king of Sweden (Snorri, *Edda*, p. 7, and *Ynglinga saga*, ch. 5).

the faint-hearted: Odin was notorious for deserting his protégés in battle and giving victory to the other side so that his favourites could join him in Valhall.

pervert: this story is not otherwise known, though Loki gives birth to Sleipnir, the eight-legged horse of Odin, after having sex with the Giant-builder's stallion, Svadilfari (Snorri, *Edda*, p. 36).

89 seid *on Samsey*: the use of drums and cross-dressing seems to be typical of *seid*, a type of magic said to be practised by the Vanir, especially Freyia (*Seeress's Prophecy*, v. 22), and by the Lapps.

Vili and Ve: Odin's brothers. Once when Odin was away on a journey, Vili and Ve shared Frigg, Snorri reports in *Ynglinga saga*, ch. 3. Snorri's account seems to be based on this passage, so it adds nothing. Saxo, *History of the Danish People*, Book 1, p. 26, tells how Othinus (= Odin) went away into exile at one point, because of his wife's disgraceful behaviour, and does not return until she is dead. There is no mention of the two brothers in Saxo, however.

Baldr: for Loki's part in the killing of Baldr, see Snorri, *Edda*, pp. 48–51.

90 *Freyia*: Freyia's affair with her brother is not mentioned elsewhere, but the fact that Niord seems to have fathered her and Freyr on his sister (v. 36 below) suggests that brother–sister sexual relations were a distinguishing characteristic of the Vanir.

pissed in your mouth: Niord is a god of the sea; the daughters of the giant Hymir are conceivably the rivers which flow down into the sea.

91 *Fenrir tore*: when the gods tried to bind Fenrir with a magic unbreakable rope, the wolf suspected them and would only submit to binding if one of them would put his hand in the wolf's mouth as a pledge of good faith. When the rope proved unbreakable Fenrir bit off Tyr's hand (Snorri, *Edda*, pp. 25, 28–9).

wife: nothing is known of Tyr's wife, nor whether Loki's allegation is true.

Gymir's daughter: see *Skirnir's Journey*.

Muspell: i.e. at Ragnarok.

92 *muddy back*: from *Seeress's Prophecy*, v. 27, we know that white loam pours down Yggdrasill to where Heimdall's hearing is hidden. As the watchman of the gods, perhaps Heimdall has to sit under Yggdrasill, waiting for the first signs of Ragnarok, though he is often depicted as sitting at the edge of heaven.

93 *gods shall bind you*: this story is told in the prose which follows this poem (pp. 95–6).

Thiazi: Skadi's father who kidnapped Idunn. Loki rescued her and thus was instrumental in Thiazi's death. The story is related in Snorri, *Edda*, pp. 59–61. Thor claims the credit for killing Thiazi in *Harbard's Song*, v. 19.

bed: this claim is not corroborated elsewhere.

Loki: Sif is not recorded elsewhere as unfaithful, although Odin suggests as much to Thor in *Harbard's Song*, v. 48. In one story (Snorri, *Edda*, p. 96) Loki cuts off all of Sif's hair: how he got close enough to carry this out may be explained by this verse.

94 *rock of your shoulders*: i.e. head.

roads to the east: Thor threw Thiazi's eyes up into the sky as stars after killing him (*Harbard's Song*, v. 19), and also the toe of Aurvandil, another giant (Snorri, *Edda*, pp. 79–80).

glove: see note on *Harbard's Song*, v. 26.2 (p. 273 above), for the story of Thor's trip to Utgarda-Loki.

95 *Hrungnir's killer*: i.e. Miollnir. See note on *Harbard's Song*, v. 14.2 (p. 272 above).

starved: this is a reference to Thor's adventure with Skrymir. Thor proved unable to get food out of the giant's pack because it was secretly fastened with trick wire (Snorri, *Edda*, pp. 39, 45).

Narfi: Snorri rationalizes the rather confusing details given here: one son is changed into a wolf and tears open the other to provide the guts for the binding (Snorri, *Edda*, p. 52).

Thrym's Poem

97 *feather cloak*: an attribute of Freyia which allows her to fly.

98 *necklace of the Brisings*: this is frequently mentioned in connection with Freyia, but we know little more about it. On one occasion Loki stole it. It was recovered by Heimdall, who fought with him for it at a place called Singastein. Both gods were in the form of seals (Snorri, *Edda*, p. 76).

99 *keys*: keys to the pantry, storehouses, and chests were the housewife's responsibility. The bunch of keys is a mark of her status as married woman.

goats: Thor always drives a chariot drawn by his magic goats.

101 *Var*: the goddess of pledges between men and women, according to Snorri, *Edda*, p. 30.

The Lay of Volund

102 *valkyries*: the women are swan-maidens, women who can fly with the aid of cloaks of swan feathers. Valkyries are not normally swan-maidens; perhaps they have been conflated here since both can fly, and both eschew domesticity. The three have ordinary human names but two—Swanwhite and Alvit—have bynames which indicate their swan natures.

103 *weather-eyed shooter*: Volund.

104 *Grani's road*: Grani is the hero Sigurd's horse, on whose back he bore off the treasure-hoard of Fafnir, the Rhinegold, alluded to in the next line. Volund seems to be claiming that the gold is neither Nidud's property, nor part of the legendary hoard, but is rightfully his.

she: Nidud's malicious queen.

105 *cut . . . the might of his sinews*: i.e. hamstring him so that he cannot run away.

106 *overcame her with beer*: this scene is illustrated on the eighth-century whalebone box known as the Franks Casket, which can be seen in the British Museum.

webbed feet: this phrase, and the crippled smith's method of escape from the island, remains obscure. It is possible that the ring which he has now recovered has some transformative power, changing Volund into a swan (hence the webbed feet), like the swan-maiden for whom it was made. The later prose account of the story, *Thidreks saga*, has Volund's brother Egil come to his rescue, shooting down geese with his bow so that the smith can make himself wings. This scene may also be illustrated on the Franks Casket.

107 *he sat and rested*: Volund, who has flown to Nidud's palace.

with child: in *Thidreks saga* Volund returns with an army, kills Nidud, and marries Bodvild. Their son, Vidia, becomes a great Germanic hero.

All-wise's Sayings

109 *sea of wagons*: obscure in the original: it probably means 'earth'.

111 *Dvalin's deluder*: Dvalin is a frequent dwarf-name. The sun is his deluder because, presumably, Dvalin was caught by the sunrise and turned into stone, just as All-wise is at the end of the poem.

112 *lagastaf*: the meaning of this word is unknown. It is also used to denote grain in v. 32.

The First Poem of Helgi Hundingsbani

114 *norns*: female fate figures who determine the lives of men. They are associated with weaving.

115 . . . *in Bralund*: there are no actual missing words here; the Norse text simply makes no sense.

moon's hall: i.e. the sky.

kinswoman of Neri: Neri is unknown, but the reference must be to one of the norns.

kinsman of the Ylfings: Sigmund, Helgi's father.

byrnie: a mail-coat.

stands in his byrnie . . .: like Vali, the son begotten by Odin to avenge Baldr, Helgi is ready to fight when one day old. The conversation between the ravens points to the hero's future prowess in battle. He will be a friend to wolves and ravens by providing corpses for them to eat.

shining leek: a sword.

blood-snake: a sword.

Sinfiotli: son of Sigmund by his sister Signy. Sinfiotli was born to help the brother and sister avenge the death of their father, Volsung, at the hands of Signy's husband, Siggeir. Sigmund and Sinfiotli spent some time in the forest living as werewolves before the revenge was achieved (see *Volsunga saga*, ch. 8).

shining-born elm-tree: humans are often metaphorically designated as trees, no doubt because the story of Ash and Embla (*Seeress's Prophecy*, vv. 17–18) tells of mankind's origin, shaped from trees. Women are 'trees of jewellery', men 'trees of battle' or some variant of this.

116 *Odin's hounds*: wolves.

breaker of rings: generous man. A successful leader would break up the big arm-rings captured as booty and distribute the fragments of gold or silver to his men.

kitten of a cat: at the equivalent point in *Volsunga saga* (ch. 9), Sigrun says that she would rather marry a young crow than Hodbrodd.

117 *river-fire*: gold, an allusion to the legend of the Rhinegold.

118 *the sister of Kolga*: Kolga is one of the nine daughters of Ægir, who rules over the sea, and she and her sisters represent the waves; v. 29.3 refers to the same belief.

Ran: the goddess of the sea, who seeks to catch and drown men in her net.

the others: allies of Hodbrodd, led by Gudmund.

pigs and bitches: an insult: feeding such low creatures was the work of slaves.

119 *crept into a stone-tip*: the verse refers to Sinfiotli's former exploits as a werewolf, accusing him of sleeping out in the forest instead of living in a hall like an ordinary man. Sinfiotli also killed his half-brother when he betrayed Sigmund and Sinfiotli as they waited to take revenge on Siggeir.

except Sinfiotli: the suggestion that two men have had sexual relations is a disgraceful one. In such taunts shame attaches to the one who takes the female role; hence Sinfiotli asserts that he was the dominant sexual partner in this encounter.

120 *home haystacks*: this seems to be another taunt based on Sinfiotli's time as a werewolf. Lying about under the haystacks may suggest an idle youth, in which Sinfiotli achieved no heroic deeds.

120 *a mare for Grani*: Grani was Sigurd's stallion. To accuse someone of being a mare was particularly insulting, implying both sexual deviancy and bestial appetite. The verse is a variation on the insult of v. 37.

as Imd's daughter: Imd seems to be a giant-name. The story is unknown, but the accusation combines transvestism and doing the tasks of slaves.

[*Helgi said:*]: it is not clear from the manuscript who speaks verses 45 and 46, and the corresponding ones in *A Second Poem of Helgi Hundingsbani*, vv. 23–4. The tone seems to be that of a commander, advising Sinfiotli to get ready for battle and judiciously summing up the nature of the opposition, so I have, like a number of editors, assigned the speech to Helgi.

Svipud and Sveggiud: horse-names.

121 *troll-woman's mount*: traditionally, troll-women ride on wolves. Here the wolf is feasting on corpses—the fodder of the raven.

The Poem of Helgi Hiorvardsson

125 *no name*: some Germanic heroes are unpromising in their youth, and their fathers do not bother to give them a name. Often called 'coal-biters' because of their habit of idling by the hearth, it takes an unusual occurrence to make them show their mettle.

burial-mound: as liminal places, on the threshold between the living and the dead, burial-mounds are places where supernatural incursions often occur.

apple-tree of strife: warrior.

with the name: traditionally, the giving of a name or nickname had to be accompanied by a gift if the name was to stick to its new owner.

126 *Helgi is his name . . .*: at verse 13 the change in style from narrative to flyting produces a change in metre from *fornyrdislag* to *ljodahattr*.

Atli . . . atrocious: this pun is in the original: *Atli* and *atall* meaning 'terrifying'.

127 *give to Ran*: to give someone to the sea-goddess is to drown them.

gelded: female–male flytings often use sexual insult; Hrimgerd suggests that Atli is sexually incapable. A comparable exchange of sexual insults can be found in Saxo Grammaticus, *History of the Danish People*, Book 5, pp. 132–3.

129 *the prince*: Alf, the son of Hrodmar. A *holmgang*, literally 'going to an island', was a single combat which might be fought to settle matters of honour.

130 *fetch*: in Norse *fylgja*, a kind of guardian spirit, usually female, who appears when the death of the hero is near.

A Second Poem of Helgi Hundingsbani

132 *piercing*: the belief that the hero has especially piercing eyes which cannot be disguised occurs often in Old Norse.

133 *goslings of Gunn's sisters*: Gunn is a valkyrie, as are her sisters. The goslings of the valkyrie are ravens, given carrion to eat by the warrior.

134 *bears in Bragalund*: Helgi talks in riddles, still disguising his identity.

'Old Poem of the Volsungs': this has not survived.

137 *grey stud-horse of the troll-woman*: the wolf.

norns: spirit women who determine fate.

138 *not go forward*: the elements of Sigrun's curse may be compared with the curses in the *Lay of Volund*, and in the *Lay of Atli*.

139 *fetch the foot-bath*: Hunding is humiliated in Valhall by being made to do the work of slaves.

hawks of Odin: ravens.

140 *slaughter-dew*: blood.

precious liquid: presumably Sigrun has brought some mead or ale into the mound with her.

Salgofnir: the cock who awakens the inhabitants of Valhall.

141 *dream-assembly*: sleep.

'Song of Kara': this has not survived.

The Death of Sinfiotli

142 [*?*]: the manuscript leaves a space for the missing name.

disappeared: the old man is probably Odin, come to take Sinfiotli to Valhall.

Gripir's Prophecy

144 *Grani*: Sigurd's famous horse.

sorrow of Eylimi: Eylimi, Sigmund's father-in-law, fell fighting the sons of Hunding when Sigmund was killed. Thus Hiordis, Sigurd's mother, lost husband and father in a single battle. *Volsunga saga*, chs. 11–12, gives full details.

145 *ride to Giuki's*: this is out of sequence. Sigurd does not visit Giuki until he has freed the valkyrie on the mountain top; v. 31 has the visit in its proper place.

the killing of Helgi: this seems to link Sigrdrifa/Brynhild with Sigrun; she represents another variant of the 'valkyrie bride' motif; as in the *Poem of Helgi Hiorvardsson* and the *Second Poem of Helgi Hundingsbani*, marriage with the valkyrie ultimately brings about the hero's death, though in the story of Sigurd it is the valkyrie herself who brings it about.

146 *Brynhild*: the poet of *Gripir's Prophecy* follows the succeeding poems in distinguishing between the valkyrie Sigrdrifa, whom Sigurd encounters on the mountain, and Brynhild, whom he first meets on this visit to Heimir. For further discussion of the complications of the doubling of Sigrdrifa and Brynhild, see pp. 172–3 above.

148 vv. 41–3: the verses are numbered in the order of the manuscript. However, logically, 42 cannot follow 41, since it is a reaction to the news (given in 43) that Gunnar will marry Brynhild despite the nights she and Sigurd have spent together. The verses have been transposed to make narrative sense.

The Lay of Regin

151 the events recounted here are also narrated in *Volsunga saga*, chs. 13 and 14.

152 *serpent's flame*: gold, because serpents, especially dragons, like to bask on heaps of gold.

norn of misfortune: norns, dispensers of fate, are not normally imagined singly, but this one seems to have put a curse on Andvari.

wound . . . with words: Loki's question seems to be a *non sequitur*, but various figures in the *Edda*, notably Sigurd in the *Lay of Fafnir*, vv. 12–15, take the opportunity when they have a supernatural being at their mercy to question him about knowledge normally hidden from gods and humans.

Vadgelmir: an underworld river, probably similar to Slid ('Cutting') in the *Seeress's Prophecy*, v. 36.

ring: according to Snorri, *Edda*, p. 100, the ring had a replicative function, generating more gold from itself. Hence Andvari is particularly reluctant to give it up.

cause of strife: Andvari puts a curse on the gold. The death of two brothers refers to Regin and Fafnir who will both be destroyed through their lust for the gold. The strife between eight princes is less easy to identify—the phrase may be a general one.

153 *princes . . . not yet born*: possibly Gunnar and Hogni, who will be killed for the gold-hoard by Atli in the *Lay of Atli*.

son will avenge: one would expect Lyngheid's descendants to be significant in the rest of the Sigurd story, but in fact this is a blind motif.

154 *helmet of dread*: exactly what this magical device is, is not clear, but Fafnir relies on it to maintain his power—see the *Lay of Fafnir*, vv. 16–17.

155 *Hnikar they called me*: Odin in disguise has come to Sigurd's rescue; *Volsunga saga*, ch. 17, tells of Odin's continuing patronage of the Volsungs.

shining sister of the moon: i.e. the sun. Not to face into the sun in the late afternoon is common-sense advice.

wedge-shaped column: this battle-formation is particularly associated with Odin, who teaches it to the hero Haddingus, under similar circumstances, according to Saxo, *History of the Danish People*, Book 1, p. 31.

156 disir: female spirits, either fertility spirits or ancestors, who concern themselves with the fates of fighting men.

the bloody eagle: there is considerable controversy among scholars as to whether this phrase simply means that the eagle perches on the back of the corpse, or whether it is a reference to the (probably not historical) practice of sacrificing a defeated enemy to Odin by breaking open the ribs and drawing the lungs out onto the back in the shape of an eagle's wings. The 'blood-eagle' rite is mentioned in the purportedly historical *Orkneyinga saga*, here, and in the legendary *saga of Ragnar Lodbrok*.

The Lay of Fafnir

158 *pre-eminent beast*: this riddling allusion still has not been satisfactorily explained, nor why Sigurd voluntarily reveals his identity in v. 4.

innate qualities: the Norse text makes little sense at this point. I follow the suggestion of La Farge and Tucker here.

159 *the judgement of the norns*: the norns are fate-figures—their judgement is the hero's doom. However, though Fafnir seems to be threatening Sigurd with drowning, this is a blind motif.

159 *tell me, Fafnir*: as in the *Lay of Regin* the hero presses the supernatural figure to share his wisdom with him, mythological knowledge which will fit Sigurd for future kingship.

choose mothers over children: the norns who preside over childbirth often have to decide whether it is the mother or the child whose life they will claim.

daughters of Dvalin: i.e. descended from the dwarfs, a fact not found elsewhere in Norse myth.

160 *sword-liquid*: i.e. blood.

helm of terror: the nature of Fafnir's magical protection is unclear.

162 *the old giant*: see note to v. 38.1 below.

163 *destroyer of rings*: generous man, who breaks up arm-rings to distribute to his followers.

I expect a wolf: a proverbial saying, meaning that savagery is to be expected from a savage person, referring either to Regin's nature or Sigurd's courage.

frost-cold giant: Regin is described as a dwarf in the introduction to the *Lay of Regin*, but he himself calls Fafnir a giant above at v. 29. Probably the tradition that the brothers were giants is the older one; Regin's dwarfishness is likely to have developed in connection with his skills as a smith.

164 *terror of the linden*: fire, for the tree is consumed by it.

thorn: a sleep-thorn as a punishment for giving victory to the wrong fighter.

goddess of flax: conventional term for a woman, who wears linen garments.

The Lay of Sigrdrifa

166 *raven's corpse-plain*: dead flesh; that of Regin presumably.

167 *acquainted with fear*: this is the condition of marriage which Brynhild makes, pointing to an original identity between Sigrdrifa and Brynhild. Certainly Sigrdrifa is not known to Snorri, nor does this name appear in *Volsunga saga*.

apple-tree of battle: warrior.

'*Naud*': 'need', the name of the rune denoting the sound 'n'. Sinfiotli, Sigurd's half-brother, had been killed by just such a poisoned horn (see *The Death of Sinfiotli* above).

168 disir: female ancestors or fertility spirits. Here they are said to help women in childbirth, a function ascribed to norns in the *Lay of Fafnir*, v. 12.

Hoddrofnir's horn: this verse is obscure; the liquid referred to here may be identical in some way with the mead of poetry (see *Sayings of the High One* above). Heiddraupnir ('Bright Dropper') and Hoddrofnir ('Hoard-tearer') are unknown. Hropt is a name for Odin.

169 *Brimir's sword*: the reference is unknown.

Mim's head: presumably identical with Mimir, who was sent as a hostage to the Vanir, according to Snorri in *Ynglinga saga*, ch. 4. The Vanir cut off his head, preserved it, and returned it to the Æsir. Odin consults it for advice, cf. *Seeress's Prophecy*, v. 46.4.

shield . . . Alsvinn: the shield must be Svalin, the shield in front of the sun, mentioned in *Grimnir's Sayings*, v. 38. Arvak and Alsvinn must be identical with Arvak and Alsvid who, in *Grimnir's Sayings*, v. 37, are named as the horses who draw the sun.

book-runes: or possibly beech-runes, but most likely an error for 'healing-runes'.

maple of sharp weapons: warrior.

171 *songs*: these seem an unlikely cause of sorrow—an early editor suggests 'quarrels' instead.

burnt inside: burnt alive in your house, a tactic used sometimes in the sagas, most notably in *Njals saga*.

coffin: the reference seems closer to Christian burial rites than the usual pagan practice of cremation.

Fragment of a Poem about Sigurd

174 *all were false*: Brynhild has persuaded Gunnar that, during the three nights when she and Sigurd slept side-by-side after Sigurd, disguised as Gunnar, had ridden through the magic flame-wall and won her, Sigurd took her virginity. This is not true; the two, as Brynhild later admits in v. 19, were separated by a sword.

Guthorm: the youngest brother did not swear oaths of loyalty to Sigurd. He needs to be fed on magical food which will increase his courage in order to become brave enough to attack Sigurd.

175 *the inheritance of Giuki*: Brynhild seems to imply that Sigurd would in time have displaced Gunnar and Hogni from their territory.

176 *blood . . . into a trench*: Sigurd and Gunnar had sworn blood-brotherhood to one another. The ceremony involved scraping a trench in the earth and pouring the mingled blood of the oath-takers into it.

destroyer of armies: Sigurd; the young prince of the next line is Gunnar. Brynhild reveals that, contrary to what she had previously told Gunnar, she and Sigurd had slept chastely together.

wound-wand: sword.

'Old Poem of Gudrun': this seems to correspond to the *Second Lay of Gudrun*, below.

The First Lay of Gudrun

178 *Gullrond*: Gudrun's sister, although she appears only here.

180 *runes of speaking*: i.e. unlocked, as if by magic, Gudrun's power of speech. Once she is able to lament, she can alleviate some of the effects of her grief.

fire of the serpent's bed: gold, as dragons (serpents) like to lie on top of gold. Atli's greed for gold, a theme developed later in the *Poetic Edda*, caused him to force Brynhild into marriage.

A Short Poem about Sigurd

182 *man from the south*: in this poem the epithet refers to Sigurd, perhaps because of his mother's connections with the land of the Franks.

183 *norns*: female figures who determine fate.

ice of the glaciers: since the events of the Sigurd story take place near the Rhine, Brynhild's walking on the glacier may be intended as much to suggest icy resolution as a realistic description of the landscape.

the son: i.e. the son of Sigurd and Gudrun who would be a likely future avenger for his father.

184 *metal of the Rhine*: i.e. Fafnir's hoard, now in Sigurd's possession. The history of the hoard is told in the *Lay of Regin*.

we four: Gunnar, Hogni, Guthorm, and Sigurd.

185 *man eager for battle*: i.e. Sigurd.

backwards: the slightly comic effect here underlines the cowardly nature of Guthorm's attack on the sleeping Sigurd.

clapped together her hands: this gesture seems to be a sign of grief.

like him: the sense is that Sigurd's oldest son is the finest boy that Gudrun could ever give birth to, even if she were to have many sons by future husbands. Her brothers will not tolerate the boy's survival. The logic is spelt out in *Volsunga saga*, ch. 32.

186 *constrained*: Brynhild points out her happiness and independence before she was forced to marry.

187 *Atli said*: Brynhild's full inheritance of her father's treasure, in particular the portion set aside for her dowry, depends upon her getting married to a suitor Atli approves of. Brynhild can either fight him over this or capitulate, as the following verse makes clear. In *Volsunga saga*, ch. 31, it is Budli who compels Brynhild to marry.

valkyrie of necklaces: i.e. woman, Brynhild herself.

188 *dead were her maids*: Brynhild's close female companions seem to have committed suicide to join their mistress in death, though in v. 50 some—less heroic—women decline to follow the same path, despite Brynhild's promises of rewards and honour.

189 *treasures of Menia*: Menia is one of the giantesses in the *Song of Grotti* who was employed as a slave to grind out gold for King Frodi from a magic millstone.

beside the king: this looks ahead to Gudrun's marriage to Atli signalled in v. 56.

190 *Oddrun*: the love of Oddrun and Gunnar is a late addition to the cycle, developed in *Oddrun's Lament*. Oddrun is unknown to the German tradition. In Norse she is a sister of Atli and Brynhild. Gunnar's seduction of Oddrun thus provides a further motive for Atli's killing of Gunnar, though it is clear that his desire to get Sigurd's treasure is the more original and important motive.

snake-pit: this exotic method of execution is to be found in several places in Old Norse, notably in the *saga of Ragnar Lodbrok*. The idea is most probably imported from the Near East.

Bikki's counsel: the reference is to the events which precede the *Lay of Hamdir*. Svanhild is sent to marry the cruel emperor of the Goths, Iormunrekk, but his wicked counsellor, Bikki, advises the emperor that Svanhild is the lover of the emperor's son, Randver. Furious, Iormunrekk has his son hanged and Svanhild trampled to death by horses. See Snorri, *Edda*, pp. 104–6.

191 *jangle at his heels*: i.e. I must not delay following Sigurd much longer. The funeral is described in *Volsunga saga*, ch. 33.

Brynhild's Ride to Hell

193 *put under an oak*: this part of Brynhild's story is unclear and not mentioned elsewhere. Most likely the motif is borrowed from swan-maiden stories, like the one in the *Lay of Volund*. Brynhild and her sisters were able to change their shape by means of the magic garments, probably into some kind of bird, in connection with their life as valkyries. A king—perhaps Gunnar, perhaps Atli—brings this life to an end by taking the shape-changing garment and forcing her into marriage. Or conceivably this is a reference to the beginning of the valkyrie's career, acquiring the magic garments from beneath the tree.

Odin was very angry: Brynhild's story is identical with that of Sigrdrifa in the *Lay of Sigrdrifa*, showing that the two figures have coalesced.

destroyer of wood: i.e. fire.

Danish viking: i.e. Sigurd, though he is normally characterized in the Volsung poems as the man from the south rather than from Denmark, pointing perhaps to a different source for this poem.

The Second Lay of Gudrun

196 *green leek*: cf. the *First Lay of Gudrun*, v. 18.2.

from the Assembly: the manuscript reads 'to' here. This poem follows the tradition pointed out at the end of the *Fragment* . . . (p. 176), that the brothers killed Sigurd at the Assembly rather than in his bed.

198 *yew bow*: Grimhild arranges a splendid formal procession to make peace with Gudrun.

199 *I could not remember*: Grimhild's drink of forgetting contrasts with the memory-drinks which Sigrdrifa gives to Sigurd in the *Lay of Sigrdrifa*, and which Freyia asks for to give to Ottar in *Hyndla's Song*, v. 45.

heather-fish: a fish of the heather is a snake.

corn-ear of the land of the Haddings: obscure. The 'land of the Haddings' is the sea—an uncut corn-ear of the sea is perhaps seaweed.

200 *Sigmund*: the son of Sigurd and Gudrun, murdered at Sigurd's death and named after Sigurd's father.

202 *white sacrificial beasts*: the meaning of the Norse *hviting* ('white thing') is obscure. Gudrun deliberately misinterprets Atli's doom-laden dreams, which presage the events of the *Lay of Atli*. In *Volsunga saga*, ch. 35, Gudrun tells Atli the truth about the import of the dreams.

The Third Lay of Gudrun

204 *foul bog*: drowning criminals under a lattice in a bog was a well-attested Germanic punishment, mentioned by Tacitus in *Germania*, ch. 12.

Oddrun's Lament

206 *bitter spells*: the idea that problematic labour can be helped with spells or runes is a common one in the *Edda*. See also the *Lay of Sigrdrifa*, v. 9, and the role of the norns in the *Lay of Fafnir*, vv. 12–13.

slayer of Hogni: Vilmund, father of the children, is not named as the killer of Hogni anywhere else.

drink for Gunnar: the significance seems to be that for a woman to prepare a drink for a man is a sign of intimacy; since the betrothal between Oddrun and Gunnar had not yet been arranged, Borgny was scandalized by Oddrun's action. Her moral stance is ironic given her own later liaison with Vilmund. Verses 11 and 12 are out of order in the manuscript but clearly belong here.

207 *Odin's beloved girl*: the dying Budli arranges a marriage to Gunnar for Oddrun and the life of a valkyrie for Brynhild, but their fates go awry.

burden of Grani: this is a common kenning for 'gold', but in this context it may literally refer to the treasure-hoard Sigurd won from the dragon and which he loaded on his horse's back to take away. The hoard had passed into the hands of Gunnar and Hogni.

208 *ring-breaker*: a generous man who breaks up gold rings to distribute to his followers.

wise king: i.e. Gunnar.

209 *the mother of Atli*: here Oddrun says that Atli's mother is responsible for Gunnar's death; in the other sources, one particularly large serpent, resistant to Gunnar's harp-playing, strikes the death-blow (Snorri, *Edda*, p. 104, *Volsunga saga*, ch. 39). Scholars have reconciled the two accounts by assuming that Atli's mother magically

turns herself into a snake and hence is immune to Gunnar's serpent-charming.

209 *goddess of the pillow*: i.e. lady, Borgny, whom Oddrun is addressing.

The Lay of Atli

210 *you two*: though Knefrod at first addresses Gunnar, as the elder brother, he makes it clear that Hogni is included in the invitation by the use of a dual form.

211 *gold on Gnita-heath*: Gnita-heath was the home of the dragon Fafnir; the gold there had been taken by Sigurd and has now passed to Gunnar. So the brothers literally do own the gold of Gnita-heath.

heath-wanderer: the wolf. Gudrun sends a ring with a wolf-hair twisted round it as a secret message which Hogni correctly interprets. The motif is subtler than the altered runes which have a similar function in the *Greenlandic Poem of Atli*.

212 *young men's court*: the manuscript has 'court of the Huns', which cannot be right. Normally the poem keeps the two tribes scrupulously separate.

Bikki: the evil counsellor of Iormunrekk of the Goths, who belongs in the *Lay of Hamdir*. Possibly Budli, Atli's father, is meant.

213 *norns weep*: even the implacable determiners of fate would have been moved to pity by the greatness of the slaughter if Gunnar and Hogni had come armed.

the russet mountains of the Rhine: this is a crux in the Norse and may refer to Worms on the Rhine, the Niflung headquarters.

prince of the Goths: i.e. Gunnar.

Hialli: a cowardly retainer of Atli.

214 *far from my eyes*: Gunnar prophesies Atli's death.

the Æsir-given inheritance: the Norse is obscure here. This interpretation, coming at the climax of the Rhinegold theme, recalls how it came to play a part in the history of the Volsung and Niflung dynasties.

the captive is in chains: v. 28 contains first Atli's order to lead Gunnar out to execution, then a commentary on the chariot's progression towards the snake-pit. Editors have assumed that the scene at Atli's hall, where Gudrun curses him (vv. 29–30), must conclude before the narrator brings Gunnar to the edge of the pit in the second part of v. 28.

215 *ship of the bit*: the 'ship of the bit' is a horse. The 'necklace-guardian' in the following line is a possessor of treasure. The elaborate metaphors work to conceal the slow horror of Gunnar's death-journey.

harp: Gunnar harps to show his aristocratic fearlessness, but the harping is also imagined to have a charming effect on the snakes in some sources.

little creatures gone into darkness: Gudrun is deliberately riddling here. In Norse the word signifying 'gone into darkness', *niflfarna*, puns on 'Niflung'. The dead children are also of Niflung stock like their mother and dead uncles.

sharer-out of swords: this type of construction, where a noun group is split up by another phrase, is very frequent in skaldic poetry, but rare in Eddic verse, suggesting possible influence from the skaldic style.

The Greenlandic Poem of Atli

218 *lady of the house*: Gudrun.

both: here, as in the *Nibelungenlied*, two messengers are sent, but the second man swiftly fades from view.

the couple: i.e. Hogni and Kostbera.

219 *burnt up*: Hogni points to some old rags ready for burning and suggests that this domestic concern is the subject of Kostbera's dream. Her other dreams are equally interpreted as domestic in reference, while Glaumvor's seem to be understood more symbolically.

white bear: that Hogni should automatically assume that the bear is white seems to confirm the connection with Greenland.

Gunnar undertook: something is missing in the manuscript. I follow Ursula Dronke's suggestion here.

221 disir: female spirits who watch over a tribe and often appear in connection with a death. Such women are often found in the sagas where they presage the death of the hero, notably in *Gisla saga* where a good and a bad dream-woman do battle over Gisli.

222 *Bera*: i.e. Kostbera, Hogni's wife.

223 *didn't tie up*: thus the boat would drift away and the party be unable to return. The detail shows the resolution of Gunnar and Hogni in the face of the knowledge of their death. Similarly in the *Nibelungenlied* (ll. 1564–81), Hagen rows very violently and does not tie up the boats after Gunther and his men have crossed the

Rhine on their fatal journey to visit Etzel, the equivalent of Atli in that poem.

223 *struck down one*: i.e. Vingi.

225 *the brave man*: i.e. Atli.

sister off to hell: Atli, with some justification, blames the Giukungs for the death of Brynhild.

wise cousin: this detail, and the suggestion that Atli was responsible for Grimhild's death, is unknown from any other sources. Some German sources, however, recount that Atli met his death in a cave where the treasure was hidden.

226 *gallows*: in fact the gallows are never used, but the detail here, and in Vingi's remarks in v. 39, seems to be necessary to fulfil Glaumvor's dream in v. 22.

fated for death: the implication is that a coward, always fearing death, is halfway dead already. Hialli will not be missed.

227 *day-labourers*: the peasants in the fields at some distance from the fortress.

foot-twigs: i.e. toes. Presumably his hands were bound.

229 *anger will not be slaked*: i.e. you will be furious with yourself if you commit this deed.

over: since the battle Atli and Gudrun must have kept to different sides of the hall.

skulls: this detail is probably borrowed from the *Lay of Volund*—Gudrun herself is no smith.

230 *Hniflung*: the son of Hogni, left behind, who has now come to seek revenge for his father.

232 *captained*: Gudrun lays claim to a martial past, explaining her courageous fighting on her brothers' side in the earlier battle.

233 *coffin*: Gudrun promises a mixture of pagan and Christian rites for Atli's funeral.

The Whetting of Gudrun

234 *Erp*: it is essential to the *Lay of Hamdir* that Erp should not be Gudrun's son. That he should bear the same name as her murdered son by Atli must be coincidence.

told the king: in *Volsunga saga*, ch. 42, a Tristan and Isolde-like theme seems to be about to emerge. Randver is sent on a wooing journey and returns with Svanhild. Bikki suggests that the two young people are better suited to one another, and Randver agrees. Bikki falsely tells Iormunrekk that Randver and Svanhild are lovers. Randver is hanged, although Iormunrekk, realizing that the loss of his heir is a serious matter, tries but fails to avert the execution at the last minute. Svanhild is trampled by horses anyway.

I: i.e. the poet.

235 *all*: Hamdir points out, ironically enough given what is to follow in the *Lay of Hamdir*, that the expedition of revenge would have been easier if the murdered Erp and Eitil had been able to join them.

237 *oak-wood pyre*: Gudrun intends to die now; the motif of the funeral pyre is clearly drawn from that of Brynhild in the *Short Poem about Sigurd*. Our last glimpse of Gudrun here, and in the parallel passage in the *Lay of Hamdir*, is of the bereaved mother, sister, and wife lamenting the terrible story which has unfolded in the last eleven poems.

The Lay of Hamdir

238 *elves weep*: if the elves (*alfar*) are ancestral spirits, as has been suggested, they would weep when they knew disaster to be imminent for the family they protect.

239 *Hamdir*: this response must be to a verse contrasting the two brothers with Gunnar and Hogni, probably much like *Whetting of Gudrun*, v. 3, rather than the preceding verse in this poem.

240 *son of a different mother*: this is Erp, half-brother to Hamdir and Sorli by a different mother. That he shares a name with Gudrun's son by Atli is coincidental.

troll-woman: possibly Hel, goddess of death, or a malevolent *dis* (see note on *disir* below, p. 294).

sister's son: i.e. stepson, Randver, whom Iormunrekk had believed to be Svanhild's lover. That he is wounded as well as hanged may suggest an Odinic sacrifice. In *Sayings of the High One*, v. 138, Odin sacrifices himself to himself, by hanging himself on a tree and being pierced with a spear. The double motif of hanging and piercing reappears elsewhere in sagas where sacrifice to Odin is mentioned.

241 *Hrodglod*: the manuscript is defective here. This is either a woman's name or else an adjective meaning 'woman pleased by glory'.

241 *spears will not bite*: the brothers are apparently invulnerable. In *Volsunga saga*, ch. 44, and in Snorri, *Edda*, pp. 104–6, this is because Gudrun had given them magic mail-coats, resistant to iron. The poet retains the detail but not the explanation.

Hamdir: the manuscript gives Hamdir verse 26, but logically Sorli needs to speak it and the one which follows. I punctuate accordingly.

opened up that bag: Iormunrekk's armless and legless torso is compared to a bag; provoking him to speak is tantamount to opening the bag from which the fatal command comes. Bags may have been traditionally thought to contain hidden wisdom, cf. *Sayings of the High One*, v. 134.6, in connection with the wisdom of the aged: 'often from a wrinkled bag come judicious words'.

242 *if Erp were alive*: in *Volsunga saga*, ch. 44, the brothers stumble shortly after killing Erp and save themselves by leaning on the other hand and foot. Thus they already understand Erp's remark and begin to regret the murder before the torture scene. In Snorri's account, it is only Sorli who stumbles, and Gudrun has already instructed each brother as to which portion of Iormunrekk he should cut off. Reserving the realization of the brothers' error until the climax of the poem, as here, is far more effective.

disir: female ancestral spirits whose influence is felt when a member of the clan is doomed.

Baldr's Dreams

243 *all together*: this line is identical to one in the *Thrym's Poem*, v. 14.

sacrifice for men: why Odin should be described as a sacrifice, twice in this poem (also at 13.2), is not clear. The reference may be to his hanging on the tree Yggdrasill to gain the runes (*Sayings of the High One*, vv. 138–9), but men are only incidentally the beneficiaries of this.

dog: this may be Garm, the hound of Hell.

corpse-reviving spell: Odin boasts of his knowledge of these in *Sayings of the High One*, v. 157.

244 *dispatch the famous warrior*: this line is disputed. Literally it reads 'Hod will send the tall glory-tree in this direction'; most commentators take 'glory-tree' as a metaphor for 'warrior', but it may conceivably refer to the mistletoe dart.

Rind: Saxo gives the story of how Odin uses magic to force himself on Rind in order to beget Baldr's avenger in his *History of the*

Danish People, Book 3, pp. 78–82. This line is also to be found in the *Seeress's Prophecy*, v. 33.

girls who weep: since the prophetess does not answer Odin's question, we have no idea of who these girls may be, though, following the pattern of other dialogues in the *Edda*, in which protagonists often ask questions about norns, it may be that they are referred to here. Alternatively, the riddling quality of the question points perhaps to a concealed kenning, denoting clouds, waves, or sailing vessels. Odin's enquiry reveals his true identity to the prophetess, who refuses to give him any further information; it seems that in the mythological poetry of the *Edda*, only Odin goes about asking such questions.

245 *Doom of the Gods*: Baldr's death is one of the first premonitions of the coming of Ragnarok. See Snorri, *Edda*, p. 49.

The List of Rig

246 *Rig*: the name is derived from the Irish *rí* (*rig* in other cases) meaning 'king'. The identification of Heimdall with Rig is not absolutely secure, since it is based only on the prose introduction, but the beginning of the *Seeress's Prophecy*, asking for attention from all 'the offspring of Heimdall', seems to suggest that the god did have some connection with the creation of mankind.

247 *coarse loaf*: typical peasant fare.

poured water over it: this action is a kind of pagan naming ceremony, often mentioned in the sagas.

248 *advice*: a gap follows here. Presumably Rig receives hospitality typical of a well-set-up farmer.

249 *exchanged rings*: the farming couple get married properly, unlike Thrall and Slavegirl who simply set up house together.

looking into one another's eyes: in the more aristocratic household the couple have some leisure for romance.

252 *young Kin*: in the original Kin's name is Kon. When modified by *ungr* ('young') it becomes *konungr* or 'king', emphasizing the young man's future role.

called Rig: Kin establishes a claim to kingly status through his superior knowledge and relationship with the founder of the dynasty.

The Song of Hyndla

254 *I must sacrifice*: in the manuscript Freyia speaks in the third person.

wolves: the traditional mount of giant women.

made for me: this beast may be identical with the boar made by the dwarf Brokk for Freyr, recounted by Snorri, *Edda*, pp. 96–7. 'Battleswine' is a name for a helmet in skaldic poetry.

turned to glass: the stone has fused into glass because of the frequency of Ottar's sacrifices.

Skioldungs . . . Ylfings: Snorri, *Edda*, p. 148, gives fuller details of these clans.

255 *Hildigunn*: presumably Almveig's mother.

256 *the two Haddings*: two brothers, heroes who appear in a list of berserk warriors in *Heidreks saga*. They were the youngest of twelve brothers and it was only collectively that they had the strength of one man.

Hiordis: Sigurd's mother and the daughter of Eylimi by most accounts. Hraudung may be an error for a tribal name like Odling in the line which follows.

257 *not of the line of Giuki*: that Guthorm was only a half-brother of Gunnar and Hogni explains his rather marginal status in the Sigurd story.

eleven: vv. 29–44 belong to another poem which Snorri calls *Voluspa in skamma—The Short Prophecy of the Seeress.* It deals with some of the same material as the first poem in the Codex Regius and has nothing to do with the tally of ancestors which Hyndla is recounting.

heir to Bur: i.e. Odin.

Aurboda: these facts accord with *Skirnir's Journey*, though there we do not learn the name of Gerd's mother.

seid-*practisers*: a particular form of magic associated with the Vanir.

258 *nine women*: it has been thought on the basis of this detail that this cryptic allusion may be to Heimdall, since Snorri quotes an otherwise lost text called *Heimdalargaldr* (*The Spell of Heimdall*), in which Heimdall declares himself to be the son of nine mothers (*Edda*, pp. 25–6).

Iarnsaxa: the mother of Thor's son Magni.

Svadilfari: the stallion belonging to the Giant-builder who was repairing the walls of Asgard after the Æsir–Vanir war. Loki had to change himself into a mare and entice the stallion away to prevent the builder from fulfilling the terms of his contract and thus winning Freyia and the sun and moon for himself.

Byleist: Byleist's brother is Loki; nothing is otherwise known of Byleist, who only appears in this kenning. The monster is presumably the Midgard-serpent, since Fenrir the wolf has been mentioned earlier in the verse.

Lopt was impregnated: Lopt is a name for Loki. This story is otherwise unknown, although in *Loki's Quarrel*, v. 23, Loki is said to have borne children.

259 *name his name*: it is not clear to whom vv. 43 and 44 refer. If v. 35 refers to Heimdall, then v. 43 may have the same referent; v. 44 has been interpreted as referring to Christ.

memory-ale: The *Song of Hyndla* proper resumes. Ottar, disguised as Freyia's boar, will have the information he needs to prove his lineage and win his inheritance in the face of Angantyr's claims. As in the *Lay of Sigrdrifa*, memory-ale is a magic potion which enables a listener to recall everything he has heard.

Heidrun: the nanny-goat of the gods who gives mead from her udder. Hyndla accuses Freyia of promiscuity.

Œdi: this may be a form of Od, Freyia's husband according to Snorri, *Edda*, p. 29, or it may be another of Freyia's lovers.

The Song of Grotti

261 *he*: i.e. Frodi.

men seized it: in their giant games Fenia and Menia created the millstone to which they are now chained.

262 *calmer of strife*: the millstone, which is still grinding out peace and prosperity.

son and brother: Hrolf Kraki, who would avenge the death of Frodi, was the son of his half-sister Yrsa. Yrsa was the daughter of Thora, whom Hrolf's father, Helgi, had raped. The mother deliberately sent her daughter to seduce her father and trap him into incest; the product of their union turned out to be a great hero. The story is told in Saxo, *History of the Danish People*, Book 2, pp. 51–4.

ANNOTATED INDEX OF NAMES

List of Abbreviations

All	*All-wise's Sayings* (*Alvissmal*)
Atli	*The Lay of Atli* (*Atlakvida*)
Baldr	*Baldr's Dreams* (*Baldrs Draumar*)
Bryn	*Brynhild's Ride to Hell* (*Helreid Brynhildar*)
Death	*The Death of the Niflungs* (*Fra Daudi Niflunga*)
DS	*The Death of Sinfiotli* (*Fra Daudi Sinfiotla*)
Faf	*The Lay of Fafnir* (*Fafnismal*)
Frag	*Fragment of a Poem about Sigurd* (*Brot af Sigurdarkvida*)
Green	*The Greenlandic Poem of Atli* (*Atlamal in groenlanzko*)
Grim	*Grimnir's Sayings* (*Grimnismal*)
Grip	*Gripir's Prophecy* (*Gripisspa*)
Grott	*The Song of Grotti* (*Grottasongr*)
Gud1	*The First Lay of Gudrun*
Gud2	*The Second Lay of Gudrun*
Gud3	*The Third Lay of Gudrun*
Ham	*The Lay of Hamdir* (*Hamdismal*)
Harb	*Harbard's Song* (*Harbardsljod*)
HH1	*The First Poem of Helgi Hundingsbani* (*Helgakvida Hundingsbana I*)
HH2	*A Second Poem of Helgi Hundingsbani* (*Helgakvida Hundingsbana II*)
HHi	*The Poem of Helgi Hiorvardsson* (*Helgakvida Hiorvardssonar*)
High	*Sayings of the High One* (*Havamal*)
Hym	*Hymir's Poem* (*Hymiskvida*)
Hynd	*The Song of Hyndla* (*Hyndluljod*)
Lok	*Loki's Quarrel* (*Lokasenna*)
Odd	*Oddrun's Lament* (*Oddrunargratr*)
Reg	*The Lay of Regin* (*Reginsmal*)
Rig	*The List of Rig* (*Rigsthula*)
Seer	*The Seeress's Prophecy* (*Voluspa*)
Short	*A Short Poem about Sigurd* (*Sigurdarkvida in skamma*)
Sigrd	*The Lay of Sigrdrifa* (*Sigrdrifumal*)
Skir	*Skirnir's Journey* (*For Skirnir* or *Skirnismal*)
Thrym	*Thrym's Poem* (*Thrymskvida*)
Vaf	*Vafthrudnir's Sayings* (*Vafthrudnismal*)
Vol	*The Lay of Volund* (*Volundarkvida*)
Whet	*The Whetting of Gudrun* (*Gudrunarhvot*)

Note: in the index below, references within each entry follow the order of the poems in the text, and two or more characters sharing a common name are listed according to the order of their first appearance in the text.

A SELECTION OF OXFORD WORLD'S CLASSICS

Eirik the Red and Other Icelandic Sagas

The German-Jewish Dialogue

The Kalevala

The Poetic Edda

Ludovico Ariosto — **Orlando Furioso**

Giovanni Boccaccio — **The Decameron**

Georg Büchner — **Danton's Death, Leonce and Lena, and Woyzeck**

Luis vaz de Camões — **The Lusiads**

Miguel de Cervantes — **Don Quixote**
Exemplary Stories

Carlo Collodi — **The Adventures of Pinocchio**

Dante Alighieri — **The Divine Comedy**
Vita Nuova

Lope de Vega — **Three Major Plays**

J. W. von Goethe — **Elective Affinities**
Erotic Poems
Faust: Part One and Part Two
The Flight to Italy

E. T. A. Hoffmann — **The Golden Pot and Other Tales**

Henrik Ibsen — **An Enemy of the People, The Wild Duck, Rosmersholm**
Four Major Plays
Peer Gynt

Leonardo da Vinci — **Selections from the Notebooks**

Federico Garcia Lorca — **Four Major Plays**

Michelangelo Buonarroti — **Life, Letters, and Poetry**

A SELECTION OF **OXFORD WORLD'S CLASSICS**

PETRARCH	**Selections from the Canzoniere and Other Works**
J. C. F. SCHILLER	**Don Carlos and Mary Stuart**
JOHANN AUGUST STRINDBERG	**Miss Julie and Other Plays**

A SELECTION OF OXFORD WORLD'S CLASSICS

	Six French Poets of the Nineteenth Century
Honoré de Balzac	**Cousin Bette** **Eugénie Grandet** **Père Goriot**
Charles Baudelaire	**The Flowers of Evil** **The Prose Poems and Fanfarlo**
Benjamin Constant	**Adolphe**
Denis Diderot	**Jacques the Fatalist**
Alexandre Dumas (père)	**The Black Tulip** **The Count of Monte Cristo** **Louise de la Vallière** **The Man in the Iron Mask** **La Reine Margot** **The Three Musketeers** **Twenty Years After** **The Vicomte de Bragelonne**
Alexandre Dumas (fils)	**La Dame aux Camélias**
Gustave Flaubert	**Madame Bovary** **A Sentimental Education** **Three Tales**
Victor Hugo	**Notre-Dame de Paris**
J.-K. Huysmans	**Against Nature**
Pierre Choderlos de Laclos	**Les Liaisons dangereuses**
Mme de Lafayette	**The Princesse de Clèves**
Guillaume du Lorris and Jean de Meun	**The Romance of the Rose**

A SELECTION OF **OXFORD WORLD'S CLASSICS**

GUY DE MAUPASSANT	**A Day in the Country and Other Stories** **A Life** **Bel-Ami** **Mademoiselle Fifi and Other Stories** **Pierre et Jean**
PROSPER MÉRIMÉE	**Carmen and Other Stories**
MOLIÈRE	**Don Juan and Other Plays** **The Misanthrope, Tartuffe, and Other Plays**
BLAISE PASCAL	**Pensées and Other Writings**
JEAN RACINE	**Britannicus, Phaedra, and Athaliah**
ARTHUR RIMBAUD	**Collected Poems**
EDMOND ROSTAND	**Cyrano de Bergerac**
MARQUIS DE SADE	**The Misfortunes of Virtue and Other Early Tales**
GEORGE SAND	**Indiana**
MME DE STAËL	**Corinne**
STENDHAL	**The Red and the Black** **The Charterhouse of Parma**
PAUL VERLAINE	**Selected Poems**
JULES VERNE	**Around the World in Eighty Days** **Journey to the Centre of the Earth** **Twenty Thousand Leagues under the Seas**
VOLTAIRE	**Candide and Other Stories** **Letters concerning the English Nation**

A SELECTION OF **OXFORD WORLD'S CLASSICS**

ÉMILE ZOLA	**L'Assommoir**
	The Attack on the Mill
	La Bête humaine
	La Débâde
	Germinal
	The Ladies' Paradise
	The Masterpiece
	Nana
	Pot Luck
	Thérèse Raquin

A SELECTION OF **OXFORD WORLD'S CLASSICS**

ANTON CHEKHOV	**Early Stories** **Five Plays** **The Princess and Other Stories** **The Russian Master and Other Stories** **The Steppe and Other Stories** **Twelve Plays** **Ward Number Six and Other Stories**
FYODOR DOSTOEVSKY	**Crime and Punishment** **Devils** **A Gentle Creature and Other Stories** **The Idiot** **The Karamazov Brothers** **Memoirs from the House of the Dead** **Notes from the Underground** and **The Gambler**
NIKOLAI GOGOL	**Dead Souls** **Plays and Petersburg Tales**
ALEXANDER PUSHKIN	**Eugene Onegin** **The Queen of Spades and Other Stories**
LEO TOLSTOY	**Anna Karenina** **The Kreutzer Sonata and Other Stories** **The Raid and Other Stories** **Resurrection** **War and Peace**
IVAN TURGENEV	**Fathers and Sons** **First Love and Other Stories** **A Month in the Country**

A SELECTION OF **OXFORD WORLD'S CLASSICS**

LUDOVICO ARIOSTO	**Orlando Furioso**
GIOVANNI BOCCACCIO	**The Decameron**
MATTEO MARIA BOIARDO	**Orlando Innamorato**
LUÍS VAZ DE CAMÕES	**The Lusíads**
MIGUEL DE CERVANTES	**Don Quixote de la Mancha** **Exemplary Stories**
DANTE ALIGHIERI	**The Divine Comedy** **Vita Nuova**
BENITO PÉREZ GALDÓS	**Nazarín**
LEONARDO DA VINCI	**Selections from the Notebooks**
NICCOLÒ MACHIAVELLI	**Discourses on Livy** **The Prince**
MICHELANGELO	**Life, Letters, and Poetry**
PETRARCH	**Selections from the *Canzoniere* and Other Works**
GIORGIO VASARI	**The Lives of the Artists**

A SELECTION OF **OXFORD WORLD'S CLASSICS**

Jane Austen	**Emma** **Persuasion** **Pride and Prejudice** **Sense and Sensibility**
Mrs Beeton	**Book of Household Management**
Anne Brontë	**The Tenant of Wildfell Hall**
Charlotte Brontë	**Jane Eyre**
Emily Brontë	**Wuthering Heights**
Wilkie Collins	**The Moonstone** **The Woman in White**
Joseph Conrad	**Heart of Darkness and Other Tales** **Nostromo**
Charles Darwin	**The Origin of Species**
Charles Dickens	**Bleak House** **David Copperfield** **Great Expectations** **Hard Times**
George Eliot	**Middlemarch** **The Mill on the Floss**
Elizabeth Gaskell	**Cranford**
Thomas Hardy	**Jude the Obscure** **Tess of the d'Urbervilles**
Walter Scott	**Ivanhoe**
Mary Shelley	**Frankenstein**
Robert Louis Stevenson	**Treasure Island**
Bram Stoker	**Dracula**
William Makepeace Thackeray	**Vanity Fair**
Oscar Wilde	**The Picture of Dorian Gray**

A SELECTION OF **OXFORD WORLD'S CLASSICS**

	Women's Writing 1778–1838
JAMES BOSWELL	**Life of Johnson**
FRANCES BURNEY	**Cecilia** **Evelina**
JOHN CLELAND	**Memoirs of a Woman of Pleasure**
DANIEL DEFOE	**A Journal of the Plague Year** **Moll Flanders** **Robinson Crusoe**
HENRY FIELDING	**Joseph Andrews and Shamela** **Tom Jones**
WILLIAM GODWIN	**Caleb Williams**
OLIVER GOLDSMITH	**The Vicar of Wakefield**
ELIZABETH INCHBALD	**A Simple Story**
SAMUEL JOHNSON	**The History of Rasselas**
ANN RADCLIFFE	**The Italian** **The Mysteries of Udolpho**
SAMUEL RICHARDSON	**Pamela**
TOBIAS SMOLLETT	**The Adventures of Roderick Random** **The Expedition of Humphry Clinker**
LAURENCE STERNE	**The Life and Opinions of Tristram Shandy, Gentleman** **A Sentimental Journey**
JONATHAN SWIFT	**Gulliver's Travels** **A Tale of a Tub and Other Works**
HORACE WALPOLE	**The Castle of Otranto**
MARY WOLLSTONECRAFT	**Mary and The Wrongs of Woman** **A Vindication of the Rights of Woman**

The Oxford World's Classics Website

www.worldsclassics.co.uk

- Information about new titles
- Explore the full range of Oxford World's Classics
- Links to other literary sites and the main OUP webpage
- Imaginative competitions, with bookish prizes
- Peruse the Oxford World's Classics Magazine
- Articles by editors
- Extracts from Introductions
- A forum for discussion and feedback on the series
- Special information for teachers and lecturers

www.worldsclassics.co.uk

MORE ABOUT **OXFORD WORLD'S CLASSICS**

American Literature

British and Irish Literature

Children's Literature

Classics and Ancient Literature

Colonial Literature

Eastern Literature

European Literature

History

Medieval Literature

Oxford English Drama

Poetry

Philosophy

Politics

Religion

The Oxford Shakespeare

A complete list of Oxford Paperbacks, including Oxford World's Classics, Oxford Shakespeare, Oxford Drama, and Oxford Paperback Reference, is available in the UK from the Academic Division Publicity Department, Oxford University Press, Great Clarendon Street, Oxford OX2 6DP.

In the USA, complete lists are available from the Paperbacks Marketing Manager, Oxford University Press, 198 Madison Avenue, New York, NY 10016.

Oxford Paperbacks are available from all good bookshops. In case of difficulty, customers in the UK can order direct from Oxford University Press Bookshop, Freepost, 116 High Street, Oxford OX1 4BR, enclosing full payment. Please add 10 per cent of published price for postage and packing.